After Shanghai

Alison McLeay

After Shanghai

St. Martin's Press ⚇ New York

AFTER SHANGHAI. Copyright © 1995 by Alison McLeay. All
rights reserved. Printed in the United States of America. No
part of this book may be used or reproduced in any manner
whatsoever without written permission except in the case of
brief quotations embodied in critical articles or reviews. For
information, address St. Martin's Press, 175 Fifth Avenue,
New York, N.Y. 10010.

Library of Congress Cataloging-in-Publication Data

McLeay, Alison.
    After Shanghai / by Alison McLeay.
        p.   cm.
    ISBN 0-312-14271-4
    1. Married women—China—Shanghai—Fiction.
    2. British—China—Shanghai—Fiction.   I. Title.
PR6063.C55A68   1996
823'.914—dc20   96-3513
                                                        CIP

First published in Great Britain by Macmillan, an imprint of
Macmillan General Books

First U.S. Edition: August 1996

10   9   8   7   6   5   4   3   2   1

After Shanghai

Part One

Chapter One

IN 1916, ON my sixth birthday, a Chinese business acquaintance of my father's gave me a nest of concentric ivory balls, pierced and carved and revolving within one another as snugly as the layers of an onion. It held all the mystery of China, pocket-size: though I had to arrange the layers with a hat pin to catch a glimpse of the innermost orb, in some miraculous way even that, almost invisible, had been cut like the rest with an outline of milky blossom.

I used to imagine my heart like the littlest of the ivory balls, keeping its secrets within a series of cool, geometrically perfect shells.

But then, I was born in that city of secrets, Shanghai. Perhaps a breeze from the east tossed the peppery scent of the incense shops in the Old City over our garden wall as I drew my first breath; perhaps the murmuring of the fortune-tellers in the narrow lanes stole into my nursery, or the whispering of the river and the furtive traffic which scurried along its margins. At any rate, Shanghai breathed in my infant face, and made me half-way hers.

My parents went off to garden parties and the races; I took my first unsteady steps in the servants' courtyard. Soon I could stumble after the bent backs of the gardeners as they picked stray rose petals from the green perfection of our lawn, or perch on a stool in the kitchen to watch Cook make a delicate butterfly from the simple sliced eggs, cucumber and meat loaf of my nursery luncheon.

I grew to share the Chinese love of small, exquisite, enclosed spaces contained within larger spaces, themselves walled off from the outside world. From the servants I heard of houses with more than a dozen courtyards but only a single gate to the highway, where all the pavilions looked inwards on quiet gardens and clear pools. Even the Emperor, they said, had lived like a precious prisoner in the red lacquer halls of the Forbidden City in Peking, shut in by walls-within-walls and a thousand layers of protocol.

Us and *the others*. Our fields and theirs, friends and enemies – China is a land of instinctive subdivision. When I was eight, my English governess told me how the Chinese had built a Wall of Walls far to the north, a great paved rampart lacing the furry hills for six thousand miles to keep out the northern barbarians. Beyond it, she said, lay such a wilderness that exiled Chinese considered themselves the living dead.

She spread out a map. I was pleased to see that Shanghai lay safely on the proper side of the Wall: yet I was pretty sure I wasn't Chinese.

'Am I a barbarian, then?' I enquired.

My governess was the widow of an up-country missionary. 'A barbarian? I should think not.'

'But if I'm not Chinese, I must be a foreign devil of some kind.'

'Good gracious, you're *English*, child – and very fortunate to be so. I hope you thank God for it every night in your prayers.' She surveyed me, her brow puckered with concern. 'One day soon your papa will take you home, and then you'll understand.'

Home. Home was Shanghai: yet apparently home also meant Britain, the tiny pink islands I'd to turn my globe so far to see. And my governess was wrong. Even now, seven and a half decades later, twisting and turning my story like those baffling ivory balls, I still don't fully understand.

'Write it all down, why don't you?' My elder son is a pragmatist and a busy man. 'I read somewhere that writing things down makes them clearer. Well then, put it all down on paper – about Liu Ling, and going in disguise to see the Great World, and that Russian dancer who went into the movies and his sister who fought your cousin Rose on the Riviera—'

'That was partly Rose's fault, you know—'

'And Great Aunt Margot and her trumpeter from the Savoy – and about meeting Father, of course, and the bombs . . . Better still—' My eldest son has a habit of tapping me on the arm when inspiration grips him. 'Go back to Shanghai and see it all again for yourself. I've been suggesting that for ages. Go back – hop on a plane. See the old places before they pull them down and put up an office block.'

Never, I told him. Only fools go back.

And here I am.

Here I am in a Shanghai hotel room, staring at the first blank page of the paper I bought with such determination this morning in Fuzhou Road. The pen in my hand is still circling like a fly, searching for a landing spot. Shanghai: surely this is the place where it all started, the same city where Liu Ling used to buy me spun-sugar monkeys twirled by the sweetmeat-maker over his charcoal stove, and where, many years later, Sammy Liu's severed head rolled out of a rickshaw under the street lamps and we knew for certain that our long, desperate party had finally come to an end.

No. I shall begin my account in a quiet cemetery in Norfolk, England, on a June morning in 1923, with the honeyed smell of freshly turned earth rising around me. We'd come there to bury Grandfather Matthew Oliver, the man I'd travelled a third of the way round the world to see, only to find them about to lower him into the ground in a wooden box.

I remember the rector's voice drawling on among the orange-tip butterflies while I wound my fingers into the stiff black dress bought hastily for me the previous day. Forty-eight hours earlier I'd still been at sea, as much of a stranger to these people as they were to me. Now already I was part of that black ring round the grave, that sombre, living wreath of Olivers, the men growing hot in morning coats and the women tall and fashionably slender, their faces downturned under the squashing brims of their hats.

The Olivers were on parade, though not altogether willingly, by the look of some of them. Christopher Oliver, my Uncle Kit, had greeted us solemnly enough, but mutiny showed in the faces of his family. Aunt Margot's coal-scuttle hat hid everything but a soft, sulky mouth, while her daughters Alice and Rose had given up watching one of the undertaker's men furtively scratching his rump to stare across at me with hard, speculative eyes.

I couldn't imagine why my brother Guy had chosen to stand among Kit's brood, on the other side of the neat slot they'd dug for our grandfather. At fifteen Guy was only two years older than I was, yet with a dozen terms of English schooling behind him he clearly thought himself too much the man about town for old China hands like Papa and me. I guessed he'd acquired that cool, disdainful expression at school – and the beautiful morning coat from his uncle's tailor. He'd long since buried the white-faced boy who'd waved forlornly from the ship's rail in the Whangpoo River, biting back unmanly tears as he left for England in the care of a homeward-bound banker.

Naturally – my father had murmured to Kit on the way to the grave – since we'd all careered off to deepest Norfolk for Grandmother Kate's benefit, Kate herself had stayed in London to spite us. Her short note had said simply that there were already too many memories in that Norfolk churchyard for her to want to add another. Matthew Oliver had seldom needed her in life and could certainly manage without her now he was dead. And that, as far as Kate was concerned, was that.

For once, Papa had told me *don't*: don't stare at the rest of the family. I stared anyway. When would I ever have a better opportunity?

I could tell Uncle Kit wasn't listening to a word of the service. He was gazing, absorbed, into the grave, his handsome face consumed by a kind of fierce satisfaction. From the other side of the excavation my father was scowling at Uncle Kit, wondering, I suppose, what had taken place between Kit and Grandfather Matthew while we were still steaming back from Shanghai and whether Guy could be made to tell whatever he knew.

Alice and Rose clearly hadn't been warned about staring. Rose was my age, but Alice was two years older and an expert starer; after a while their brazen scrutiny made me so uncomfortable that I let my gaze wander round the leafy churchyard instead. That's when I became aware of two people watching us from beside a weatherstained stone angel some distance away. They were very much a couple, by which I mean they were standing side by side, close together, as two people stand who've decided to defy the world; yet the woman must have been in her thirties and the boy at her elbow hardly a year or two older than I was.

People from the village, I thought at first. The woman's face was guarded by the brim of her hat and I couldn't see much of the boy except that his hair was the shade the superintendent's daughter in Shanghai called 'dirty fair' – a glinting straw colour which caught my eye at once, accustomed as I was to a multitude of blue-black heads. After a few seconds it occurred to me that the pair might not be from the village after all: the woman seemed too citified and she and her companion stood straight and level-eyed, with no hint of that respectful, round-shouldered deference the villagers adopted in the presence of the Oliver family.

I'd long since lost interest in the progress of the burial, completely absorbed in watching this new distraction, when the woman suddenly detached herself from her companion and walked towards us with calm, purposeful steps. Kit noticed her before my father; perhaps the movement of her almond-coloured silk coat attracted his attention amid the cluster of seemly black. At any rate, his head snapped up at once. He stared at the advancing woman and then across at my father, who by now had seen the stranger for himself. To my amazement, I saw a glance of perfect understanding pass between them, a sudden, unlooked-for unity in the face of this startling development.

Yet almost at once my father's gaze slid away. While my Uncle Kit glowered openly at the intruder, cramming down his brows until they hung on the bridge of his nose and jutting his jaw in silent outrage, my father studied his gloves; he seemed to be relying on the hunched black shoulders of his morning coat to make him invisible. I guessed he was praying that no one would speak and force him to become involved.

Yet the rector's head was still bowed in reverence and his

eyes were closed, while the footsteps of the stranger continued to fall soundlessly on the soft turf. Quite oblivious to the disturbance around him, the rector droned on, his voice rising and falling in the mellifluous sing-song of words repeated so often they'd long since been bleached of all meaning.

The woman paid no attention to any of it. Her gaze was directed solely at the yawning earthy pit at our centre with Grandfather Matthew Oliver's coffin suspended above it on wooden staves. Everyone was staring now: Kit, Margot and the girls, Guy and I, and behind us the more distant family members, the shipping company men, the senior masters and all the black-clad crowd who'd deemed it proper to be there.

The unknown woman walked right up to the edge of the grave, watched from a distance by the fair-haired boy. For a moment she stood, staring down. I was near enough to see the muscles of her lips twist and compress for a moment; her chin trembled and she tightened her jaw to stop it – and then, with a violent shrug of her shoulders which took us all by surprise, she turned and walked swiftly away across the grass to where her companion waited by the stone angel.

I suppose the service must have continued afterwards, though I remember nothing of it now, nor of Matthew Oliver's swallowing up in the brown mouth of his grave, nor of the flowers, nor the village itself on that summer morning. My memory of it contains nothing but that rigid, creamy figure, dappled with leaf shadow, disappearing among the headstones alongside another, broader back and a paler head inclined towards her own.

I buried a shrew, once, in our Shanghai garden, under the ancient magnolia by the verandah whose creamy summer blossoms floated, fragrant and luminous, in the evening lamplight. I made the garden boy dig a hole and sent my amah to find a lacquer box for the stiff little corpse; yet in spite of all my efforts it was an odd, unsatisfactory funeral, dull where I'd hoped for drama. What it needed, of course, was a mystery woman in an almond-coloured coat to stare into the grave with that strange expression of mingled loss and contempt, and then to stalk away with a toss of her head, arm in arm with her young companion.

Not that I understood that then. On the day of the shrew burial my distant family in England were still only names, a list recited whenever letters were delivered: Uncle Kit Oliver-and-Aunt Margot followed by Alice-and-Rose, always in order of descending importance like the procession of ivory storks on our dining-room chimneypiece. I'd been taught to recite the genealogy of our family as faithfully as any Chinese: how Grandfather Matthew Oliver had produced two sons (no mention of wives in these dynastic matters), one son to take charge of each of the two divisions of the Oliver Steam Navigation Company.

Edward, the elder son and my father, had chosen Oliver Oriental. At the time this had seemed a shrewd choice, since it had allowed him to go off to Shanghai and build an empire of his own, leaving Kit to labour as his father's messenger boy, managing director of Oliver Atlantic in name alone.

Then, gradually, as the years passed, old Matthew Oliver withdrew into his chairmanship, taking less interest in the day-to-day business of the shipping line. One by one, Kit the messenger boy gathered the levers of power into his own hands, first the business of Oliver Atlantic and then, increasingly, policy affecting the company as a whole. Edward might be emperor in Shanghai, but Kit was in London and Matthew was in London and the line between what Kit had decided and what Matthew had decided became more and more difficult to detect.

By then, if Papa noticed that documents had begun to pass over his desk with Kit's signature where his father's should have been, he was too taken up by other matters to be concerned.

Shanghai suited Edward Oliver. Our house suited him, with its sprawling, airy verandah and its garden planted with willow and yellow ginkgo, with roses and tulip trees whose spade-shaped leaves fluttered in the breeze like an explosion of flags. The only problem, I believe, was that Shanghai didn't suit my mercurial mother, who grew bored in a house which seemed entirely the property of its Chinese staff. If she laid down her magazine for a moment she'd find it again, miraculously restored to its place on the shelf with a marker where she'd stopped reading; cushions would be smoothed the instant her dainty, restless shoulders had left them and necklaces put away in their leather cases almost before she'd had time to try them on. If she rose from her deckchair on the verandah for more than a few seconds, she'd find it when she returned, pushed back to within a quarter-inch of its appointed place.

My mother was too much of a butterfly to be a home-maker. Her fingers had never yearned to straighten a picture and she hadn't the faintest idea of cooking, but it offended her to live in a house where she felt she belonged as little as a muddy footstep in the hall. Reduced to invisibility in her own home, my mother, the dazzling Sylvia, took to travel instead. Soon after I was born, she left me in the care of my nurse, Liu Ling, and sailed from Shanghai aboard the Oliver ship *Oceania*, bound for London, Paris and the brightest amusements New York could offer.

Seven days after my mother sailed away a young Chinese woman joined our household with the official designation of Steward's Niece. I remember wondering, when I became old enough to notice, why, since the girl seemed to have no domestic duties, she was so often in our part of the house. It wasn't until several years later that I realized she'd come to us as my father's first concubine.

By the time my mother returned six months later, Steward's Niece had been joined by Gardener's Little Sister, a girl so young she was happy to play among the tulip trees with Guy and myself as Steward's Niece never did. I've no idea what my mother thought of these decorative additions to our staff. Perhaps she'd even suggested them herself, following time-honoured Chinese tradition – for who can ever be sure what goes on in the private heart of a marriage?

Yet for all that, I believe Sylvia, who sparkled and throbbed with nervous energy, was the sole spiritual love of my father's life, his sun and stars wrapped up together. The only occasion on which I saw him weep was when he came to tell us our mother had died on the liner *Lusitania*, torpedoed by a German submarine on her way back from her latest swing through the salons of New York.

Lusitania had not been an Oliver ship, which at the time seemed to me a far more likely explanation of her sinking than the convulsions of a distant war of which I knew nothing. My five-year-old world was bounded by the wall of our Shanghai garden. I'd never seen the sea, which was rumoured to lie far away, beyond the mouth of the Whangpoo River, but I tried to imagine it all the same. For days I sat on the topmost verandah step, scowling with concentration as if I could force the ocean to give up my mother like Venus on a scallop shell, a glass in one hand and a theatre programme in the other, laughing as though the whole episode had been no more than another delicious lark.

I understood nothing of death: only that a shimmering, perfumed meteor which periodically lit up my infant sky had now spun into immortal orbit, never to return. I was saddened, but not bereft. Sylvia had been a bringer of costly gifts, something to marvel at from a distance. I'd never been hugged to that *chypre*-smelling bosom in case I thrust sticky fingers into her hair or corsage; even now, my clearest memory is of watching her push a mother-of-pearl inlaid stretcher into the fingers of a pair of white kid evening gloves – not her maid, for some reason, but Sylvia herself, sliding the beak of the stretcher into each narrow channel and then laughing with me at the croak of the spring as she squeezed the handles.

She was an icon, something to be worshipped from a distance. Yet one must feel love, in order to mourn – which is why, I suppose, my shrew-burial was so unsatisfactory.

It was Liu Ling who gently explained to us that my father had been made too ill to answer our questions about Mama. I'm sure he was devastated, but on a spiritual level which had no effect on his physical needs. Little though I was, I noticed that by the end of the year Steward's Niece had left our house and Steward's Cousin's Daughter, with her heart-shaped face and mouth as moist and intense as the heart of a fig, had come to giggle under the magnolia with Gardener's Little Sister.

11

I assumed this was how everyone lived and that thousands of miles away my unknown cousins Alice-and-Rose led exactly the same existence. I never fastened a button for myself until I reached England; it didn't occur to me for a moment to put my pencils back in their drawer when I'd finished with them, or to pick up the scattered pieces of my latest jigsaw. And on those days when Liu Ling took me to play with the daughter of the Oliver engineering superintendent, we travelled in a lacquer sedan chair carried by four bearers and filled with cushions and I looked out at the footsore hordes we passed on the way, wondering why their amahs didn't care for them as well as mine did.

Sometimes, on long, silent afternoons when it was too hot to sleep, Liu Ling would take me to call on her own family, who lived on a sampan in Siccawei Creek. It always seemed such an adventure to squeeze in with her parents and grand-parents and brothers and sisters under the curving roof of a boat moored side by side with a legion of others; it never dawned on me that this was as much living space as they ever had – and that only because Liu Ling's two elder brothers pulled a city rickshaw in alternate twelve-hour shifts and were never at home at the same time. Her younger brother Tung was the great hope of the family, a clever boy who worked as a messenger for the *North China Daily News*, where the journalists tipped him in cigarettes and affectionately called him 'Sammy'.

Yes, on the whole, Shanghai suited us. Most young British men came out to China on four- or five-year postings, but my father stayed there for sixteen, travelling back to London less than half a dozen times, and reluctantly even then. In those days, as a foreigner in Shanghai you could have anything you wanted, literally anything at all. The one thing Shanghai couldn't provide, apparently, was a fox, and so there was a 'paper hunt' for those who were incurably horsey.

Not that the Olivers had ever denied themselves luxury in England, or anywhere else for that matter. But Shanghai was like no other city: self-indulgence was simply taken for granted. For us children, birthdays meant jugglers and stiltwalkers and mighty eruptions of skyrockets; winter meant coats lined with soft rabbit fur or beaver, and even when Guy and I were older and had to endure lessons with our respective tutors, our likes and dislikes were still deferred to by everyone – until the day when Guy sailed away to England at the age of eleven, to be educated as a gentleman under Uncle Kit's supervision and made ready, as the only grandson, to inherit both divisions of Matthew Oliver's empire.

My father had the long, smooth fingers of an aesthete, slightly drooping at the last joint: his weakness was beauty, but not the sort to be found in opium dreams, or in antique jade or exquisite silks, not even in the heavy silk of that startling coat, that pale banner flown so defiantly at Grandfather Matthew's funeral. Ah now . . . the dignity of that unknown woman as she advanced, the bony poignancy of the hand that clasped her coat just above her waist and the brave tilt of her chin have brought to mind another woman, two years before we returned to England, a woman of similar grace and self-containment whom my father saw and wanted.

In Shanghai, whatever my father wanted he could have. I've no idea what arrangement was made with the lady's family, but as soon as she came to us, tottering unsteadily on bound 'lily' feet, it was clear this was no Gardener's Sister or Steward's Niece. Flat-footed Liu Ling went in awe of Sumei, and so did I once I understood the nature of foot-binding in childhood, the crushing and breaking which had created those tiny fist-like feet, a torment outlawed one year after my birth. I've heard that the sensation of those two mutilated crescent moons caressing a man's penis could drive Chinese males to ecstasy: at any rate, Sumei brought a cool pride to her position and occupied a special place in our household.

There was even a moment when I believed my father might bring Sumei to England with us when the summons came in 1923. He could force himself to leave Shanghai and our magical house and even his empire of ships, but to leave Sumei, who'd come nearest to entrancing him as my mother had done . . .

'I want Liu Ling to come to England with us.'

'No, Clio.'

'But she must!'

'The answer is *no*.'

'But I want her to come.'

'I dare say you do. The answer is still no. Liu Ling is Chinese, all her family are here. She'd hate it in England.'

. 'And what about Sumei? Won't she hate it too?'

'Probably.' My father stared out of the window, absently stroking his knee.

In the end we each travelled to England without the one person we needed most in the world.

My father rushed off to see Grandmother Kate as soon as we'd reached London and discovered that Matthew Oliver's illness had killed him in a matter of weeks rather than the months he'd expected. Immediately after the funeral Papa was suddenly very anxious to talk to his mother again, alone, without Kit or Margot or their staring daughters listening to all that went on. He must have wanted to see Kate quite badly, since we were hardly back in our hotel suite when he telephoned to arrange a time. Then, at the last moment Kate upset all his careful plans.

'Bring the girl.' Kate shouted so loudly into the telephone that I could hear her imperious buzzing from the next room. 'Bring what's-her-name – Clio, is it? It's high time I had a look at her.'

A maid in a frilled cap showed us into the tall, hushed drawing room where a wealth of churned plasterwork lost itself in the dimness overhead. Grandmother Kate looked at me and I looked back. I imagine she saw a solemn, putty-coloured creature with a pair of dark pigtails and knitting-pin legs, while I saw a scrawny little bird of a woman with a combative jaw and white hair held up on top of her head by an old-fashioned aigrette of paradise feathers.

'Now go and play.' His annoyance multiplied by the echoes, my father shooed me into the purple-shadowed, lavender-smelling vastness of the house.

Play? I was thirteen years old – not that my father ever noticed such details. Resentful, I lingered, or at least, I moved away in reluctant stages, certain something significant was about to be discussed as soon as my father thought I was out of earshot. Instinct sharpened by a lonely girlhood told me it had something to do with the mysterious woman who'd appeared at the funeral and, since Guy had already been sent back to school and my father had brushed all my questions aside, I was aching with curiosity. Yet dawdle as I dared, by the time I'd reached the drawing-room door they were still discussing the weather.

There was a tiger-skin rug on the dining-room floor with which I occupied myself for a while, drawing the dry bunches of claws across the skin of my arm and examining the hard, heavy head with its bared teeth and plaster tongue which reared up, snarling, at one end of the mothy hide. The teeth reminded me, oddly enough, of my Uncle Kit. Kit Oliver was an attractive man in a pale-eyed, tigerish sort of way, but he had the prominent, elongated lower teeth I've always associated with villainy and when he shook my hand for the first time I noticed that he wore his nails unusually long. I hoped Guy hadn't begun to copy him in that, too.

Kate's house seemed remarkably sunless and full of heavy pictures of people and ships. Gradually, I wandered back towards the drawing room and since the door was still open as I'd left it I was able to slide silently inside, more or less invisible behind a large glass cabinet near the entrance.

I didn't mean to eavesdrop, not really, though since Kate was quite deaf I knew I might well not be able to prevent myself overhearing some of what was said. If challenged, I'd say I'd only returned to have a closer look at the mermaid, half-monkey, half-fish, who peered warily out at me from the depths of her glass case, her skin yellowed by the years and her scaly tail dried to the roughness of a tiled roof. Nothing could have been less seductive than her grotesque face and the wrinkled arms coyly ruffling her plaster surf, but I was so fascinated that for a moment when my grandmother spoke I imagined she was talking about the little sea creature.

'Offered her money? Of course I've offered her money.' Kate's voice was sharp with indignation. 'I'd have given her anything she wanted, whether Matthew liked it or not. But that

15

fellow of hers wouldn't let her take a penny and after he'd gone she was always too proud.'

'Oh Mother, for heaven's sake.' Uncomfortably, my father flexed the toe of one shoe. 'I'm not saying you shouldn't try to help her – goodness knows, I never suggested we should leave her to starve. But I wish you hadn't gone behind our backs like that.'

'Don't treat me like a child, Edward. Your father never did and even Kit knows better.'

'I only meant—'

'You're a fool, Edward, if you think you can bully me, when even Matthew failed.' Kate gave a loud, contemptuous snort. 'Thank goodness someone in this family still has a bit of backbone left. *And* a conscience.' She smoothed her black skirts with arthritic fingers and her rings rattled.

'What could I have done?' For a moment, my father met his mother's gaze, then wearily shook his head. 'Neither of them ever listened to me. And now – to come to the churchyard like that, without a word to anyone, and to bring the boy—'

'Don't you think they had a perfect right to be there?'

The point was evidently unanswerable. A profound silence fell, while I scarcely dared to breathe.

'Kit says Catherine's to get nothing.' My father's voice, unusually loud and decisive, cut through the failing light. 'So it's out of our hands now, in any case.'

'And how would Kit know that?'

'He's seen the will.'

'I don't believe it. Years ago, Matthew promised me you'd all get equal shares, no matter what. That was agreed.'

'Then he must have changed his mind.' My father's hands gave a dry hiss as he rubbed them. 'It's a wretched business, I know, but if that's how Father arranged things, it's hardly our fault.'

'And what about the boy? What about Stephen? Even if Catherine were to get nothing, Matthew would hardly have forgotten the boy.'

'There's no mention of Stephen Morgan.'

'Pooh – Kit says.'

16

My father's chair creaked as he shifted uneasily on its delicate canework. Ever since word had reached us in Shanghai that Matthew Oliver was in failing health and had demanded our immediate presence in England, my father had fretted over the six weeks it would take us to reach London. For six vital weeks Kit would be alone with his dying father: who could tell what he might persuade the ailing Matthew to do before Edward could arrive to secure his and his son's interests?

'You might have made Matthew see reason, if you'd come in time.' Kate shouted the words, cupping an ear for the answer.

'A day earlier and I'd have been able to speak to him. One day less in that confounded Canal.'

'He went down very quickly, at the end.' I heard Kate give a brief sigh. 'I asked him if he'd like to see Catherine, just once more. But no.' Her dress rustled as she shrugged. 'I doubt if Catherine would have come, in any case.'

My mouth had been hanging open, my breath misting the mermaid's tank, but now I closed it, losing interest. My Shanghai-trained mind had settled upon a mundane and disappointing solution to the mystery: clearly this *Catherine*, this woman who'd appeared in a flamboyant coat at my grandfather's funeral, had merely been one of the old man's concubines, too upset by her protector's death to remember her place in the order of things. If the memory of that eloquent, speechless mouth suggested any other interpretation, I pushed it away, together with the image of a fair head waiting beside a stone angel in a Norfolk churchyard. Whoever Stephen Morgan and his mother might be, they were clearly of no real importance to the Olivers.

'For all your sakes, I hope Kit's wrong.' Kate Oliver's voice broke into my thoughts. 'If that boy gets nothing, I suspect you'll both come to regret it.'

For a while I puzzled over the word *regret*. My reclusive world had never contained much sadness of any kind – except frustration, perhaps, when for some reason I hadn't got entirely my own way, or a vague disappointment when my father had been too busy as usual to look at a picture I'd drawn specially for him. I was entirely self-absorbed, yet Liu Ling had taught

17

me that the sadness or happiness of one individual was of no importance. Duty to the family was everything, especially for girl children. I must have been a cold creature in those days: but what example of warmth had I been given? Even my mother's death had only brushed me like the loss of a delightful dream.

And now I'd come to a strange country where people openly showed shame and anger and spoke of *regret*. Perhaps regret was what I was feeling for my absent Liu Ling, my rock, my refuge. Her place was surely with me and I missed her dreadfully. That must surely be regret: not something to be wasted on a concubine's child, even one who'd watched us so boldly among the tombstones.

My Shanghai governess, the missionary's widow, used to make me copy from a book of old Chinese legends. Day after day, I transcribed them in my careful hand, until one in particular, translated from verses by the poet Tao Chi'en, became linked for ever in my memory with the warm, tawny breath of our midday verandah, sweet with the faded glory of crumpled magnolia blooms.

Once upon a time, said Tao Chi'en, in that part of China where water buffalo flounder among the rectangular mirrors of the rice fields and the hills leap up from the river in blueing ranges of limestone stumps, in a magical valley beyond a forest of blossoming peach trees, an old man and his daughters led a life of eternal pleasure, with no knowledge of toil, or sadness, or conflict.

One day a poor cormorant fisherman stumbled upon their miraculous peace. Though they begged him to keep their secret, he couldn't resist letting in the outside world and at its touch the valley and the peach-blossom forest vanished, never to be seen again.

The moral of the tale escaped me, but I knew that flowery forest well. Now I wondered if Liu Ling was thinking of me, far away in our magic valley in Shanghai, and how soon I'd be returning to her. I wondered if Sumei was weeping for my father in the humid, greenish light under the tulip trees.

Chapter Two

THREE MONTHS after the funeral, my father returned to Shanghai. I didn't. Instead, in England, I was sent to a school whose motto was *Onward and Upward* – a strident, bracing college which specialized in the taming of pubescent girls. My father must have made the arrangements immediately after Matthew Oliver's funeral, simply choosing the school which already held Alice-and-Rose among its lolloping herd.

That's when I discovered we wouldn't be living in Shanghai any more, in the enchanted security of our house and garden. My father was only going back to tie up the loose ends of our existence there.

I stormed and sulked and was sent to my room, astonished, to storm and sulk alone. I became frantic with despair. I'd almost never been refused something I'd set my heart on and at that moment all I wanted was to go home with my father to Shanghai and Liu Ling.

Instead, Hallowhill School undertook to form my character, never understanding it had begun at least seven years too late. I was hopelessly accustomed to total indulgence – there'd never been anyone else to 'fit in' with – and from the very first, the mistresses regarded me as a dangerous deviant. At Hallowhill a passion for one's own way was the sign of an unwholesome mind, and heaven knows how often I was banned from games for insisting on it. Fortunately the ban was no punishment. I suppose I must have been truly degenerate: I even preferred lonely labour over pages of *I must not* to all that hearty thundering over the lacrosse field.

If I'd only realized it, my father must have longed to stay in China as much as I did; but the head office of the Oliver Steam Navigation Company was in London and Kit was in London, and now Matthew Oliver had made it necessary for the two brothers to keep looking for all eternity over one another's shoulders. Shortly before his death Matthew had told the Oliver board that he wished Edward, as his elder son, to take over the chairmanship of the company with my Uncle Kit as managing director. He'd joined them at the hip, as he'd no doubt intended, yet my father held one winning card which even Matthew couldn't take from him – my brother Guy.

Through Guy, Edward Oliver had provided the next generation of Oliver shipowners, while Kit's daughters would soon become Mrs Somebody Somethings with no more interest in the shipping line their grandfather had built than the ownership of a parcel of shares. As brothers, Edward and Kit had been forced to divide the business between them, but lucky Guy was the sole heir apparent, and though for years now he'd spent his school holidays with Uncle Kit and Aunt Margot, he remained by blood my father's son.

Perhaps it was the sight of Guy standing with his uncle's family at Grandfather Matthew's funeral which wakened my father to potential danger. At any rate, from that day forwards nothing – not Shanghai, nor Sumei, nor his daughter's happiness – was too great a price for winning Guy back to his side. As soon as the start of the school term arrived I was packed off with my trunk to Hallowhill, while my father returned to China to break up our household and prepare the Shanghai office for a new master.

I couldn't see why I needed to go to school at all, except that no one else wanted me. It wasn't as if I was uneducated by the female standards of the day. The missionary's widow who'd taught me in Shanghai had introduced me to Wordsworth and *Lamb's Tales from Shakespeare*, and made sure I could count up a purseful of dollars and the copper dross we called 'cash'. Liu Ling had encouraged me to paint, letting me daub away with the beautiful Chinese brushes designed for calligraphy. And as

for dancing – for dancing there'd been Igor Andreevich Starozhilov and his sister Nina.

You might say the Starozhilovs were a tiny, dazzling piece
of the outside world allowed in to enliven my cloistered
existence, like jugglers at a birthday party. Engaged to teach me
social dancing, they astounded me with their glamour. Merely
by being Russian exiles, they trailed into our house a barbaric
magnificence which transformed their much-mended clothes
into Tartars' robes and lit their hollow, hungry faces with a
nobility all the more romantic for having nothing but poverty
to support it.

The Starozhilovs' father had been an artist at the court of the
Tsar and they'd been born into a cultivated, Europeanized court
that was as much a world within a world as the Forbidden City
in Beijing. They'd been as cut off as the emperors from the
troubles of ordinary mortals, until the day the Bolsheviks came
and smashed their complacency to atoms. Starozhilov the artist
was shot against his own studio wall, leaving his wife to drag
her children for months across the frozen steppes towards the
uncertain sanctuary of China; their first shelter across the border,
Nina recalled, was an icy cave whose walls, painted with a
thousand ancient Buddhas, had long since been savaged, like the
Winter Palace, by an unbelieving horde.

Yet despite their present aching need, Nina insisted the
Starozhilovs were still a cut above the rest of the White Russians
who'd flooded into Shanghai; their mother, she said proudly,
was a countess. But weren't they all countesses, those sad-eyed
women who gave piano lessons or made hats, or daydreamed
behind the cash-grilles of down-at-heel restaurants?

When my father discovered them Igor and Nina were
dancing in a cabaret in one of the big hotels, as lithe as cats,
sliding over one another with a liquid ease that made the purest
ballet steps seem unspeakably wanton. Nina's fringes and span-
gles glittered like flame in the spotlight, but her glory was sadly
tarnished when she came out to the kitchen door, a coat flung
over her bare shoulders, to suck for a moment at a customer's
Turkish cigarette. In those days she wore her dark hair scraped

back into a knot at the nape of her neck, which pulled out the corners of her eyes and made her look like a gypsy: it was hard to believe that Nina, in 1922, was still only fifteen years of age and her brother barely a year or two older.

They came once a week to our house in the French Concession, always together and always during their rest hours from dancing in the hotel. Our dining-room table had already been pushed to one side of the polished parquet floor and a pile of records laid out by our fashionable new gramophone. Liu Ling was supposed to stay in the room as chaperone, but the first strains of a Strauss waltz were enough to send her scuttling away to mutter to Cook in the kitchen.

At the start of each lesson, Nina would take on the role of instructor, seizing her brother in an impassioned grip to demonstrate a new step while I marvelled that two separate human beings could move so closely as one. Then it would be my turn to dance with Igor, while Nina stalked wolfishly round us, darting forward now and then to twist my shoulders with her strong little hands, shouting guttural instructions.

'*Won*-two-zree, *won*-two-zree . . . *Bend* yourself, girl! Lean back a little more, let your partner see your beautiful eyeees! Odderwise *wy* are you dancing at all?'

Then, without warning, Nina would vanish – to collect their fee from my father, she always claimed later – leaving me alone with her brother, my nose level with his middle shirt-button and my twelve-year-old legs splayed over his hard, dancer's thigh. In the polka or the two-step, of course, we stayed properly apart and Papa had forbidden the tango; but the waltz was another matter, and the foxtrot – the smooth, undulating English foxtrot where two bodies glue along their length and move together – then Igor would stretch me against him, stretch and glide, supporting my spine with his hand while his longer stride parted my knees for that heart-stopping sway on the eighth beat.

Above my head, his handsome face gave away nothing at all. If it hadn't been for a glow like live coals in his dark eyes and the faint quivering of his over-long lashes, he might have been carved in alabaster. Yet I could tell Igor was just as aware of me as I was of him. He gave off an earthy, animal smell, he and his sister, which they didn't trouble to wash away, and there I was, with my baby breasts squashed to his ribs and my legs tangling with his own. The pressure of his hand on my spine was thrilling and frightening at the same time: pretty soon I'd made the appalling discovery that young men of seventeen or so cannot control every part of their bodies as easily as they can govern their faces.

I sometimes wondered if Liu Ling sensed my agitation, like a silent cry for help. Always, before long, her round, watchful face would appear at the dining-room door, causing Igor to thrust me out abruptly to arm's length.

'*Now* we do mazurka, I think.'

Shortly after that Nina would return, grimly pleased with herself and a little flushed, clutching what I always thought was a very large amount of money for a dancing lesson, however much I might have learned from it.

Once a week they came to repeat the ritual, licensed to enter our magic valley, bringing with them a gust of the forbidden, bitter-sweet scent of the outside world. They were my only glimpse of it. How was I to know that beyond our walls, famine had swept across China and children who could not be fed were being sold to strangers or flung into rivers to drown?

Onward and Upward.

There were no birthday stiltwalkers at Hallowhill School and precious little dancing either. At Hallowhill we slept ten to a dormitory and washed ourselves at a row of basins fed by greenish plumbing which dripped on the frigid tiled floor. The mattresses were horribly thin, the porridge was thin, and the headmistress, apart from a small, wadded bust which pushed out like a bowler hat under her stockinette jumper, was as skinny and unwelcoming as everything else.

Enough of Hallowhill. Even to describe it fills my nose with the smell of chalk and musty books and Mabel Browne's carbolic tooth-powder.

At least at Hallowhill Alice-and-Rose lost the hyphens which had joined them like Siamese twins during my years in Shanghai.

Rose, the younger of my Oliver cousins, was bewitchingly pretty and affected a kind of passionate dottiness which made everyone cry fondly, 'Oh Rose! What a priceless creature you are!' I'd have fussed over her too, just for the sake of friendship, but although we were the same age, my educational shortcomings had banished me to a lower form and she preferred to pretend we weren't related in any way. Even in private she treated me with scorn, especially on days when a letter arrived for me from my father.

'For God's sake, Clio. It's pretty pathetic, snivelling in the bootroom like this, don't you think?'

'I c-can't help it.'

'Well you better had help it, if you don't want everyone calling you a cry-baby. Most of them think you're pretty peculiar already.'

'I don't care what they think of me! I don't want to be here at horrible Hallowhill, I want to be home in Shanghai—'

'But you stupid thing, Shanghai isn't *home*. No one's at home in Shanghai unless they're Chinese and you aren't that, I presume. Well, then – you can't possibly be homesick for China.' Rose tossed her head theatrically. '*England*'s home. Everybody knows that. Now come on, Clio. Think how it looks for me, having a cousin who's such a weed.'

Late at night, at the risk of being made to scrub the washroom floor as punishment, I examined my father's letter again by torchlight under the bedclothes.

'My dear Clio, I'm afraid we shan't be together for Christmas after all, as I can't possibly leave Shanghai just yet. However, your Uncle Kit and Aunt Margot say you must definitely spend Christmas in London with them – and of course, Guy will be there too, and the girls, so I'm sure you'll have a much jollier time than we used to have on our own in Shanghai.

'By the way, Liu Ling sends her love, and has shed a tear or two over the letter you gave me to read to her. You'll be pleased to know I've found her a position with a family from the

American consulate who have a house near the Avenue Joffre. She should be perfectly happy there.'

Far from being pleased, I was utterly wretched. I didn't want Liu Ling to be happy in a strange house in the Avenue Joffre: I wanted her to be happy again with me, sitting on our verandah steps near the magnolia tree, or painting, or burying shrews, or whatever diversion had come into my head at that moment. I *needed* Liu Ling. Sometimes, lying sleepless on my lumpy mattress, I'd make bargains with God; if only He would let me go back to Shanghai, I promised I'd dress myself every morning, even the little hooks down my back, and tidy my room and fetch my own coat when we went out and never throw my shoes on to the verandah roof, just for the fun of watching Gardener's Assistant scramble up for them.

I needed Liu Ling. And I was pretty sure that as long as my father remained in Shanghai, Sumei wouldn't be sent away. Sumei would still be there, shuffling across the polished floors on the crippled 'lily' feet which completed her perfect beauty.

Alice . . . Alice was quite different from Rose. She was fifteen when I arrived at Hallowhill, old enough not to feel ashamed by her odd cousin, but young enough to remember what it had been like to be new. It was Alice who patiently explained the rules of lacrosse, Alice who secretly taught me to tie my own shoelaces and only Alice with whom I could speculate on the identity of the woman in the almond-coloured coat who'd startled us so much at Grandfather Matthew's funeral.

'She was very pretty, wasn't she?' Alice's own hair was the colour of old tennis-balls and cut in a straight fringe over her forehead which made her eyes look eternally anxious and her mouth very small above her pointed chin. On the day in question she'd found me condemned to clean brushes in the art room and had stayed to help.

'Yes, she was pretty.' I passed her another matted handful. 'But then, I suppose Matthew Oliver was rich enough to take a beautiful mistress whenever he wanted one.'

'Oh Clio, you don't know anything of the kind!' Alice

blushed furiously at the very idea. 'How can you possibly know?'

'Who else can she have been? You could see by the expression on her face that she'd once loved him to distraction. Loved him and borne his son.' I paddled the stiff hog's-hair in the stained sink and thought of Igor's manly arms.

'Do you really think she was his mistress?' Alice's eyes ate me up in awe.

'Definitely.' For a moment I experienced a novel feeling of sophistication. Here, at last, was something I knew about. Years before, Guy had discovered where our father kept the antiquarian books he collected and I'd traded my clockwork camel for the secret. The illustrations were exquisite – richly dressed men and women, their robes parted to expose lovingly detailed sexual organs, enjoying one another in various bizarre ways with the faintly bored expressions of dowagers indulging in an afternoon's bridge.

For a long time, I couldn't imagine why they should want to do these curious things to one another.

'Oh God, you're stupid,' snapped Guy, going pink, when I asked.

It was only after the menarche that I understood, when Liu Ling explained the reason for my bleeding with delicate precision and I fled to re-examine the pictures in all their riveting awfulness.

Now I imitated Guy's most world-weary tone. 'With important men it's quite usual, you know.'

Alice stared at me for a moment and then took refuge in her seniority. 'When you've finished those brushes, they go in the cupboard by the window. And don't be too long about it, or you'll miss tea.'

Alice was destined for Guy. I realized that at Christmas, when I went to Uncle Kit and Aunt Margot's house in Belgrave Square, just as Guy had done for the past four years. There, thank goodness, I had a room of my own again – though of course it wasn't really mine, any more than the maid I shared with Alice and Rose or the enormous Hispano Suiza which Aunt Margot ordered up to take us to a celebratory tea at the Ritz.

I'd assumed that at least Guy was mine, even with all his new airs and cleverness, but I soon discovered Uncle Kit had important plans for him.

'Guy, you must take Alice in to dinner.' This was Aunt Margot, languidly arranging a very long taffeta scarf. To my admiring gaze, Margot Oliver seemed long all over – endless limbs, soaring cheekbones and narrow, elegant hands. Even her eyes were long, giving her face a classical perfection: the lazy swing of her pupils under their heavy lids added to that languor which many men confessed to finding irresistible. But Margot was also wise, and understood when romance needed a helping hand.

'Guy, has Alice shown you her watercolour of the Chilterns? Oh, but you must ask her to let you see it. If you hurry, you might find her in the conservatory.'

Soon after this I made a point of catching Guy alone one morning, before anyone else had come down to breakfast. 'Tell me, do you really like Alice?'

For a moment he continued to rattle about among the silverware on the sideboard. 'Alice? Oh, she's good fun, I suppose.'

'You certainly seem to spend a lot of time with her.'

'It's sort of expected. I think the Governor and Uncle Kit would like us to hit it off one day, for the good of the company. That sort of thing.'

'To keep Kit's family involved in Oliver's.'

'Something like that.' Guy sat down at the table, his plate piled high.

'And is that what you want?'

'Oh God, not yet! I'm not sixteen until April, thank you very much. The world's full of pretty girls, it seems to me, and I dare say a few of them will come my way.'

'Don't you think Alice is pretty, then?'

Guy waved his fork ambiguously. 'Besides, there isn't only Alice. There's Rose too. I reckon she's going to turn out quite a beauty.'

'But Alice is nicer than Rose.' I'd turned my back on him, torn between my loyalty to Alice and possessiveness of my brother. Unable to choose, I concentrated on fishing an egg out of the silver steamer. 'Alice is nicer, I said.'

'I heard you the first time.' Guy's voice was thick, his mouth full. He swallowed a gulp of tea. 'In any case, there's years and years before I have to decide. I haven't even joined the company yet.'

'What if Alice marries somebody else before you've made up your mind?'

'She won't.' Guy reached out for the toast rack, drawing it right up to the edge of his plate. 'Alice thinks I'm pretty bloody marvellous.'

My father wrote again from Shanghai, complaining about missing the family Christmas and trying to sound as if he'd made a determined effort to be with us.

'Oh, by the way, I saw Liu Ling last week, with a funny little American baby up to its ears in fur, like a dormouse. And do you remember the Starozhilovs?' My father swept on with bland indifference. 'Nina and Igor, who taught you to waltz? Nina has set her heart on a place in Diaghilev's dance company in Monte Carlo, but of course she hasn't a penny to get herself there, so as a favour to the poor girl I've promised to arrange a passage to Europe for her on the *Alexandria* when I leave for England myself. Her mother, the countess, insists Igor must stay in Shanghai, so at least this way Nina will have someone to look after her on ship-board.'

I was puzzled. I thought of Nina's bright eyes and grim little mouth as she pushed each thick pad of dollars into the pocket of her coat: surely Nina was clever enough to take care of herself – and Igor too, if it came to that. I couldn't imagine what had possessed my father to take such a ferocious young woman under his wing.

I didn't see a great deal of Aunt Margot that Christmas – never, in daylight hours, much before the great dimpled gong in the hall was struck to announce the imminence of lunch. Even then, it only meant lunch for 'the young people', since Kit lunched at his club and Aunt Margot invariably had an engagement of some kind. From lunch she flowed serenely through a programme of massage, manicure, hairdressing and bathing which culminated in her appearance in some astounding creation, ready for the theatre or a dinner party, or whatever excitement offered that evening.

I should really have said *un*excitement, since it was Margot Oliver's trademark, in an age when every stylish woman had to have one, never to be stirred by anything. If it didn't imply effort, I'd say Aunt Margot had conquered the summit of indifference and *ennui*. Even when her prized Hispano was rammed by a charabanc in Regent Street she emerged coolly from its carpeted depths to be whirled away by an acquaintance whose own motor had conveniently been brought to a halt by the gathering crowd.

Margot Oliver, I understood from the pages of old *Tatlers* in the conservatory, flitted from luncheon at the Savoy, with Guinnesses and Grosvenors to shopping in Paris at Patou and Chanel, or to costume parties in Venetian palazzos, dressed as Diana with emeralds in her hair and a pair of greyhounds dyed the exact beetle-green of her chiffon tunic.

'Oh darling, *that*. . .' she murmured when I showed her the pictures one day. 'Oh, that was such a disaster. Cleopatra's panther came round too soon from its morphia and ripped up Juno's peacock at the foot of the stairs, just where everyone could see.' She gave an elegant shiver. '*Too* horrid.'

Uncle Kit seemed content to wear his wife like a jewel in his lapel. The more she glittered, the more he was envied, which apparently satisfied him. For her part, Margot Oliver kept Kit at her side, casually, wittily, like the rope of enormous pearls she'd inherited from his grandmother and wore knotted like an afterthought round the strap of her evening gown. Nothing mattered except style; and the most stylish thing was to show that nothing mattered.

All of which made Aunt Margot's behaviour twice as strange, on the day we went to call on Grandmother Kate.

'By the way darling, Mother says she hasn't seen the girls for months.'

For once we were all present at dinner, when Uncle Kit suddenly bared his tiger teeth in a charming smile and uttered the remark with deceptive unconcern. At the opposite end of the table, Aunt Margot regarded him coolly from under half-moon eyelids.

'And I'm expected to take them over there at once, I suppose.'

'When it's convenient, I'm sure Mother would appreciate a call.'

'And if it isn't convenient?' Aunt Margot's pencilled brows rose by the merest fraction.

Kit's voice was silken. 'Oh, you must have an hour or so free.'

'Chester Square isn't very far away,' Alice pointed out. 'We could go on our own. In the motor, with Dickson.'

'No, my dear.' Kit laid down his fork and spoon, perfectly aligned. 'I don't think that would be quite the same.'

'I could look after the girls, Uncle Kit.'

'Thank you, Guy, but that won't be necessary. Your Aunt Margot will take them.'

Margot Oliver's lower lip bulged infinitesimally. 'Then it will have to be next week. I've nothing but engagements until the fifth.'

'Then cancel something, darling.' Kit's eyes met his wife's along the length of the table. 'One of your little afternoon jaunts, perhaps. I'm sure the gentleman concerned won't mind.'

Aunt Margot flushed under her pearl powder, opened her mouth as if to say something mutinous, then glanced round the table, changed her mind and pressed her lips together instead. She gave a swift shrug. 'I'll see what I can do. If I must,' she added under her breath.

'Oh, I think you must. Mother was quite specific. Besides—' Kit appealed to the table at large. 'You girls enjoy calling on your grandmother, don't you?'

'Oh yes,' we chorused dutifully.

'Then I think you should go as soon as possible.'

'Oh, very well.' Aunt Margot dabbed at her lips with her napkin, leaving a blood-red stain on the linen.

'Excellent.' Uncle Kit showed his teeth once more. 'Now, if Rose has had as much of that brûlée as she wants, I think we might ring for them to clear away.'

Aunt Margot took us to Grandmother Kate's the very next day, Rose and I stiff in new fur-collared winter coats and Alice wrapped in seal coney from her neck to her ankles. Aunt Margot seemed to have dressed for the role of warrior queen, draped in several silver-furred dead animals of some kind, complete with tails, paws and glassy-eyed snouts swinging at her knee. It's just as well Grandmother Kate hasn't a nervous disposition, I thought as we emerged from the Hispano, though I was pretty sure that anyone who could tolerate that freakish mermaid in her drawing room could also stand the sight of Aunt Margot's furs.

I was still brooding about the mermaid when the most extraordinary thing happened.

Rose, bounding ahead, had just reached the area railings when Kate's door suddenly opened and a female figure hurried out and down the steps, causing Rose to jump backwards in surprise and collide with Alice. The woman's shoulders were hunched against the cold; her head was bowed and one skeletal hand held her collar closed at her throat, but even so none of us doubted for a moment that this apparition was Catherine of the almond-coloured coat, the woman we remembered so vividly from Matthew Oliver's funeral.

This time she was huddled in a long grey waterproof – but what shocked us most was the colour of her face and her drawn, haggard appearance. She glanced only once in our direction before hurrying away, but that single glance was enough to show us eyes which gazed out of great tunnels of shadow and the ridge of her nose glistening white through her skin. For an instant she held her chin high, searching our faces; then she was gone, drawn in on herself, stooped over her lonely secret.

I remembered how Catherine and her young companion had instinctively drawn together in the churchyard, united against the world. Where was he now, that light-haired young man? For clearly Catherine needed him.

Rose, unconcerned, was already at the top of the steps. 'Shall I ring, Mama?'

No one answered and I glanced over my shoulder. To my astonishment, Margot Oliver was staring after Catherine's dwindling figure, while her extravagant furs slid slowly to the pavement in a jumble of limp paws and glass eyes.

Chapter Three

OF COURSE Margot, being Margot, managed to recover her poise even before Dickson had rescued her sprawling foxes from the gutter. As he wrapped her once more in their soft embrace I watched her construct that tight, vague smile which signals *pas devant les enfants* as if nothing of the slightest moment had happened. And by the end of the afternoon, when we all piled back into the motor to go home and I was at last able to ask my question, it was already too late to expect an answer.

'What lady, Clio dear?' Absently, Margot flicked a stray snout from her knee. 'Oh, I expect she was a friend of your grandmother's.' With calculated indifference she turned to gaze out of the Hispano's window. And that was that.

Yet not even Margot could banish every awkwardness so easily. From the very first days of that Christmas holiday with my aunt and uncle, I'd sensed a tension behind Kit's suave good humour and Margot's indolence that I was quite unable to fathom. Of course, I was a poor judge of marriage: the only home I'd known besides my own had been that of the Oliver engineering superintendent and his wife in Shanghai, whose family seemed to amble along in easy, mutual tolerance. Yet in Belgrave Square I could feel a brittleness in the air which filtered through the house like the sharp notes of Margot's perfume. Conversations were broken off when I entered a room, or became loud discussions of something impossibly banal; glances flew to and fro over the cocktail glasses, Kit's hard with warning, Margot's brightly defiant.

'There's something wrong between them,' I told Guy one

morning. I'd come down to breakfast early again; it was the best time to catch him, before Alice and Rose arrived. 'Something's definitely up – and I bet it's all connected with that woman we saw at the funeral.'

Guy put on his irritating, man-about-town expression. 'I very much doubt if that's the cause.'

'Why shouldn't it be? Guy, if you know something, you'd better tell me.'

All Christmas Guy had been modelling himself more closely than ever on his uncle. Now his smile was a perfect copy of Kit's: easy, urbane and impenetrable.

'It's nothing you need worry yourself about, little sister.'

'Don't be so condescending! I demand to know what's going on.'

'Go ahead and demand. You're still too young.'

'That means you don't know any more than I do. You're a fraud, Guy. You pretend to be so grown up, but nobody tells you any more than Alice or me.'

Guy shrugged scornfully and rose to leave the room. 'Kit's right,' he remarked from the doorway. 'Little girls are an utter bore.'

The spring term at Hallowhill was a month old by the time my father returned to London and set about finding us a house of our own. Summoned to the headmistress's study to take his telephone call, I found myself suddenly tongue-tied. My father was back in London: all I could think of was that our last contact with Shanghai was lost, and my past, my childhood and all my familiar landmarks had gone with it. Eighteen inches away across the desk, Miss Aspinall held a letter rigidly before her eyes.

'Clio – are you all right?' My father's voice seemed diminished by distance. 'You aren't ill, or anything?'

'I'm not ill.' I was far from being all right, but I couldn't bear to share the details with Miss Aspinall's telephone. It wasn't as if he'd even understand. 'How was your trip home?'

'We had a storm in the Med, of all places. Darling – are you sure you're quite well?'

'I'm fine.' His persistence embarrassed me. In the past he'd always left the details of my health to Liu Ling; now he felt obliged to ask, but was afraid of hearing something indelicate.

It was safer to talk about ships. Hadn't Nina Starozhilova sailed with him to Europe? I felt a sudden, unlikely surge of affection for Nina and her sultry brother, for anything at all which might keep a link with Shanghai.

'What about Nina?' I blurted out. 'Is she in London with you?'

'Nina Starozhilova? Of course not. She left the ship in Marseilles. She was going to Monte Carlo. Didn't I tell you?'

'Perhaps you did.'

'She wants to dance with Diaghilev, or something of the kind.' My father's voice crackled irritably down the telephone line, as if he were anxious to change the subject. 'At any rate, Clio, I just wanted to let you know I've already found a house for us all. A new home for you and me and Guy – all together, just as we were in Shanghai.'

'That sounds nice,' I agreed cautiously.

Miss Aspinall laid down her letter and coughed meaning-fully, hiding her mouth behind a small, blanched fist.

'I have to go now.'

'Very well, darling. If you're sure you're all right. I must say, you sound a bit down.'

'Goodbye, Papa.'

Miss Aspinall held out her hand for the receiver and, with a sudden feeling of emptiness, I returned my father to her keeping.

The house he'd chosen was in Rutland Gate and quite enormous, considering that for most of the year he'd be living there alone and at best there'd only be three of us rattling around in its multitude of rooms. It was seven storeys high, its sombre grandeur making it perfect for the town residence of the chairman of the Oliver Steam Navigation Company.

I first set eyes on it at Easter 1924, when our gleaming new Rolls drew up before its portico and Robbins, our just-engaged butler, solemnly opened the front door. My trunk disappeared round to the mews, to be taken upstairs by passenger lift, while I wandered into the hall, the clomp of my school shoes echoing among the pillars and striking a soft ringing note from the two cloisonné vases, each taller than a man, which had come back with Papa from China.

Our house in Shanghai had sprawled, half-timbered and wide-gabled. We – and our furniture – had been accustomed to the half-light of a verandah beyond the windows and the wagging green fans of windmill palms. In this house everything was either upstairs or downstairs, in light or darkness, and the brisk London glare fell harshly on our inky lacquer and our pieces of jade and ivory, making a tawdry bazaar of our treasures.

Still, nothing was missing which could add to our comfort. Upstairs on the second floor I had a bedroom, a sitting room and a marble-lined bathroom all of my own, filled with flowers on Papa's instructions. After the horrors of Hallowhill it was delightful to wallow late in bed, cocooned in stiff and blinding linen, summoning tea and platefuls of hot buttered toast, crustless and trimmed into perfect triangles. When that novelty wore off, the electric bell would bring a maid to fill the huge porcelain bath next door, where a row of cut-glass toilet-water bottles promised a further half-hour of anointing.

Guy, who arrived two days after me, immediately thought of improvements.

'Looking-glasses,' he announced at breakfast. 'Did you know all the doors in Kit's dressing room are made of mirror-glass, with lights over them? Back view, side view, any way you please. Makes dressing a darn sight easier, I can tell you.'

My father frowned and stirred his tea. 'And that's what you'd like here?'

'Absolutely. Kit says he couldn't manage without it.'

'Very well, then. Tell Robbins exactly what you want, and he'll arrange for the tradesmen. I want you to feel at home here, after all.'

His mouth full of bacon, Guy mumbled a casual thanks.

'By the way – d'you think you could ask the kitchen to send

up devilled ham for breakfast while I'm home? And halibut, with cream – you know, with all the bones taken out. We always had it at Kit's and I've rather acquired the taste.'

Encouraged by devilled ham and dressing-room mirrors, by the end of the week Guy had demanded a superb new table for the billiard room and the latest thing in Zeiss roll-cameras for himself. He'd also presented his father with a tailor's bill for a breathtaking amount (much of it for a motoring coat lined with fur) and another from a jeweller concerning a monogrammed gold cigar-cutter.

I was astounded by this last excess. 'What on earth did Papa say about the cigars?'

'Nothing much.' Guy swaggered over to the window. 'All the fellows at school smoke nowadays. And Kit lets me take his Partagas.'

'Oh Guy, it's hardly fair to keep throwing Uncle Kit up to him.'

'Why shouldn't I?' Guy swivelled round combatively. 'Kit and Margot have been jolly decent to me since I came to England. My life here would have been pretty bleak without them, I can tell you – and the Governor couldn't have given a toss. All he ever cared about were his ships and having fun in Shanghai.' He swung back to the window. 'Well, now I'm giving him a chance to make it up to me. He should be grateful I let him.'

'It wasn't Papa's fault.' I struggled to find an adequate excuse. 'I'm sure he cares about us in his own way.'

'Let him prove it, then, now he's got us here.' Guy's voice was cold, but his back was still towards me and I couldn't read the expression on his face.

A couple of days later he vanished to Somerset to spend the rest of the holiday with the Hooker-Catchpoles, whose son was a friend from school.

If my mother had still been alive, she'd no doubt have marched me off on a round of frock-fittings, hairdressing appointments and social calls, as Margot did for Alice and Rose. But even in the school holidays my father's life revolved round the Oliver building in Leadenhall Street and it was left to various dusty great-aunts to carry me off in their immense, rug-filled landaulets to doze through 'suitable' matinées or torpid teas at the Hyde Park Hotel.

For ten days I tried to believe I was enjoying myself. I peered out of every window in that vast house, bothered the wits out of the servants and bathed in my marble bathroom until my skin began to crinkle like a prune. In truth I was bored, bored, bored – and yet the thought of going back to Hallowhill was less appetizing than ever.

Then, barely a week before I was due to return to school, I was wakened in the middle of the night by the shrilling of the telephone at the foot of the main stairs, two floors below. Normally it gave a single, discreet trill and then waited for Robbins to divert the call to whichever internal instrument was appropriate; this time, however, it rang for ages before anyone reached it, its clamour bouncing insistently from pillar to pillar.

Wrenched from sleep in the half-light, I took the voile draperies of my bed for the mist of a mosquito net and imagined for a moment I was back in my old room in Shanghai. Then the telephone pealed again, the room resolved itself into its familiar pattern of mahogany and chintz and the luminous dial of my bedside clock showed it was only a few minutes past three. Emergency! I hopped out of bed, snatched up my dressing-gown and pattered out to the top of the stairs.

Far below, I could make out the polished pink crown of Robbins's head, a pale disc against the dark blue wool of his dressing-gown and the shadows of the hall. Beside him, my father was a patch of silk paisley and a hand delicately holding the receiver to his ear.

I reached the hall in time to see him return the instrument to its stand. 'Who was that? Was it Uncle Kit? Has there been an accident? Has an Oliver ship been wrecked?'

'No, no, nothing like that.' He gazed at me absently for a moment, smoothing his ruffled hair. 'It was your grandmother, that's all.'

'At three in the morning? Is Grandmama ill?'

'No, she's perfectly well. It's just that she needs me there right away.'

'But what for?'

'Nothing that concerns you,' snapped my father suddenly. But it did concern me, all the same. I could see that the tiny muscles under my father's eyes were tense with distaste, ribbing the bridge of his elegant nose and drawing down his brows as if something very unpleasant had occurred to disturb his well-regulated existence. For some time I hovered by the balustrade on the second-floor landing, straining to catch any further clue, but all I heard were the sounds of my father coming upstairs to dress and then, later, the tap of his hand-blocked heels in the hall as he departed in the Rolls.

By the time I went down for breakfast that morning, my father had been home to change and had left again for Grandmother Kate's. Robbins had no explanation to offer and for the rest of the morning I mooned through the silent wastes of the house, where even the ticking of the clocks seemed to have slowed to a crawl. My father returned briefly in the afternoon. From my sitting room on the second floor, his voice downstairs sounded unnaturally soft, like the murmur of water at the bottom of a well; by the time I'd reached the hall he was speaking on the telephone in his study.

'. . . whatever is necessary,' I heard him say as I halted at the door, my finger curled to knock. 'I realize, of course, there's no hope of improvement . . . No. Quite so. Well, then, we must do whatever we can in the meantime. I fear it won't be for long.'

At this point I knocked and went into the room. My father swung his back to me and briskly brought the conversation to a close.

'What won't be for long?' I wanted to know.

'Nothing for you to bother about, darling.' The preoccupied look had returned to his face. He sat down heavily in the chair behind his desk and passed a hand over his eyes.

'Is someone ill? Is it Grandmama?'

'No, I told you.' My father waved away the suggestion.

'Your grandmother's perfectly well. However—' He took a breath, and I guessed he was composing a lie. 'One of her friends has been taken ill, and she needs our help.' His face brightened as if the fiction pleased him. 'Yes, a friend. An old friend.'

'Not Great-Aunt Louise?' I asked. Great-Aunt Louise was the widow of an eminent medical man and enjoyed a lurid range of symptoms. 'Perhaps I should call at Grandmama's with flowers.'

My father's head snapped up at once. 'No. Absolutely not. You are not to go near your grandmother's house, do you understand? It would be quite—' He groped for the word. 'Inappropriate.' With sudden inspiration, he added, 'There's infection, you see. You might catch the disease and fall ill yourself.'

'What about you? You went there last night and again today.'

'Don't question me, Clio! You're interrogating me as if I were a criminal.'

Just at that moment I heard the front door slam and Kit's voice in the hall. My father leaped gratefully from his seat and flung open the study door.

'Good heavens, is it four o'clock already? I do apologize, Kit. I'll be with you in a second.'

Uncle Kit tossed me a fleeting smile. 'I don't suppose a few moments will make a great deal of difference.'

'I wonder what it's like to die,' I remarked, suddenly and loudly. The reaction was everything I could have wished.

'What?' Kit stared at me in concern and then glanced at my father. 'What have you told her?'

'Only that *one of her grandmother's friends* is very ill.'

'Ah. Oh yes, that's true.' With cat-like agility, Kit recovered his self-possession. 'Poor old lady,' he murmured, laying a hand on his waistcoat. 'Heart trouble, you know. Very sad.'

'Perhaps Clio could spend tomorrow with Alice and Rose,' hazarded my father. 'I dare say Margot could find something to amuse the girls.'

'I'm sure she'd be delighted.' There was velvet malice in

Kit's tone. 'Margot is always pleased to have youthful company.'

Poor old lady, I thought to myself as the front door closed behind them. It was the first time I'd heard of heart trouble being infectious.

The following afternoon, Margot Oliver hit upon the simple entertainment of letting us three girls loose among her vast collection of hats while she disappeared to a tryst of her own.

'We'll take great care of them, Mama,' promised Alice, overawed.

'Oh, don't worry, darlings.' Margot flung a cream chiffon scarf over one shoulder and pinned it with an enormous Tutankhamun-style brooch. 'It's high time those hats went off to the poor. They've all been *seen*, my dears, every one of them.'

'I reckon she's almost dead.' Alice's voice issued from under a flowered coracle which Margot had worn to Ascot the previous year. 'Grandmama's friend,' she expanded. 'The lady who's so ill at Chester Square.'

'What makes you think that?'

'I overheard Papa tell Mama.' Alice raised her brim. 'Papa said, "I doubt if she'll last more than a few days," and then Mama said, "At least no one can blame your family for this," and Papa said, "The boy does. I'm sure of it. He blames us for everything."'

'*The boy?*' I had a sudden vision of a straw-coloured head among the tombstones and of two people united against the world. Hadn't I heard Grandmother Kate say of Matthew Oliver's will, *If that boy gets nothing, I suspect you'll both come to regret it?* Stephen Morgan, that had been the name she'd mentioned.

Alice had moved to a velour toque from which a pigeon appeared to be trying to escape. 'Do you think the beak goes to the front or the back?'

'Never mind that,' I exploded. 'What did Aunt Margot say next, for goodness' sake?'

'I didn't find out.' Alice preened her feathers in the looking-glass. 'Mason came upstairs just then with a pair of Papa's shoes and I had to pretend to be going to my room.'

'In any case, what does it matter who's ill?' Rose had made herself ravishing in a matinée cap fringed with jet beads. 'We don't know this lady, do we?'

I groaned in frustration. 'But don't you see? *The boy* – that could be the boy who was at Grandpapa's funeral, Stephen Morgan, or whatever his name was. Which means the lady who's dying could be Catherine, the woman we saw at Christmas at Grandmama's house. She looked jolly ill then, I must say.'

'Pretty ghastly, it's true.' Alice skewered the pigeon with a hat pin. 'But why should Grandmama care what happens to a woman who made such a scene at Grandpapa's funeral? Why should my father care, or yours?'

'Because Catherine was Grandfather Matthew's mistress!' I declared triumphantly.

Under her bugle beads, Rose's lip curled in contempt. 'You do talk a lot of rot, Clio. What on earth do you know about mistresses? Besides, I can tell you, if my husband took a mistress I'd *poison* her. I certainly wouldn't nurse her if she fell ill.'

There was an awful silence. 'You don't suppose they have, do you? Poisoned her, I mean?' My own voice trembled in my ears. 'Though why else should Uncle Kit say she had heart trouble, when Papa told me there was an infection?'

Alice was gazing at me aghast, her eyes peering from under the edge of the toque and her mouth like a mousehole. Even Rose looked thoughtful.

'Oh, come,' Alice managed at last. 'This isn't China, you know. British people don't go around poisoning all and sundry, no matter what Rose says. At least, I'm sure my father never would, nor Uncle Edward either.'

'No, perhaps not.' I suspected Edward Oliver was too squeamish to poison anyone, though to tell the truth, I wasn't so sure about Kit. 'But even if the poisoning business isn't true, either your father was fibbing, or mine was. Heart trouble and infection are two different things.'

'Parents always tell lies,' observed Rose darkly. 'Like pretending midwives bring new babies in their leather bags, or picking your nose gives you appendicitis.'

Yet I couldn't forget my father's discomfort as he fended off my questions. Something shameful was being covered up, I was sure of it.

'Maybe this Catherine was born the daughter of a duke and Matthew Oliver seduced her and ruined her life—'

'Oh, surely not.' Alice screwed up her face. 'I can't imagine Grandfather Matthew seducing anybody. He was so old.' For a moment she reflected on the possibility. 'Poor Catherine,' she concluded. 'And poor Stephen Morgan too.'

The woman died, I'm sure, the day before I was supposed to leave for the summer term at Hallowhill.

'What d'you think?' I asked Guy, who'd returned fleetingly from Somerset, raving about the new Burndept Wireless Apparatus which had filled the Hooker-Catchpoles' conservatory with crackling dance music. Unthinkably, that morning, our father had refused outright to give Guy a wireless of his own and when Guy pursued him into his study, extolling the virtues of 4-valve receivers and Ethnovox horns, he found himself unceremoniously thrown out and the door shut firmly in his face.

'The Governor's in a real bate,' he complained. 'What have you been doing to him while I've been away, Clogs?'

'You'd know, if you ever bothered to listen.' If there was one thing I hated, it was this new and unlovely name Guy had invented for me. 'He's worried about this friend of Grandmother Kate's who's dying.'

'Well, she's dead now,' concluded Guy ungraciously. 'So I'll write him about the wireless from school.'

'How do you know she's dead?'

'I heard the Governor telephoning Kit as I went into the study. "Mother's desperately distressed," he was saying, "but it can't be helped. A quick end to a nasty business."'

'There you are, then!' I pounced on the words. 'There *is* a scandal about it, just as I thought.'

'Codswallop. Look, if you want to be useful at all, Clogs, go and tell Robbins my trunk's ready to go down to the motor.'

I was supposed to go back to school the following day, back to a regime of hard beds, endless prep and a running battle with Miss Pittenweem, the Latin mistress, a stringy little creature with mad eyes and the soul of a sucked lemon. But then, somehow, on my way to the motor, with my trunk packed and my horrible felt hat squarely on my head, I tripped over my clumsy school shoes and ended up sprawling across the doorstep. My left ankle swelled up most satisfactorily; on doctor's orders I was installed on a sofa in the drawing room, with no prospect of school for at least a week.

So it was only by the merest chance that I was at home when the doorbell jangled at six o'clock and a voice I was sure I recognized rang through the hall. Frowning faintly, my father brought our visitor into the drawing room.

'Look who's called to see us, Clio!' He cleared his throat and took refuge behind my sofa. 'Isn't this extraordinary?'

I'd forgotten how young Nina Starozhilova was – no older than those girls in the Upper Sixth who hadn't yet gone off to be finished in Switzerland. Not that she'd have thanked me for the comparison. She was wearing a tea-dress of clinging crêpe de Chine, a perfume far too old for her and so much make-up that it only drew attention to her youth, like a child who's spent a wet afternoon at her mother's dressing-table.

'My darling!' She kissed me on both cheeks with uncharacteristic affection. 'So well, and with roses in the cheeks! Absolutely the young English lady.'

'Hello, Nina. I thought you were in Monte Carlo with Diaghilev.'

'Ach!' Nina's hand flew up like a firework. 'I cannot work always. And my new English friends tell me over and over again, "You must see London, everything there is *such* fun." And so here I am.'

She dropped into the deep cushions of the sofa opposite me, crossed her legs and flung her arms wide with a sigh of delight – seventeen passing for twenty-five. She was staying with her English friends, she confirmed, and circled an ankle dismissively. 'They only have a little, little house in *Maryle-bone*. Not nearly so nice as this.'

To my astonishment, my father rang for champagne, and Nina, that dangerous child-woman, sipped it like a veteran, her lips crushed to the rim of her glass and her supple dancer's body curling forward among the cushions.

'Papa, may I have—'

'Good heavens, no, darling. You're far too young.' My father gave a quick bark of a laugh and bent over Nina's sofa to refill her glass. I watched Nina lean back towards him, laughing deep in her throat, her eyes half-shut with pleasure and the happy superiority of those who are old enough to drink champagne – and I suddenly yearned to be free of school myself and to have slim, hard limbs to show off inside the softest of garments.

A wriggling warmth began to kindle in the pit of my stomach, just as it used to do sometimes when I danced with Igor, pressed tightly against his body. Now that I was a year older the memory made me more excited than afraid – or at least, that's how I thought I'd feel, if I ever got the chance to dance with him again. Nina hadn't mentioned his name once, but now I was dying to know whether he'd joined her yet on the Riviera.

She sighed. 'Poor Igor, he'd so much like to come to Monte Carlo. *So much*. But then our mother, the countess, would be all alone. So he must stay for the present with her.'

'And my brother would do so well in Monte Carlo, don't you think?' Nina turned enquiring eyes on my father. 'Or in Nice, or Cannes? Though Cannes, you know, is still very quiet in summer, except for the Americans.' She waved a contemptuous hand, revealing blunt, nibbled, little-girl nails. 'But oh, the villas! Clio, you should see the villas they are building, these rich, beautiful men.'

'Not all beautiful, surely,' murmured my father, perching on the arm of her sofa.

'Beautiful as peacocks! All of them, in wonderful, expensive clothes.'

Nina re-crossed her legs extravagantly to the other side,

spilling the sash of her tea-gown over the cushions. At that moment I'd have given anything to be heading for Monte Carlo in a week's time, or Cannes – anywhere but back to Hallowhill School. With difficulty, I crossed my own legs under my rug and tried to pretend my lemonade was champagne.

'To think you're dancing with Diaghilev, Nina, just as you hoped!'

'Ah.' She ran a finger round the edge of her glass. 'To be exact, I am not quite *at present* with Diaghilev. Though, of course, I see him most days in the Café de Paris – as we all do. Dear Sergei Pavlovich,' she added swiftly, 'was most anxious I should dance in *Les Noces* next month in Paris, but I said it was not for me.'

'Where are you dancing just now, then?' I couldn't imagine what stroke of fortune had inspired her to turn down the great Ballets Russes.

'Oh, here and there.' Nina flashed my father a brilliant smile and as she turned her head I noticed for the first time a small diamanté buckle pinned to the shoulder of her dress. The clip was unusually discreet for Nina and I was surprised. Paste costume jewellery was so cheap at the time that most people wore huge, stylish pieces.

'Here and there.' She shrugged her shoulders and the brooch sparked blue fire. 'But for now—' Her smile became sweetness itself. 'I am here, as you see.'

My father cleared his throat again and ostentatiously studied his watch. 'Good gracious, is that the time? Early to bed for you tonight, Clio. I've told them to send supper up to your room.'

'But can't I have dinner with you?' I was utterly dismayed. During that Easter holiday I'd begun to feel my father noticing me for the first time as a person in my own right – and perhaps, even, as a tolerable, marginally interesting person at that. He dined so often in town that I'd been looking forward to having him all to myself for a whole unexpected evening. 'If it wasn't for this silly ankle, I'd be perfectly all right,' I assured him.

'I've no doubt you would, but I shall dine at my club, all the same. I've one or two papers to pick up from the office before it closes for the day.'

At once Nina fixed him with tragic eyes; I'll swear her lower lip quivered.

'But *Édouard* – you said you'd take me to dinner when I came to London.'

'Did I? I can't imagine—' My father glanced quickly towards me, clearly uncomfortable. 'I've really no recollection . . .'

'On the boat, sailing back from Shanghai. You told me when to come here. You promised we'd dine at the Savoy Hotel and I was so looking forward to it.' Nina was straining towards him, her hands pressed together in supplication, and somehow the sash of her dress fell across my father's hand. She glanced down – and drew it back between his fingers, exquisitely slowly. 'Please,' she whispered.

There were, it's true, a great many things I'd yet to learn; but in those few, embarrassing seconds I discovered more than in a whole term at Hallowhill – about the money-making possibilities of dancing lessons, and diamond brooches, and about lonely men and determined young women too.

Chapter Four

AT HALLOWHILL, on the first of June each year, Miss Aspinall brought out a sky-blue ribbon to bind up her greying hair. From then until the start of the school holidays, we girls were allowed the frivolity of straw hats instead of felt.

My grandmother, Kate Oliver, spent her summers in Norfolk, where she had a house, Hawk's Dyke, which had been hers long before she married Matthew. Kate adored her country home, refusing to have it changed in any detail until the house had become so old and dilapidated that even my Uncle Kit had lost interest in inheriting any part of it and had bought himself a country place of his own, Easton Broome in Surrey.

Unlike her mother-in-law, my Aunt Margot lived for change. In her first year as chatelaine of Easton Broome she was reputed to have spent a fortune on the place, installing sunken marble baths and laying acres of carpet in her favourite ivory white. After that she deserted it. Winter in Surrey was too cold and besides, there was Cannes; at Easter she played tennis at Deauville, then went to Paris for clothes, to dine and to gossip with friends; by then the London season was calling, the siren voices of the Royal Academy and Ascot and Henley, and finally Cowes, where the most amusing people went to wave to one another from the sterns of little boats.

Fortunately Margot didn't feel obliged to hunt or go out with guns and so she was able to spend a restful autumn visiting other Margots in Venice or Newport: and then – *quel ennui!* – it was time for Cannes all over again.

Kate Oliver went to Norfolk with the first of the sunshine

and stayed until the yellowing leaves forced her to admit another summer had gone.

I don't suppose she anticipated having my company, or Guy's, in that summer of 1924, but we had nowhere else to go. The Oliver directors had become nervous at the amount of transatlantic shipping business being sucked in by the American Mercantile Marine combine and Norddeutscher Lloyd. Recent moves by the United States government to limit the horde of migrants flocking to their shores had almost emptied Oliver's third-class berths to New York and with the Italians insisting that their own people should travel to the New World on Italian ships, the future of Oliver Atlantic suddenly looked less rosy.

Under the circumstances, it seemed prudent for Oliver's chairman to make an appearance in the United States of America – and for his children to spend the summer in Norfolk with their grandmother. I wondered if my father had taken Nina Starozhilova with him to New York. I knew no one would tell me if he had: already, I'd noticed that the English have a truly oriental ability to ignore anything they don't care to acknowledge, even when it winds its hungry little body in rose crêpe de Chine and clings to a gentleman's arm.

Instantly, Margot invented an excuse for sending Alice and Rose to Norfolk, too, though I assume Grandmother Kate must have been quite pleased to have them. Kate Oliver never did anything she didn't enjoy.

As for Hawk's Dyke, it was old and cockeyed, with sharp gables, chimneys like the prongs of a fork and low doors which had been altered to windows only to be turned back into tall doors again a century later. The house lay drowned in the countryside like one of the cloying Victorian paintings in Miss Aspinall's study where cottages swam in a green succulence spattered with hollyhocks, dripping with artistically tattered thatch. At Hawk's Dyke only a sweep of gravel kept the tide of growth at bay; beyond this moat was a lawn and a grove of ancient oaks among whose whispering skirts tea was served each afternoon in a ritual involving wicker chairs, white damask and paper-thin bone china.

It must have rained more than once during the summer, but I can't remember it happening – only the drunken droning of bees gorging among the roses and the rich golden scent of the stocks in Kate's borders.

At some time in the past Matthew Oliver had added a tennis court by the stables, not because he played the game, but because he was determined to leave some mark on the place and it was all that Kate would allow. It was the four of us who played that year: Guy conscious of looking well in white flannel, smugly knocking dolly shots to 'the girls', Alice pink and earnest, nibbling her lower lip, Rose pretending the sun was in her eyes whenever she missed a shot and I . . . revelling in the *rightness* and safeness and sheer other-worldliness of it all.

I suppose Hawk's Dyke reminded me of another place of eternal delight whose spell was only disturbed by occasional visitors from a different, half-acknowledged existence. Margot whirled in one day in time for lunch, found a greenfly on her lettuce and complained at dinner that her bathwater had been almost cold. Next morning she appeared briefly on the tennis court in a Patou dress and hat, patted a few balls to and fro as vigorously as *chic* would allow, applied cream to her forehead in case of 'tennis frown' and then departed in a shower of air-kisses towards the next set of friends on her schedule. For the rest of that afternoon the atmosphere seemed to shimmer with the ferment of her passing. Not until evening did the dust-motes in the air settle back to their customary golden drifting.

There were four of us at the start of that summer – perfect for tennis, perfect for whist, perfect for the old dog cart with its two bobbing ponies which carried us down to the village. We fell comfortably into four-cornered familiarity – Guy and Alice bickering casually like a long-married couple, Rose and I like tolerated children – content with our tennis and our well-worn jokes. Then, one day, we were suddenly five.

Kate broke the news at the tea table under the oaks, gravely and carefully, as if she'd spent a great deal of time choosing precisely how much to tell us.

'I expect you all to do your best to make him feel at home. Guy, you especially, since I imagine you'll see more of him than the girls.' Kate peered at Guy, who was lying on his back in the grass, to make sure he was listening. Alice had taken her usual place by his head, popping morsels of sesame cake into his mouth at regular intervals – Guy liked to dream up these menial tasks to demonstrate his proprietorship.

'Guy – did you hear me?'

'Oh, absolutely, Grandmama. I'm to be particularly decent to Stephen Morgan, because he's had a rotten life and hasn't any place to go home to.'

'That isn't what I said and you know it.' Crossly, Kate twisted round to glare at her grandson. 'And remember, Stephen mustn't know I've said anything at all behind his back. I'm sure he'd hate it, if he found out.'

Alice and I exchanged glances across the tufted grass beneath the trees. Stephen Morgan, in person. *The boy.* Who else could he be but the fair-haired youth we'd seen at a distance at Matthew Oliver's funeral? And now he was coming here to Hawk's Dyke because his mother was dead and he'd nowhere else to spend his shore leave. I added the words 'shore leave' to the elaborate fantasy in my head. Had Kit and my father bought him off, then, this mistress's child, with a seaman's berth on an Oliver ship? Was it possible they'd had the young man shanghaied aboard some Australia-bound vessel to keep him out of harm's way? I hoped devoutly he wasn't coming to Norfolk bent on revenge. Surely he couldn't believe the four of us had taken any part in his mother's death.

'What I don't understand – ' Guy swallowed a piece of cake ' – is why he has to come *here*, to Hawk's Dyke, in the first place. He isn't family, is he?'

'I told you.' Kate's voice was sharp. 'His father, Captain Morgan, was an Oliver officer, though he died when Stephen was hardly more than a baby. And now that his mother's dead too, the poor boy has nowhere to stay while he's ashore. The least we can do is offer him a fortnight's holiday – and I intend those two weeks to be as pleasant as possible. I shall count on you, Guy, to make a friend of Stephen.' Kate frowned at Guy's elegantly sprawled limbs. 'As a favour to me, if nothing else.'

I wondered why Kate should care so much about her

husband's 'mistake', since I didn't for a moment believe her face-saving tale about a dead Oliver officer. Sailors had drowned from time immemorial. In the normal way of things, the survivors of Oliver crewmen accepted their loss as the price of seafaring and that was that. I'd never heard of one being invited to *visit* before. Clearly, Stephen Morgan was different – and I was pretty sure I understood in what way. We'd been instructed to like him: I very much doubted if he'd be prepared to like us.

Stephen Morgan arrived two days later by train at Downham Market and Kate sent her motor-landaulet to fetch him. Guy, Alice, Rose and I had been invited to tea with Great Aunt Alice at nearby Wellborough Abbey that particular afternoon and so, frustratingly, we didn't set eyes on the enigma until he came down to dinner with Kate on his arm.

Subconsciously, I suppose, I was expecting the boyish figure from the graveyard, certainly not the tall, upright young man who stood before us in a brass-buttoned uniform, with a gold-badged cap pressed closely under his elbow.

I heard a sharp intake of breath from Alice; and even Guy, splendid in a new double-breasted dinner jacket, seemed taken aback for a moment.

But only for a moment. Almost at once he leaned over to hiss in my ear, 'So it's Admiral Morgan now, is it? Well, splice the mainbrace and stand by your fore-scuttles.'

Not that Stephen Morgan was exactly dashing, not in a matinée idol kind of way, yet he was certainly striking enough for me to feel an instant of doubt that twelve months at sea could have wrought such a change. The boy in the churchyard had seemed smaller and slighter and for all his rigid defiance there'd been a vulnerability about his slim frame which had stayed in my memory. This Stephen Morgan was no boy, but a well-made young man with sunburned cheekbones and the dark gold hair of a medieval angel. Perhaps it was the wariness in his face which deceived me, an animal vigilance which moulded his features into sharpnesses and hollows and made him seem older than his years.

I stared, just as I'd always been told not to, while Stephen

Morgan's eyes examined each of us in turn as Kate made introductions, searching for the marks of friend or foe. He stood uncannily still, that same stillness I'd noticed among the tombstones, that disconcerting absence of the tiny, involuntary movements of life. Only his eyes moved, examining, judging and drifting on.

'Sit here by me, Stephen.' Kate indicated the chair which had been Alice's, directly opposite Guy. 'Alice, sit next to Clio, if you please. You have a good, carrying voice. I shall hear you perfectly well from there.'

I can remember very little of that meal except some talk of Valparaiso and of Kate's birthplace, New Orleans, which Stephen Morgan had seen but Guy hadn't. I certainly don't recall eating very much, too absorbed in watching this stranger whose mere existence had made me so curious.

'Stephen is an apprentice officer with the Blue Castle Line.' Kate twisted her ear-trumpet in its white lace stocking towards her new guest. 'How long does your apprenticeship last, my dear?'

'Four years, in all.' His voice was low and matter-of-fact, with a hint of long, round West Country vowels. 'I've just over three years to go, then I should get a berth as second mate.'

'I say, pass the salt, will you, Alice?' Guy managed a creditable imitation of Kit's drawl, the disdain of a man who in a few years would eat second mates for breakfast. But for once Alice didn't hear him. Her eyes were fixed on Stephen Morgan and it was Rose who held out the salt-cellar.

After dinner Kate sent us out into the formal garden at the side of the house, where the night was warm and heavy with honeysuckle. No doubt she knew she was throwing Stephen to the wolves. I expect she was satisfied he'd survive us.

We strolled to the fountain in silence with Guy in the lead, his shoulders thrown back and his hands thrust casually into his trouser pockets. Lounging on the stone rim, he slid a slim gold cigarette case from the breast of his dinner jacket and offered its contents to Stephen.

'They're Turkish.'

Stephen glanced down at the row of black cylinders, each with its single gold band. His eyes swept up towards Guy. 'No thanks.'

'You don't like Turkish?' Guy selected one for himself.

'I don't smoke.'

Guy closed the case with a soft *click* which spoke volumes.

'How old are you, Stephen?' Alice moved out of the shadows to stand at Guy's shoulder.

'Almost sixteen.'

'Guy's older,' said Alice. 'Next year he'll have a motor car of his own.' After a moment she asked the inevitable question. 'Do you drive?'

'No.'

'Play tennis?'

'No.'

Guy blew a smoke ring which became a writhing loop of silver in the fading light. 'Where were you at school, Stephen?'

'I've finished with school.' Involuntarily, Stephen Morgan had balanced himself like a prize-fighter, his hands loose and his feet a little apart. 'I'm going back to sea in three weeks' time.'

Guy's tone was deceptively casual. 'Grandmother said your father was *Captain* Morgan.'

'That's right.'

I watched Stephen's face closely for signs of the lie I knew this to be, but his expression was drained of any emotion.

'And he was drowned at sea.'

'*Guy!*' For once Alice was shocked into criticism of her champion.

'I don't mind.' Stephen Morgan's eyes swept from Alice to Guy. 'If you want to know, my father's ship disappeared in a typhoon in the South China Sea. They found one of the boats a few days later, but nothing else.'

'Golly,' murmured Rose. 'Imagine one's father drowning.'

'I was just a baby at the time.'

'I know about typhoons.' This was my chance at last. 'We lost two trees in our garden, once, when a typhoon came ashore. In Shanghai,' I added, to give my tale a touch of exotic interest.

'Shut up, Clio.' Guy threw me a glare. 'Nobody wants to hear about stupid trees.'

'Some junks in the river were swept ashore,' I muttered, aware that my moment of glory had passed.

Guy had Stephen in his sights once more. 'And now your mother's dead too, Kate said.'

'*Guy!*' squeaked Alice again. Outraged, she slipped away round the fountain.

'That was damnable luck,' continued Guy, unperturbed. 'To lose both of them, I mean.' He touched the cigarette to his lips and blew out a delicate stream of smoke. 'What happened to your mother?'

'She died.' Stephen Morgan never moved, but a narrowing of his eyes and a slight, faint, hardly perceptible tilt of his chin warned Guy to give up his interrogation. Now I was more certain than ever that Stephen's mother was the woman we'd seen, the haunted Catherine, the one who'd died at Easter in Grandmother Kate's care.

'I do think you're frightfully rude, Guy,' pronounced Alice, emerging from behind the fountain. 'Take no notice of him, Stephen, he and Clio grew up in China.'

'I don't mind.' Stephen Morgan stared at each of us in turn, as if daring us to believe he did mind. 'My parents are dead and I'm on my own. That's all there is to it.'

'Oh, absolutely.' Guy tossed his half-smoked cigarette down behind the box hedge. 'Absolutely all.'

'My God, what an oik!' he hooted a couple of days later. Stephen had gone to the village with Kate, and the rest of us, a foursome once more, had returned to the tennis court.

'Why is he an oik?' Alice wanted to know.

'Because he just is. Can't you tell?' Guy shaded his eyes with a hand and frowned at Alice. 'I mean, he went to some peculiar school in Southampton and he doesn't seem to know anyone. I've asked.'

'Just because he doesn't know all your smart friends,' objected Rose. 'Like these Hooker-Catchpole people you're always talking about and the fellow whose father owns most of

Monmouthshire. Look, are you going to serve, or do we have to stand here all day?'

Sulkily, Guy sauntered back from the net and unleashed a cracking shot which whistled past Rose's ear to smash into the netting behind her.

'The sun was in my eyes,' bleated Rose, squinting.

'Rot,' said Alice. 'You never saw it.'

'I think tennis is a silly game,' Rose snapped in return. 'Stephen Morgan's quite right not to bother with it.'

On the far side of the net Guy served again, this time sending the ball sizzling past Alice's shoulder into a distant corner of the court.

'Thirty–love, I believe.' Grimly, Guy swatted the air with his racket.

'Look here, Guy.' I padded across. 'This isn't fair.'

'What's the matter, partner? Don't you want to win?' Ball in hand, Guy strutted back to the service line. 'Go and practise knots with Admiral Morgan, if you're tired of playing tennis with me.' Once more the ball screamed across the net. This time Rose made an awkward attempt to return it, then dropped her racket, nursing her bruised fingers.

'*Guy!*' Alice ran over to inspect the damage. 'What on earth's got into you today?'

'That's forty–love.' Guy's voice rang out cold and clear. 'Go back to the house, if you want to play pat-ball.'

'I might very well do that!' Rose wailed back. 'I don't know why you're being so beastly to us this morning, showing off all the time.' Her eyes flashed with sudden malice. 'You're just jelly-bags because Grandmama spends so much time with Stephen these days. That's what's really put your nose out of joint, Guy, isn't it?'

'Oh, do you think so?' Guy came forward to the net, twitching his racket with annoyance. 'Do you really think I give a damn for an oik like that? I'll tell you one thing, Rose – if you're too much of a baby to play tennis with grown-ups, then you'd better go and find your precious Stephen Morgan and ask him to take you on one of these long walks he's so fond of.' For a moment Guy and Rose glared mutely at one another across the net. 'Oh, what's the use!' Guy set off for the gate in the fence, furiously kicking a ball out of his path. 'I'm going in.'

Alice peered through her fringe at his retreating back, vaguely dismayed. 'What's happening to us, Clio? We were perfectly happy when we first came to Norfolk, all four of us, but now we seem to do nothing but quarrel. And it isn't fair to blame Stephen, because he really hasn't done anything at all.'

Alice and I took Stephen round the vinery and into the scented warmth of the peach house, where the peaches were still hard and covered with silvery down. Alice kept pushing her hair back behind one ear, as she did when she was excited. I was sure Stephen Morgan must have noticed, with those quick eyes of his, and I reflected gloomily on the great gulf that existed between a young woman of sixteen and a mere girl two years younger.

Alice's chest would have been quite respectable, if she hadn't been so round-shouldered. Her breasts were slightly pendulous and turned up at the tips like the udders on one of Kate's goats. I imagined a man would find them attractive, while I still had very little more than the adolescent swellings which had first showed themselves in Shanghai.

Now it seemed I was destined to play gooseberry, in the velvet heat of the peach house. I glanced at Stephen Morgan. He didn't play tennis, or drive: I wondered if he danced.

Stephen and Alice had already passed through to the next section of the glasshouse, where Alice reached up to caress one of the fuzzy, half-ripe globes, arching her back. I heard her laugh – a nervous, girlish sound at first, but already soft with the lower notes of womanhood.

Peaches can do strange things, peaches and summer. Liu Ling used to say that when the Chinese godlings wish to make you immortal, they offer you a peach. Take a single bite and you'll live for ever in a state of bliss, like the old man and his daughters glimpsed by the fisherman in the peach-blossom forest.

I hurried to catch up with Alice and Stephen.

'If they ripen in time,' I heard her promise, 'you must take some back to your ship.'

'Alice likes Stephen. Quite a lot, I'd say.'

'*Nostalgie de la boue*,' declared Guy, who'd heard Kit use the phrase.

'What on earth does that mean?'

'It means some women can't resist a low-life,' observed my worldly brother. 'But they don't marry them. So Kit says,' he added blandly.

I was cross with Guy and jealous of Alice. I was also unaccountably cross with Stephen Morgan. There was a fierce elusiveness about him I'd never encountered before and, of course, the thrilling facts of his history – yet every so often a subterranean anger would erupt in a savage remark or a flash of those slate-grey, conversation-killing eyes and I'd decide I hated him after all. Guy could be rude – oh dear me, yes – but he managed to be offensive in such a charming, silken manner that it often took a few moments for the insult to sink in, by which time it was too late to retaliate. With Stephen Morgan I sometimes felt as if the very fact of my existence was being tumbled in the mill of his resentment and ground up small.

I decided he must have inherited his bad manners from Grandfather Matthew Oliver.

'Do you see any resemblance?' I asked Alice one afternoon. Stephen had been with us for almost two weeks and we were taking tea under the oaks as usual, Guy lounging in a wicker chair a little apart from us girls, Kate at the table and Stephen himself wandering restlessly among the trees, returning fleetingly for fresh tea as the impulse took him.

'You don't still believe all that nonsense about Stephen's mother being Grandpapa's mistress, do you?' Alice, stretched out in a deckchair, had shaded her eyes with one hand in order to watch him through her fingers. 'Honestly, Clio, it's time you grew up, it really is. You heard Stephen say his father was drowned in a typhoon and his mother had recently died. It all sounds perfectly reasonable to me.'

'But if that's true, then what was he doing at Grandfather Matthew's funeral? And why does he keep dodging any questions about his family?'

Alice leaned back and closed her eyes. 'How would you like to be thrown in with four complete strangers who keep asking impertinent questions? I think he's been jolly forbearing, considering Guy's hardly given him a chance.'

'I shouldn't let Guy hear you say that.'

'Say what?' enquired Guy, who'd caught the last couple of words. He'd got to his feet to pull back his grandmother's chair as she went indoors for her pre-dinner rest. 'What is it I'm not supposed to hear, then?'

'Nothing,' said Alice.

'Nothing but the truth.' Rose, who'd been listening at our feet in silence, sat up and hugged her knees. 'Alice was simply saying she thinks Stephen's pretty terrific and you've been perfectly bloody to him.'

Guy stared at Alice with the astonished expression of a man who's just been bitten by his horse. 'Did you?'

Decent, honest Alice struggled to be fair. 'Not exactly. But it's true you could have been nicer.'

'Well, I like that! You've changed sides very quickly, haven't you?'

'I haven't taken anyone's side,' insisted Alice, her cheeks flushing pink under her freckles. 'I mean, there aren't any sides to take. Grandmama said we ought to make Stephen feel welcome, that's all.' She broke off as Stephen's tall figure appeared among the trees nearby.

'Oh, so you want me to chat to him, do you? A bit of small talk, perhaps?' Guy's tone was savage. 'Hey, Stephen!' he called loudly, 'you haven't told us where you're sailing off to next.'

Stephen raised his head sharply, like a deer scenting danger. He continued to walk towards us, but his expression was wary. 'I don't know where I'll be going, yet. It depends on where the company sends me.'

'Ah yes,' agreed Guy smoothly. 'You're still only an apprentice. I'd forgotten.'

'Everyone has to start somewhere,' Rose pointed out. 'Even

you, Guy. Uncle Edward is hardly going to hand you a shipping line to run, as soon as you stroll in from school.'

'Why not, since it's all going to be mine in the end?' Guy thrust out his chin. 'And for your information, Rose-nose, your father reckons I've a natural talent for the business. "You can cut your teeth on the Clyde–Canada trade' – that's what he said at Christmas.' Guy flung himself back into his chair and half-closed his eyes, savouring victory. 'Tell you one thing—' With lazy insolence, he propped his feet on the tea table. 'The apprentice officers won't half snap to it when I'm in charge.'

Stephen Morgan halted suddenly, a few feet from Guy's chair, and for a moment I thought anger had at last got the better of his icy control. Then I saw his jaw tighten, a grim little spasm of self-denial.

'Pity help them, then,' he said quietly.

It must have cost him a great deal and I was furious with my brother. 'Guy, how could you? That was a dreadful thing to say.'

'You're *such* a stinker, Guy!' Rose let go of her knees and planted her fists indignantly in the grass. 'I'm sick of hearing how clever you are and how rich your friends are, as if those were the only things that mattered. Let's face it, you've never earned a penny in your life – and here's poor Stephen having to make his own way in the world because his parents are dead and all you can do is sneer at him. It would serve you right if he bashed you on the nose.' She glanced hopefully at Stephen and then back to Guy, disappointed. 'As it is, he's clearly got better manners than you, even if he did go to a perfectly ordinary school—'

'He's pretty hard up if he needs *you* to protect him,' said Guy scornfully.

'I don't need anyone to protect me.' Stephen Morgan's voice cut like sleet through the soft shade of the oaks. 'Not you.' He pointed at Rose. 'Nor you.' He pointed at Alice and then swung round on me. 'Nor you either. Not against spoiled, stuck-up little runts like him.'

He wheeled round to face Guy. 'As for you, you'd better hang on tight to your father's coat-tails, because you wouldn't last a single day on a ship. There's no place at sea for nanny's-boys. By God, I've known wharf-rats from the Liverpool docks worth two of you.'

There was a dreadful silence. I half-expected Guy to come out with some smart reply, but he seemed utterly stunned – not so much by the words as by the frightening venom which had inspired them.

For a moment longer Stephen Morgan stared down at Guy in silent disgust; then he turned and set off for the house. 'You sicken me,' he said. 'All of you.'

Guy watched him go and then let out an uneasy, braying laugh.

'Well, *he'd* better not come begging for a job with the Oliver Line in future.' He glanced at the three of us for agreement. 'A trouble-maker, that's what Stephen Morgan is. An oik and a scrounger, just as I said.'

Alice got to her feet. 'Dash it all, Guy. You never learn, do you?'

Dinner that evening was a ghastly affair. Stephen Morgan had given up any attempt to make conversation, while Guy drawled more loudly than ever in an attempt to fill the silence. Once or twice I caught Stephen watching my brother keenly as he floundered on, clearly adding to whatever poor opinion he'd already formed.

I didn't want to be included in that opinion. I'd never set out to be one of 'the enemy' and I resented the way Guy had managed to blacken us all with his spite. Whatever lies Stephen had told about his father having been drowned at sea, it was probably true he'd been left with no home and no family, and little enough to live on, judging by his ill-fitting dinner jacket and department-store flannels. I felt we'd been inexcusably beastly to him, or at least Guy had, and the more I thought about it, the more I wanted to explain.

Immediately after dinner Stephen disappeared so suddenly that if I hadn't been watching for an opportunity of speaking to him alone, he'd have gone before I realized it. A second or two after he'd left the room I heard the front door close with the softest of clicks.

Rose was reading aloud to Kate and I could hear Alice and Guy quarrelling about something in the library as I let myself out into the dusk. As the door closed, swallowing its rectangle of light, the pink of the gravel turned to grey and the shrubs by the step transformed themselves into a tangle of blackish spears. But at least it was obvious which way Stephen had gone: the mist which had drifted across the fields in late evening had loaded each grass stem with moisture and his footprints made a dark chain across the silvered lawn. I decided he'd gone down by the old dyke itself, the wide, water-filled channel which had given Kate's house its name.

The evening had turned to indigo in the copse beyond the lawn, where the trees filtered the mist to a damp, mossy breath, cool against my flushed cheeks. On the far side of the copse, the vapour had tumbled into the dyke itself to lie in whorls on the water's surface. I'd often followed that path before, rambling with Alice and Rose, but now solitude and the strange, disorientating miasma had turned the butterfly highway into a cloudscape. Like the finest of ink-strokes, delicate branches leaned from the hedgerow to trace the outline of hills and pavilions on the virgin haze.

Stephen Morgan was sitting on the misty dyke bank, as still as the windless reeds. He didn't say a word as I approached, but simply watched me draw nearer, his silence making me feel like an intruder, blundering along the grassy track. When I stopped beside him, he went back to throwing pebbles, one by one, into the water.

'May I sit down?'

'I shouldn't. The grass is wet.'

'You're sitting on it.' I slithered inelegantly down on the bank beside him. 'It's a bit spooky out here at this time of night, isn't it?'

'It was quite peaceful until now.' His hand moved, pale in the half-light, and another couple of pebbles plopped into the invisible water below us.

'Do you mind my being here?'

'Not if you're quiet.'

'All right.' It wasn't what I'd intended, but at least he hadn't asked me to go. With an effort I sat in silence, feeling the dampness of the grass soak through my thin frock and cotton knickers. For several minutes I watched Stephen out of the corner of my eye, reflecting once more on how stark his features were for an almost-sixteen-year-old and how little of the boy remained. That was what frightened me: to find the vigour of a man and the rage of a man and – who could tell? – the needs of a man in a male creature not much more than a year older than I was myself, with boyhood still raw upon him and none of the smooth sexlessness of the only men I was used to, my father's middle-aged acquaintances.

A violent rustling broke out at our feet and a flurry of muffled squeaks. I jumped in alarm and only just saved myself in time from clutching Stephen's arm. I was glad I had, when I saw a glimmer of amusement cross his face in the failing light.

'An otter, probably, catching a shrew for his supper. Not a ghost, at any rate.'

'I didn't think it was a ghost, actually. It just gave me a fright, that's all.'

'Then why are you shivering?'

'I'm a bit cold, in this mist.'

'You'd better have this, then.' With a twist of his spine, he slid out of the ill-fitting dinner jacket and dropped it over my shoulders. It was still warm from his body; for some reason I hadn't expected that – it was almost as if he'd put one of his lean, brown arms round me. I was about to throw off the jacket indignantly when it occurred to me that he might think I'd rejected it because it was old and shabby and so I sat on my confusion and my damp skirt and tried to simper like Alice did when Guy was being particularly gallant. Yet I was more bewildered than ever.

'How do you know about otters?'

He glanced at me sideways, wary again. 'Why shouldn't I know? Just because I work on a ship doesn't mean I don't know anything about the countryside. I'm not a complete idiot.'

'I realize that.'

'And if you're sitting there feeling sorry for me, then you can go straight back to the house.'

'Why should I feel sorry for you?'

'Because I probably earn about the same in a year as your chauffeur. That's a pretty good reason for feeling sorry for me, isn't it?'

'Of course not. I don't feel at all sorry for our chauffeur.'

He burst out laughing at that, a low, harsh laughter I'd never heard before. I'd never suspected he could laugh; I wished I could understand what he'd found so funny. After a few seconds he fell silent again, drew up his feet and rested his folded arms on his knees.

This was my moment. I took a deep breath. 'Look, Stephen. I didn't actually come out here to talk about otters.'

'No?' He was watching me again, with that maddening expression I couldn't read, half-way between amusement and contempt.

'I wanted to say – well, to say I'm sorry Guy was so awful today.' Honesty drove me on. 'Actually, he's been pretty ghastly for the last fortnight, if it comes to that.'

There was the faintest of pauses. 'Can't say I'd noticed.'

I examined Stephen Morgan's profile, that stern intensity of planes and hollows. I was certain he noticed everything.

'It's good of you to be so decent about it.'

'Guy's a fool. I don't listen to fools – they can say what they like.'

'He isn't so bad once you get to know him. He's terrifically clever at billiards.'

'Well, good for him.' Stephen's tone was scorching. 'In any case, it doesn't matter. In another couple of days I'll be away from here. I go back to Liverpool on the twelfth.'

'So soon?' I tried to decide if I was disappointed or not. I suspected Stephen might be relieved to be free of us. 'And you really don't know where you'll be sailing to next?'

'Haven't a clue.'

'I don't think I'd like that.' I squinted dubiously into the dusk.

'I prefer it that way. Nothing behind me – and heaven knows what in the future. Anything's possible.' He lifted his head to stare into the distance over the dyke, a misty expanse of hedges and pasture. 'If I were a bird I'd spread my wings whenever I wanted, and fly away to . . . anywhere the wind took me.'

'You'd have to be brave to do that.'

'There's nothing *brave* about it. Sometimes it's easier to go than to stay.'

I glanced at him in surprise. It was the first time I'd known him give any hint of having hopes and fears like the rest of us. Even his quiet breathing, soft in the still air, seemed more human, somehow.

Stupidly, I went too far.

'Look, Stephen, I ought to tell you . . . You see, I *know*. About who your real father was.' He turned his head at once, baffled, outraged, but in my foolishness I ploughed on. 'I guessed, you see, after I saw you at the funeral. But I just wanted to say it doesn't matter a bit to me and I won't tell a soul if you don't want me to.' Guiltily, I remembered my discussions with Alice. 'Well, almost no one.' My voice trailed away, suddenly stilled by the cold fury in his eyes.

'What the hell are you talking about?' With dreadful distinctness, he added, 'My father was Captain Robert Morgan, born in Exeter, who once worked for your family's damned company. His last command was the steamer *Shanxi*, until she was lost with all hands in the South China Sea on the twenty-seventh of July, 1909. That is a fact. Go and look it up, if you don't believe me. I was less than two years old at the time – and no, I can't remember anything about him, but I do know he was my real bloody father!'

The fathomless pain in his face convinced me that every word of it was true. Yet he still wasn't satisfied.

'What else do you want to know? That I've no brothers or sisters? That my father's people have no interest in me? Go on, ask your questions, since that's obviously what you came out here for.'

'It wasn't.' My voice had shrunk to a dismal whisper. I made one last, despairing attempt to touch him. 'My mother was drowned too, you know. When the *Lusitania* was torpedoed, years ago. So I do know what it's like.'

This time, somewhere deep inside Stephen Morgan, all the hoarded resentment exploded. 'You don't know! You and your brother and your precious cousins, you don't know anything at all.'

'But I want to know! I want to understand.'

He was staring at me with fierce intensity. And he was right – I knew nothing at all about love and loss, but that surely wasn't my fault. I sat there, hopelessly mixed up, willing him to speak.

'No.' He turned away, dug for a pebble and hurled it into the ditch. 'Go back to the house.'

I scrambled to my feet, throwing off his coat.

'Go on,' he snapped, 'get out of here.'

'You and Guy deserve each other, do you know that? You're both pretty hateful, if you ask me.'

I'd forgotten, when I first came out through the gathering dusk, that I might have to go back alone and in full darkness. But I was no longer cold; instead I was burning with anger and embarrassment and I pounded off along the path to the copse, heedless of brambles, or mist, or the sounds of the night. After a dozen steps I heard his voice call bitterly out of the blackness behind me.

'It's the irresistible charm of the Olivers. Why should I be any different?'

It wasn't until I'd reached the lighted windows of the house that it occurred to me to wonder what he'd meant.

Stephen Morgan left Hawk's Dyke two days later, as abruptly as he'd arrived. With Kate looking on, we staged forced and perfunctory farewells after breakfast was over, and the last I saw of him was a modest leather suitcase with his uniform cap laid on top, waiting in the hall for the landaulet to take him to the station.

One of us, however, was genuinely sorry to see him go. Watching through the open library door for the arrival of the motor, I saw Alice come into the hall and glance round. Satisfied that she was alone, she went quickly to the leather suitcase, picked up Stephen's cap and held it for a few seconds against her face, her fingers pressing the fabric urgently over her nose and lips.

I couldn't believe my eyes. Alice – mousy Alice who refused to go stockingless, even on the hottest of days – standing there, inhaling so deeply that her breasts seemed about to burst from her blouse, relishing the smell of a savage young man who despised us all.

Beyond the door, the landaulet's wheels ground slowly over the gravel. Instantly, Alice restored the cap to its place and scurried away, secure in her secret. But I'd seen enough to know that Guy's power in that quarter was broken for ever.

Chapter Five

I DON'T seem to have said very much about Rose, which is surprising, considering she was the cause of so much that happened later. No one was ever indifferent to Rose. Long before she officially came of age it was hard to ignore her, since she'd already begun to turn into a dramatically beautiful young woman; besides that, she'd learned that people tend to listen to the words which come from a lovely face and to find them more persuasive than if they were spoken by someone plainer. Rose had inherited all Margot's love of the limelight and quite early in life she discovered her own way of securing it. She became a revolutionary.

Not that Rose was a thinker. Sometimes I wonder if she even listened to the phrases she repeated with such conviction – or ever applied them to herself and her own comfortable circumstances. It was the thunder and roar of the words she enjoyed, and their power to shock. Revolutionaries of Rose's stamp melt away long before the armoured cars arrive; it's never they who stand alone in the boulevards like the last, guttering candle-flames, waiting to be snuffed out under the rolling tracks of the tanks.

'Do we know this creature MacDonald?' The country's first Labour Prime Minister took office in January 1924 and I remember how Margot Oliver struggled to recognize the name. Kit explained, and Margot shuddered in elegant horror. 'I suppose the next thing will be Bolsheviks in the streets of London, with their nasty, twisted faces and dirty fingernails.'

Rose had observed her mother's distaste with interest. Normally, Margot took no notice of politics. Clearly, this Ramsay MacDonald was more intriguing than the usual herd who said 'pardon' and combed their hair in public places.

In due course copies of *The Workers' Weekly* began to arrive for Rose at Hallowhill School – smuggled in, it was whispered, under the pig's feet in the butcher boy's delivery cart. When Zinoviev's leaked letter urging British Communists to revolt brought the MacDonald government down again, the general panic struck a romantic echo in Rose's bosom. She'd no interest in the proletarian struggle or the ownership of the means of production – but oh, to be one of those picturesque women who went out with loose hair and burning eyes to blow up bridges!

Margot Oliver was introduced to Mussolini at a party in Rome and assured her friends in London he was charming. Rose called her mother 'shallow' and pinned lines from Eliot's *Waste Land* to the wall of her room at Hallowhill. Soon she was inventing a regular Sunday headache to avoid worshipping in chapel. She became a vegetarian, refused the school shepherd's pie and wore her hair in a bun, copying a newspaper photograph of Sylvia Pankhurst.

By the spring of 1926 Rose had earned the nickname which was to last until she left school – Red Rose. And when a General Strike was called in May to support the militant miners, Rose alone, in a school full of mineowners', millowners' and shipowners' daughters, triumphantly proclaimed the Revolution – though only when her mistresses were out of earshot.

Guy, on the other hand, came down early from school to drive an omnibus to Peckham under the noses of the pickets.

'Philip Hooker-Catchpole's been delivering milk,' he reported proudly after it was all over. 'His uncle fixed it up for us. Actually, I haven't had such a good time for ages. They can all strike again tomorrow, as far as I'm concerned.'

'The miners are still on strike, so Rose says.'

'They are, the bloody fools. Just as well Oliver's have gone over to oil. Kit was quite right when he said we'd get back the cost in the long run.' Guy frowned as a complication occurred to him. 'Mind you, the boilermakers' strike has held up the launch of this new refrigerated ship we're building on the Tyne.'

I was impressed: recently, Guy had begun to make quite businesslike noises.

'Are you really going straight into the shipping office, Guy? No Oxford?' Our Uncle Kit, who'd spent most of his time at Eton beagling but had still carried off the King's Prize for French, had gone up to Christ Church before joining the company. My father, as elder son, had gone straight into the business from school and had often said he regretted the missed opportunity. He'd advised Guy to wait, but Guy would have none of it.

'Naturally I'm going in right away.' He stared at me, astonished. 'What's the point of hanging around for three years at Oxford? No fear. Oliver's is my future and I want to get my hands on it as soon as I can.'

Alice had left Hallowhill the previous year, at the age of seventeen. Aunt Margot had heard of a perfectly *divine* finishing school in Munich and had decided Alice should go there for two terms before making her début the following season. Alice was almost hysterically desperate to stay in London.

'This isn't a bit like Alice,' reported Rose. 'She's usually such a sheep. Actually,' she went on, 'I reckon Alice is sweet on some fellow she met at the Headingtons' tennis party last Easter. She's had that silly, moony look on her face a lot recently.'

I had also noticed Alice's wistful, preoccupied expression, but I was certain it dated from long before the previous Easter. Watching her pack to go home from school for the last time, I'd seen the old copies of *Lloyd's Register of Shipping* she'd hoarded at the back of her locker. In each one the same vessel's name had been circled in red – the SS *Tintagel*, a twin-screw Blue Castle steamer on the London–Sydney run – and I was sure that if

Alice was wallowing in romantic dreams, a Headington tennis party had nothing to do with them.

Poor Alice. She might as well have hidden her tender heart in her locker along with her *Lloyd's Register*. When he left Hawk's Dyke, Stephen Morgan had made his opinion of us brutally plain and Alice had had to be content with very little. Yet twelve months had made no difference to her feelings. It seemed enough for her that Stephen existed and that his ship existed, and that occasionally Grandmother Kate would mention that he'd been in London and had called to see her. At least while Alice was in London the object of her passion inhabited the same city every few months: Munich meant total exile and Alice couldn't bear the thought of that.

'But of course you'll go!' Aunt Margot cast her eyes heavenwards as the argument broke out for the hundredth time. 'She's such a silly girl, isn't she, Clio? Don't bite your nails, Alice. It's common.'

'You'll get jolly bored,' I felt bound to say, 'hanging around at home all the time.'

'I'm going to get a job,' insisted Alice. 'I'm going to work in the Oliver offices. And why not?' she demanded, seeing her mother's horrified expression. 'Guy will be there next year, won't he? Why should it be all right for him, but not for me?'

'Yes, why not? There's nothing shameful in having a job.' Rose had spent her holidays reading the *Daily Herald* conspicuously around the house, after hearing her mother call it 'that socialist rag'.

Margot struggled with the unfamiliar maternal role. 'Guy must spend time in the office, darling, because one day he'll take his place at the head of the company and he must learn something about business. Obviously, that will never be necessary for you. No, Alice—' she raised a graceful white hand. 'Your task in life is to become a clever and ornamental wife. There's no point in discussing it any further.'

Margot settled back into her impregnable calm and a month later Alice departed miserably for Munich.

She was launched, like an Oliver ship, at a lavish coming-out ball in summer 1926 and trailed unhappily through the usual programme of presentation at court, fork luncheons, private views and At Homes. Guy, now free of school, was dragooned by Margot into squiring Alice at picnics and Maidenhead boating parties; but she could do little for her daughter at balls, where Guy could legitimately divide his attention between a great many girls. Alice, with no talent for chatter, spent much of her time in the cloakroom, pretending she'd caught her heel in the hem of her gown.

'Oh God, this is awful,' she wrote to me in October from a rain-lashed Wellborough Abbey. 'My toes have gone mushy from wearing galoshes, because Lady W insists we go out every day to have lunch with the guns – beastly game pie with the rain running down one's neck in some tumbledown cattle-shed. Bertie Headington shot one of the Earl's birds yesterday, which I gather is a fearful howler, and was lucky not to be sent home forthwith. Give me a gun and I'd shoot them all, if only to be released from this hell.'

At that moment, I couldn't imagine anywhere worse than Hallowhill School, where the fireplaces would contain nothing but sooty fans of paper until the second week of November and where Rose was rumoured to have tempted one of the under-gardeners to familiarities in the shrubbery, all in the name of free love.

I didn't see Alice at Christmas, but in March she wrote to me from Easton Broome, where Margot had organized a weekend house party of her own. A late frost had made the artificial lake too cold for the pink flamingos, but at least if sleet drove guests from the nine-hole golf course, they could take refuge in the Chinese billiard room or admire the paintings by Fragonard and Zoffany which lined the walls. Every evening, said Alice, the flowers which filled the principal rooms were changed to match Margot's ensemble.

I could tell something had excited Alice, though I was pretty sure it wasn't the flamingos.

'By the way,' she added with elaborate casualness, 'do you remember Stephen Morgan, the boy who stayed with us at Hawk's Dyke a couple of years ago?'

I remembered him well. The memory of that disastrous conversation beside the dyke still had the power to make me hot and embarrassed all over again.

'You'll never believe this, but quite out of the blue, Grandmama has made our fathers give Stephen a job at Oliver's.'

I imagined Alice staring blissfully out of the window at Easton Broome, watching the sleet whistle across the sunken garden.

'Isn't that amazing?' she said. 'No wonder Guy's been in such a filthy temper lately – but you know what Kate's like when she's set her mind on something. The men might huff and puff, but none of them would dare to refuse her.'

Alice's letter made me horribly restless. It was spring 1927, I was almost seventeen and I suppose the sap was rising and everyone except me seemed to be *doing* something. Alice was 'out', Guy had bought himself a two-seater Alvis and even Rose would be free of Hallowhill by summer, though she'd refused point-blank to follow Alice to Munich. And now that strange, wild creature Stephen Morgan had actually been given a job in the family firm.

Rose and I were almost the same age, but I suspected my father intended to leave me at Hallowhill until I was eighteen, simply for the sake of convenience. I felt as if I'd been abandoned, forgotten, in a jail from which everyone else had escaped.

Rose paid absolutely no attention to me at school these days. In the last half-year she'd found a soulmate in Polly Cadzow, the daughter of the well-known artist Leonard Cadzow, whose picture *The Riveter's Supper* had caused such a sensation at the Academy the previous year. Margot was deeply suspicious of the Cadzows and grew more so when Rose came back from a visit preaching about having discovered 'the brotherhood of mankind'. Shortly afterwards Margot heard a whisper that Cadzow routinely slept with his daughters and Rose was forbidden to visit again.

She felt humiliated by the ban – and worse when it became known at school that a young man named 'Cad' Langham had driven his Bentley tourer into a Hyde Park tree after a champagne lunch, tipping Margot Oliver out of the passenger seat at the feet of an astonished policeman. The newspaper gossip columns claimed Langham had been driving Margot to visit an old lady in hospital, but no one believed it. 'Old lady be damned,' said Guy. 'More like an afternoon with the Widow Clicquot.'

As it happened, I knew, because Alice had told me, that 'Cad' Langham, with his Bentley, his flannel blazer and his shock of red hair, had meant more to Rose than all the revolutionaries and left-wing painters in the world. Her head might be communist, but her heart was quite ordinary; and to discover that her mother had been seeing – and no doubt having an affair with – the object of her first, aching adoration was almost more betrayal than she could bear.

After the crash in the park Rose seemed to withdraw into a dark abstraction of her own. To the school staff she was silently docile and to the rest of us simply silent, and when one day I found myself briefly alone with her in the common room, I was totally at a loss for anything to say.

'Aunt Margot wasn't hurt, was she, when the car hit the tree?'

'Of course not.' Rose glanced up savagely from her book. 'Her kind are never hurt. It's the rest of us who have to suffer – and she doesn't care at all.'

That seemed to be the end of the conversation. Rose had hidden her face again, bent over her book, and it was impossible to tell from the back of her dark, vivid head what emotions might be filling it. Then I noticed her fingers tremble as she turned a page – but not before a great, wet blot had plopped on to the print. All at once, Rose's head flew up, her eyes sparkling with the tears which clung to her long lashes.

'They never stop telling us here how we ought to be upright and honourable – but it's nothing but words, worthless words.' Impulsively, she slammed her book shut. 'I don't know what to think any more – except that I don't believe in right and wrong and God in a long white beard watching to see if we behave ourselves. If God really exists, why does Mama get everything she wants, no matter how bad she is? I tell you, there's no God and no honesty in the world and no one gives a damn about us. It's all lies they tell for their own selfish reasons.'

It was beautiful, that bitter passion which illuminated her face. Recently, the sweet flesh of childhood had begun to fall away swiftly from Rose's cheeks, leaving a pale oval dominated by great, dark, speaking eyes. It was hard not to be beguiled, when Rose talked like that.

'It *is* a waste land,' she insisted fiercely. 'It *is*.'

Two evenings later, a handful of us were dawdling back from prep across the central courtyard of the school when Mabel Browne, wandering ahead, came to a sudden halt and pointed dramatically to the chapel wall. Painters had been at work in the courtyard for the past week, covering the doors and window frames in a colour which used to be known as Dust of Paris; but now four-foot cream letters had mysteriously appeared between the leaded windows of the chapel, like the prophesy at Belshazzar's feast. *No God in the Waste Land.*

'No . . . God . . .' Frowning madly, Mabel Browne began to read out the words as if she expected a divine instruction to reveal itself. She pressed her podgy hands to her cheeks. 'But what does it mean?'

'The paint's still wet,' someone pointed out. 'Look, it's running down by the sill there. It can only have been done a few minutes ago.'

We gazed, shocked into whispers by the enormity of the crime. There was nothing timid in its wickedness: a great deal of paint had been used and the letters were bold and defiant. *No God in the Waste Land.* It didn't take a genius to know whose hand had held the brush.

'Golly, Red Rose won't half cop it this time.'

'Bother Rose – I bet we'll all catch it for this.'

Yet I couldn't help feeling a sneaking admiration for Rose. It takes courage to plaster your feelings of betrayal across a public wall in letters four feet high.

Rose herself was standing just inside the boarding-house door. Her face was ashen and she seemed dazed, as though the consequences of what she'd done were only just beginning to sink in. I just hoped she'd had enough sense to put the paint pots and brushes back under the tarpaulin where the painters had left them, so as not to leave absolute proof of her guilt.

'Oh, good grief—' I suddenly realized the palm and fingers of Rose's black glove were smeared with Dust of Paris which had run down the handle of the brush like blood from a murderer's knife. I remembered the passionate, tragic Rose of two days earlier, with teardrops spiking her long lashes, and my heart ached to save her.

'Quick, quick, give it here.' In a second I'd stripped off my own glove, pulled the paint-daubed one from her unresisting hand, stuffed it deep into my coat pocket and given her mine instead. Rose smiled at me a little wildly and I felt a glow of reflected heroism. Perhaps now, at last, she'd like me.

The storm broke after supper, just as the upside-down pudding was being cleared away. Miss Aspinall, who'd been called outside by the school secretary five minutes earlier, returned with a face as grey as her iron fringe and rapped a spoon on the nearest table for silence.

'Some girl,' she began in a voice which throbbed with outrage. '*Some wretch* has perpetrated an abomination on the wall of our beloved chapel. I desire the girl – or girls – who were responsible for this desecration to step forward instantly.' Miss Aspinall's terrible eye swept over the rows of tables.

Nobody moved. I was dying to twist round to glance at Rose, but I managed to keep my eyes glued to a board on the far wall bearing the names of former lacrosse captains. The Aspinall would have been bound to notice.

'Well?' The headmistress glared round the hall, her cavernous cheeks quivering. 'Be assured I shall find the culprit, if I have to punish the whole school in order to do it.'

Still no one moved.

'Very well. Miss Pittenweem, would you be so good as to identify those girls who came in from the courtyard at six?'

The Latin mistress lunged zealously forward. 'Mabel Browne,' she called out. 'Georgina Eresby . . . Isobel Wyckham . . . All the late prep class and one or two others, in fact, head-

mistress. Clio Oliver . . . Gladys Tenby-Williams . . . Rose
Oliver . . .'

One by one, Miss Aspinall scanned our faces. 'We shall start,
then, with these girls, since they were the last to be present at
the scene of the crime. The entire school will remain seated at
table while the prefects search the belongings of these pupils for
evidence.'

She kept us there for three-quarters of an hour while I
wondered if they'd find the tin of humbugs hidden behind the
sponge-bag in my locker. I hoped devoutly that Rose had
remembered to take *The Waste Land* down from her wall.

At last Miss Aspinall swept back, flanked by the head girl
and deputy head girl like lictors attending an emperor. Every
eye in the hall followed her progress.

'School—' Miss Aspinall held up a hand. 'I am satisfied that
I have discovered the culprit. The rest of you may rise from
your places – quietly – and proceed to your common rooms or
your dormitories. I shall address you again tomorrow morning
on this shameful matter. Not you, Clio Oliver,' she snapped
as I clambered over the wooden bench. 'You will come to my
study.'

'Me?'

'Don't insult me by feigning surprise, girl. I suspected you
from the start.'

'But I had nothing to do with it!' I stared round desperately.
'I was in prep with the rest of the class. Ask the others, if you
don't believe me.'

'Silence!' Majestically, the headmistress pointed to the door.
'Proceed.'

'But I didn't do it – honestly!'

Rose was standing by the door, her eyes wide. I waited for
her to say something, to call out that she and not I had painted
that defiant message. But she dropped her gaze to her hands and
when Miss Aspinall followed my glance there was nothing to
see but solemn, beautiful Rose, the very picture of pure Hallowhill womanhood.

Miss Aspinall's face assumed a soppy smile – and I was
marched away between the lictors to the headmistress's study.

The worst of it was that Miss Aspinall thought I'd used Rose's glove in order to put the blame on my cousin. 'You didn't expect me to believe,' she said, 'that *Rose* would do such a thing? Rose is a quiet, industrious girl, whereas you – you have been a disruptive influence ever since you arrived at Hallowhill. You are a sly, secretive, selfish creature, Clio Oliver, who lives only for herself. You have an unwholesome nature, without the slightest spark of comradeship, sportsmanship or the feminine virtues.'

She's going to expel me, I thought with relief and began to cheer up a little. Then, at the last minute, the headmistress seemed to remember that several hundred pounds in fees hung on my continued presence at Hallowhill.

'On the other hand, you are, of course, motherless. It is our duty to make every effort to redeem you.' She stared at me for a moment, weighing up my iniquity. 'You will spend the night alone in the sick bay, where I hope you will realize the enormity of what you have done. Tomorrow morning you will confess your wickedness at assembly and after that I shall announce your punishment. Get out of my sight.' Miss Aspinall averted her scrawny head and waved me out of her presence.

In silent rage I gathered together a few belongings and went to spend the night on a narrow iron bed in an isolation room – finally confined to the prison I'd always known Hallowhill to be. Well, I wasn't staying – not any longer. Exciting things were happening in the world outside and I had a right to be part of them.

At four in the morning I squeezed through a window on to the washhouse roof, dropped down by way of the dustbins to the kitchen yard and set off for the railway station to catch the milk train to sanity.

Chapter Six

I WAS already half-way to London by the time I remembered my father was in New York again (or Philadelphia or Boston or somewhere of that kind), Guy was dividing his time between Kit's house in Belgrave Square and Easton Broome, and our house in Rutland Gate would be shut up for another fortnight.

Squashed into my third-class corner, I counted the coppers in my pocket. I must have enough left for an omnibus fare to somewhere – but to where? Kit and Margot were quite likely to send me back to Hallowhill, just to be rid of me. In fact, I could only think of one place that might offer a refuge. As soon as the train pulled into London I marched up to one of the vehicles waiting outside the station and gave the driver my grandmother's address.

I didn't know anything about omnibuses, except for a few remarks that Guy had dropped about double de-clutching and the fun of honking at pickets. The driver of this one enquired whether Lady Muck's chauffeur might conceivably have the day off, then peered down from his seat at the few coppers in the palm of my hand and sneered, 'You'll get off at Hyde Park Corner, girlie, and like it.'

Hot with mortification, I tramped the rest of the way to Chester Square, where Kate Oliver, thank heavens, took me in. She listened, frowning intently, while I poured into the bell of her ear-trumpet an account of my flight from school. Then she left the drawing room and somewhere beyond the door I heard her shouting into a telephone. At last she returned, looking thoughtful.

'Will you give me your word you didn't do it?'

'Yes, of course. Though I wish I had done it, now.'

'And you know who the culprit was?'

I nodded in silence. I had some notion of loyalty, even if Rose didn't. I could still hardly believe she'd stood there, treacherously silent, and left me to take the blame for her crime – me, especially, who'd tried to help her. So much for Rose's soul-melting tears! Liu Ling had been right: without thinking, I'd followed an impulse of my heart and had learned a bitter lesson.

'At any rate—' Kate installed herself in her favourite chair and smoothed her skirt over her knees. 'What's done is done. I've told that Aspinall person to dispatch your trunk to this address.'

'You aren't sending me back!'

'I can't see the sense in making you stay where you aren't happy. What would be the use of that?'

Bless you, Kate, I thought, *you wonderful, crazy old thing.* Then a dismaying thought occurred to me. 'Papa will expect me to go back. He thinks I should stay at school for another year.'

'Leave your father to me. He's never understood the first thing about women. Your grandfather was just the same – he believed the less he understood, the easier his life would be. You and I know what nonsense that is.' And Kate reached out to wind the old-fashioned bell handle and make arrangements for my stay.

'I've been trying to decide what to do with you,' she remarked next day at breakfast. Even at eighty-one, Kate never lingered in bed after half-past seven.

'Can't I stay with you until Papa gets back?'

'You may stay as long as you wish, though I can't imagine how you're going to fill your time. No, I think it would be far better if you went to Antibes with your Aunt Margot. I'll explain everything to your father.'

'Antibes?' I gaped at her. 'In France? On the Riviera?'

I knew Margot usually took a villa in the south of France for the few weeks between tennis at Deauville and clothes-buying in Paris. 'For recuperation,' she said. Alice had told me that this year, in the absence of any beaux or an engagement ring, she was being taken south to recuperate too.

'Aunt Margot may not want me.' This seemed highly likely. And there was a further unpleasant possibility. 'Won't Rose be there as well?'

'Rose will finish her term at school, I should think.' Kate gave me a shrewd glance, then went back to crumbling a roll between her knobbed fingers. 'Besides, any villa good enough for your aunt must be so enormous that an army could live there without treading on one another's toes.'

As I'd suspected, Aunt Margot didn't want me, but Alice was desperate for companionship and Kate's insistence finally carried the day – provided, said Margot, I was outfitted in 'something suitable'. All my previous holiday clothes had been a great-aunt's choice, not mine – and not Margot's either, it seemed.

'I've told her she may choose it all herself,' said Kate. 'Every stitch, if she pleases.'

Margot Oliver arrived next day in the Hispano with Alice in attendance.

'Naturally, Alice's gowns come from Paris these days.' Margot worked a wrinkle from her glove as the motor swept us towards Bond Street. 'But there's no time for that now. I just hope you won't look like a shop girl in ready-made.'

'This is a bit of a wheeze, isn't it?' I murmured to Alice as we plunged into the White House to look for blouses and lingerie. 'Just imagine – weeks on the Riviera instead of beastly Hallowhill.'

'To tell the truth,' Alice flashed a brief smile at the uniformed lift boy. 'I don't really want to go at all.'

'Oh, Alice—' Her constancy amazed me. 'Not still Stephen Morgan?'

Behind her mother's back, Alice shot me an anxious glance. 'Is it terribly obvious?' she whispered. 'Oh, damnation.'

She kept her head lowered and her face hidden by the brim

of her cloche as we marched over the soft carpets and down an aisle lined with glittering glass counters. Margot disposed herself on a bentwood chair with careless regality and within a few moments every vendeuse in the place had begun to spread heaps of garments in moirette and crêpe de Chine before our eyes. None of it was *sensible*; none of it was even remotely *warm*. I was half-blinded by the blizzard of splendour, drunk with the notion that most of it was going to be mine.

'Georgette evening knickers, I think.' Margot's voice fell on my ears like the smoothest silk, rolling out at five guineas a yard.

'Guy's furious with me,' Alice confessed in a low voice. 'He says I keep asking about Stephen – "that oik" or "that clown" as he calls him. Even if it was true, Guy doesn't own me, does he?' Unhappily, she fished in the pool of silk and satin.

'Guy's jealous, that's all. You ought to be flattered.' I held up a lacy camisole for her approval. 'You know how it's always been taken for granted—'

'I won't be taken for granted! I won't Clio – I don't care what anyone says, Guy or Mama or anyone. I'll do as I please.'

'This silk Milanese peignoir is really quite handsome,' Margot called out. 'But absolutely not in apricot. We can't have you looking like something out of *Hay Fever*.'

'Good grief, Alice,' I hissed, 'you aren't going to elope, are you?'

Alice shook her head, neat in its simple cloche. 'Stephen doesn't even notice me. I drop in on Papa in Leadenhall Street sometimes and occasionally Stephen's there. But he only says hello if I say it first – and never any more than that.'

'Oh, Alice . . .' I couldn't understand her enslavement. If that was how love took hold of you and made you wretched and prevented you from finding any pleasure in all the excitements the world had to offer, then save me from it! 'Things are bound to be better in the south of France,' I suggested. 'There are sure to be lots of fascinating people on the Riviera.'

'And we shan't know any of them. Not one.'

I thought of Nina Starozhilova, a peppery serpent in rose

crêpe de Chine, dancing in Monte Carlo for her beautiful millionaires. 'You can never tell,' I assured Alice hopefully. 'I might.'

At least Hallowhill was over and done with.

As soon as I got back to Chester Square I burned my horrible serge in the kitchen boiler and gave my cotton blouses and my stout school shoes to the cook for her niece. Then upstairs, one by one, I tore the tissue paper from the various garments Margot had approved, slid into them and surveyed my seventeen-year-old self in the pier-glass.

The transformation was startling. In a silk taffeta afternoon dress, the mirror offered me a vision I hardly recognized: no longer a lanky schoolgirl, but a slim, nonchalant creature, supple where before she'd been gawky, hinting at graceful curves where, as recently as that morning, all had been angularity.

If my nose had only been a trifle more fashionably retroussé . . . But my mouth was generous, with a fascinating little blue shadow under my lower lip, my skin was good and my eyes held such a sparkle . . . *Dazzling*. I decided I'd settle for *dazzling* or *bewitching*, even. *Miss Clio Oliver looked truly bewitching and was quite the centre of attention.*

I spun before the mirror in cloudy gossamer georgette and knew I could pass for twenty-one. In a beaded cocktail gown *à la mode King Tut* I almost achieved mystery. You could say what you liked about Margot (and many women did), but her taste was superb.

I sat down suddenly on the bed. The pier-glass showed me a young woman doing the self-same thing. Apparently the woman was me.

'Does this mean I've come out now?' I'd asked Margot eagerly as we climbed back into her motor outside Liberty's.

'You're tugging at the door, darling. Tugging at the door.'

Yet now, all of a sudden, I wasn't sure I was ready to be a woman, if it involved things like those horrifying illustrations in Papa's books and whatever it was one did in return for diamond brooches. Growing up had seemed so simple when

Liu Ling explained it to me in Shanghai: duty to the family was everything, especially for girl children – so safe, so straightforward. But Liu Ling had gone and here I was in England, trying to live up to a beaded cocktail gown and georgette evening knickers.

The next day Margot sent me off to her own hairdresser to have my plaits transformed into a dashing bob which clung to my cheekbones and made my eyes look almost as big as Alice's.

'I don't travel with children,' she'd warned me coolly.

We were to leave in less than a week, but Alice's gloom refused to lift.

'Gosh, Alice, you'll make yourself ill, you know. And all for someone who doesn't care a bit.'

'It's all right for you. You've never been in love.'

That was something to which I'd been giving a great deal of thought. I hadn't forgotten that wriggling, warm feeling in the pit of my stomach whenever Igor and I became tangled in a foxtrot. Perhaps that had been the first stirrings of passion.

'I think I used to be in love with Igor Starozhilov. The Russian who taught me to dance.'

'That was a crush,' Alice explained patiently. 'You can't fall in love at thirteen. Not like this.'

'Well then, I reckon what you need is someone else to fall in love with. What about Bertie Headington? He's good fun, isn't he?'

'Oh yes! If life were nothing but a round of scavenge hunts and costume parties, then Bertie would be perfect. But Clio, you've no idea, he's such a ghastly ass!'

Poor Alice. I was sorry for her, but I couldn't really see why being miserable over Stephen Morgan was so much more satisfying than training to be a spoiled and complacent wife for Guy.

I wondered if Kate had ever been in love with Grandfather Matthew. There seemed very little to love in the portrait that hung over the sideboard in her dining room, which gave him an obstinate mouth, its corners drawn down by a bowstring of sour ideas, and eyes as hard as farthings, linked by a cruel crease across the top of his nose. No doubt the artist had meant to convey solid worth and dignity and mastery of the tiny ships which sailed to and fro beyond his client's shoulder. All the same, I didn't think I'd have cared to marry such a man and I'd often wondered about the life Kate had led.

Now, however, for the first time, I noticed that Matthew Oliver had been moved aside to allow another portrait to share his space over the sideboard: the likeness of a man in an old-fashioned frock coat which had previously hung on the library wall at Hawk's Dyke. Seeing them together like that, I realized that while the stranger's features showed the same stubborn arrangement of nose and prominent cheekbones as my grand-father's, the artist had caught a glint in his eyes of something more – a wildness, a sort of elusive, pagan sensuality which the sitter's respectable clothes did nothing to disguise. The portrait reminded me of a nursery print of the Big Bad Wolf in top hat and tails.

'Who's that?' I asked Kate as we left the room after lunch. 'No one in our family, surely.'

Kate halted in front of the heavy gilt frame. 'That's Adam Gaunt.' For a few seconds she considered the picture thought-fully. 'Adam was Matthew's father.'

'Though his name was Gaunt, not Oliver?'

'Matthew was born a Gaunt. He took his Oliver stepfather's name when he inherited the shipping company.'

I digested this for a moment. 'Then Adam Gaunt must have been my great-grandfather, and Guy's.'

'He was.'

'And you actually knew him?' I was still fascinated by those enigmatic, anarchic eyes.

'I knew him – as well as anyone did. He was a restless man, a compulsive wanderer in his younger days. He hadn't much time for family. And yet—' She indicated the picture-filled walls of her house. 'He read Latin and Greek and he bought all these. Many of the artists were his friends.'

I couldn't imagine Matthew Oliver ever buying a picture, not with that hard, acquisitive scowl and that small mouth so like Alice's. Beside him, Adam Gaunt returned my stare, daring me to follow wherever his demons might lead. And then, for a strange instant – one of those moments quite outside time – an entirely different face stared back from the frame, every morsel of flesh and bone defying me to feel pity for him as we sat together on a damp dyke-bank in Norfolk.

Suddenly I knew I'd been right from the very beginning and every one of them had lied.

'Stephen Morgan *must* be Matthew Oliver's son!' I burst out. 'He couldn't possibly look so much like Adam Gaunt and not be related to us.' I didn't mean to sound so accusing, but here was yet another betrayal, another layer of the lies which seemed to bedevil our family. 'That's why you made them give Stephen a job at Oliver's, isn't it? And the story about his father's ship sinking in the China Sea wasn't true at all!'

'It was perfectly true, do you hear?' Kate rapped her stick on the floor. 'Stephen's father died in a typhoon in the China Sea. He had nothing to do with this family, nothing at all.'

She closed her mouth suddenly. Her glance darted round the room – to the window, to the door, anywhere but straight ahead, where I was waiting. Yet I'd had enough of falsehoods. This time I was determined to know the truth.

'Then why does Stephen Morgan look so much like my great-grandfather? It can't possibly be a coincidence.'

Kate shook her head. 'I can't tell you, child. I promised.'

'Promised *who*?' I was eaten up by curiosity. I felt as if, ever since leaving Shanghai, I'd been stifled by half-truths and meaningful looks and sudden silences. 'Promised who, Grandmama? Please, this isn't fair. I'm not a child any more and you shouldn't treat me like one.'

The door opened and a maid came in with a tray to clear the table.

'That's all right, Mary. We were just leaving.' Striking out with her stick, Kate set off for the drawing room, but I ran after her, refusing to let her escape.

'Tell me! You must! Does Guy know? Because I could make him tell me. Guy's hopeless with secrets, you know.'

'Oh, my stars!' Wearily, Kate dropped into her favourite

armchair and lifted her hands in despair. 'What am I supposed to do?'

I knelt at her feet, imprisoning her. 'Just tell me the truth, that's all. If Matthew Oliver wasn't Stephen's father – then how are we related?'

Kate glared at me and for a few seconds her mouth remained an obdurate line.

'Through his mother, you ninny!' The words burst out of her in an explosive hiss. 'Through his mother, Catherine Oliver – my daughter, and Matthew's.' Kate smiled grimly at my astonishment. 'You didn't think of that, did you? By heaven, you're as bad as your grandfather. D'you think only men matter in this family?'

She shook her head. 'You'll have to learn to look out for yourself, among the Olivers.'

'So the woman who came to the funeral – was Catherine—'

'In a sassy silk coat, so they told me. Just to show them all.' Proudly, Kate raised her head. In the light from the window I saw the faint freckles which still, after decades, dusted her skin. 'That's the sort of daughter I raised. My middle child, born between the two boys, with more spirit than either of them. Matthew's favourite, by a long way.'

Kate spread her frail, blue-veined hands on her knees and regarded them gravely. 'Matthew loved Catherine best because she stood up to him – until the day it began a war between them and he never spoke to her again, right to the instant of his death.'

That cruel crease on the bridge of my grandfather's nose had hinted as much. I'd have asked the artist to paint it out.

Kate had laid her ear-trumpet on the table, as she did whenever she didn't mean to be interrupted. 'When Catherine was small, you know, Matthew used to call her his little siren, because she could ask him for anything in the world and get it – they were almost like lovers, those two. Then, when she grew older, Matthew terrified any young fellow who came near her. No one was good enough for his daughter – no one but himself, of course, though he couldn't see that. And then, one day, when she was twenty-one years old, Catherine met a man called Robert Morgan and discovered what love was really all about.'

Love. I leaned forward intently. Here it was again, that insistent chimera.

Kate turned her eyes up to the ceiling and sighed. 'I promised Stephen I wouldn't tell you any of this. How am I going to explain to him?' Her eyelids began to quiver with a sudden welling of tears. Impatiently, she brushed them away, leaving a glistening trail on her hand.

'You see, Robert Morgan was a married man, which was bad enough. But what Matthew couldn't forgive was that Morgan was one of his employees – first officer on the *Severn Valley*, I seem to remember. He was a handsome fellow, too, though Catherine would have loved him if he'd had no looks at all.

'If it had just been a passing affair, I believe Matthew would have bought off Morgan's wife – they were separated by then, anyway. He'd have *bought* the man for Catherine – like a new hat or a grand piano. But what he couldn't stomach was the fact that she was desperately in love with this sailor of hers. She'd set the fellow above Matthew himself – a seaman he'd hired for a few pounds.

'So he made her choose: Robert Morgan, or her father. And of course, Catherine chose Robert and went to live with him in two rented rooms in Southampton.' Kate shook her head sadly. 'And after that, Matthew was determined to destroy Morgan and force Catherine to crawl back to him, begging his pardon. First of all, he had Morgan thrown off his ship and then he blacklisted him with the other shipping companies so that he'd never find another berth on a British or American-owned vessel. He was a powerful man, your grandfather.'

For a moment we both sat in silence, shocked by the dark face of passion.

'Robert – ' Kate clasped her hands ' – found work of a kind, as a crewman on a collier, or mate on a coasting schooner, but he was earning next to nothing and by this time Catherine was expecting a baby. I tried to make them take some money of mine, but Robert was every bit as proud as Catherine and they wouldn't hear of it. Even when the baby was born and they almost starved, they wouldn't let me help. That's when Robert went to Hong Kong and became master of the *Shanxi*.'

Kate's voice filled with disgust. 'A rusty old tramp, with a hold full of rice and rubber and an engine that was broken down as often as it was running. But what else could he do? He had to provide for Catherine and his baby son.' She made a gesture of helplessness. 'Poor Robert. When the typhoon caught him, he didn't have a chance. And, of course, Catherine blamed her father – blamed him and hated him. She found work in a dress shop, and somehow managed to support herself and Stephen.' Kate managed a smile of bleak pride. 'She was good at her job, too. She was manageress by the time she died.'

I remembered the silk coat worn so defiantly at Matthew Oliver's funeral. Catherine had been determined to look her best.

'She was so proud of her son.' Kate's eyes had misted again. 'She used to call here sometimes to show him off, if she was sure Matthew was away. Eventually she let me send Stephen presents at Christmas, but she'd never take anything for herself.'

Kate paused for so long that I was startled when she spoke again. 'Catherine's dead now, of course. Cancer – she'd had it for months before she came to me. She wouldn't accept my help, you see, even after her father was dead. Not until the very end.'

This time there was no more. Kate remained motionless in her chair, her gaze fixed on something far beyond the tall glass panes of the drawing-room windows.

My mind was filled with questions I didn't have the words to ask. How could you tell when another human being was worth such a sacrifice? Why had my grandfather been driven to such savagery? His portrait hung in the next room, with its tyrant's mouth and cruel crease: where had his daughter found the courage to defy all that? Surely, it must be a fearful madness, this love that rushed gladly to embrace banishment and ruin.

For several minutes I sat silently at Kate's feet – bewildered and feeling once more very young.

Then I remembered others whose names hadn't been mentioned. 'What about Catherine's brothers – my father and Uncle Kit? Didn't they try to help her?'

I had to repeat the question. Kate stared at me for a moment and then snorted in disbelief. 'There was a time when I had some hope of your father, certainly – until he went off to Shanghai and washed his hands of the whole affair. He was ashamed of himself – and still is, I suspect – but he was never strong enough to stand up to your grandfather. Matthew held the purse-strings, you see, and he was quite ruthless. Edward and Kit had to do as they were told, or give up any future with the shipping line.' She sighed deeply. 'Neither of them was prepared to risk that.'

To tell the truth, I wasn't surprised. Would Guy put my happiness before his inheritance? I doubted it. Women were of small account among the Olivers – and women who forgot their duty to the family of no account at all.

Kate leaned forward, hooked a finger under my chin and turned my face up to her own. 'You must hear the rest. Guy knows everything, so it's time you were told, or you might cause a great deal of hurt, without meaning to. What you must know—' she spoke very slowly and deliberately, as if spelling out a lesson '—is that my daughter Catherine and Robert Morgan were never married, because Robert's wife wouldn't divorce him. So Stephen, their son, is illegitimate. A bastard.'

She pronounced the ugly word with precision, leaned back and examined me narrowly. 'So now you know Stephen's secret. If it weren't for that, I wouldn't care who knew the story – and let the Olivers live with their guilt, if they could. But that would hurt Stephen and so I've never told anyone outside the family. Do you understand?'

'Of course.' I hardly heard her; I was thinking about Stephen, the child of that reckless, overwhelming love. For the first time I understood what he'd meant when he'd said he had nothing behind him, no past. And yet he had as much Oliver blood in his veins as I did. I tried to imagine how I'd feel in Stephen's position.

'Being a bas–, being illegitimate isn't so awful, is it?'

'It is, if you're young and you have a great deal of pride. Remember that, the next time you see Stephen.'

I was wondering how Alice would react when she knew. Perhaps I shouldn't tell her. Fond though I was of Alice, I had to admit she was awfully conventional. On the other hand, maybe this would cure her, once and for all.

'I'm not likely to see Stephen,' I said. 'Our paths never cross.'

My cousin Stephen came for dinner the evening before I was due to leave for Antibes. Kate had invited him, I suspect, as a test of my loyalties: whose side would I take – Catherine's, or my father and uncle's?

I thought about Stephen Morgan as I dressed. The love-child. Kate had said love-children were often beautiful, but Stephen would have had a special place in her heart, even if he'd been as ugly as sin. Which he wasn't. I called up an image of him in his apprentice's uniform, and again, sitting in the dusk on that Norfolk dyke-bank, staring over the hedgerows and longing to be able to fly like a bird, free of bitter reality.

I supposed I ought to feel sorry for him – my memories of Rose's treachery at Hallowhill were still so fresh that I could imagine exactly how Stephen must feel about our family – but instead I found myself desperately jealous. Stephen Morgan, for all the hostility surrounding his birth, was still the child of strength, blessed by that intense, exultant love for which Catherine had given up so much. I was the child of weakness and cold-heartedness, of a man who'd seen his sister suffer and simply walked away.

No wonder Kate loved Stephen dearly. Alice had loved him from the first moment she saw him. Why should anyone love me?

Piece by piece, I put on my shop-bought finery, until my crystal fringes glittered round me like armour and I began to understand why Margot had chosen them. I brushed my bobbed hair to a severe, glossy cap of indifference, shimmied my dinner dress into place over my hips and went downstairs to prove I didn't care.

Stephen was older, too: of course he was – how stupid of me not to have thought of that, as I welcomed my own escape from girlhood. He was more than two years older than the last time I'd seen him – and taller, with good shoulders and a dinner jacket that fitted, but that same speculative expression in his grey eyes when he tilted his head back to regard me.

'Well, well.' Curiously, he looked me over from head to toe. 'I don't think I'd have recognized you.'

He'd certainly inherited the Oliver talent for staring, though there was none of Guy's swagger or Kit's subtle relish in that cool examination. Stephen simply inspected me as a male creature inspects an almost fully developed woman, with the kind of scrutiny that makes her aware of every inch of her skin.

I flicked out my fringes for reassurance. 'You haven't changed so much.'

'Well, you certainly have.' Calmly, he rested a foot on the fender. 'You don't look so much like your brother any more.'

'I suppose that's a good thing. You never thought very much of Guy, as I remember.'

He gave a crooked smile, but didn't answer. Stephen Morgan, the love-child. The favourite.

There was a short silence and then we both spoke at once.

'I said, I hear you've left school. In something of a hurry, according to Kate.'

I glared at Kate. What was the point of all my dressing up, if she was going to tell everyone I was a runaway schoolgirl? Especially, I wished she hadn't told Stephen.

'I've finished with school. I'm going to the south of France tomorrow. To a villa,' I added, in case he thought I was going to stay in a hotel.

'Dinner,' called Kate at that moment. 'Come on now, everything gets cold if it's kept waiting.'

★

'I hope they've been making you feel at home in Leadenhall Street.' Kate had taken the top of the table, with Stephen on one side and me squarely opposite.

Stephen swirled the wine in the bowl of his glass. 'I didn't exactly expect a welcoming committee.'

'And didn't get one, by the sound of things.'

'I'll cope,' he said quietly. 'And with business the way it is, Oliver's may find a use for me yet.'

'What's wrong with business, may I ask?' The question snapped out before I could prevent it, but I felt as if I were eavesdropping on a conspiracy. I could guess how Guy and my father must be treating Stephen in the office, but my father was still my father and Guy was my brother, and the struggle to be fair to them all was setting my nerves on edge. I made an effort to sound reasonable. 'Oliver's is one of the biggest shipping companies in the world, you know.'

'And shipping's in trouble all over the world.' Stephen Morgan put down his wine glass. 'Oliver's have already lost a large part of their third-class transatlantic trade and now first and second class numbers are down too, and eastbound cargoes with them.' He leaned back in his chair. 'On top of that, the bottom's dropping out of the rubber market, taking more of Oliver's profits with it. You'll find it all in the figures,' he added, meeting my gaze. 'It's no secret.'

Kate had been watching him thoughtfully. 'You've obviously been busy.'

'Not officially. I'm not supposed to "poke my nose into company policy" – and since just about everything seems to be classified information, that leaves me a great deal of spare time.'

Suddenly I lost the struggle for impartiality. 'Then perhaps I should ask Papa to find you more to do.'

'He already has.' Calmly, Stephen ran a finger along the rim of his plate. 'He's packing me off to Australia in a week's time.'

'Australia?' I stared at him. 'Why Australia?'

'Because I know it – Sydney, Melbourne and Victoria, at least. And because there are strikes in the Sydney docks and the Oliver agent seems to be making a hash of things.' He raised his eyes suddenly to meet mine. 'And, I imagine, because it'll get me out of the London office.'

Kate snatched the napkin from her lap and flung it on to the table. 'But that's monstrous! They're sending you off to Australia like a remittance man. Refuse to go,' she instructed, 'and tell them to send someone down from Singapore.'

Stephen looked amused. 'I'm an employee, Kate, not a director. I have to do what I'm told. Besides—' He stretched his legs out under the table, inadvertently pushing one foot between mine. I noticed that he didn't apologize. 'I'm bored to death, hanging round the Oliver office, trying to keep myself occupied. At least there'll be some action in Australia.'

'And you'll get back to sea,' Kate pointed out tartly. 'I suppose that's the real attraction.'

'Not at all. I'm going to fly a good part of the way. Between flying-boats and short hops on other aircraft, I should be able to get as far as the Cape before I have to take a boat.'

'Good God!' Kate flung up her hands in exasperation. 'You're supposed to be in shipping! What am I going to do with you, Stephen?'

'Nothing at all, I hope. You've done enough for me already.' His smile was bland, but his lowered eyelids implied a warning. Stephen Morgan would go so far along the road Kate had opened up for him, but no further. After that he'd travel alone, wherever the fancy took him.

I knew Kate understood by the briskness of her tone. 'We'll have coffee in the conservatory, I think. Pour for me, Clio. I'll join you in a moment.'

The conservatory was lit by a cluster of electric lanterns which dangled from its darkened dome through the leaves and branches of a wisteria almost as old as the house itself. Under glass, the wizened climber burst into blue cascades twice a year, like a hag in a bridal veil. Even now, though it was hardly in bud, its heady, fragrant breath clung to the shadows between the palms and round the brass grilles of the heating channels.

Stephen Morgan didn't sit. Instead, he planted himself in the middle of the tiled floor, his jacket pushed wide and his hands in his trouser pockets, and solemnly watched me pour two cups of coffee. By now my beaded dinner dress seemed poor protection against that direct stare and yet I couldn't resist stealing a glance at him from under my lowered lashes. He was standing with his legs slightly apart, stiffly combative; a greenish light seemed to be pouring down on the crown of his head like the aureole of an avenging angel. He didn't bother to take the cup I held out to him.

'You know, don't you? Someone's told you the whole story.' His voice was soft with controlled anger. 'Did Guy tell you? Or was it Kate?'

To my annoyance, a trickle of coffee slopped into the saucer in my outstretched hand. 'I can't imagine why you should think that.'

'I can see it in your face. You've been watching me all evening as if I were a spider in a jar.'

'Of course I haven't. I've made a particular effort not to stare.'

'Oh, have you? Well, how very thoughtful!' He rocked backwards and the light caught a hard glitter in his eyes. 'And now you're kindly pouring me coffee. Another handout from the Olivers. I suppose I ought to be grateful for that, too.'

'Certainly not.' I smacked the cup down on the far side of the table, leaving the saucer awash. 'I don't suppose you take sugar in it.'

'You're right. I don't.'

I was too angry to respond. Stephen flung himself down in a rattan armchair, his face hidden from me by the knotted stems of a bamboo palm but his breathing shallow and rapid with annoyance. So much for tact and delicacy – but at least the whole business was out in the open now. There was no longer any reason for avoiding the subject and I even felt a kind of relief.

'In any case,' I challenged him, 'does it matter so much, if I know the truth? I don't see what you've got to be ashamed of.'

'It's none of your damned business – that's the point.'

'You're my cousin, aren't you? Kate's your grandmother, just as she's mine, or Guy's – or Alice and Rose's.'

'Apart from a small matter of a wedding ring.'

'That isn't your fault. I don't see what difference it makes.'

'Don't you?' There was sarcasm in his tone, but at least his anger seemed to be dissolving. He reached forward for his coffee cup. 'Your brother Guy knows it makes all the difference in the world – and your father and Kit. It means I've no claim to a share of my grandfather's company. Not legally, at any rate. And, let's face it, what's *morally* right has never concerned the Olivers very much.'

It was true; I didn't even try to deny it. 'Is that what you want? A share of the company?'

He shrugged, shivering the palm-fronds. 'Kate thinks I ought to want it. She still reckons I could challenge Matthew Oliver's will on my mother's behalf. "Fight for it," she says.'

'And are you going to fight for it?'

He leaned forward and regarded me quizzically round the palms. 'Are you asking for your own sake, or for Guy's?'

'I don't spy for my brother, if that's what you think.'

I held his gaze directly, defying him to disagree. He allowed me another of those crooked, fleeting smiles which gave away nothing and moved back in his chair. 'I haven't made up my mind yet.'

In the silence that followed, I examined him covertly through the foliage. As cousins, Guy and Stephen were utterly different – I couldn't imagine them sharing anything, let alone a shipping company. For one thing, Guy was a sugar addict. I'd seen him pile as many as five spoonfuls of the stuff into a coffee cup, his gold Cartier wristwatch flashing among the porcelain. Yet there was no sweetness about Stephen Morgan. His pleasures, I suspected, were as spare and simple as his own lean, hard-muscled body. His possessions probably fitted into a suitcase.

He seemed such an unlikely figure for Alice to worship – and yet, sitting there in the green gloom below the wisteria, I fancied I could understand the perverse fascination of someone so determinedly unreachable. It was his dogged refusal to yield which had seduced Alice: the solitary dignity of the outcast, the bleak mystery of an Ishmael.

His profile was a pale mask now between the green straps of the palms, where the shadows clung deeply to the stark hollow under his cheekbone. Perhaps Matthew Oliver had looked much the same at that age, before dwindling into a lonely old man with cruelty etched on the bridge of his nose. I felt an odd rush of regret: perhaps Alice could save Stephen, if anyone could.

I reached for the coffee pot. 'Have you seen Alice recently, by any chance? I believe she comes into the office, sometimes.'

'Alice?' Stephen frowned vaguely. 'I've seen her there, yes.'

'She's very nice, Alice. Very gentle and sincere. We're going to the Riviera together tomorrow.'

'Really.'

'She's been out for almost a year now and she's awfully popular. I'm sure you'd like her, if you got to know her.'

'Look, what on earth is this all about?' Stephen sat forward in his chair, creaking the rattan, and held out his cup. The lanterns overhead had veiled his eyes with unreadable darkness. 'I'd like some more coffee, if you've quite finished matchmaking. I take it that is what you're doing?'

'Of course not.' I could feel the colour rising in my cheeks and wished to blazes I'd kept my pity to myself. 'I must say, Stephen, you can be jolly rude sometimes.'

'I don't like people interfering in my affairs, that's all. No sugar, please.'

'Oh, *no* sugar. Absolutely not.' I snatched his cup and accidentally sent the little coffee spoon spinning towards the tiled floor.

Except that it never reached the floor. How Stephen Morgan intercepted it I still don't know – simply that one instant the spoon was in mid-air and a split second later it was in his hand and he was replacing it on the tray.

A little shiver ran down my spine. At least now I knew

Stephen Morgan was definitely not the man for Alice. Love-child or not, no one had a right to move as quickly as that.

There was a rustling among the palms and Kate came in. 'I do like the conservatory in the evenings,' she murmured. 'So peaceful, don't you think?'

Chapter Seven

IT WAS more difficult than I'd expected, telling Alice what I'd found out, almost as if Stephen Morgan were listening resentfully to every word.

I made the story as matter-of-fact as I could. I pointed out gently that Stephen seemed quite wrong for her and she'd be far better off with some calm, countrified chap, a decent sort with a solid family and several thousand acres. Then I got rather carried away and reminded her of someone's joke about Lord Brougham – that if he'd been a horse nobody would have dared to buy him, since with an eye like that no one could answer for his temper. Alice pretended she didn't understand. She said absolutely nothing while I talked, hunched on the edge of her bed, her eyes downcast and her hands pressed together between her knees.

'So that's the end of the mystery,' I concluded. 'You can stop fretting about Stephen Morgan and start thinking about all the terrific young men we're bound to meet on the Riviera.'

For a moment Alice remained silent. Then an enormous sob broke through her silence.

'Australia . . .' she murmured and scrabbled in her sleeve for a handkerchief.

Her eyes were still pinkish next morning, when our little party arrived on the platform at Victoria to begin the journey to Cap d'Antibes – though 'arrive' hardly conveys the full drama of the scene. Margot Oliver never simply arrived anywhere in her life: Margot *happened* to places like an earth tremor, claiming everyone's attention and leaving the same turbulence in her wake as the passing of a tidal wave.

On the fifteenth day of April we duly *happened* to Victoria Station, preceded by the station master himself, stepping out in frock coat and top hat, cutting a path through lesser travellers with a rolled-up copy of his timetable. Behind him stalked Margot, glancing neither to right nor left, and followed by Alice and me, rushing along in a flourish of pleats and the lowest possible cloche-brims. At our heels came Margot's maid Briggs, clutching Margot's jewels in a black morocco case, Dickson the chauffeur, weighed down with rugs, and Wilkins, newly promoted to Alice's maid (and by extension temporarily mine), her arms wrapped anxiously round Margot's outsize crocodile dressing-case. Behind us came nine porters wheeling towers of Vuitton luggage: steamer-size wardrobe trunks, hat-boxes, shoe-cases, umbrella-and-parasol-cases, sundry tea-baskets, and lawn tennis bags, a box of massage oils, cosmetic mud, Oxford marmalade and Cheltenham Spa water, and a leather box containing a gramophone and a dozen records of Margot's melodies of the moment, all to be packed into the gleaming womb of a Pullman coach, en route for Dover and the fast Calais packet.

In view of what Stephen Morgan had said about the state of Oliver Line profits, I'd watched intently for any slackening in Margot's spending. Yet she seemed to have shopped for the south of France as magnificently as ever. While her husband's Wellborough relatives saved the pieces of string from the joints cooked for their servants' hall, Margot had thought nothing of buying a rare Kakiemon vase to show her decorator the precise shade of blue she required for a bedroom at Easton Broome.

Yet even Margot couldn't eclipse the glamour of the 'through' carriages of the Blue Train which awaited us at Calais, the *train de luxe* of the Compagnie Internationale de Wagons-Lits, which would whisk us through the night to the sparkle of the Mediterranean. It was a grand hotel on wheels, its tables crowded with silver and fresh flowers, its sleeping compartments loaded with impossibly starched linen and engraved mirrors, and enough blinds and draperies and curious little doors opening on secret taps and basins to keep one opening and shutting and pouring and flushing all the way south.

But more exciting, even, than all this was the Gallic night which descended on us somewhere near the tail of the Paris *Ceinture*, a darkness stuffed with dangers through which our softly lit capsule of luxury plunged unscathed, sloughing murder and mayhem from its gleaming cobalt flanks. The following morning there was just enough time for croissants and coffee and a glimpse of a blue ribbon of sea beyond the window, before we were out of the train and installed in an enormous Delage with silver-plated towel-rail bumpers, heading for the villa Margot had rented.

The Villa Oléandre . . . To me, the house was a joy, as ancient as the promontory on which it sat, all plum-coloured dimness behind its tall shutters, rich with the scent of lavender and thyme blown in from the sun-baked slopes below the pines. This was the kind of house I understood: mellow wooden floors, thin needlework carpets wrinkled like ancient skin, chandeliers sagging in dewy webs . . . all of it airy, shadowed, peaceful and self-contained.

A terrace ran along the sea side of the house, its stone rampart overgrown with Hottentot fig and stained by the marks of old downpours. Below it lay a garden created for no one in particular, an impersonal exercise in palms and clipped shrubs and hard-beaten, lion-coloured earth, its furthest edge marked by a balustrade. Above that stone rim the eye launched itself like a gull into a strip of bright ultramarine – our slice of the Mediterranean at last.

And the weather had excelled itself for us – balmier and warmer than anyone could remember in Antibes at that time of year. '*Une vraie chaleur d'été,*' the chauffeur had called it, resentfully running a finger round his tight uniform collar.

'There's no beach!' Alice leaned over the parapet in dismay, surveying a cascade of rock with the texture of Madeira cake. Below us, a flight of steps fell fifty feet through a damp and dizzying cleft to a tideless inlet. The stench of weed puddled round roasted rocks rose up to greet us: clearly there was no bathing to be had just there.

Not far along the headland, however, the sea had carved a small cove from the rocks and sprinkled it with sand. As Alice and I made our inspection from a corner of the balustrade, two sun-umbrellas bloomed in its centre and miniature figures marched to and fro before finally creeping into the pool of shade.

They were Americans, as it turned out – to no one's surprise, since the move to extend the Riviera season was chiefly an American affair. Traditionally, under British influence, the hotels began to close in April and the modish world melted away to play golf at Le Touquet; but lately a younger, more adventurous set had begun to linger round Cannes in the hotter months, persuading the restaurants to stay open and creating a new craze for tanned, firm, sun-warmed flesh.

Margot Oliver, whose instincts for changing social fashion were sharper than anyone's, knew to the instant when to set off firmly and quite devastatingly in a new direction, dragging a scampering herd of imitators. The Riviera in summer was poised to become chic: and where there was chic, there was Margot.

Quite by chance, there also was Mrs Longbaugh Karp.

By the time Alice and I reached the little strip of beach, Mrs Karp, enveloped in a striped peignoir, looked as if she'd already had more than enough of the unseasonable sun. Holed up under her parasol like a red-faced and disenchanted tortoise, she was bored by the beach and badly in need of someone to talk to. Within minutes she'd told us that Mr Longbaugh Karp – Poppa – had been too busy making motor cars in Chicago to tear himself away for a tour of Europe, but that she, determined to be more than the consort of a provincial millionaire, had set out across the Atlantic with her son and daughter to broaden the family's horizons. She waved a fistful of rings to where Honor and Chester Karp strolled at the water's edge, as long-limbed and well-nourished as a couple of Great Danes, with wide mouths and bright, appreciative smiles.

Alice and I put up our own umbrella and privately agreed not to tell Margot the Karps had rented a shiny portable bathhouse. Through lowered lashes I watched Chester Karp lunge up the beach, kicking up little puffs of sand, and fling himself down on his bamboo mat. Chester, I decided, was just what Alice needed: a wholesome young millionaire of twenty or so with easy manners and a body which, even in an all-over swimming costume, looked hard and games-playing and transatlantic.

Mrs Karp plunged into fulsome introductions. '. . . and, believe it or not, their daddies own the ship we came over in, Honor – isn't that just amazing?'

'Well, my goodness.' Honor Karp looked us over with critical interest while her mother picked up the story of their trip once more.

'—and in the Paris Ritz we had the very great felicity of being presented to the King of the Belgians—'

I nudged Alice. 'He has nice teeth, don't you think?' I could see Chester Karp was bored to death by his mother's recital. He was a good deal darker than Stephen Morgan, but he glowed with the confident gloss that only a great deal of money can achieve and I knew he'd be perfect for Alice, if only she'd make an effort to be agreeable.

But Alice was staring fixedly at the sky. 'Do you know,' she murmured, 'Stephen could be somewhere up there at this very moment. And I'd never even be aware of it.'

Margot had disappeared by the time we returned to the Villa Oléandre, but in the *petit boudoir*, a note had been pegged down under a Meissen Psyche. 'Eat when you please, darlings. Don't wait up for me, M.'

'I warned you,' said Alice. 'We're on our own here now.'

The following morning brought someone called Couscous, with oiled, heavily perfumed hair and an armful of lilies, who sipped coffee on the edge of Margot's bed and gossiped about the previous night's party. Alice disliked him on sight, but I couldn't help noticing that his brilliantine and plucked eyebrows contrasted curiously with the tough, wiry body he hid in cotton peasant overalls and with his eyes, which remained as hard and round as a macaw's. I wondered what scandal had exiled him to the south of France, to preen and chatter on Margot's bed.

Unlike the international gypsies who came and went with the Riviera season, many of the permanent residents had been lured there because the living was cheap. Couscous's conversation was studded with famous names: a retired *grande horizontale* ruined by the bottle; a Russian princess who sold English newspapers on the Promenade des Anglais in Nice; a former Balkan grand duke and his duchess who dropped in most days at *le five o'clock*, gently formal and faded, to drink the sweet champagne Margot despised and complain about rising prices on the Côte d'Azur.

'*Chère Margot*,' they'd murmur. '*Comme elle est divertissante.*'

These were people whose lives I understood: Shanghai had been full of the penniless and the dispossessed, clinging to the threads of former glory. Such a place was Nina Starozhilova's natural home. I had no doubt that sooner or later I'd find her.

Naturally, Couscous, who knew everyone, also knew Nina, or knew *of* her, at least. 'A Russian young lady, yes. A dancer – certainly, that's what I heard. But not with Diaghilev. The mademoiselle I have in mind dances in the cabaret at the Coq d'Or, and lodges with the Platonovs in Cannes. As for her brother . . .' Couscous shrugged extravagantly. 'I have met him, yes – but I can't tell you where to find him, *mon ange*.'

'Igor Starozhilov is here!' I told Alice, greatly encouraged. 'Here, on the Riviera. You remember, Nina Starozhilova's brother, the Russian who used to give me dancing lessons in Shanghai? Isn't that exciting?'

'Terrific.' Alice regarded me dolefully from under her fringe.

To tell the truth, I'd begun to feel that something was missing, even from this demi-paradise. Sometimes, in the early mornings, I'd seen Alice out on the mist-hung terrace, leaning her thin, bare arms on the corky lichen of the balustrade and contemplating something a million miles removed from the Cap d'Antibes. There was no doubting what, or who, was at the heart of that yearning silence: and yet I had to admit that Alice, for all her unhappiness, had come better equipped than I, since the Villa Oléandre was surely made for *amour* – of the tender, wistful, star-crossed variety which lingers for decades as a faded rosebud, long since scentless but treasured in the hidden drawer of a jewel-box.

Margot, I suspected, was already deep in some languorous affair. Alice was content to wander under the pines, dreaming of Stephen Morgan, while I, with no one of my own to sigh over, was missing half the pleasure of being in such a place.

Chester Karp kept inviting us to swimming parties, but since he seemed immune to the exquisite melancholy in the air and didn't seem able to stay on the beach for more than ten minutes without having to whack balls around or race in the surf, Alice and I usually made excuses, preferring to laze on the rocks and let the salt surge whisper among our thoughts. Alice's mood was subtly infectious. Pretty soon I couldn't wait to be the whole, grown-up woman my London looking-glass had shown me. I desperately wanted to fall in love, as Catherine and Alice had done: what use were Liu Ling's careful precepts, except to keep me a child for ever?

And thanks to Couscous I knew there was someone on that dreaming coast with whom I already imagined myself half-way enchanted.

Couscous became my courier, falling so effortlessly into the role of go-between that I realized it was his profession. Nina was overjoyed to hear of my arrival: *malheureusement* her brother was not at that precise moment available, but she herself longed to meet me (and my delightful cousin, if she cared to come) at the Café des Allées overlooking the square in Cannes, at such and such a time on such and such a day.

I lured Alice to town with an afternoon's roller-skating at the Miramar. Margot had left before lunch, allegedly to play bridge, in ivory silk pyjamas and a straw hat from the market pinned with a huge diamond crescent. In spite of what Nina had said I nursed a tremulous hope that when we got to the café Igor would be there too; but when the Delage with its towel-rail bumpers pulled up outside, there was only one person waiting at a table among the trees, her chin high and thrown out aggressively in Nina's unmistakable profile.

The vaulted branches splashed the tables with lilac shadow. In their shade Nina looked thoroughly pleased with herself – pleased with her neat little hat with its ribbon *chou*, with her twinkling strappy feet and knees made rosy and inviting in pink silk. She was only a year older than Alice, but there might have been a century between them, for all they had in common.

Nina had already embarked on cognac; Alice and I ordered *citronnades*, and sipped discreetly, side by side, watching the taxis fly to and fro beyond the edge of our leafy umbrella and letting Nina fill our ears with all the gossip of the coast. No, she was not yet dancing with Sergei Pavlovich and the Ballets Russes – she snapped her fingers dismissively – but then, poor Diaghilev was so utterly besotted these days with that charlatan Stravinsky's twangs and bangs, which no one in his right mind could call *dance* music . . .

But enough of that! Nina flung herself back in her chair, crossed her legs with her usual abandon and lit a cigarette, drawing on it deeply as the smoke foamed up around the ridiculous little nose-veil attached to her hat. Ah – the Riviera! So much *life*, so much *art* – I must know Bonnard, of course, who'd bought a house in Antibes where he meant to paint, and the Murphys at the lighthouse, whose home was permanently *full* of American writers – charming sober, but so often drunk – and, of course, the darling, *divine* Isadora, writing her memoirs in Nice, though frankly she hadn't a penny left to live on, would you believe it after *all* those men?

'And Igor?' I took advantage of one of Nina's gasps for air.

'Igor?' She rolled her eyes and her pencilled brows arched in mock despair. 'I sent money to Shanghai and I said, "Igor, I long for you to come here." But now he has so many friends, I hardly see him.' She leaned forward and seized my hand. 'But I have many friends also – artists, sculptors. I think they would like to meet you and your cousin and perhaps your very rich aunt. I expect she buys many beautiful things, *n'est-ce pas?*'

'Sometimes,' I agreed.

'Bravo!' Nina clapped her strong little hands, creating a zig-zag of cigarette smoke above our table. 'I shall take you where there are things to see.'

We didn't even bother to ask Margot, worldly creatures that we were. Nina became our guide and took us to garrets and cottages thick with cigarette smoke and the stench of turpentine, full of canvases of open windows 'after Matisse' or sturdy nudes 'in the style of Gauguin'. She bore us off down narrow, sun-dried lanes to *estaminets* ringing with the sound of mechanical pianos, where we drank fierce black coffee with the artists and the women who might have been their lovers, their models, their landladies, or even their mothers, for all anyone seemed to know.

In these places *amour* swirled so thickly amongst the garlic and the stink of cheese that even Alice's face became flushed with excitement and she no longer gasped at petrol-green nudes with hugely inflated buttocks and tiny heads, or limbs which turned into strawberry trees or crimson violins.

In the end, I spent most of the money Kate had given me on a rather daring figure of a reclining woman with no head or feet, and Alice, who had a generous allowance of her own, bought an expensive *nature morte* of a cane chair and pink apples. Encouraged by this burst of sophistication, we climbed down to the rocks of the shore with a packet of the vicious local cigarettes and made ourselves sick amongst the seaweed.

And yet, in the end, it was Mrs Longbaugh Karp who reunited me with Igor, over cocktails in the grand salon of the Villa Oléandre, with its glass doors open to the terrace. The Grand Duke Dino and his wife were there as usual, with a snuffling black *bouledogue* which flung itself lasciviously on the gentlemen's shoes. There were film people from the hills behind Monte Carlo, and Couscous hovering possessively over a young potter from Biot, and the local Anglican priest who surely must have been there by mistake, and a couple of male Gould relatives, surreptitiously kicking the *bouledogue* from their feet.

I'd never liked champagne much before; but the evening was hot and I was thirsty, and I polished off several glasses before realizing it. Then all at once I saw him – Igor Starozhilov, beyond doubt – coming into the salon with Mrs Longbaugh Karp on his arm. He looked amazingly elegant, in a blazer of some soft woollen stuff, a putty-coloured silk shirt and impeccable flannels which clung to the curve of his thighs as he moved. When he offered a cigarette, there was a blaze of gold from case and lighter and another from the cuffs of his shirt. Yet there could be no mistaking those great dark eyes in their wells of mauve shadow, or the deep, eloquent, Slavonic clefts which ran from cheekbone to jaw.

Ellie Karp had come in a turban and smoking-pyjamas which made her resemble an untidy parcel.

'Look.' Alice was standing near by: I grabbed her by the sleeve. 'That man walking towards your mother with the Karps, just ahead of Chester. That's Igor, from Shanghai.'

Alice squinted short-sightedly.

'Isn't he the most glorious thing you ever saw?'

Across the room I watched Margot inspect Igor with interest and felt a surge of proprietorial pride. If Igor was dancing for a living, he must certainly be the star of the show. I've seldom seen real beauty in a man, but Igor Starozhilov was blessed by it without effort.

At last, I saw him walk alone through the glass doors to the terrace. Weaving through the crowd, I followed.

He turned when he heard my step on the paving and gave me the polite, impersonal smile of a man who finds himself in conversation with a stranger.

'Hello again, Igor.'

'Hello there.' His smile widened automatically, but his eyes remained hesitant.

'You haven't forgotten me, have you? Clio Oliver, from Shanghai? You used to give me dancing lessons, you and Nina.' The rising fumes of the champagne were going to my head. Swirling my filmy georgette, I held out my arms, danced a few paces of a foxtrot over the terrace and fluttered back to him, breathless.

'Ah!' Now he remembered, nodding. He held his hand out at chest height. 'But you were only *so* big, surely. And your hair was in tails.'

'Pigtails – yes, of course it was. I was only twelve years old when you started my lessons.'

'And now you are . . . twenty? Twenty-one?'

'Twenty-one,' I agreed without a blush, hoping his arithmetic was weak. Why not? The copper stems of the honeysuckle on the parapet were twining with one another on pairs of grey-green wings, perfuming the evening all around us; the last thing I wanted was for Igor to think I was still a child.

'And so Mrs Oliver—' he gestured to the salon behind me – 'is your mother, yes?'

'Oh no, only my aunt.' I rushed to confirm my status as a free spirit. 'Margot goes out with her own friends and Alice and I do as we like.'

I found myself smiling – a wide, sunny, champagne grin. 'Nina told me you were here, on the Riviera. I was hoping to see you.'

'Were you?' He examined me curiously. Emboldened, I moved closer and his gaze slid from my face to the bodice of my dress, where I'd pinned the yellow diamond butterfly brooch Margot had lent me for the evening ('So no one will notice the frock, darling'). He reached out to touch it.

'Very pretty.'

And then, without any warning, his fingers left the brooch and skimmed my throat, flitting to the point of my chin. 'You too. Though you are more than pretty. You are quite . . . enchanting.'

That moth-wing touch was enough to blow all my sophistication to the breeze. I stared at him, idiotically tongue-tied, wondering how Margot would have responded. Should I deny it? Should I say thank you? Should I move out of reach and demand *How dare you?*

In the end, I simply smiled my happy smile. It was the first time a man had ever paid me a proper compliment.

Igor glanced over my head at the glass doors to the salon. 'I tell you what – why don't we go into the garden for a little while? I want to hear all about you – and about your father, who owns all the ships, and this Mrs Oliver who rents the villa.' Without waiting for an answer, he took my arm and steered me down the steps from the terrace towards a path bordered with tufted dragon-trees in whose shade night had already begun to gather.

Somewhere – half-way down the path, perhaps, where shrubs hid our wanderings from the house – I discovered his arm round my waist and found myself magically leaning against his side with my heart setting off on a wild tango of its own.

'Happy?' He inclined his head.

'Oh, yes.'

The evening was still soft and warm and after a while we sat down, close together, on an iron seat among the camphor bushes, to recapture the past.

'Your house in Shanghai was so big – as big as a hotel.' Igor drew aside a strand of hair which had tangled with my eyelashes, his fingers caressing my temple. 'And everywhere, there were servants, the same as when I was very young in Russia.'

He'd stretched his arm round my shoulders and I nestled dreamily against him, convinced that something familiar and very dear to my heart was being restored to me. Was it Shanghai – or was it Igor? Memories had begun to flood back irresistibly.

'Do you remember the funny, perfumed smell of the wooden floors? And our gramophone record of Strauss waltzes that used to hiccup—'

'And all the wonderful pieces of jade.' Igor's voice was a deep, thoughtful murmur above my head. 'They used to say your father's collection was worth millions of dollars.'

'Did they?' I wasn't interested in jade. In my mind, I was foxtrotting again round the cleared space in our dining room, close enough to feel the warmth of Igor's chest against my cheek. I could feel the strength of it again now, thrillingly resonant when he spoke.

'Your cars, too. You went everywhere in enormous cars, with a driver to drive you. I used to see you, sometimes, staring out of the windows like a little prisoner.'

He printed a fleeting, fly-away kiss on my forehead – as soft as a butterfly alighting – and then, before I could recover from my surprise, disconnected us. 'Let's walk a bit more.'

By the time we reached the algae-crusted pool at the end of the garden, it was a circle of slate in the dusk and his lips were moving against my hair, whispering endearments. 'So you hoped you would see me again . . . I, too, because even in the old days, in Shanghai, you were very special, very different . . .'

His lips found my ear and caressed it; now I could feel the old, wriggling warmth flooding the pit of my stomach and spreading outward like the slow radiance of a live coal. Igor's words fluttered in the labyrinth of my ear. 'And now I've found you again, my Shanghai dancer.'

A little way beyond the pool there was a natural cleft in the rock, a cool vault roofed by the leathery leaves of a fig tree. We slipped inside and at once Igor pulled me powerfully against him. I felt utterly helpless and yet excited, just as I'd dreamed I would. Wonderfully imprisoned, I closed my eyes and savoured the touch of his lips on my brow and then lower, brushing my eyelids.

'My darling—'

I slid into willing surrender, tilting my face up to be kissed, but he teased me by nibbling the hollow of my throat – greedily, while I shivered in his arms.

I was overwhelmingly, blissfully happy. Now, all at once, it seemed that I, too, had a love like Alice's – a love like Catherine Oliver's, to be clung to and sighed over under the rustling pines. My loneliness would be quenched in the joys and despairs I'd never known; I might even share Alice's tears and the dreams that went with them.

At last Igor kissed me: and I, who'd never known more than a great-aunt's peck, was left breathless and dizzy with astonishment that a kiss could be so much more than a mere melting of mouths. As it happened, one mouth had been knowing and determined and the other innocent, offering itself softly for plunder – but even so: nothing so possessively intimate, so *internal* had ever remotely happened to me before.

When I opened my eyes, Igor was staring down at me, his face filled with something like satisfaction.

'How odd to find you such a grown-up, rich young lady.'

'*Rich?*' It was the last thing I'd expected him to say. Still giddy from champagne and his kiss, I was suddenly seized with the fear that he might see the Oliver wealth as a barrier between us, as it had been for Catherine and Robert Morgan. I rushed to reassure him. 'Papa's rich, I suppose, and my uncle and aunt. But I haven't any money of my own – nothing at all. Not until my father gives me an allowance, that is.'

'Absolutely nothing?'

'Not a bean.'

I saw him glance, puzzled, at Margot's yellow diamond brooch. So that was the cause of the trouble! 'Oh, the brooch isn't mine – it belongs to my aunt. She only lent it to me for this evening.'

Igor's face registered some strong emotion I took for relief. 'But in any case, money makes no difference, honestly.' I tilted my face up again, hoping for another of his devastating kisses, but he seemed preoccupied.

'So you are not rich . . . but your aunt, she must have plenty of money, to stay in a house like the Villa Oléandre.'

'I suppose so.'

'More money than Mrs Karp, yes?'

'Possibly, yes. Does it really matter?'

'Not to you, maybe, because you've never been poor.' Almost absently, Igor had begun to massage the small of my back with hypnotic warmth, circling down to explore my backside through the flimsy georgette. The play of his hand was irresistible, yet his mind was still engrossed. 'It isn't good to be poor. I don't like it. People walk past in the street as if they can't see you. They're embarrassed, if they know you have nothing.' His massaging hand halted. 'I don't suppose you understand.'

'But money isn't important, Igor, really it isn't.' I laid my cheek against his chest, willing him to believe that I'd care for him just as much, rich or poor. A feeling I couldn't comprehend was eating me up inside and his pride was heartbreaking.

Gravely, he detached me, peeling me from his shirt-front and taking a step backwards.

'It's time we went back now. Your aunt will think I have kidnapped you.'

'So soon?' I couldn't believe he really wanted to go back to the villa; but he was already staring out of our refuge to where the house sailed like a great ship in its silent garden. I only realized there were tears in my eyes when he brushed one gently from my cheek.

'Don't cry.' He put an arm round my shoulders and drew me out into the dusk. 'We can't always have everything we want.'

'Igor,' I whispered, 'I think I love you. Is that possible, do you imagine?'

'I hope it is.'

'Then shall I see you again soon?'

'Very soon. I promise.' Without missing a step, Igor bent his head and kissed me fleetingly on the lips.

'When shall I see you?'

'I don't know. Soon.'

'But you will come?' For the first time, I knew the anguish of love.

'I gave you my word. If you love me, then you must believe me.'

He said it so sternly I didn't dare to ask again.

'Darlings.' Margot swam out of a buzz of moving picture people as we came back into the salon. 'Mr Starozhilov, forgive me – Honor Karp tells me her mother's motor is waiting. Mrs Karp has been looking for you everywhere,' she added archly.

Igor sighed. 'Mrs Karp is always afraid of losing me.' He clasped Margot's hand between his own and for several seconds unaccountably forgot to give it back.

'Poor Mrs Karp, waiting in her motor.' Margot retrieved her fingers and favoured Igor with a brilliant smile. 'How will she ever forgive us?'

I followed Igor to the door. 'It's quite safe to come here, you know. Aunt Margot's out a great deal and Alice won't mind.'

'I will call as soon as I can. Haven't I sworn it?' He bent to kiss my palm, his lips moving softly in the hollow of my hand. A moment later, he was being received with squawks of relief into the deep red luxury of Mrs Longbaugh Karp's motor.

As I got ready for bed I found an elegantly curling dark hair on my shoulder, twined it with one of mine and wrapped it tenderly round the pencil I'd chosen to write a journal of our affair, fixing them both with candlewax. *Igor Starozhilov came to the villa tonight and kissed me wonderfully* . . . The pencil spent the night under my pillow.

I was terrified to leave the house now, in case Igor called while I was away. By the worst possible luck he always seemed to arrive on those afternoons when Alice and I had been obliged to go out, and I'd return home to find him formally drinking coffee with Margot on the terrace, or relaxing with a cocktail among the cushions of the *petit boudoir* while she changed for dinner in her dressing room next door.

'I can't believe it!' Igor would linger sadly over my hand. 'I always seem to choose the wrong day. And now we have such a short time together.'

Then, in a moment or two he'd consult the slim gold watch on his wrist and exclaim, 'So soon! I must be in Cannes by seven – I promised.' Then Margot would offer the Delage, Igor would protest and Margot would insist, and the only time I'd manage to snatch alone with him was the few seconds it took us to walk from the salon to the front door.

Alice became quite resentful when I refused to go shopping with her in Nice. 'Now perhaps you understand how I feel about Stephen.'

Shortly before we were due to leave the Villa Oléandre, Rose arrived, having used a mild bout of 'flu to get herself sent home from school to recuperate, and persuaded Riviera-bound friends called Charneywood to bring her down in the train. A few weeks earlier I'd have been furious to see Rose again, but now I was almost too preoccupied to resent her presence and contented myself with pretending she simply didn't exist. In the end, Alice made us bring the whole Hallowhill business out in the open at bedtime one night.

'Why didn't you *say* something, you rotten coward?'

Rose fixed me with huge, injured eyes. 'I was going to own up, honestly. I would've told them the truth at assembly next morning, only by then you'd disappeared.' Her long lashes trembled with sincerity. 'After that, there didn't seem much point in landing both of us in trouble.' She touched my arm. 'I'm awfully sorry, Clio, really, I am.'

'There you are,' declared Alice, presiding. 'It was all a misunderstanding. Rose never meant to let you take the blame.'

'Didn't she?' I was still suspicious, but it was hard to look into Rose's ravishing face and not believe every word.

'Best friends,' pronounced Alice, and made us shake hands.

At least now Alice had someone to go roller-skating with, or down to the beach, while I haunted the villa, waiting for Igor. In spite of Alice's reproaches, I was still wary of Rose. Temporarily free from the repression of school, my younger cousin had an air of restlessness, a kind of fermenting excitement, which warned me she was on the lookout for adventures of her own.

'Guess who we met today at Rumpelmayer's!' she announced on the third afternoon of her stay, bursting into the stately shade of the salon and flinging her hat on to a silk-upholstered canapé. 'Polly Cadzow – and her mother and father, too! Isn't that extraordinary? Leonard's taken Henri Matisse's old studio in the Place Charles-Félix in Nice and he says the light there is like nowhere else in the world. Do you know, Leonard Cadzow is actually a friend of Matisse's – well, more of an acquaintance, really.'

She whirled across the salon and flung open a pair of shutters. 'Leonard says the light in the south of France does perfectly extraordinary things to a woman's skin. He says I'd make a perfect model because my spirit shines so transparently from my body—'

'No,' Margot interrupted with finality. 'No, Rose. I will not have my daughter acting as a model for Leonard Cadzow or anyone else.' She shuddered at the notion. 'Didn't you ever see his painting of Bobo Delahaye, with one breast like a blanc-mange and the other like a lamb chop, and perfect tree-trunks

115

of legs – not to mention wearing the kind of hat one wouldn't care to be *buried* in? Oh, it was supposed to be a masterpiece, but the stupid woman has never, ever, lived it down.'

'I didn't expect you to understand.' Rose sniffed her contempt. 'Leonard Cadzow says artists never really paint naked women – just impressions of the emotions the women produce in them.'

'All the more reason to stay away, then.' Margot inspected her perfect manicure. 'The last thing I want is a framed souvenir of Leonard Cadzow's droolings over my daughter.'

'You see? I *knew* you wouldn't understand!' cried Rose, and stormed out, slamming the door so hard that the brass knob dropped on to the parquet.

Predictably, Rose despised the Karps – though we hardly ever saw them these days and I suspected Mrs Karp of harbouring some mysterious grudge against Margot. The Grand Duke Dino, of course, represented the debased class which had kept its foot on the throat of the masses: Rose loathed the old couple on sight, hated their lecherous *bouledogue* and refused to flatter their faded nobility by addressing them as 'Highness'.

'Disgusting old things!' She sulked on the terrace after our visitors had left, still outraged by the grand duke's tales of peasants beheaded for failing to salute his carriage and valets flogged for leaving creases in his evening shirt.

'I'd like to flog the two of them, for a change, so they'd know how it feels! They treated their people worse than that revolting, snuffly black dog they're so fond of.'

'I suppose that's the way they were brought up,' Alice suggested mildly. 'But in any case, Rose, Mama will expect you to be perfectly sweet to everyone at her party, whether you approve of their politics or not.'

It was to be Margot's last party of the season and a matter of great agony to anyone not included. 'I expect you'd like me to invite your young Russian, would you, Clio? Yes, I thought you might.'

★

116

The evening got off to a glittering start. Margot looked breath-taking, draped from one shoulder in a cascade of something metallic which revealed her back right down to the cleft in her buttocks, dripping with string upon string of antique pearls. As she passed among her guests she shimmered like a cataract flecked with foam.

Her guests were the cream of the current Riviera crop. For once, the Karps were there, along with a pack of the inevitable movie people from Monte Carlo, a deaf great-great-Bonaparte grandson to add a certain cachet, and Barr Fletcher the author, wearing a soft shirt with his dinner jacket, which Guy always claimed was absolutely the mark of the Beast. There was a fair sprinkling of comtes and comtesses and, of course, the grand duke and grand duchess – with their *bouledogue* shut out on the terrace, his nose pressed damply against the glass of the door and a look of desperation in his bulging eyes.

Did I mention Nina? I couldn't think why Nina was there, unless Igor had mentioned her in passing to Margot and she'd invited his sister as a kindness to me.

Nina was seated quite near me at dinner, just beyond Jonathan Charneywood in a raffish version of *le smoking*. Opposite us, Rose had been safely penned between the deaf Bonaparte and the owner of the largest yacht in the harbour, who kept complaining about the effect of sea air on his Titian. Yet as the meal wore on, I could see that Rose was becoming dangerously bored – and worse, since her yachtsman neighbour was automatically filling her glass with wine as soon as she emptied it. On my side of the table, I noticed, Nina had quietly commandeered a bottle of champagne all to herself.

At last one of those odd general silences fell – allowing the whole table to hear the Grand Duke Dino, his moustaches clogged with profiteroles, loudly mourning the decay of the great cathedrals of the imperial past, which he blamed on the scoundrels Marx and Freud.

'What's he saying?' cried Mrs Karp, whose French was limited.

'He says ordinary working chaps have been encouraged to

believe the sun shines out of the seats of their trousers,' called Jonathan Charneywood. 'So no one bothers to light candles any more in the Orthodox churches.'

'Shame,' declared the yacht owner firmly. He raised his glass in Duke Dino's direction. 'With you there, dear fellow. With you there.'

Rose leaned forward, her eyes unnaturally bright. 'And what is religion,' she demanded, 'except groundless superstition designed to keep the people from demanding their rights?' She leaned further over the table to get a better view of the grand duke. 'Christianity is a bourgeois conspiracy, with the church as its mouthpiece. It's taken the Bolsheviks to show us the truth.'

Some distance away I heard the grand duke noisily demand a translation and then Margot's voice, lazy but with a hint of steel. 'Why don't you go to bed, Rose dear? I suspect you're about to become boring.'

'Bugger the Bolsheviks,' muttered a sudden, thick voice to my right. Nina, now hugging two empty champagne bottles like outlandish breasts, was glaring at Rose across the width of the table, her chin thrust out. 'The Bolsheviks shot my father!' She detached a fist and smacked it down on the board, rattling the glasses. 'Your precious friends made my family beggars! But *you*—' Nina's voice dripped scorn. 'You're no revolutionary. You're a nasty, spoiled child, shouting for attention!'

'Oh, I say!' Jonathan Charneywood pressed his napkin to his mouth in genteel shock. 'That was a bit hard, wasn't it?'

But Rose had already launched herself across the table with a howl of rage, toppling candlesticks and scattering flowers in her blind determination to reach the enemy. Crawling among the compôte dishes, she lunged forward and grabbed Nina by the hair; but Nina had been raised in a harsher school and in a few seconds Rose lay flat on her back on the floor with Nina straddling her chest, slapping hard.

'How very tedious!' Margot's voice sliced through the uproar. 'Someone, please stop those silly girls.'

Somebody screamed – Mrs Karp, I believe – and slumped from her chair. Chester opened the terrace door to give his mother some air and the *bouledogue* rushed in to fling itself on Barr Fletcher's shoes with grunts of bliss. This suddenly woke us all from the trance that had gripped us. Strong male hands intervened: I saw Igor lunge at his sister, shouting in Russian, tugging at her shoulders and trying to haul her to her feet while someone else tore Rose's hands from her hair. But Nina was almost mad with rage and continued to scratch and lash out wildly in her brother's arms until his face, too, was marked with blood.

It was, inevitably, the end of the evening. As soon as a flutter of napkins had mopped up the blood and tears and something like calm had been restored, the guests sped off, awe-struck, into the night, to spread the gleeful news of the brawl at Margot Oliver's dinner table. Igor, alas, seemed to have vanished without a word – disgraced by his sister, I supposed, and too ashamed to face me. Rose was snivelling in a corner, nursing a great weal on one side of her face, but I could have set about her myself for having ruined my evening. For once I'd had the chance of snatching some precious time alone with Igor. Now I only had two more days in France, two days in which to persuade him to follow me back to London. Every time I'd broached the subject he'd raised so many problems I was almost in despair.

Alice had gone to bed. Tired and dispirited, I'd have liked to go too, but my conscience wouldn't let me rest. Margot had only invited Igor for my sake and Nina only as Igor's sister; I was the one who'd brought Nina Starozhilova into the Villa Oléandre and one way or another, I felt responsible for the havoc she'd caused. Margot had been kind to me in her own way. The least I could do now was to say I was sorry for what had happened.

The door to Margot's bedroom was open and the lights were on; I could see part-way across, as far as the doors to her bathroom and dressing room, but just as I was about to knock I heard her voice downstairs, giving instructions to the men carrying Mrs Karp to her motor. For a moment I hesitated, wondering whether to wait or to leave my apology until morning. Then, all at once, I realized that the door to Margot's bathroom was ajar and the sound of humming and splashing was coming through the opening, as if a substantial body were wallowing in Margot's bath.

Rose? Alice? Impossible – they were in another part of the house. And now, to my misery and horror I heard an unmistakable male voice echoing among the tiles and the porcelain.

'Margot – is that you? You aren't still cross with me, are you, darling? How was I to know my stupid sister would get so drunk? And to be fair, Rose was just as much to blame.'

There was a pause, while I listened in anguish, and then the voice continued, 'You know you can't ever be angry with me for long. When I hold you in my arms, it's a different story – then you only want more.' More splashing followed and a low, conspiratorial laugh.

I wanted to run – as far away and as fast as I could – but my limbs wouldn't answer and I had to stand there, sick with humiliation. In my misery, everything had become clear – the ill-timed calls, always when I was out, Igor's reluctance to be alone with me, Ellie Karp clinging to his arm, absorbing the culture of Europe, and now Margot, who'd lured him from Mrs Karp's bed with the prospect, no doubt, of richer pickings and better presents. Igor had simply exchanged one sleazy business venture for another, while I'd deluded myself that someone, in this world of indifference, actually cared for me.

Igor was – I'd heard Kit use the words – a *damned gigolo* and I'd been a stupid, lovesick fool.

A huge Bohemian vase of lilies stood on a nearby table, so heavy I needed both hands to pick it up. Igor must have heard something, because he called out, 'Margot? Why don't you come and talk to me?' just before I crashed into the bathroom to confront him.

He was stretched out in the marble bath, examining his scratched cheek in a silver hand-mirror, utterly relaxed and . . . oh dammit, more downright, gut-wrenchingly gorgeous in his nakedness than I'd even imagined. Why did he have to be such a squalid, despicable louse?

As I hurled the contents of the vase over him he gave a yell and tried to scramble out of the bath, covered in a wreckage of lilies. For some reason this feebleness annoyed me more than anything, so I threw the vase at him too for good measure.

And then, since there didn't seem to be any point in staying, I went to bed.

Chapter Eight

I TOLD Alice everything. I felt so wretched, I had to tell someone. Fortunately, that catastrophic evening was the last time I saw Igor Starozhilov – for the time being, at least. Goodness knows what story he told Margot to explain her bath being full of pieces of broken vase, but Margot said nothing to me and for the remaining two days of our stay at the Villa Oléandre, Igor was mercifully invisible.

Alice was very sympathetic. 'It can't have been the real thing. You wouldn't be able to sleep at night, if you'd really loved him.'

After a while I began to think Alice might be right. It was true, I slept: I looked forward eagerly to that nightly oblivion, a respite from the shame of knowing I was still just a child in the ways of the world. If I could, I'd have cut out that stumbling, naïve part of myself and yet, although I was furious with Igor and furious with Margot, too (the thought of Margot and her lover laughing together at my simple bliss was enough to make me squirm with humiliation), nevertheless . . . I wasn't broken-hearted.

In fact, in more rational moments I was disturbed to find I didn't feel empty or desolate or purposeless. I still had a future – oh, how my hands longed to grasp it and put the Villa Oléandre behind me! No – if I felt anything beyond the pain of having behaved like a fool, it was a vague, puzzled realization that I'd also been cheated by life itself. Like my shrew-funeral a decade earlier, the loss of this great love of mine hadn't *touched* me at all, not in the way I longed to be touched.

Not for the first time, I began to wonder if the isolation of my Shanghai childhood had allowed my heart to die of neglect inside me.

Guy, on the other hand, seemed to have no such fears. Guy and London were made for each other.

'Oh good, you're back,' he crowed as soon as Margot's motor had brought me back to Rutland Gate from the railway station. 'Nice time? Thought you would. Now, just you come and see this.' Without even letting me take off my hat, Guy dragged me round to the mews to admire his new toy: a bright green three-litre Bentley tourer with headlights as big as hat-boxes and a horn which made itself heard over five counties.

'Isn't she a gem? There's a bigger engine coming along, of course, which will be awfully tempting—' He sucked a breath through his teeth. 'But this baby will see the boots off pretty well anything she's likely to meet round here.'

I suggested that the front of the vehicle had the earnest, bespectacled look of Miss Marsh, our father's secretary, and Guy scuttled round anxiously to see for himself.

'Course it doesn't.' Guy patted the gleaming radiator. 'Though, talking about the office, your friend Stephen Morgan seems to be causing no end of bother in Sydney. We've had complaints. "Unorthodox" was the politest word they used. D'you know—' He stood back, squinting at the motor. 'I think I might need the four-and-a-half-litre engine after all.'

'Stephen Morgan's no particular friend of mine.' Nevertheless, I lingered, wondering what else Guy might have heard about Stephen's adventures.

'I suppose you know Alice has got some silly soft spot for him.' Guy had already unbuckled the strap and folded up the side of the Bentley's bonnet and his voice echoed from somewhere amongst its plumbing. 'Wait till I tell her he's just fired our Australian agent without so much as a word to London. Still, he's less trouble down there than he would be back here. Kit reckons it was only a matter of time before he put in a claim on his mother's behalf for a share of the company.' Satisfied with his inspection, Guy emerged from the oily grotto and reverently lowered the bonnet. 'I hear Kate told you how Cousin Stephen came to be one of the family.'

Guy's flippancy made me angry. 'I happen to know he only took the company job in the first place because Kate made him do it.'

'So he says. Just goes to show how clever he is.' Guy installed himself in the driver's seat and began to run his hands greedily over the wheel. 'Hop in and I'll take you for a spin.'

'Guy, I honestly don't believe Stephen wants any part of the shipping line.' I slid into the leather-lined space beside my brother, Papa's chauffeur came over to wind the handle and after a couple of convulsions we were able to roar off into the traffic. Guy was grinning, all thought of business banished, but, having found myself in the unusual position of defending Stephen Morgan, I was determined to make my point. 'Guy, are you listening? Just because Grandfather Matthew wanted nothing to do with him, I don't see why that automatically makes Stephen a villain.'

'Hah.' Noisily, Guy changed gear and veered close enough to a baker's van for me to smell the yeasty tang of new-baked bread. 'What would you do, if you were Matthew Oliver's grandchild and felt you'd been cheated of a fortune?'

'I thought you were only supposed to do twenty in this thing!' I snatched at the side of the motor to keep my balance as we charged past a horse and cart in the middle of the road.

'Of course, I had his measure from the start. If it had been left to me, he'd never have got over Oliver's doorstep.' Grimly, Guy swung us round a corner and missed the clutch in a grinding of gears. 'Damn and blast! Still, Kit would have it his own way. Better in than out, he said, then we can keep an eye on the blighter. The first sign of trouble and our Mr Morgan won't know what's hit him – and no amount of oiling up to Kate will save him then.' He sucked his teeth again. 'Maybe this row in Australia's just what we need.'

We swerved round another corner, missing a lamp-post by inches, the car swinging on its springs like a dinghy.

'Watch this!' Opening the throttle, Guy sent the Bentley thundering up behind an unsuspecting cyclist, clearing him by a hair's breadth and making the poor man steer into the gutter in fright. 'Gangway!' Guy shouted triumphantly.

'Stop the motor!' I turned furiously towards him. 'Stop it this minute, and let me get out.'

'Don't be silly, Clogs. This is half the fun.'

'Stop the motor – and don't call me Clogs. If you're going to drive like a maniac, I shall walk home.'

'You're such a bore!' Guy made a face. 'What a shame, my goody-goody sister doesn't like the way I drive.'

I stepped down to the pavement and slammed the door behind me. 'I don't like a lot of things you do these days, Guy.'

Guy might sneer, but his pride was injured, all the same. Young women didn't generally object to being whirled around London in a bright green three-litre Bentley – a weakness Guy was currently exploiting to the full. Almost every night, a different female face seemed to simper from his passenger seat as a succession of Chloës and Jills and Dianas were whisked off to pyjama or bottle parties, or on crazy swings round London in search of such side-splitting trophies as a policeman's helmet or a brace of Trafalgar Square pigeons.

'And what about Alice?' I demanded one morning, when Guy had turned up for breakfast in white tie and tails, still festooned with pink streamers and a single silk stocking.

He shrugged, rustling the streamers. 'If I'm going to be stuck forever with Alice, then the more women I get through now, the better. Come on, Clio, a chap's got to have some fun in life, hasn't he?'

None of this was lost on Alice. Guy's girls were racy and striking and looked well with the Bentley, while Alice . . . Alice could certainly make herself pretty, but in a fugitive, fussy sort of way. Margot, who favoured dramatic simplicity, used to sigh over the puffs and ruffles and rustic floral prints Alice preferred. 'Think *line*, darling. Think *perfection* – think of a *blade of grass*.'

As for me – Margot's opinion, when we returned from France, was apparently that I hadn't *come out* so much as escaped. She said so to Bobo Delahaye, who told Fay Standish, who, loathing Margot, told me. I thought this was pretty rich, coming from Margot, but I forgave her when she volunteered to bring me out officially, along with Rose, the following year, when we'd both be eighteen.

'It's no more than your mother would have done,' she murmured dismissively when I thanked her. 'At least, I assume Sylvia would have attempted something.'

As it happened, the following year began with my father being knighted for services to shipping.

'Kit's positively chewing the carpet,' reported Guy, who'd been forced to break the news to his uncle. 'It's a pity no one suggested giving them a knighthood apiece, instead of simply tossing one to the Old Man as chairman.'

The truth of the matter was that our father, quiet and clubbable, shared the prime minister's ambition for a peaceful life, while Kit, with his noisy ideas and his tiger grin, only made Baldwin uneasy.

I went to the palace too, of course, to make my curtseys in tulle and feathers, but without my cousin Rose. Rose had waited until all the arrangements were complete – flowers, photographer, pearls sent to the jeweller's for cleaning – and then, at the last moment, refused to go.

'You can't make me.' She struck a pose, lips and eyes very bright in her pale face and her fists by her sides.

'I wouldn't dream of it, I assure you.' Margot's drawl was as lazy as ever, but I knew her well enough now to recognize the crocodile droop of her eyelids and the sharp white hollows on either side of the bridge of her nose which indicated extreme anger.

'What about you, Clio?' Rose turned to me, still hoping for an argument. 'Are you going off to kow-tow to the parasites at the palace?'

'Well, yes, I am, actually.' In the last few months I'd become acutely aware of the milestones to be passed on my way to womanhood and I couldn't wait to reach another and know it was behind me. I don't know what I was hoping for – a magical transformation, perhaps, a dropping of scales from the eyes, a sudden bursting of wings – but if a curtsey to Their Majesties could set it off, then a curtsey they should have.

'Thank you, Clio darling.' Margot inclined her head graciously towards me. 'Of course you must go. Rose will regret her silliness one day.'

In that, I suspected, Margot was wrong. Although Rose's much-vaunted communism had always been a thing of her own making, a theatrical hotch-potch of borrowed ideas, never too closely examined, she had a very clear image of herself and the path she intended to follow through life. She could easily have warned Margot twelve months earlier that she'd no intention of being presented – but then, no one might have noticed. This way everyone knew that Margot's daughter had flown in the face of her mother's wishes. Red Rose, romantic Rose, courageous Rose of the flying hair and passionate words – 'Oh Rose, what a priceless creature you are!'

I didn't waste a second on concern for Rose. I'd even stopped worrying about the profitability of the Oliver Steam Navigation Company – something that had bothered me vaguely ever since Stephen Morgan's gloomy report at Kate's dinner table. By now I was attending too many parties to think of anything more complicated than whether to wear taffeta or black lace, and besides, Margot continued to spend as if the turbines of the Oliver ships were puffing out ten-pound notes instead of steam.

I was dimly aware that somewhere beyond the chandeliers which glittered over my first season, there were nearly two million people unemployed – the newspapers reported the fact from time to time, but the reasons for it and what it meant to the people concerned might as well have belonged to a different planet. It wasn't that we were greedy, you understand: it was simply that the capacity to spend money had always been part of our lives, like the ability to move a hand or a foot, and we'd never had to consider it. Money simply existed, like oxygen. In those days we breathed it in and sighed it out and assumed everyone else did the same.

For several months I saw less of Alice than usual, since she'd already been out for two years and spent her time with a different crowd. Because of that I was as astonished as anyone when, in August, Alice suddenly announced her engagement to Bertie Headington, by which I mean she produced him like a rather dazed rabbit after the Longthorpe ball and simply sprang it on everyone out of the blue.

Kit was the most taken aback; it had never occurred to him that Alice might object to his dynastic plans for her to marry Guy. At five a.m., angry and dressing-gowned, he took Bertie aside and demanded to know on what, precisely, he proposed to keep a wife, hoping for an excuse to call the whole thing off. Bertie grinned guilelessly and admitted it had all been Alice's idea, though he'd begun to think it was rather grand. I was surprised, but I didn't blame Alice a bit: she'd always said she didn't intend to be taken for granted.

Margot immediately commissioned Patou to design the trousseau. As far as she was concerned, Bertie Headington would do as well as anyone for Alice. His father, Lord Brace-burn, owned the soundly Tory *Daily* and *Evening Arbiter* and presumably one day Bertie would become an amiable non-executive chairman, fully occupied in playing golf, sailing his yacht and lavishing little attentions on his wife – altogether a perfect husband, in Margot's estimation. Kit's objections were ground down by the persistence of his wife and daughter, the wedding was arranged for the following March and the cocktail cabinets and canteens of cutlery began to arrive by the lorry-load.

The sketches for Alice's wedding gown were quite enchanting. There was something absolutely Alice – very sweet and modest – in the simple headband securing the flowing, virginal veil and the purity of the pearls which glowed among the embroidery at the neck and sleeves. I could already imagine her gliding slowly up the aisle with her eyes meekly downturned, resolutely sacrificing herself on the altar of . . . not of Bertie Headington, that was certain.

I was sure Alice didn't love Bertie; she was only marrying him because she'd given up hope of the man she really loved and, Alice-fashion, had made up her mind to hurl herself over the cliffs of marriage in a kind of emotional self-destruction. I'd no particular fondness for Bertie, but it seemed a hard fate to begin married life as Alice's precipice.

'Are you sure this is what you want?' I asked her one evening, watching Bertie come into the drawing room after dinner, wearing an expression of expensive idiocy. 'Are you really sure? I mean, you aren't rebounding, or anything?'

'It doesn't always have to be grand passion, you know.' Alice's face was set, her pinched little mouth pulled in smaller than ever. Much as I longed to save her from herself, I could see she was determined not to listen. For a very sweet person, Alice could be extraordinarily pig-headed.

'What about Stephen Morgan?' I persisted. 'And what about Guy?'

She shrugged, brusquely, like someone dislodging a fly. 'It's quite obvious that all Guy wants to do is enjoy himself.'

'And Stephen?'

She shrugged again, in the same curt, distant manner. 'Water under the bridge, that's all.'

Stephen Morgan returned from Australia in December of that year. Alice met him by chance at Christmas, at Kate's, and from that moment he apparently set out, quite coolly and deliberately, to break up her engagement.

'So much for not being a villain!' Guy kicked a braided pouffe across the drawing room at Rutland Gate. 'Doesn't mean any harm, *you* said. Yet here he is, hardly back a month and already he's discovered a way of causing trouble.'

'It can't be as simple as that.'

'Why can't it?' demanded Guy and kicked the pouffe again.

I didn't know whether to be relieved or afraid for Alice. Somewhere inside, she had a need to love with all her heart and soul, to drench some living creature in sustaining sweetness as the passion-flower overwhelms the bee. It was her métier, her career in life and I could only see that love being stifled and turned in on itself in a marriage to Bertie Headington. At the same time, I was sure Stephen Morgan didn't care in the least bit for Alice – couldn't care for her, I suspected, or for anyone, much, except himself. *Like me*, I thought: empty, untouchable. I felt an odd rush of kinship; not that it excused what Stephen was doing.

'Alice is engaged to Bertie,' I reminded him once, when he called at Kit's house to take her to dinner.

Stephen gave me a level stare. 'If she gave a damn for Headington she wouldn't come out with me.'

'But how did you *know*?' I demanded furiously. 'How did you know about Alice?'

'You told me, when I met you at Kate's, just before I went off to Australia.' The suspicion of a smile flitted over his face. 'Don't you remember?'

Stephen's opening moves had been so subtle – a ride to town in his two-seater roadster, a casual meeting at the office – that he'd become a force in Alice's life before any of us realized it, least of all Bertie, who, after his initial astonishment, was beginning to take to the idea of engagement with gusto. But then, Stephen had to do so little, merely to exist and let Alice's adoration do the rest.

By the time Kit woke up to what was happening it was already too late to salvage the situation. When her father suggested sending Stephen to Japan, Alice warned him she'd go too. When he reminded her of her engagement to Bertie, she promptly slipped the big diamond solitaire from her finger and left it on her dinner plate for the butler to find.

In February, after a dreadful row between Alice and her mother, her engagement to Bertie Headington was formally called off, the church and reception were cancelled and the presents returned – including, to Margot's frustration, a French bronze and ivory lamp she'd particularly coveted.

I believe I was sorrier for Bertie than Alice was. The humiliation of discovering Igor Starozhilov in Margot's bath was still raw enough in my memory to make my cheeks burn when I thought of it. I could imagine exactly how poor Bertie must feel – first of all swept up in an engagement which was none of his making and then left flat like a bad joke, alone and foolish, the object of everyone's pity and scorn.

Alice let me read the poor, bewildered, dignified little note he sent her. I wished she hadn't. I'd become uncomfortably aware that under all the softness and yearning there was steel in Alice.

After this, most people expected Alice to withdraw from society for a decent interval, but Stephen Morgan wasn't 'society' and so Alice felt free to meet him and walk and dine with him as often as she pleased. He'd recently taken up flying and had saved enough to buy himself a small De Havilland Gypsy Moth; now Alice began to spend her weekends at the airfield, watching Stephen looping and coiling across the heavens which had always seemed to her his natural element.

If Guy had been mildly put out by Alice's engagement to Bertie Headington, he was utterly incensed by the sight of her arm in arm with Stephen Morgan. It wasn't as if he particularly wanted Alice for himself, but over the years she'd come to function in his life like a spare wheel – always there in case of accidents, probably necessary at some point in the future – and while he'd been irritated to have this useful fixture filched by Bertie Headington, he was damned if he was going to stand for having Alice stolen by Stephen.

'For God's sake, Clio, he's nothing but a jumped-up sailor!'

'Oh Guy, that isn't true. And anyway, you've hardly paid any attention to Alice in the last year or two. I don't see what right you have to complain about whom she sees.'

'But Stephen Morgan! Kit's absolutely livid, did you know that? The trouble is, Alice is so stubborn that anything Kit says only makes matters worse.'

'And in the summer she'll be twenty-one and able to do as she likes.'

'Kit's sure Stephen reckons if he can persuade Alice to marry him, we'll have to give him a slice of the company.' Guy's face was dark with resentment. 'It's either that, or leave Alice to live on whatever lover-boy can earn.'

'I don't believe Stephen wants anything to do with your blessed company. He as good as told me so himself. He isn't interested in working in a shipping office.'

'Well, that's a bloody lie, for a start. For a fellow who isn't interested in Oliver's, he's put the dickens of an effort into

ALISON McLEAY

fixing the Australian agency end of things. All of a sudden, the
people out there seem to think he can walk on water.'

'Stephen sorted everything out? Even the strike and the
missing money?' I was genuinely surprised. 'I thought the
Australians were yelling for his blood.'

'That was months ago. Later on, he managed to settle the
whole business, blast him. By the time he left they were eating
out of his hand in Sydney harbour – even the Aussie stevedores,
and you can imagine what they're like to deal with.'

'Golly. And he's younger than you, by a few months.'

'I know that!' Guy was clearly eaten up with jealousy. He
strutted across the drawing room to stare out of the window,
his hands in his pockets and his shoulders aggressively square.
'Of course, he's no better than a wharf-rat himself, when all's
said and done.' Guy wheeled round to face me. 'In fact, Stephen
Morgan *is* a rat, a first-class trouble-maker, and now he's got
his hooks into Alice, just as his father ruined Catherine Oliver's
life. Well, I'm saying exactly what Grandfather Matthew said
then. Stephen Morgan gets a piece of this company over my
dead body, I can promise you that.'

I tried to find out how things stood between Alice and Stephen.

'Of course he's kissed me.' Alice studied her shoes, torn
between shyness and pride. 'More than once, actually. And no,
I'm not going to tell you what it was like.' Her tongue slipped
out to moisten her lips. 'You know I haven't done much of that
sort of thing. Bertie used to apologize afterwards, every time.'

After Igor Starozhilov I had no faith in kisses. 'Stephen's
much younger than Bertie, you know.'

Alice's head flew up at once. 'I don't see why that matters.
No one could be more juvenile than Bertie.'

'Perhaps not, but Stephen's hardly in a position to marry
you, is he?'

I expected her to leap to Stephen's defence, to tell me that
many people married on less and were blissfully happy, but she
didn't say any of that. Instead, after a moment, she sighed.

'I don't expect him to marry me,' she said quietly. 'I just want to be with him, on any terms at all.'

'And you threw Bertie over for that?'

Alice glanced at me in surprise. 'Well, of course.'

Now I really was afraid for Alice. I'd been right all along: it was the very *otherness* of Stephen Morgan which had bewitched her, his contempt for the rules the rest of us cherished. His fascination lay in the fact that he wouldn't play fair: and in the end, it would be Alice who'd suffer, just as I'd suffered with Igor, but far, far worse.

'Perhaps you shouldn't see so much of Stephen, then, if you don't think it's going to come to anything. I mean, you know how people talk and you've been seen together all over the place.'

A dangerous light glittered in Alice's eyes. 'Let them say what they like. It'll give them something to talk about besides Mama.'

It always amazed me to find Alice so unmoved by her mother's 'adventures'. I was the cousin who'd been raised in the voluptuous East and yet conventional, modest Alice accepted Margot's continual affairs without surprise. 'After all,' she'd pointed out coolly when Igor's status at the Villa Oléandre had become clear, 'Papa's got three children by his lady in St John's Wood, so I suppose it's only fair.'

Yet that wasn't the sort of future Alice wanted for herself, I was sure. What she wanted was someone to absorb the great flood of her love and now that Stephen was back in her life, his very unlovability challenged her to redeem him, to conquer his indifference with the boundless outpouring of her heart. He never sent flowers: it was enough for Alice that he made himself available to be worshipped. I was sure there was nothing she mightn't do, if he asked her.

In the end I went to my grandmother for help.

'What makes you so certain Stephen doesn't love her?' Kate leaned forward to catch my reply. 'You know absolutely nothing about him, it seems to me.'

'I'm certain he's only doing it to make Guy angry.' I was

disappointed by Kate's lack of concern. 'I'm desperately worried about Alice, you know. This is far worse than before, when Stephen didn't care at all. How will she feel when she finds out he's only been using her?'

'And what do you expect me to do about it? Tell Stephen he should marry the girl to save her reputation?'

'You could tell him to leave Alice alone, if she means so little to him.'

Kate leaned back in her chair. 'Or I could mind my own business and tell you to mind yours. If there's one thing I've learned, it's that meddling only makes things worse. So be warned.' And she folded her hands firmly in her lap to indicate that the subject was closed.

Adam Gaunt stared down at me from his frame on the dining-room wall, his face alight with lawless resolve.

'This is all your fault,' I told him.

For Alice's sake, I couldn't let the matter rest. I went to Leadenhall Street, made sure from the front desk that Mr Morgan was in and sent up a note asking him to meet me at four in a tea shop near by. To my annoyance, he didn't turn up until twenty past, no doubt to put me firmly in my place.

At last I saw him arrive, hatless and breathing heavily, with an odd, left-over smile of satisfaction on his face which irritated me even more. He ran his hands through his hair, sweeping it back from his brow as he glanced round, the gesture drawing various female eyes to follow his progress between the tables towards me.

'I'm late, I know, and I'm sorry.' A slight inclination of his head acknowledged the fault. 'I was held up on my way here.' He remained standing, waiting for my invitation to sit.

I was still certain he'd kept me waiting on purpose and I decided to let him stand for a few more seconds.

'I'm afraid this tea has gone cold – but then, I ordered it twenty minutes ago.' I signalled to the hovering waitress and was disgusted by the round-eyed eagerness with which the girl scurried to take his order.

When the waitress had gone, he turned back to me. 'I did apologize for being late.'

'So you did.' I gazed round the room with a little sigh, more in sorrow than in anger. The effect was electrifying.

'If you really want to know—' Stephen suddenly leaned forward over the table. 'Your brother has paid a detective to follow me around and I didn't think you'd want the man tracking me here. I had to run through a shop to shake him off.'

I stared up at him, completely taken aback. 'Guy wouldn't do a thing like that, I'm certain he wouldn't.' Yet in my heart I suspected he would.

Stephen sat down in his chair opposite me and his voice softened. 'I wasn't going to say anything about it. I just didn't want you to think I'd come late on purpose.'

'It never crossed my mind.' I hid my guilt over the teacups and the pot of fresh tea the waitress had brought. 'Though I still can't believe Guy would do such a thing. Are you sure?'

'Sure I'm being followed?' Stephen's eyes narrowed in amusement. 'I'm quite certain of it. The fellow's hopeless at his job – but at least I have the satisfaction of knowing that whatever Guy's paying the man, he's wasting his money.'

The waitress returned, straightened the plates in the cake stand and wanted to know if everything was arranged to the gentleman's satisfaction.

'It's fine,' said Stephen. 'Thank you.' The waitress beamed and retreated, twisting her apron between her hands. Her agitation reminded me of Alice.

'That's one young woman you've made happy, at least.'

Stephen looked up with guarded curiosity. He glanced at the retreating waitress and then back to me. 'Do I take it we're talking about Alice?'

'That's why I asked you to meet me.' I'd never been brought up to look boldly and coolly into a man's eyes, so I reached for a scone I didn't want and sawed at it with a tiny, ineffectual knife.

Now, for the first time, I found myself wondering what sort of company Stephen had kept during the year he'd been in Australia. As I struggled with my scone I could feel him examining me across the table as he'd once done at Kate's – slowly and minutely, making my skin tingle with the sensation of stroking fingertips. I couldn't believe he'd spent sixteen months in the exclusive company of stevedores.

'Look, Stephen—'

'Before you say any more—' He raised a hand. 'Forgive me, but there isn't a polite way of putting this. Is it any of your business, Clio, what Alice and I do together?'

'Of course it is. I'm Alice's friend.'

'Don't you think I'm her friend, too?'

I took a breath. 'No, I don't think you are. You see, I can't believe, if you really cared at all about Alice, you'd go on using her for this silly game you're playing with Guy.'

'So that's what this is all about.' Stephen pushed himself back in his chair, stony-faced. 'You've made up your mind, even though you know nothing whatever about it.'

'For heaven's sake, Stephen, it's obvious what you're doing. You took Alice away from poor Bertie, just to show that you could, and then you set out to make Guy so jealous and suspicious that he's paid a private detective to watch you. It's perfectly clear you're enjoying every minute of it.' Indignation stiffened my throat and forced me to swallow. I leaned forward, pushing my teacup unevenly aside over the cutwork cloth. 'I'm not concerned about Guy – he probably deserves whatever he gets. But Alice is hopelessly in love with you, Stephen. Don't you realize how badly she'll be hurt, when she finds out you're only seeing her to win some silly victory over her cousin?'

Stephen's gaze was as unblinking as a cat's, flecked with angry light. 'You seem very sure that's all there is to it.'

'Can you honestly tell me there's more?' I didn't blame Stephen for being bitter: he was more alone in the world than even I was and he'd no reason to love any of the Olivers.

'Alice's wedding gown was almost finished,' I blurted out.

'For heaven's sake – do you really think she'd have been happy with that idiot Headington?'

'She might have been.' I tried to believe it. 'Bertie's a decent sort, you know.'

'Then maybe one day he'll thank me for saving him.' Stephen's resentment rang sharply among the preserve jars.

'How can you say that? Saving him from what?'

'You see? You don't understand the smallest thing about all this. Yet you came here today to lecture me on the subject.'

'It wasn't meant to be a lecture. I simply thought . . .' The sentence trailed away. A disturbing possibility had just occurred to me, something I hadn't considered and didn't want to consider, something unfair and surely impossible . . . Had I imagined that raw edge to Stephen's voice, that hint of pain which suggested he was more involved than he'd ever admit? I sat unhappily between the brass-hooped cake stand and the jar of tired freesias, wondering if the world had passed me by again.

'Are you—' I hesitated. 'Are you telling me you do feel something for Alice?'

Stephen's right hand was resting on the cloth between us. The fingers were slim, with disproportionately large finger-joints, as if a boy's hand had been forced to turn early to a man's work. For a moment the sight of it almost convinced me that somewhere in Stephen Morgan a spark of tenderness remained to take pity on Alice's enslavement.

He removed the hand. 'I don't see why I should tell you anything.'

'If I thought you cared for her . . .' The hand had gone, so I searched his face instead and found nothing there but self-will and impenetrability – no softness, no affection, no hint of doubt. Clearly, I'd been mistaken. I moved on, reassured, to my carefully prepared appeal.

'Please, Stephen, will you promise me something?'

'That depends on what it is.'

'I know you say I don't understand what's going on and maybe that's true. But I do know Alice would do anything for you, anything at all – just the way Catherine Oliver gave up her home and her family for your father.'

I paused, prepared for an angry denial, but he said nothing and I pressed on. 'Your father would have married Catherine if he'd been free, I know. All I ask is that if you don't feel the same way about Alice as Robert Morgan felt about Catherine, then please don't let her destroy herself for your sake – because she'd do it, willingly. Find a way of setting her free without hurting her.' The image of Igor, wallowing voluptuously in

Margot's bath, crawled into my mind unbidden and the pain of it sharpened my entreaty. 'Leave Alice some self-respect, leave her some pride to cling to.'

He considered me for a moment across the tea things, then his eyes slid away towards the panorama of hats and animated faces and teacups in motion. 'If I'm such a scoundrel, what makes you think I'll pay any attention to what you've said?'

His right hand had returned to lie between us, brown and boyish, with its prominent knuckles.

'But I don't think you are a scoundrel, Stephen. Not completely, at least.' The tea shop suddenly seemed a very shabby place for such an admission, squandered amid the smell of toast, the cheap curtains and the scuffed wooden chairs. Yet Stephen waited, his eyes on my face, as if he sensed there was more to be said; and perhaps there was, except that the thoughts lay, unformed, somewhere behind my concern for Alice.

To break the silence, I asked, 'What will you do now?'

'That's my business, I think.' Briskly, he centred the knife on his unused plate.

'Promise me, Stephen—'

'No.' He abandoned the knife and reached out to silence me with a fingertip which burned my lips where it touched. 'No,' he repeated softly. 'No promises. I've told you, you're meddling in things you don't understand.'

He rose to go, as if driven by an irresistible need for action. 'You've had a wasted afternoon, I'm afraid, Clio. I'll settle the bill on my way out.'

It all ended in tears, as I'd feared it would. Guy was the first to spot Stephen at the opening night of a new musical, with an unknown, ebony-haired, bugle-beaded siren on his arm. Shortly after that, Bertie Headington ran into him at the races with a long-legged blonde in a shamelessly short skirt. Bertie, honourably, said nothing to Alice, but plenty to Connie, his sister. Still smarting from the collapse of her brother's engagement, Connie met Margot at a charity luncheon and passed on the news with relish.

'Someone called Vanity, apparently,' Margot recalled later. 'Too dreadfully bleached.'

'Oh, come on, Aunt Margot. No one can be called Vanity.'

'Something else with a V, then. Virtue? Velvet? No – *Verily* Somebody.'

'Really? Verily, I say unto you?'

'Absolutely.' Margot's expression indicated refined distaste. 'She was all over him apparently, like a fly on a Pêche Melba.'

Alice let out a low moan and covered her face with her hands.

'Don't sniff, darling, it's common.' Margot surveyed her daughter in vague distress. 'I do think you should have stuck with Bertie, you know. There's a great deal to be said for predictability.'

'And there were others.' Guy tapped his nose, importantly mysterious. 'I can't tell you how I know, but I do know. A young woman in a green hat was seen leaving his rooms at five a.m. and there was a weekend party on a yacht in the Solent, when he was supposed to be in Liverpool.'

How much, I wondered, had it cost to send a private detective to Southampton?

'Of course, you mustn't repeat any of this to Alice.' Guy tried hard to conceal his satisfaction.

'I should think not.'

'Though the fellow's clearly a blackguard of the first water. Even if Catherine Oliver was his mother, he obviously doesn't know how to behave.'

'Oh, *absolutely*.' There was such sharpness in my voice that Guy glanced at me in surprise. I was furious with Stephen, but I was furious with Guy, too. 'Naturally,' I snapped, 'a real gentleman would keep a mistress in St John's Wood and everyone would call him a pillar of the community.'

'What's that?' Guy looked shifty. 'What have you heard?'

'Nothing,' I told him. 'Nothing at all.'

★

Alice wept for days and then made a great effort to pull herself together.

'I've been very stupid.' She gulped determinedly. 'Stephen Morgan is an utter snake and I should have realized it. You're quite right, Clio, there's no point in crying over a man like that.' Fiercely, she wiped her eyes with her sodden handkerchief, leaving her fringe spiky with damp. 'He's been perfectly bloody and I'm lucky to be rid of him. I've written to him, you know.'

'What on earth did you say?'

Alice sniffed enormously and straightened her back. 'I told him I thought he was a rotten swine and not fit to polish poor Bertie Headington's boots. I told him he'd no right to make up to me when all the time he was seeing other women and that in view of his behaviour I never wanted to speak to him again.'

'That sounds pretty final, I must say.'

'Being angry makes it easier.' Alice sniffed again and managed a ghastly smile. 'I told him I hoped his beastly Gypsy Moth would fall out of the sky. That would teach him.'

'Oh, I expect it would.'

Two days later, still pink and swollen-eyed, Alice lifted her chin and hoisted the social smile she'd been taught in Munich. *Custard*, Alice – pull back the lips to expose the part-opened teeth in a grimace of bright, intelligent interest. It was true, there was definitely steel in Alice.

It was time, Margot decided, to leave London for a while, especially since charming Mr Baldwin's government had recently fallen and that odd, wild-looking Ramsay MacDonald had come back with his socialist hordes. As it happened, friends in New York, the Ransome Spencers, had once more begged Margot to spend part of August with them at their 'little place in Newport'. What could be more convenient than for Margot and her daughters to cross the Atlantic on the Oliver flagship *Concordia* to spend a few weeks by the sea?

Rose, however, claimed to have plans for Cowes Week and refused outright to go. As a result, Margot enquired if I'd care to travel with them instead, as company for Alice. For fully five seconds I debated whether to go or to stay and continue my search for something possible among that season's singularly uninspiring batch of young men – then the glorious, tempting glamour of the Oliver flagship *Concordia* tipped the scales.

The very name *Concordia* called up visions of making an entrance down swirling staircases, outlined against bronze doors and reflected from a thousand mirrors. It whispered of dangerous midnight flirtations in the Turkish Grill and being photographed cheek to cheek with a nameless lover, framed in a lifebelt, in a mid-Atlantic dawn. And for Margot, as the wife of the Oliver managing director, it meant the sumptuous Sovereign Suite redecorated throughout in ivory silk and filled with the lilies she adored.

Even Alice cheered up a little at the prospect.

'Think of the dancing, Alice,' I urged her. 'Think of the champagne and the parties – and think of the men!'

'Oh yes,' said Alice, and tried.

Alice and I, aboard the *Concordia* – it seemed the ideal way to Forget. It didn't occur to either of us that there'd be a fourth member of the party until a steward knocked softly at the door of our suite as we were settling down to a pre-sailing cocktail.

'Excuse me, madam,' he said to Margot, 'but where shall I put the gentleman's luggage?'

Chapter Nine

FROM SOMEWHERE, he'd bought a large bunch of Margot's favourite lilies and their vanilla scent preceded him into a cabin already crammed with floral arrangements. Margot received the blooms indulgently, admired them for a few seconds and then dropped them on a side table: 'I'm sure Briggs will find a corner for them when she has a moment.'

He glanced at me rather apprehensively – I dare say he'd expected Rose, not her vase-throwing cousin – while I stared at those features I'd hoped never to see again. Igor Starozhilov was still, I had to admit, just as sickeningly handsome as he'd seemed on the Riviera two years earlier, all soaring cheekbones and hooded obsidian eyes. One might criticize Margot's morals, but one could never fault her taste: Igor was a Hispano Suiza among men, an exotic, flawless, beautiful machine for the gratification of obscenely rich women.

'Darling—' said the machine, capturing Margot's hand and conveying it to his lips.

'Silly boy,' murmured Margot, making no attempt to withdraw her fingers. Apparently, at twenty-one and nineteen respectively, with two thwarted love affairs and a ruptured engagement between us, Alice and I were now supposed to be women of the world.

Alice rose from her chair. 'Shall we go and see if Wilkins has finished our unpacking yet, Clio?'

'Just what I was going to suggest, actually.'

★

Margot was the star of the Commodore's cocktail party that night, supple as a panther in the simplest and most appallingly expensive of black gowns, all smoke-smudged eyes and dramatic, milky shoulders. Across the room, I watched her accept the homage of countless young men, flaunting her forty-three years like an aphrodisiac cloud, and longed to learn the secret of her mystery. It was contempt, I now believe, for every part of a man except the one which satisfied her physical desire. She treated men like wayward children and bedded them like stallions at stud, and somehow they scented her disdain and found it an irresistible challenge.

Afterwards we dined at the Commodore's table on lobster and Egyptian quails, while the gold braid of the officers' uniforms glittered among the champagne glasses. Later, there was a stir like a breath of wind as we departed, a frisson which followed us down the length of that enormous, colonnaded hall and rose up to whisper round the cupola: *Who? Where from? Are they really? Well, I never . . .*

Copying Margot, we didn't turn our heads. After all, the *Concordia* was ours, down to the last bolt and cake fork. Her passengers had a mere five days in that enchanted kingdom, but we were the Olivers and this ship was our birthright. Cunard liners might be full of aristocrats, tramping the decks in tweeds, and the French Line might tempt film stars and American new money, but everyone agreed that the Oliver ships were where Hollywood and the peerage fused in a white heat and where all the best scandals and alliances were born.

There was sea, it was rumoured, somewhere beyond the shell of onyx and glass and silver marquetry which enclosed us. Someone – Mr de Mille, or Miss Swanson, perhaps – had definitely spotted a large expanse of ocean from the rail of the sun deck, and identified it as the North Atlantic. But as the *Concordia* continued to crush it under her forefoot at a steady twenty-five knots, the sea soon receded to the realm of make-believe, an ingenious backdrop of ultramarine Lalique to match the marble and the bronze.

None of us needed a bromide for seasickness on that crossing. Alice and I shopped ourselves silly in the First Class

Arcade, invaded the bridge, had our faces mud-packed in the beauty parlour, lounged in the Tutankhamun Pool, sipped Sidecars in the Hall of Mirrors – squeezing the little spiral of lemon peel between our teeth when no one was looking – and still, somehow, found enough energy to dance into the small hours to the stomping of the jazz band in the Turkish Grill.

'Remember,' I told Alice. 'You're expressly not to think about Stephen Morgan.'

'I hadn't since breakfast, until you said that.'

'But it's only half-past nine, Alice.'

'And you were the one who brought him up,' she reminded me tartly. 'Forget him yourself, if it's so easy.'

In mid-Atlantic, on our third night aboard, there was a costume party in the Winter Garden. Margot went as Venice, in a shimmering lake of sequins and a campanile headdress made out of silver paper from our Fortnum's basket. Igor, as her escort, was splendidly dressed – or rather, undressed – as Canova's Orpheus, his muscular torso barely concealed by a fleecy rug from our stateroom floor and his hair scattered with a few silver leaves.

Alice made a passable Nell Gwyn, clutching a basket of the steward's best oranges, while I went as Greta Garbo, with Briggs's mackintosh tightly belted, a beret crammed slant-wise over my hair and some of Margot's eye-shadow smudged under my cheekbones. When I last saw Alice she was disappearing on to the dance floor with Charles II in a dressing-gown and black paper curls, while I was borne off to the buffet by an earnest crocodile who'd seen *Flesh and the Devil* sixteen times and insisted I was the exact double of its star.

After supper, as the Winter Garden became hotter, I peeled off my waterproof like a rumpled skin and danced in the little black crêpe marocain frock I'd worn underneath.

'It's a foxtrot next,' said a deep voice in my ear as the band scraped up the first chords of a fresh tune. 'This is our dance, I think.' And there was Igor-Orpheus in his Grecian sheepskin, holding out the arms of a sculpted godling to carry me off.

I turned my shoulder towards him. Even if I'd forgiven him for making such a fool of me at the Villa Oléandre – which I certainly hadn't – I had no intention of dancing with him. Igor was as thoroughly Margot's now as her toothbrush and I'd never have dreamed of borrowing that.

'You should be dancing with my aunt. Isn't that why you're here?'

He continued to hold out his arms; a passing pierrot glanced at me with envy. 'I'm here to do what I do best. If I were a doctor, I'd heal sick people. If I were a painter I'd make pictures.' With some dignity, he spread his hands. 'But I can't do any of those things and so instead I make women happy. Why do you expect me to be ashamed of that?'

When I didn't answer, he simply drew me into his arms with a little hiss of exasperation and set off with me across the dance floor.

'Besides,' he pointed out, 'now we are even – all square. When you threw the vase – remember? – you cut me pretty badly. I still have a scar, just because of your temper.'

'You deserved to be hurt.' I strained up to look him directly in the eye. 'How could you make up to me like that, when all the time you were on the lookout for rich old women? You're contemptible, Igor, no better than a leech.'

To my surprise he threw back his head and laughed. 'And you're a spiteful girl, do you know that?' Grinning, he pressed me closer – *absorbed* me would be a better word – and slid into the familiar, undulating glide we'd rehearsed so long before.

'You ask "How could you make up to me?" and I say "Because you are a very attractive young woman." *Very* attractive. Irresistible. Yet I also have to live and I like to live well. Sensible women understand that.'

'Oh, I understand perfectly. And I still think you're an unprincipled louse.'

'Ah, you remind me of Nina,' he sighed. 'So fierce! Like a cat.'

His thighs skimmed mine, recalling the old days in Shanghai. Even though I was taller now, he had a trick of keeping me off balance as we danced, forcing me to depend on him, binding me to the movements of his own sinuous body as we whirled and dipped. This, I supposed, was professional seduction – this temptation to abandon oneself to unreason, to a sensation as thrilling as slipping naked into a warm sea at midnight.

I almost wished it were possible to be deceived a second time. Why, oh why was this ecstasy of the senses always make-believe, never the real thing? Curiously detached, I allowed Igor to lead me where he pleased, to capture the music inside himself and manipulate its rhythm for my pleasure; and for a few minutes I pretended to believe there was passion in it. No one had danced with me like that since Shanghai and I doubted if anyone ever would again.

And then, when the foxtrot ended and the band slid into the heady, dangerous march of a tango, I left him there and went off to join a pirate with a burned-cork moustache in the safety of the buffet.

It was after one o'clock when I returned to our suite, with my crocodile escort shuffling tenaciously at my heels. He left me with a rubbery kiss on the cheek and a promise of deck tennis next day and I let myself into our vestibule, opened the door of my cabin and slipped inside.

As soon as I'd closed the door behind me, I realized I wasn't alone. Instinctively, I reached for the light switch.

'Don't touch it.' The words flew like a sigh in the darkness. 'We don't need to see one another, you and I.'

'Igor?' I'd recognized his voice at once, yet his presence in my cabin was almost beyond belief. Thank heavens I hadn't switched on the light! What on earth would Margot think, if she came in to wish me good night and found me with her lover?

I peered into the dimness. My windows looked out over the promenade deck, and the vessel's lamps had printed two pale, cherry-coloured rectangles on my closed curtains.

'Igor, what on earth are you doing here?' Surely he'd only come to borrow something, or had missed his own door in the dark. Anything more was unthinkable.

'I've been waiting for you. What else?' Amazingly, he made it sound perfectly straightforward, quite manifestly rational that he and I, impatient male and ripening female, should want to be together. He moved confidently towards me across the room, a rapidly enlarging silhouette against the windows, and I stepped aside, fumbling for the doorknob.

'Go away, Igor! You must be drunk, or something. Margot will go mad if she finds you here.' I managed to open the door an inch or two, letting in a sliver of light from the lobby. It rippled over him, barely inches away now: a satyr striped with pale gold, regarding me with ancient, wild, knowing eyes. He reached over my shoulder and gently pushed the door shut again.

'Margot,' breathed his voice at my ear, 'is playing bridge in the lounge with a beautiful boy from Harvard who makes sheep's eyes at her between tricks – I saw them myself. So there's no danger of her finding us.'

His body touched mine with each breath; the feral scent I remembered from my childhood – sweetish, not unpleasant – had begun to overwhelm the spicy notes of whatever perfume he was wearing. I struggled to focus my senses on that detail. Already the whole episode was beginning to seem as unreal as the marble Sphinx in the swimming pool, just another mirage of that great Palace of Nowhere as it sailed through the night.

Igor ran his hands lightly over my shoulders, skimming Garbo's raincoat to the floor. I pulled away, found myself backing softly into the side of a cupboard and did my best to sound stern.

'It's no good, Igor. You won't fool me a second time with your lies about love.'

'Clio—' He held out his arms. 'Clio . . . I won't even try to lie to you. Why should I? You are grown up now – you know how things are between men and women – so I simply say I want to *make* love to you. I want it and I know you want it too. Nothing more is necessary.'

He reached for my hand and began to draw me across the cabin to the satin-covered bed. 'Come.' He led me gently, but his fingers were firm against my palm, and I'd no choice but to follow or topple over on knees already softening with excitement.

It was the firmness of his grip that unnerved me.

Suddenly afraid, I tried to wrench my hand from his grasp. In that instant he'd seemed enormous, raw, man-size, thrilling and frightening at the same time in his determination. Gracious heavens, how would it be – the actual *business* of it, the act, the physical doing of all those bizarre things I remembered from my father's hoarded books? It made me dizzy, even to think of having such a giant inside me without the least veil of affection or even friendship. How did I know it wouldn't all be coarse and animal and absurd, leaving me sad and violated, weeping for the girl I'd been before?

'It's time,' he said and pulled gently on my hand. The fear remained – and yet even that fear was compelling. Hopelessly confused, I played for time.

'What about Alice?'

'Alice is still a child,' he whispered contemptuously. 'You are a woman.'

'I mean, Alice might come in at any moment.'

'Not if it's dark, she'll think you're asleep.' He reached out to imprison me against him and kissed me – letting that mouth of his and his treacherous body do their work, until I became aware of a longing whose intensity took me completely by surprise. It was as if my mind and all the womanly organs inside me were simultaneously at war. My mind said *beware* but its small, cavilling voice was overwhelmed by the clamour of the rest: *join – unseal – release – rejoice!*

'Stand here,' he whispered. 'Here, where there's a little light.' For a moment his lips hovered, swollen with kissing, over mine; then he began to cover my forehead and cheeks with fierce, snatched, pin-point kisses. This was no performance, as it had been at the villa: his breathing was deep and uneven with desire. As I twisted my head to speak, he moved down to my throat. 'Igor – wait, wait—'

My black skirt was riding up round my thighs: I felt his hand, confidently exploring and experienced, and heard the faint pop of a suspender. His voice rustled in my ear. 'See, like this.' Smoothly, he lifted each of my legs against his thigh and slid the stocking over my toes.

'Don't be afraid. We'll go slow. I know this is your first time.'

I attempted a careless laugh, which came out like a gasp. 'Why should you think that?'

'Because I know you're a virgin. I can tell from the way you move.' He drew me against him again, leading me into my seduction, like a slow pas-de-deux.

'That's impossible,' I gasped. 'How can you tell?'

'Because' – he slipped his fingertips inside the waist of my silk knickers and sent them slithering to the floor – 'women are my life, remember?' His words came in whispered bursts, in long, sighing exhalations. 'And I promise you, there is a looseness, a tiny vulgarity, in the walk of a woman who has been with a man – and in the way she holds herself. But I don't see it in you, so I know it is the first time.'

He tore the sheepskin from his shoulder and was suddenly as naked in that rosy dimness as I'd ever longed to have him on the Côte d'Azur, a shameless and virile Pan.

If my head still counselled caution, I was no longer listening. Even my terror had become part of the urgent tumult raging in my body: I wanted to run headlong upon the spears that frightened me, to be pierced and possessed by that perfect, skilled machine. Where was the virtue in saving my ignorance for some Bertie Headington on his wedding night, fuelled by champagne and his own blundering need? If I could not love, at least I could ride this demon of sexual hunger to the last shivering, glorious instant.

Our legs were already intertwined. Now Igor's practised fingers began to unhook the black marocain, like inexorable footsteps pacing down my spine.

Then all of a sudden, I *heard* footsteps – two taps, unmistakably, beyond the door of my room, made by a pair of high-heeled shoes crossing the single strip of bare parquet in the vestibule, followed by the opening of a bedroom door.

'It's Margot! Oh, my God – she's come back.' I tried to push myself away from Igor, at the same time scrabbling between my shoulder blades for the sagging hooks, but he pulled me back.

'Shhh. She won't come in here.'

'You don't know that! For heaven's sake, hook me up again.'

'Don't worry, I tell you. She'll go to bed in a moment.' Then Igor himself froze against me as the footsteps returned to the passage, followed by the soft creak of the drawing-room door handle. My desire was cooled in an instant, drowned in a cataract of icy horror.

'Oh, my God!' I squirmed out of Igor's arms; I could hardly hear Margot's footsteps now for the blood thumping in my ears.

'She's looking for you. She must be.'

'For her cigarettes, maybe.'

'No, for you.' I began to push Igor in the direction of the door. 'Get out of here! Quick! While Margot's in the drawing room!' His skin was smooth under my fingers and startlingly warm. 'What on earth are you doing?' For he'd dropped to his knees on the blackness of the floor and begun groping about near the bed.

'My sheepskin—'

'There's no time for that!' I heard Margot close the drawing-room door, and imagined her standing in the hallway, the first stirrings of suspicion dawning in her face.

'Hurry, oh hurry!' I dragged Igor to his feet, tripping over one of my discarded shoes. 'You'll have to go out another way. Look – my bathroom window opens on to the promenade deck. It must be big enough for you to squeeze through.'

I started to drag him towards the bathroom door. In my haste, I couldn't think why he resisted.

'What? Just look at me!' He indicated his nakedness. 'You want me to go out like this?'

The pad of Margot's steps on the carpet was louder now and the sound of her voice calling 'Igor?' sharply in the doorway of his room. I heard the click of the light switch and then a pause as she surveyed his empty bed and considered its implications.

The realization of what would certainly follow hurled me into action. 'If you won't go, then I will.' Pushing Igor aside, I bolted into the bathroom, climbed on to the lavatory seat and wrestled frantically with the window-catch. It had a butterfly-screw fitting – designed, I suppose, for safety in hurricanes – but at last, whirling the nut on its thread, I managed to force open the window as far as it would go and hoisted one naked leg over its brass sill.

I had to bend almost in two to force my body through the small, rectangular opening; yet even stretching desperately down as far as possible, I still couldn't feel the solid surface of the promenade deck under my toes. I couldn't see anything either, since my head was still inside the bathroom, which made my fright all the worse when I felt someone outside grip me firmly by the elbow, and heard a male voice murmur, 'Don't worry, I've got you. Just let yourself fall against me.'

I fell. What else could I do? Behind me I'd already heard Margot's knuckles rap on my bedroom door and her voice call 'Clio? May I come in?' She wouldn't wait, I knew, for an answer.

'Oh, golly.' I tumbled out on to the promenade deck and into a pair of masculine arms – not wearing, thank heavens, a crocodile suit or a pirate hat, but safe, orthodox and desperately welcome evening dress. Shoeless, bare-legged and virtually naked under my frock, I'd still somehow kept enough presence of mind to press the bathroom window as nearly closed as I could behind me.

'Are you all right? Can I help in some way?' The gentleman in the dinner jacket was still supporting my arm. He was young, thank goodness – perhaps only three or four years older than I was – and seemed more amused than concerned. 'If there's a fire,' he suggested solemnly, 'we really ought to call a steward.'

'There isn't any fire – thank you.' My chest was still rising and falling like a hand-pump and from somewhere behind the bathroom window there came the muffled sound of raised voices. My rescuer glanced towards it briefly and then back to me; I fancied I saw him stifle a smile.

'A small misunderstanding,' he suggested.

'A silly quarrel, that's all.' I managed a little gasping laugh, as if squeezing out of bathroom windows was by far the jolliest way of spending one's time at sea. Fortunately the promenade deck was almost empty at that hour, except for a few couples loitering by the windows or lying in the shadows, heads close together, in adjoining steamer-chairs. No one seemed to have noticed my sudden appearance except for the gentleman at my side.

Margot's voice was quite clear now behind the bathroom window, conducting a low, dangerous duet with Igor's indignant bass. Any moment now, she might notice the half-open window and look out. To be honest, I was surprised she hadn't done it already.

Perhaps the same thought had struck my rescuer, since he glanced along the sheltered gallery, where the lamps wore the misty haloes of the witching hour. With formal politeness, he offered his arm.

'Perhaps you'd care to take a look at the sea before turning in? I'm told it's quite spectacular at night.'

The deck felt wonderfully cool under my bare feet and, once we were out in the open air, velvety with damp. At the ship's side, suddenly unsteady, I clung to the wooden rail and leaned out into the breeze, sucking in great reassuring draughts of stinging, salt-laden air. I was still light-headed and, thanks to Igor, all mixed up inside – still gripped by a kind of unfulfilled yearning, still tumbled in a flood of left-over lust.

My new friend followed my gaze. 'No sign of icebergs, at least.'

I twisted round to examine him. He was exactly the sort of chap John Buchan might have chosen to rescue a damsel in distress: decently tall, properly broad in the shoulder, admirably clean-jawed and with the kind of sandy hair which seemed to spring in picturesque ripples from a virtuous brow. In spite of the darkness, it seemed to me that he even had blue eyes.

'Ewan McLennan,' he said and held out a hand.

'Clio Oliver.' When I took it, his hand was warm, dry and resolutely firm.

'Ah, of course. You're one of *the* Olivers. I thought I'd seen you somewhere before – in the restaurant, on the night we sailed.'

'I'm afraid so. We have to travel on our own ships, you see.'

The blue eyes swept over me. 'Business must be bad, if the Olivers can't afford shoes.'

'Oh, that—' I glanced down at my naked toes, thanking heaven he didn't know what else I'd lost. 'It was the costume party,' I said quickly. 'The Little Match Girl.'

One sandy eyebrow twitched. 'You mean the little match-seller who was so poor she was down to her last string of pearls and didn't even have a maid to hook up her dress?' He laughed as my hands flew involuntarily to the nape of my neck. 'Here, let me do it.'

Efficiently, he restored the hooks Igor had undone.

'Thank you.'

'A pleasure, I assure you.' He rested his elbows on the rail beside mine.

'It wasn't as bad as it looked, you know. We weren't – I mean, I wouldn't—'

'Don't worry.' He smiled at the ocean. 'I have a remarkably innocent mind.'

The moon had emerged from behind a cloud, staining the sea with spilled silver. All around us, the *Concordia* floated in a pool of her own reflected radiance, a minor moon in a nebula of dancing wavelets.

The grandeur of the night made me unexpectedly shy. I glanced at the man beside me. 'Your name's Scottish, but you don't speak like a Scotsman.'

He turned his head to regard me. 'How many Scots do you know?'

'And you aren't wearing a kilt.'

'I must be a great disappointment to you.'

'No, not at all.' To tell the truth, he wasn't in the least disappointing. I already liked his calm confidence and his faintly ironic air. I could just imagine him at some outpost of the Empire – in a kilt, of course, and probably smoking a pipe – quelling a native rebellion with no more than a sardonic lift of those sandy brows and a copy of the King's Regulations.

'So here you are!' Margot, a little breathless, stalked up behind us, enveloped in a plum-coloured velvet wrap. She gave me a sharp stare which took in my bare legs and shoeless feet, but her voice was all honey. 'I've been looking for you every-where, Clio, darling. I was quite certain you'd gone to your cabin, but I must have been mistaken.'

'I did go there, but I came out again.' It was, after all, the perfect truth. 'It seemed too early to sleep.'

'Indeed?' Margot's eyes were slits of suspicion.

'I must take the blame for that, I'm afraid.' Ewan McLennan moved to my side. 'After the costume party I persuaded Miss Oliver to come out to look at the sea. The phosphorescence on the water was supposed to be particularly fine tonight.'

Margot's gaze flicked at once to the moonlit ocean, searching for phosphorescence.

I moved swiftly to distract her. 'Margot, this is Mr Ewan McLennan. Mr McLennan, I don't think you've met my aunt, Mrs Oliver.'

'I've seen Mrs Oliver from a distance, certainly. No one could possibly be unaware of her presence on board.'

Automatically, Margot extended a hand. 'Too kind.' She surveyed him critically and I imagined her conclusion: too conventional to lie. 'Have you been out here for long, then? I hope you haven't taken a chill, Clio.'

'My fault again, alas. We lost track of time.' Ewan McLennan managed to sound genuinely apologetic. 'Our tour of the promenade deck must have taken longer than we thought. Miss Oliver had never seen the fountains before, or the tropical fish.'

'Too many other excitements, I dare say.' Margot's eyes probed my face, her expression hard. At last she drew her velvet wrap more closely round her throat. 'It's becoming cold out here, Clio, and you hardly seem dressed for it, I must say.' For a significant moment her bright gaze held mine. 'You may stay for another ten minutes – but no longer. Girls of your age need sleep as well as parties, you know.'

'Ten minutes, I promise. And then I'll turn in.'

'Good night, Mr McLennan. Perhaps we shall see more of you tomorrow.' With a regal inclination of her head, Margot swept away towards her troubled bed. I wondered if Igor was in it.

Chapter Ten

NEITHER MARGOT nor Igor appeared for breakfast next morning; I tiptoed to the door of our little dining room to make sure Alice was there, alone, before going in to join her. Especially, I couldn't have borne the sight of Igor's face with its black satyr's eyes regarding me across the coffee cups, reminding me of the ignominious yielding I'd been about to make of myself to a man I despised.

At least I'd learned something: that love wasn't necessary to the rising up of that fierce, hollow longing – not even the least affection or liking. But I was no Margot: I'd also learned that love, with its tenderness and its compassionate blindness, must go hand in hand with it, if I were not to hate myself.

Alice was drinking orange juice, evidently with no inkling of the dramas of the previous evening, and I tried hard not to look furtive.

'How was the crocodile?' she enquired, reaching for a croissant.

'Oh . . . toothy. And a bit smelly, I'm afraid. Like a wet mackintosh in a train.'

'It must have been hot, in all that rubber.' Alice yawned and stretched. 'You'd all gone to bed by the time I came back, even Mama. King Charles lost his sword playing Camels and Horses in the gymnasium and it took us for ever to find it.'

'Blissful evening?'

'Passable, I suppose.' Alice poured herself more coffee, securing the pot-lid with a mindful finger.

'And King Charles?'

'Quite nice, if you like that sort. He's something in the Foreign Office, I think – all nervous coughs and Latin jokes.'

My heart sank. I'd wanted nothing but the best for Alice, but a *nice* Foreign Office chap was no good at all. Even if Stephen Morgan had proved faithless, I could see that every moment of Alice's evening had been measured against the exultation she'd felt in his company, and found wanting. *Nice* was impossible. Now, if there'd been a penniless student, or a hopeless rake . . . Alice needed an undeserving object for her love.

'Do you know,' she remarked suddenly, 'there's a poor man in third who goes everywhere with a couple of policemen? He's being taken back to America, apparently, to be tried for embezzlement. I saw the three of them out on the boat deck this morning and he has such a sad, white face, he can't possibly have done it.'

'Oh, Alice!' I murmured.

Later that morning, my new friend Ewan McLennan and I played together in the deck-tennis tournament and acquitted ourselves surprisingly well, only finally put out by an American pair rumoured to have been college lawn tennis champions. I hadn't expected such success: as Ewan escorted me back to my cabin the previous night I realised he had a slight limp, a legacy of childhood polio, he said, which had partly wasted the muscles of one leg. Yet on the deck-tennis court his only handicap was an awkward hopping lunge to return shots which went deep. Most of the time I was amazed by the quickness of his eye and his unerring instinct for guessing where a shot would land next.

It was almost inevitable, I'd thought, that the clear morning light would uncover a flaw or two in my new discovery, but Ewan McLennan triumphed over even that. If anything, his eyes were a trifle paler than I'd imagined them the night before – harebell rather than forget-me-not – his cheekbones a fraction heavier and his wrists thinner and more flexible: yet all of these only helped him to step out of the pages of fiction and be himself, less of a cardboard champion.

We'd just flung ourselves into deckchairs to drown our defeat in something long and mildly alcoholic when a thin, earnest man in a Fair Isle sweater materialized indignantly at my side. 'Excuse me, but I thought we'd arranged that you were to be my partner this morning.'

'I beg your pardon, but I don't seem to . . .'

'Last night. At the party. The *crocodile*.' He made gnashing movements with his arms.

'You were the crocodile? Oh, I'm most awfully sorry. It's just that without all the rubber and the teeth, I'd no idea which one you were.'

'Oh, I say!' For a moment the reptile looked as if he might have said more. But with a black glance at Ewan, solidly in possession, he drifted away.

'Thank heavens for rubber teeth.' Ewan followed the man's retreat with satisfaction and then patted my hand. 'We make a pretty keen partnership, you and I.'

'Don't we just?' The elation of our success at deck tennis was still with me. I knew we'd looked well, my flashing dark head next to his tawny waves. Groups of passengers on their way to the verandah bar had stopped to watch us play.

'How about dinner tonight, and then maybe a spot of dancing? I'm not a great dancer, with this leg of mine, but I can manage the slow ones pretty well.'

'I'd love to.' It was perfectly true. After all, I'd had more than enough of the foxtrot. A waltz might do just as well.

Margot took her revenge on Igor at luncheon in the Grill, though the lesson, I'm sure, was meant for both of us. It was the first time I'd seen him that day and I noticed his cheeks had a bluish, spectral look, as if his head had been chipped from some particularly gloomy marble.

Margot barely gave him time to sit down. 'Igor darling, run back to our suite for my sunglasses, will you? I'm almost certain I left them on my dressing-table.'

Frowning, Igor strode off in the direction of the bronze doors and the long walk beyond, but he'd hardly returned before Margot had him on his feet again. 'Be a dear – fetch me a little asparagus from the buffet.' And then, a few minutes later, as he snatched a glance at the menu: 'A mineral water, Igor, if you'd be so kind.'

As luck would have it, the glass was warm and another had to be fetched, and then, just as Igor's soup was brought, Margot gazed lazily round the table. 'Do you know – I seem to have left my cigarettes in our drawing room. Igor, would you?'

Igor rose bitterly from his chair once more, while Margot watched him from under heavy, implacable lids. Would he refuse to slave for her, my Orpheus, my would-be seducer? For a moment his lips parted as if an angry retort were about to fly out. But this was mid-Atlantic, not the accommodating Riviera and Igor's mouth closed again, leaving only his burning eyes to cry mutiny.

'While you're on your feet,' murmured Margot, 'ask them to serve us coffee in the bar. And bring some of their almond biscuits.'

By the end of lunch, Igor's destruction was complete. His consommé had gone cold, his escalope had been whisked away in his absence by the table steward and he returned from his last mission (to discover if rain was forecast) in time to see Margot sweep off among a band of young admirers to play bridge in the Winter Garden.

'Igor darling, you're such a *slow* eater!'

It was as delicate a castration as one could ever hope to see – and there was no doubt I'd been meant to see it. After that little exercise no one could be in any doubt as to where Igor belonged – waiting behind Margot's chair, or in her bed. She who paid the piper would be the only one to enjoy his tune.

By the following morning – our last day at sea before New York – I'd learned a great deal about Ewan McLennan. He was twenty-three, four years older than me, the only son of Sir Cato McLennan of Achrossan (which sounded very Scottish and grand and bleak) and was currently studying for accountancy exams while working in his uncle's international trading business. This was his sixth visit to New York, where he seemed to know all sorts of people in the financial world.

'I'm going there on business, of course,' he confided over dinner, 'but if I get off the mark right away, I could have it all tied up in ten days or so. Suppose after that I wangle myself an invitation to Newport – will you still be there, do you think?'

I thought I most decidedly would be, and just before we docked, Alice and I hunted out a map of Scotland in the *Concordia*'s library.

'Ewan says his father owns most of the Conachan Peninsula.' I ran my finger over the maze of inlets and islands which fretted the west side of the country. 'Look, that must be Conachan – that lumpy bit there, a little way up from the Sound of Thingummyjig. And look here – Achrossan, in teensy writing, just where the blue turns to that rather cheap green.'

'Let's see.' Alice craned over the map. 'Gosh. It must be a jolly big estate. Though I expect lots of it will just be mountains and bogs and things. And it's awfully far from London.'

'But you don't have to spend all your time in a place, just because you own it. In any case, one of the Wellborough cousins has shot with Sir Cato, so he must be all right.'

We stayed for two days in the Ambassador Hotel in New York, where Margot's shopping for 'little essentials' was so extensive that poor Briggs almost got altitude sickness, zipping up and down in the lift from her room on the eighteenth floor to repack our fleet of steamer-trunks (each one of which would have held a fair-sized steamer).

I had no objection at all to the delay, which allowed me two blissful evenings to dine with Ewan in the Persian Roof Garden of the Ritz, on brook trout and alligator pear salad, accompanied, since Prohibition was still in force, by lemonade served in the deep blue glass goblets which were the hallmark of Ritzes everywhere. Yet who needed champagne? It was intoxication itself to be there with Ewan in that softly lit Arabian paradise, where the maître d'hôtel greeted him as Mr McLennan, and led us to a spot perfectly designed for an assignation under the palms.

Inevitably, I suppose, we compared our pasts – not so dissimilar, when I realized how much of Ewan's growing up had been done in the heart of a near-feudal tradition of clans and ancient customs in which every man had his time-honoured place in the scheme of things. Most of the tenants on his father's land had known him as a toddler who would one day be their laird; and in return he knew them all by name, and their children, and their tales of their grandfathers and his.

Impossible not to trust a man who understood such things! I found myself pouring out all sorts of stories, about our home in Shanghai and coming to England for Grandfather Matthew's funeral, and about horrible Hallowhill and – in confidence – about Alice's engagement to Bertie and how our cousin Stephen had made her break it, and how we'd come to the USA to help her Forget.

Ewan looked grave, as I'd known he would. Marriages were dynastic transactions, not to be made or broken lightly.

'If you'd only *seen* her dress! She'd have looked so lovely, with her delicate little shoulders and the veil falling down like a shower of blossom . . .'

Since the Night of Igor – I couldn't think of it any other way – the idea of Alice's wedding gown had seemed to me like a symbol of hope, like a white chrysalis, within which, in the space of a day, she'd have metamorphosed into a wife – adored, desired, half of a couple, secure in a husband's arms. There, surely, was the ultimate token of love – a marriage veil, hiding the grossness and urgency of physical desire behind a sweet haze of devotion. Now, when I thought of Alice's wedding gown it was my own wistful face that was delivered up by the lifted lace, and my uncertain hand that was placed in another, firmer palm.

Remember your duty to the family, to the right way of things, and all will be well. My own inner nature had brought me back to my childhood. Liu Ling must have been right – the path to love did lie through duty, after all. For if it didn't, there was truly only emptiness ahead.

Beside me, I'd become aware of Ewan's voice. 'I'm sorry, I was miles away.'

'Dreamer.' He smiled and inclined his head as a tall man does to a child. 'I was saying that as soon as I saw you in the restaurant on our first night aboard the *Concordia*, I thought how different you looked from all the others.'

'Different?'

He reached for my hand and enveloped it in his own. 'More natural. Unaffected. And much, much prettier.'

'Oh, I see. How lovely of you.' I smiled at him, reassured; and we continued to sit at adjoining sides of our corner table, shoulder to shoulder, looking out on the world in satisfied conspiracy.

At first, Newport, without Ewan, seemed awfully flat. Unlike poor Mrs Longbaugh Karp, Leonie Spencer was a transatlantic Margot, sleek where Margot was languid, glossily enamelled where Margot was elegant, and when it came to social matters, governed by all the charitable impulses of a gun-runner. She recognized precisely where Igor Starozhilov fitted into the scheme of things and accommodated him with tact in the room next to Margot's. Mr Ransome Spencer, I gathered from his son David, was something on Wall Street, only released from the money-factory at weekends to join his wife and guests beside the sea.

David Spencer and Alice seemed to hit it off rather well. David, I decided, possessed all the good points of Chester Karp with the added bonus of sensitivity and, when Ewan MacLennan arrived ten days later to stay with friends near by, we made up a foursome of 'young people', playing tennis together at the Casino, or attempting golf, at which I was a rabbit and Ewan pretty good, or lying in the sandy shade of the parasols on Bailey's Beach, watching the daily fashion parade saunter among the tea tables.

Most of all, I liked watching Ewan – Ewan in an authoritative tweed cap on the golf course, kicking up a brisk spout of sand with his niblick; Ewan in broad-shouldered flannels fitted closely over his narrow hips, cutting a dash at the beach with his fine straw Panama; Ewan everywhere, fitting in so well –

always effortlessly *right*, always ready with easy conversation or a sturdy return at tennis.

Only swimming embarrassed him, though he swam reasonably well, pulling himself through the water with powerful arms. I guessed it was the haul from bathing-hut to sea which he hated, the sight of a leg appreciably wasted below the shorts of his swimming costume, like a cable of uneven thickness.

'There's nothing the matter with me, you know.' I was sitting in my beach coat on the steps of our hut as he returned from the surf one day, and he fancied I'd been watching his progress across the sand. 'I'm not crippled. I can do pretty well anything I set my mind to.'

'Well, of course you can.' I was surprised by his sharpness, but not offended. It was the first time I'd seen anything break the smooth surface of his composure and I found it strangely exciting. I liked the idea of his having deeper feelings, shared only with me, though I'd long ago accepted his limp as a battle-scar, so much part of his quietly heroic bearing that he might almost have seemed lacking without it. 'Honestly, Ewan, I hardly ever notice.'

'But you find it ugly. Like this, on the beach.' He dropped down at my feet and began absently to shovel sand over the imperfect limb.

'Most of the time, I forget all about it.' I couldn't think what else to say; besides, I'd suddenly noticed how the hair at the nape of Ewan's sun-browned neck curled into an almost imperceptible line, like a dart bisecting the wide bow of his shoulders. I'd have liked to touch it, to follow its silken thread with my finger, but this wasn't the time.

Ewan continued to dig at the yellow grains, until, little by little, the wasted leg disappeared from sight.

'Sometimes I wish they'd cut it off,' he muttered at last. 'God, how I hate it.' He scrambled to his feet, scattering sand, and disappeared inside to change.

There was only person who didn't share the generally golden opinion of Ewan, and that was Igor, who brooded darkly whenever Ewan was around and whose resentment seemed to swell along with Ewan's popularity.

'I don't think you've met Igor Starozhilov,' Margot had announced at their first meeting. She wafted a careless hand. 'Igor is my fitness instructor.'

'Secretary,' insisted Igor, glaring at Margot. 'I write all her letters.' The lie seemed to inflate him to his full six feet. 'I am the son of a countess.'

'My dear fellow,' said Ewan, who understood perfectly. 'Of course you are.'

By the end of August Ewan McLennan had altered his plans in order to sail back with us to England.

'He isn't really my style, darling,' Margot confided one day in the *Concordia*'s steam room. 'A little too *narrow*, I think, and too tweedy. He reminds me of windy houses with antlers on the walls and icy beds – but he's charming, certainly, and he does keep you out of trouble.'

Igor, catching me alone in the corridor, was more forthright. 'What the devil do you see in this man?' He laid his hand against the wall, barring my path. 'This McLennan is *nothing*! You're wasting yourself on a fool of a Scotchman!'

'Let me pass, Igor.' Oddly enough, while I could still appreciate the beautiful symmetry of Igor's face and body, it already seemed hardly credible that I'd once desired him as a lover. His allure was gone, utterly destroyed by Margot's sharp lesson in economics in the *Concordia*'s Grill.

I put my hand on his chest and pushed. 'There's only one fool round here, it seems to me, and that's the one who was caught without his trousers in the wrong woman's bedroom. Ewan McLennan would never be so stupid, I'm sure.'

'You wait!' Igor hissed wrathfully as I barged past him. 'No man is too clever for bad luck, I tell you. No man!'

Six weeks after we returned to England, news broke of a monumental crash on the New York stock exchange. On the third day of the calamity, Ransome Spencer, whom we'd last seen with his family on the beach at Newport, shot himself in the head in his Wall Street office, leaving his wife and son to salvage what they could from the ruins of his fortune. I knew Alice had written to David two or three times since we'd left Newport, but the romance had petered out and now she felt guilty.

I thought of hard, glossy Leonie Spencer, whose life's work had been wiped out in a matter of forty-eight hours, and I began to wonder all over again about the nature of my own comfortable Oliver world. No man, as Igor had said, was too clever for bad luck.

'Could the same thing happen here?' I asked Guy.

'There's nothing for you to worry about, if that's what you mean. Oh, I admit we've had to tighten things up here and there, but selling off the old Rodgers Line has kept us as solid as anyone else in shipping.'

He thought for a moment. 'And then, of course, we had that dock boycott and the fire in Calcutta, when we lost four warehouses – that cost us a bit. And with trade slowing down all over the place, we've had to cut our rates to pick up cargoes. But we'll get it all back on the Atlantic run, when we get the Heavenly Twins into service.'

The Heavenly Twins, as I'd explained proudly to Ewan, were to be the means by which Oliver's would once again dominate the transatlantic passenger trade – two giant ships of staggering tonnage and enormous length, whose hull models were currently being tested in a huge tank near Glasgow. Zipping along at almost thirty knots, they'd give Oliver's a guaranteed weekly service between Southampton and New York which would, according to Guy, 'knock the dear old Concordia – and all the other fellows' ships – into a cocked hat'.

There were other developments, of which I wasn't so proud.

'Would you believe it?' Guy passed on the news with disgust. 'Rose has taken up with that old faker Leonard Cadzow – ran off as soon as Margot's back was turned and fled to some sort of camp the old devil has set up for the ruin of young women. She's mad, that girl, if you ask me.'

It was virtually true, as Alice confirmed later. With Margot abroad and Kit absorbed in his new ships, Rose had accepted an invitation from Polly Cadzow to visit her family on the sprawling Gloucestershire farm where they lived – the artist and his wife, together with an ex-wife, uncountable children, and an ever-changing swarm of pupils and hangers-on. There, in a complex of ancient, gently decaying buildings, they'd set up a nest of ant-like creativity where potters potted, carvers chipped and painters could sit for days in contemplation of infinity without anyone demanding they dip a brush into colour or make the smallest mark on canvas.

Three generations worked together at the farm, ate together – and, according to Alice, made love to one another in a spirit of haphazard generosity, Leonard Cadzow himself being the most generous of all. In fact, the enveloping fog of creativity was such that every female creature in the place seemed constantly pregnant, from the dogs and cats to the ex-Mrs Cadzow, who was incapable of reaching her potter's wheel for four months out of every twelve.

In Rose, Leonard Cadzow had apparently recognized a 'great soul' which had only to shed its inhibitions to realize its true glory. Rose, he declared, had risen above the petty tyranny of the bourgeoisie and was ready to plunge into a life of *feeling*. He might have added that Rose, at nineteen, had grown into a ravishing beauty with a ripening, slender body which no doubt also seemed ready for a certain amount of feeling.

At Kit's insistence, Margot travelled down to Gloucestershire, where she was confronted by an unrepentant Rose in a smock ('Perfectly *furtive*, darling!'), absolutely refusing to come home. Kit had wanted Cadzow arrested for everything from child-kidnap to procuring, but wisely, Margot left without making a scene. As she pointed out later, Rose might easily have run off with a grocer's assistant from Pinner and flagrant black sheepery did at least bring a certain *succès de scandale* to the family name.

'If Rose has a baby,' mused Alice, 'do you suppose it will look like ugly old Leonard Cadzow?'

I thought she was being flippant. 'I doubt it – you don't hear of many babies with beards and gold-rimmed spectacles. In fact, I heard your mother say Rose is just as likely to have a baby goat or a kitten at the Cadzows' place. Everyone there seems to get at everyone else.'

I don't believe Alice even heard me, lost in a dream of her own. 'I'd like a baby,' she confessed softly. 'Not any old baby – not Bertie Headington's, for instance, or David Spencer's, but—' She fell silent and glanced down at her hands, as if an image of the lover she couldn't name were somehow contained between her palms. 'I know he's a devil,' she whispered. 'I know it and I won't ever forgive him. But the memory – you can't force a memory to go away, can you?'

It shocked me to the core to think she'd ever considered having a baby by Stephen Morgan. Alice, my cousin Alice, of all people, in her fussy prints and little-girl bows, dreaming of – well, of all the shaming, feverish things that had gone through my mind in the arms of Igor Starozhilov.

'Thank goodness you didn't,' I said.

'Didn't what?'

'Didn't take it into your head to start a baby.'

'I thought it would be a disaster, at the time. Now I'm not so sure. A baby needs his mother, after all.'

'Not if you have nurses and nannies and so forth. I never saw very much of my mother – and I can't imagine yours with an apron over her knees, changing nappies.'

'I wouldn't let anyone look after my baby.' Alice stuck out her chin. 'I'd keep him for myself, all day and all night.'

'Just as well there was no chance of babies with Stephen, then.'

Alice eyed me thoughtfully from under her fringe, but said nothing.

It amazed me that after his treatment of Alice, Stephen Morgan was still employed in Leadenhall Street, doing whatever it was he did for the Oliver Steam Navigation Company. I'd fully expected Kit to throw him out and yet he'd survived, in that doggedly uncaring way of his, carrying out, I suspected, whatever tasks the others thought beneath their Oliver dignity.

'He's in Glasgow,' Guy told me carelessly when I asked. 'There's a bit of trouble brewing with the boilermakers and the platelayers on the Clyde just now – something to do with piecework rates, I think. Kit sent clever-dick Morgan to make sure it won't hold up the building of the Heavenly Twins. You wouldn't think there were two million unemployed in this country, would you?'

'Why didn't you go, if it's so important? Or Kit himself – or even Papa?'

'It's hardly my sort of thing, is it? Arguing the toss with a handful of bully-boys in a shipyard?' Guy waved his cigarette, leaving a smoke trail in the air. 'No, thank you – let our Mr Morgan from head office go and represent the company, if there's going to be a row. Besides—' Guy drew confidently on the little gold-banded cylinder. 'He's bound to sort it out. He always does.'

I began to understand the secret of Stephen's survival. 'Is that why Kit didn't sack him, after he was so beastly to Alice? Because he's prepared to do all your dirty work for you?'

'Well—' This time Guy looked faintly embarrassed. 'I wouldn't put it quite like that. After all, no actual damage was done. Alice simply learned what comes of getting involved with a fellow with no background.' Guy drew the ashtray towards him with a single, well-kept finger. 'And it's true, Morgan has turned out to be useful, in a sordid sort of way. He has a knack of spotting trouble while it's brewing and moving to stop it before it can do us any harm. It's the common touch, I've always said so. Not that I like him any better,' Guy added quickly, 'or trust him, for that matter. But he does have his uses.'

I wasn't looking forward to bringing Ewan McLennan and Stephen Morgan together; they hardly seemed likely to get on well and I badly wanted everyone to share my good opinion of my shining knight. After Rose's example, my father was prepared to approve of anyone not connected with the art world – and even Guy, who'd tested Ewan severely on the subject of six-litre Bentleys, pronounced himself satisfied. Igor Starozhilov had loathed Ewan, of course, but then, Igor had vanished, dispatched to the Paris train as soon as the *Concordia* docked: Margot was always very tidy-minded about her dalliances.

I'd been surprised to find how much I cared what people thought, and that, almost without my realizing it, Ewan McLennan had come to occupy an entirely different place in my life from any other man I'd known. When he kissed me (we'd reached the kissing stage unexpectedly one night on the Spencers' porch) it was thrilling, but also, in an odd sort of way, protective. Unlike Igor, who'd somehow seemed to draw every last restraint from my lips when he assaulted them, Ewan's kisses were warm and considerate, and seemed to insulate me from the outside world. I'd come to trust him, recognizing an instinctive reverence for the right way, for custom and for duty which so much resembled the one with which I'd been brought up.

'I really believe you're a Scots Confucian,' I told him, laying my head contentedly on his shoulder. 'Are you sure you weren't born in China?'

In spring, when an invitation arrived from Lady McLennan, Ewan's mother, to visit Achrossan, I wasn't unduly astonished. I imagined they were as anxious to inspect me as I was to see the home Ewan had told me so much about. I spent a small fortune on cashmere and tweed and went north with eager anticipation.

In return, even the Scottish weather smiled on me. After twenty-four hours I was convinced I'd never sniffed such luscious air or known such illimitable peace as filled that blue and ancient paradise. And when it rained – soft, fresh and scented, like falling petals – I relished the bounty as much as the thin, resolute soil.

Achrossan House was – and still is – a delight of white rough-cast walls and pepperpot turrets, nestling in a crescent of flat land at the head of a sea-loch. From the lochside road, the house seems cradled in the lap of bare-headed mountains, wrapped in pines and cushioned with clumps of alder. Even now, the silence of the place makes one afraid to breathe; it brushes the skin like velvet, disturbed only by the rising of an occasional crow or the kissing of the loch on its breast of boulders.

Sir Cato wore a kilt to greet me. I'd have been most disappointed if he hadn't, or if the motor which met me at the railway station had been anything but a venerable Daimler with a creaky tonneau, or if Lady McLennan hadn't worn a plaid scarf pinned on her shoulder with a silver brooch the size of a tureen lid.

Here Ewan was in his element. I still have a photograph of him, taken on that visit beside a rocky outcrop on the shore of the loch, leaning on the gnarled trunk of an old pine, with the craggy skyline behind his head and a look of absolute rightness on his face. There's no other word for it – *rightness* – the same quiet reserve that made him order every shirt from Beale and Inman and every hat from Lock's, and smoke plain Morris's Blue instead of Kyriazi or some gold-tipped frivolity, clamping each cigarette firmly between his knuckles instead of letting it droop from his fingertips as Guy did.

Rightness: perhaps that was what he saw in me – someone who would not be out of place one day, leaning on a gnarled pine by the shore of the loch.

When a morning mist hung, trapped, in our glen, he introduced me to his ancestors on the walls of the dining room. 'And then there was Black Roderick – Roderick *Dubh*, who fought at Culloden – and his father, Sir Alexander, who was supposed to have been more than seven feet tall. That's his sword on the wall by the front door, as a matter of fact – it takes two of us just to lift it. Now this glum-looking fellow here, in the long wig . . .'

From their frames, the dead McLennans examined me sternly, weighing my fitness. It was something to which, as it turned out, Ewan had also been giving some thought.

'I don't quite know how to put this.' We'd gone for a walk by the loch shore near the end of the second week of my stay and it was almost the first time he'd spoken since we'd left the house. Half a mile from the gates of Achrossan he'd helped me up on to a stony promontory and we sat there side by side on the tussocky grass, our matching brogues dangling over the water.

After a moment Ewan extracted a cigarette from his case and lit it – largely, I suspected, to give himself a few more seconds' grace.

'The fact is – it's a silly thing, really, and I shouldn't have left it so late—' His gaze slid away, over the loch. 'But I have to ask, because I really am awfully fond of you, Clio. No, more than that – to be honest, I'm darned well in love with you.' He leaned his arm on one raised knee and watched the smoke from his cigarette become a ragged blue spiral against the green-gold of the afternoon.

I'd turned, my heart rising like a fish, expecting to be taken in his arms and given impassioned, physical proof that I was loved and wanted. But Ewan hadn't moved; he was still staring across the water, leaving me with his fixed, steadfast profile.

'The trouble is, you see, I'm rather an old-fashioned type and I've always hoped – I mean, I think it's important – though nowadays we're all supposed to be *modern* about these things—' Here the hand holding his cigarette out over the loch described a strangled arc. 'What I have to ask you is . . . When I met you first, that night on the *Concordia* when you squeezed through the window and your aunt was angry—' He rubbed his cheek, leaving it flushed. 'Were you, I mean, had you *done* anything in there?' He swallowed and added quickly, 'Because you were pretty well half-dressed, you know. All unhooked, and no stockings.'

At last he turned his face to me, his eyes bright and the skin across his cheekbones tight with stubborn resolve. 'I have to know, I'm afraid.'

'But I told you what happened!' On the brink of losing my dream, I forgot to be indignant. 'Nothing happened – because I escaped out of the window, just as you saw.' Desperation assured me this was the truth: I'd been Igor's helpless victim, never willing, struggling to save my honour. Of course that's how it had been! Hadn't I been saving myself, all my life, for this moment?

'I am a virgin, Ewan, if that's what you're asking.'

His expression cleared, to be replaced by a schoolboyish relief. 'I was sure, of course.' He swept up my hand and kissed the tips of my fingers. 'But I had to ask – you do understand? If it had only been me – but there's the estate and all that . . . I've more to think of than just myself alone.'

Of course I understood! In the elation of the moment I almost admired him for his scruples. I was so sure I was falling in love with him that I never thought of asking why it should be important to a chunk of Scottish moor and mountain that Ewan McLennan took a virgin bride. I squeezed his hand. 'I do understand.'

He threw the half-smoked cigarette into the loch and leaned over to kiss me, cupping my cheek in one hand. His lips were firm and warm and tasted of tobacco. After a few seconds we slid into the grass, still entangled; I'd never known him so voracious, as if the knowledge of my inexperience had excited him, or banished a private insecurity. For a moment I wondered if he intended to possess me, there and then, on the lake shore, in full view of the loch: the idea was oddly thrilling.

Then he rose up on one elbow, breathless. 'You must know what I'm going to ask next.'

'I can't imagine.'

'And if you refuse, I'll just go on kissing you until you say yes.'

'Oh, well!' A little tingling shiver ran down my spine, compelling me to roll my hips. 'Maybe I shall refuse, then.'

He laughed, and kissed me purposefully again. 'See?'

His lips were rosy and voluptuously curved – engorged from feeding on mine. I reached up to trace their outline, prolonging the moment.

'I want you to marry me, Clio. Be Mrs Ewan McLennan and have a home here, at Achrossan.'

A gentle breeze ruffled the pine trees overhead, stirring the small, baby-fair curls at Ewan's temples. Beyond, the ragged skyline of the mountains framed his head.

'I love you,' I whispered – certain at last.

Later that evening, Ewan gave me his great-grandmother's ring to seal our betrothal, a row of large diamonds set in carved gold. We'd agreed nothing could be official until he'd spoken to my father, of course, but I was too wrapped up in being Ewan's Highland bride to mind. I'd found a sanctuary I recognized in the bosom of those mountains, which I could share by right of marriage – and when we travelled south again, though London felt as alien as ever, I no longer cared.

Shortly after I returned from Achrossan, Stephen Morgan came back from Glasgow – flying down from Renfrew, so Guy informed me contemptuously, in the spare seat of someone's Moth.

'Why the dickens can't he take the train, like any sensible person?' Guy peered through the drawing-room window into the silver mist of an April shower. 'He'll cop it, one of these days, with this silly flying nonsense.'

'I didn't think you cared.' I was busy unwrapping the first of our wedding presents, digging through layers of tissue paper to discover unappetizing epergnes donated by great-aunts and inscribed mahogany boot-jacks sent by Ewan's tenants.

'You're right. I don't care.' Guy whirled the translucent porcelain jug of a coffee set from one finger. 'I don't care about Morgan, anyhow. If it wasn't that he sometimes comes in handy at the office, he could splash himself all over the landscape as soon as he liked.'

'Please don't mix up the cards, Guy, or I won't know who's sent what.' I retrieved the little jug, restored it to its family and wrote the details down on the list I was preparing for Ewan. I wanted very much to impress him with my efficiency.

'I take it Stephen has managed to soothe the boilermakers in Scotland, then?'

Guy snorted. 'Oh, he's poured water on the fiery cross, or whatever it took to get the tank-testing finished. Though, personally, I wouldn't have wasted my time in talking to the blighters. If the Jocks want to make piddling conditions, we can always give the work to Belfast or the Tyne. The yards there would be glad enough to have it.'

'So things are getting harder.'

'Could say that, I suppose.' Guy stirred the crumpled wrapping paper with the toe of his shoe. 'Nobody much wants cotton these days and nobody at all wants rubber, so freight's getting harder to come by. And the Americans aren't helping matters, calling in loans and pulling the rug from under half of Europe. But it'll sort itself out before long, I dare say – and after all, in a couple of years we'll launch the first of the Heavenly Twins.'

The distant tolling of the front door bell interrupted him. 'That'll be another old trout, come to say how she dandled you on her knee as a baby.' Nimbly, Guy vaulted over the back of the sofa and made for the door. 'I'm off. If it's Great-Aunt Louise or Great-Aunt Alice, remember – you haven't seen me.'

It wasn't a great-aunt. The visitor turned out to be Stephen Morgan, carrying a large flat parcel which he slid on to the sofa table a little awkwardly, as if he'd found it by chance in the street. I hadn't seen him or spoken to him for months, not since his despicable treatment of Alice. I'd begged him expressly not to hurt her and he'd paid no attention at all: I was almost more upset about that than I was about Alice.

I didn't see why I should hide the fact that I'd expected him to stay away and after a few minutes he took possession of one end of a sofa like a man preparing to defend his position to the last. Ewan would never have sat like that – as still as a cat, with every nerve-end alive to the atmosphere in the room. Stephen was like a powder keg primed to explode; I could feel his tension from several feet away, where I knelt among the discarded boxes and drifts of tissue paper. To make matters worse, he was watching me with that fixed, curious expression I hated so much.

'You'll break your decanter if you hold it by its neck like that.'

I immediately turned the fragile vessel the right way up – and then became furious with myself for minding. 'It wouldn't matter if I had broken the blessed thing. It's the eighth today.'

A hostile silence descended. To fill it, I fussed with the knot of a parcel.

Stephen had been picking at the braid on the sofa arm. 'How was America?'

'Smart, I suppose.' Head down, I tugged at my knot. 'Very social. Though not now, of course. It's all been spoiled for them by this business on the stock exchange.'

'Did Alice enjoy the trip?'

'Alice?' I was so startled that for an instant I dropped my guard. 'Why should you care about Alice?'

'I simply want to know.'

This was too much. 'Well then, if you want the truth, she enjoyed the trip as well as anyone could, with an utterly broken heart.'

'Oh.' He considered this for a moment. 'I'm sorry she's still upset.'

'Upset? When you treated her so appallingly? What on earth did you expect?'

His eyes widened and his face flushed with resentment. 'You were the one, I seem to remember, who ordered me to give Alice up, because you believed – in your infinite wisdom – that I was only using her for some kind of attack on Guy. Well – now you have everything you asked for. Are you telling me you still aren't satisfied?'

I couldn't believe he was trying to make me share the blame for Alice's unhappiness. Did he really expect me to think all that larking about with ghastly women had been his way of curing Alice of her infatuation?

'I begged you to leave her some pride.'

'She told me she hoped I'd crash the plane. Doesn't that prove it?' After a second, his eyes slid away from me. 'I was fond of Alice. I still am. But all she wants is to give, without asking for any return.'

'Isn't that what love is supposed to be about?'

This time he stared at me directly, puzzled that I hadn't understood. 'Alice's kind of loving turns a man into a prisoner. It piles up a debt that's impossible to repay – unless you're an out-and-out rat and simply take her for everything.'

174

'You are a rat, if you're trying to tell me Alice brought it all on herself.'

'I didn't say that. Oh, I suppose it's true – to begin with, I was trying to make Guy jealous. I'm not proud of that. But then, later—' He leaned one elbow on the arm of the sofa and ran his fingers through the pale mass of his hair. 'When a young woman puts herself in your hands, body and soul, asking nothing, except that you take what she badly wants to give . . . She must know only a saint would have the strength to refuse. And after that it's too late. The debt is there – the obligation exists.'

In the silence which followed I heard the dry, swift booming of my heart.

'Are you saying Alice *slept* with you?'

He showed neither surprise nor embarrassment. He simply asked, 'Does it matter?'

'She can't have. She'd have told me if she had.' Distantly, I was aware of my own voice, sharp and accusing.

'She would not have told you. And if you can't understand why, you're a good deal less perceptive than I thought.'

I stared at him – gripped by a wave of such pure, savage jealousy that it shocked me to the depths of my soul. Sweet, spinsterish Alice, with her careful finger on the coffee-pot lid: what blazing thing had she discovered that had led her on beyond fear, beyond modesty, beyond salvation? What could have bound her so fatally to this bitter, barbarous creature that even now she could still dream of bearing his child?

Across the room, Stephen was watching me almost with an expression of pity. Could he hear the blood banging in my ears? It was fear – the fear that Ewan McLennan would come to me on our wedding night in his well-regulated, utterly proper manner and I'd never know this stormy rapture Alice had discovered – if she had discovered it: I clung to that doubt. Stephen Morgan's face gave nothing away.

'I'm sorry – I shouldn't have mentioned all this.' With embarrassed briskness, he consulted his watch. 'I can't stay much longer, I'm afraid. I have to be down at the airfield at four.'

'You're flying somewhere?' I had to clear my throat in order to be civil. *Alice,* said a voice in my head, *mousy, secretive Alice, has probably slept with this man.*

'I'm selling the plane.'

'Selling it!'

'Don't worry, I'll buy another before long. But at the moment I need the money to buy a picture.' He gave a fleeting smile. 'Unlike you, I don't have unlimited cash.'

'It must be a pretty special picture.'

'It is. It's quite small, but it is by Renoir, and I want it very much.'

I felt a sudden, fierce curiosity to see the object which had drawn passion from such a stone. 'You must show it to me one day.'

He hesitated. 'One day, perhaps.' He twisted in his seat and slid the large, flat parcel from the table behind him.

'I brought this for you.'

Politeness obliged me to cross the room to take it from him and, after that, to sit down next to him in order to slip off the string and the wrapping. It was an untidy package with an inner layer of newspaper, and I fumbled and tugged at it in my vexation. It had been unfair of him to bring a gift: I hoped he'd brought something I wouldn't like.

'You might tell me what it is.'

'That would spoil the surprise.'

'I don't like surprises.' Crossly, I tore off the last veil of newsprint.

In the nest of old *Expresses* lay a rectangular screen, a whisper of almost transparent silk framed in mahogany and painted – no, microscopically stitched – with a supple cormorant chasing two fish. The embroidery was a Chinese speciality: I knew that to turn the inner frame on its pivots would reveal another cormorant and two more fish, magically back to back with the first.

It was clearly very old and miraculously fine, worked in silk filaments no thicker than a hair so that each fat scale and each air-trapping barb of the cormorant's feathers rose distinct, offering itself to the disbelieving touch.

'It's absolutely wonderful.' It was: I could almost taste that Chinese river.

'I found it in a Glasgow antique shop.' Stephen dismissed the place with a twist of his hand. 'I imagine some sailor brought it home for his sweetheart about half a century ago. I thought you might like it because it was Chinese.' He indicated the chaos of wrapping paper on the floor. 'Now you can have it as a wedding present.'

I examined him over the rim of the screen. 'I wish I knew what to make of you, Stephen Morgan. One minute you're utterly contemptible and then the next you do something kind like this.'

I held the screen up to the light, where the silk gleamed like a pool of petrol and the fish and their cormorant twisted more wildly still. If it hadn't been for the ribbons of river-water which curled along their sides, split and curdled by the power of their passing, all three might easily have been flying.

Chapter Eleven

I NEVER said 'Did you?' to Alice. Instead, I convinced myself it was her secrecy that had hurt and if there were moments in the weeks that followed when I noticed her watching me in thoughtful silence, I deliberately ignored them. Clearly, Alice and I were only to be cousins in future, not best friends. I accepted this new coolness as a rite of passage, marking my translation into Mrs Ewan McLennan of Achrossan, whose closest confidant, naturally, would be her husband.

Ewan and I were married in June, at St Margaret's, Westminster, in the usual monsoon of flowers and awnings and sunshine and so forth. My gown was by Molyneux, a sleek column of satin and pearls trailing a fifteen-foot georgette train as white and pure as satin could be, for by now I was certain that some ineffable fate had conspired to keep me virginal for Ewan and I wanted the world to know it. Hadn't Ewan guessed as much himself? My reward, I knew, would be an outpouring of tenderness – of guiltless, virtuous, heaven-sent love, culminating in a rapturous defloration at the hands of my husband.

Ewan, needless to say, looked absolutely perfect and made all his responses in a voice which seemed to ring with such steadiness and sincerity that it brought tears to my eyes to think he was now entirely mine. In the end, it was quite hard to pull him away from the reception, he'd charmed everyone so much. The great-aunts clustered round his elbows like pigeons, pecking and cooing for crumbs of his attention; Grandmother Kate conceded that he'd 'do' and even Guy, glazed with champagne, informed me I'd married a 'jolly fine chap', as if I wasn't thoroughly aware of the fact already.

Stephen Morgan was the only member of the family not to come to my wedding. Instead, he sent a note, pleading a last-minute crisis meeting in Liverpool and after a few seconds' disappointment I decided it was probably just as well. I couldn't imagine him being comfortable in a room full of Olivers and McLennans in full cry and having to flirt roguishly with the great-aunts and flatter the bridesmaids into giggles as Ewan did. I couldn't even imagine him in a church, which was rather more startling, and I began to be quite thankful he hadn't come.

Alice was pink-eyed by the time Ewan and I roared off in his Rolls tourer. I wondered what she was thinking, but our paths already seemed to have diverged too far for me to ask: I doubt if she'd have told me anyway. In the end, I threw her my bouquet and left her to Rose, who'd turned up in an odd, hand-woven tubular garment in which she managed to look infuriatingly beautiful. Everyone stared, of course; the Cadzows' talent for pregnancy was common knowledge all over London, but Rose had one of those bony midriffs which show up even a spoonful of rice pudding and there wasn't so much as a bulge.

The spectre of pregnancy, I gathered, had been the real purpose of Margot's hasty mission to the Cadzows' farm in Gloucestershire, to ensure that Rose, if no one else in that ramshackle community, understood how to avoid making her a grandmother.

She produced the farm as an awful warning on the day she came to repeat her contraceptive lecture to me. 'There were babies rolling about everywhere!' Her pencilled brows soared in distress. 'Wiping their sticky faces against one's skirt, dribbling over one's shoes – there was absolutely no escape from them. One only had to look round to see the ghastly results of carelessness, and fortunately, Rose is no fool.'

Margot's pre-nuptial advice was as explicit and meticulous as her attitude to life, without coyness or nursery words. Certainly, no one could accuse her of hypocrisy; Margot Oliver had always done as she pleased, wantonly, but with such elegant discretion that it almost amounted to virtue. If only by example, she taught me a lifetime horror of the squalid, scrabbling, ill-conducted love affair, made up of hasty couplings in corners and haunted by fear of discovery, which to Margot was the nadir of vulgarity.

'If you do decide to sin, my dear, you must sin honestly and beautifully. Then everyone knows where they are.'

I hadn't the least intention of sinning, but I was grateful for her unexpected kindness and said so.

'One does what one can.' She surveyed me for a moment, her brow gathered into a critical line. 'For instance, I shall wear something quite modest for your wedding. Anything else would be unfair.'

Ewan and I planned a honeymoon at Achrossan, driving north in easy stages, which meant that our first night together was passed in an ancient, secluded, half-timbered hotel near Oxford which had seemed the very stuff of romance when we'd chosen it weeks earlier.

'Are you sure this is it?' I asked Ewan as we pulled up outside the lopsided black and white porch. 'This one seems smaller, somehow – and I don't remember those lions at the door.'

'Of course this is it.' Ewan swung himself confidently out of the driving seat. 'You're just tired, darling, that's all. A drink and a good dinner will soon set you up. Goodness me—' He flexed his stiff back and stretched himself out, star-fashion, swelling to fill the entire space beside the motor. 'It's been quite a day, hasn't it?'

It had. It had been a long day, starting at seven with the arrival of a hairdresser after a night of excited sleeplessness. Now I found I'd developed a nagging constriction behind my eyes, like the start of a headache, so that when I stupidly broke a fingernail on the lock of my jewel-case, I had to run off to the bathroom to weep because suddenly I was all alone, and married, and in a strange place, and tired, and confused that the elation of the day seemed to have been left behind with the cheerful, convivial crowd in London of which we'd so recently been the shining centre.

And then, remembering Ewan, I hastily dried my eyes before my face could become blotchy with tears, wiped away the powdery rivulets with a licked finger and resolved that at all costs, Ewan shouldn't know. Secrets already! We'd promised one another, at Ewan's suggestion, never to keep secrets; yet here, especially for his sake, was the first lie of my married life – that I was nothing less than blissfully, ecstatically content. In the mirror, I assured myself that it didn't count: before long, after all, I would truly be in seventh heaven.

'Happy, darling?'

'Wonderfully. You?'

'Couldn't be happier.' Ewan smiled, showing strong white teeth. 'You're a marvellous girl. I'm so lucky.'

'And me, darling.'

'Tired?'

'Just a little.' I pushed my plate away, almost untouched.

'Me too, a bit.'

It was comforting, that game of *me too*. It turned us into conspirators, like a long-married couple, yawning in unison, instead of what we were – two people who hardly knew one another, preparing uncertainly to become lovers. For a moment Ewan allowed his gaze to wander round the room, idling from table to table as if there was something fascinating in the sight of the other diners scraping up slices of chicken in genteel silence, or murmuring over red and white peaks of strawberries.

He cleared his throat. 'Early night, then?'

His eyebrows made innocent arcs, as if the idea had just occurred to him. Yet I noticed with sudden alarm that his pupils were swollen with expectation, almost eclipsing the blue of his eyes and giving him a startling air of menace. He rose to his feet and held out one of his heavy, masculine hands: for the first time, I noticed the fair hairs which sprang up among the freckles with the lusty vigour of weeds.

'Come on, darling. We've a long way to drive tomorrow.'

★

181

Our bed was a four-poster, built to hold a medieval family of six. As Ewan moved over to the side where I waited apprehensively in lace and peach-coloured crêpe de Chine it creaked abominably.

'Oh, Ewan, the noise—'

'It's nothing. Just a loose joint.' He buried his face in the warmth of my neck. 'Mmmm . . . I like that perfume. It tastes of chocolate, or ice cream – or one of those huge old roses. It's just as if I could eat you up in one gulp—' He began to kiss me, slowly at first, but soon more invasively, moving his body against mine . . . Whereupon the bed squealed like a soul in torment and, horrified, I pushed against his chest. 'Ewan, we can't! The whole hotel will hear.'

'Don't worry about it.'

I wished I hadn't pushed him back. His face was slack with desire and there was irritation in his voice. 'We'll be gone after breakfast and we'll never stay here again. If they do stare at us, it'll only be out of jealousy, because we've been having such a good time.'

'But they'll all know—'

He placed a finger on my lips. 'Darling, what does it matter?'

I didn't want to hear that reproach in his voice and feel scolded – not then, at such a moment. I'd so much wanted everything to be noble and sublime. He took my silence for acquiescence and began to move against me again, more urgently now, exploring my body with determined fingers and hungry lips.

'Oh . . .' His sigh was a warm wind on my throat. 'You can't believe how much I've longed to have you all to myself like this. . . . to show you how much I love you . . .'

And I wanted to be shown – passionately, desperately – to be made to forget the heavy, hasty, masculine hands with their curled hairs that were crushing my crêpe de Chine, to be taken to that wild place I'd glimpsed before and to which I now surely had a perfect right of entry, sealed by the bright new ring on my finger.

Ewan made a valiant attempt to carry me with him. 'Tell

me if I'm hurting you, darling. I wouldn't hurt you for all the world.'

'No – honestly – it's all right.' But inside it hurt, yes – oh, yes – it hurt like the devil in my hopeful, bewildered, ransacked heart, still waiting for the magic which was meant to have taken place, the magic of the wedding veil and the falling blossom.

I tried: heaven knows, I did my best to lose myself in my headlong, herculean lover – to glory in his strength and the extremity of his desire and to rise above the rough heat and the effort and the scent of two striving bodies. But all the time that sordid *creak, creak, creak,* echoed like the scream of some huge and demented bird round the bare walls of our chamber.

In my delirium of frustration I was absolutely certain that the sallow-faced waitress who'd brought our dinner and the gangling wine-waiter and the receptionist and the porter and the grinning old man who polished the windows must all be bent double in the corridor outside our door with their ears pressed to the panelling, hugging themselves and counting.

The bird seemed to circle for such a hell of a time, too, before crashing to earth, exhausted.

'I didn't go on too long, darling, did I? Only, you didn't seem to be sore and I thought, maybe—'

'Not at all, darling, it was wonderful.' Ewan didn't even notice that my voice was stiff with fury. I lay there in that dreadful bed, rigid, naked and plundered – and all the more angry because I couldn't even identify the thief. Was Ewan to blame? He'd done his best to be considerate, as far as I could tell, so perhaps it was my fault: on other occasions, in other places, I'd almost died for the touch of his naked skin against mine and only the thought of the wholeness to come – the perfect unity of marriage – had kept us from going further.

'It gets even better when you're used to it.' Ewan encircled me with an arm and pressed my head, like that of a loyal little wife, down against his shoulder. Yet I wanted to bite that shoulder, to sink my teeth into his hot, salty, post-coital flesh as I'd have bitten an apple, to punish him for leaving me behind. Secrets! So far, married life seemed to contain nothing but secrets!

I guessed I shouldn't ask Ewan why he was so sure it got better. It was the kind of thing men were supposed to understand and new little wives weren't.

It did get better, in fact, the following night in the Lakes, after a bottle and a half of champagne and a glorious stroll by a twilit Windermere; tipsy and emboldened, we undressed together, fumbling seductively with hooks and buttons. Then it slipped a bit in Glasgow, when we quarrelled over who'd left Ewan's slipper wedging open our Lake District window and a great well of tears finally burst from me which had nothing at all to do with lost slippers and everything in the world to do with shattered hopes and trampled expectations.

'Darling – don't. Oh, please don't.' Ewan stood before me, stricken and out of his depth. 'Oh, God – I wish I'd never mentioned the blessed slipper in the first place. It was only one of those wretched, embroidered things, too. I've at least one other pair in the trunks we sent on to Achrossan. Forgive me, darling? Clio? At least look at me and say I'm forgiven.'

We'd made things up by the time the white pepperpots of Achrossan poked into view through their palisade of pines. Lady McLennan had put us in 'Princess Mary's Chamber', a huge room in the oldest and most distant part of the house where, even in June, a log fire blazed in the enormous grate and a dusty card by the bed reminded us not to offer gratuities to the servants. Which Princess Mary had slept there I never discovered; however, her bed was mercifully silent and Ewan, completely at ease in his family home, seemed to draw patience from the timelessness of his surroundings. There, amid the leaping fire-shadows and the resinous scent of the logs, it was possible to imagine myself romantically sated at last.

We spent three weeks at Achrossan, and then, since Ewan had only been given a month's leave of absence, we returned to London and the pretty little house in Cheyne Walk which had been our wedding present from my father. It was an ideal house for two people and I enjoyed it like a doll's house, kissing Ewan goodbye each morning when he left for the office and then spending the day rearranging the furniture and lunching with acquaintances before scurrying home to kiss Ewan again when he returned.

We seemed to lead much the same life as our other married friends and its routine reassured me. Now, surely, I had everything – as much as anyone could have. If you'd asked me to categorize love, I'd have done it with confidence: to be valued, to be esteemed, to be needed, to be one person's particular confidante and to have the power to make and to destroy that person's contentment. I had all of that and, I congratulated myself, the wisdom to recognize my good fortune.

In the mornings, sometimes, I'd watch Ewan shaving, his body still rosy from bed, invigorated by the swift satisfaction of sexual hunger, and feel as proud of that naked back, flushed with well-being, as if I'd given life to it myself. I'd no objection to those early awakenings. Drowsy and languorous, I accepted Ewan's ardour as I'd have welcomed a child at my breast, for the warmth and intimacy of it and the enjoyment of giving: I liked to see him bound away, happy and revitalized, to begin his day. It was only at night that the old resentment sometimes returned – when I wanted to howl and scratch and demand the impossible, even though, for the life of me, I couldn't have told Ewan precisely what it was I wanted so much.

Because we were such a tiny household, we managed with only a cook and a daily woman in addition to my maid and the manservant who'd been with Ewan for years – and even then, we ate in so seldom that our cook turned to ironing shirts out of boredom. But as Margot would have said, faultless shirts are more important than meals, especially when you go out dancing three nights a week, motor down to Easton Broome or some other country house every weekend, attend parties by the dozen, drink rather a lot and generally have a riotous time.

'It's *so* much fun, being married,' I told Alice one day, meeting her by chance outside the Savoy. 'I never realized.'

'I suppose that's why I haven't seen you for so long.'

'Haven't you? Oh dear, I suppose not. Terribly busy, you know.' I dug in my bag for a diary. 'How about lunch on the twenty-third?'

'If you like.' Alice didn't seem to need to write it down. 'How's Ewan?'

'Oh, a perfect duck. Aren't I lucky?'

'You are.'

She looked so dismal that her unhappiness at last penetrated my cloud of serenity. I reached for her hand. 'There'll be someone, Alice. One day, right out of the blue, when you least expect it. And then everything will be perfect.'

She let me clasp her fingers, but didn't return my pressure. 'Is it possible to fall in love twice, do you think? Do we get more than one chance in a lifetime?'

'But of course we do! I mean, Ewan's a darling and if something happened to him I'd be utterly inconsolable, but I dare say if I hadn't married Ewan I'd probably have found someone else to be happy with. If there was only one "right" person for each of us, it would be chaos – like trying to find an empty taxi in the Strand at midnight.'

'Ah,' said Alice and tucked her hand carefully away in her pocket.

I'd never asked Ewan exactly what kind of work he did for his uncle's company, though I was dimly aware that Fraser, Dunsinane & Co. had trading interests which stretched into almost as many corners of the world as those of the Oliver Steam Navigation Company. If a length of cotton was sold for kitchen curtains, it was ten to one that Fraser, Dunsinane had had a hand in it somewhere – and in the bags of flour and sugar on the kitchen shelf, the aluminium stewpan on the stove, the pine boards of the table and the tobacco in Guy's cigarettes. Lady McLennan's brother, old Garnock Fraser, had never been honoured by his grateful country (his second wife had been a thirteen-year-old Malay and Queen Mary disapproved), but he'd had the consolation of seeing his influence grow to a point where the displeasure of Fraser, Dunsinane & Co. could shake a tropical throne, or at the very least remind whoever sat on it where the true power in the land lay.

To be honest, I'd never taken Ewan's accountancy exams very seriously – after all, Achrossan would always be waiting in the background and Sir Cato couldn't live for ever. In fact, I thought it was rather quaintly Scottish of Sir Cato to insist that Ewan should have a profession at all. 'He'll be none the worse of it,' my father-in-law used to growl whenever I teased him.

It wasn't as if Ewan needed a salary: one or other of us always seemed to have enough money for whatever we wanted to do – or as much as any of the other 'young marrieds' with whom we spent most of our time. Six months after our marriage, when Ewan happened to mention he'd finished his examinations and acquired some letters after his name, we opened a bottle of champagne, but I soon forgot the exact details. In the same week, Bertie Headington had somehow managed to persuade an ambassador's daughter to marry him and at the time that seemed a much more incredible achievement.

It all seems rather mindless, looking back, though I don't believe any of us thought the life we led then was *it*, the ultimate purpose of our existence. It was more like an agreeable interlude, a way of passing the time while we waited for something to happen – in our case, for Ewan's father to die and for us to take up the management of Achrossan and produce a string of heirs and become grave and responsible members of society.

Perhaps that was why I was so completely unprepared when, over dinner one evening, Ewan dropped his bombshell.

'By the way—' He helped himself to buttered carrots with his usual precision. 'The old man's offered me Singapore or Shanghai as a posting – and knowing how much you love China, I've told him I'll take Shanghai. Should be fun, don't you think?'

I felt as if I'd been dealt a sharp blow to the head. I dropped the spoon back into the creamed potato, his favourite, and stared at him stupidly. 'You're going to Shanghai?'

'*We're* going to Shanghai. You and me.'

'For how long?'

'For as long as the old man says, I suppose. Not for ever, of course. There's always Achrossan.'

I could hardly believe it: Shanghai – the city of secrets, the city of my birth. My heart still fluttered at the mention of its name, those two sighing syllables, that breath of the scented, whispering Orient. To go back . . . to see it again . . .

At the same time, I was shocked that Ewan should have given his answer without even a word to me. Did I matter so little in his life, when he was the very centre of mine? My bright assurance trembled – and out of my fear there came anger.

'You've told Garnock Fraser we'll go? Without even asking me?' My voice began to claw its way up the sonic scale.

'I thought you'd be delighted! You're always telling me about Shanghai and how happy you were there.'

Involuntarily, my eyes fled to the cormorant screen Stephen Morgan had given me, with its tumultuous, sinuous pursuit. The taste of that river came to me irresistibly, like a long-suppressed thirst, but my fear refused to be assuaged.

'That was years ago – when I was just a child.'

Ewan fished for the serving spoon and doggedly helped himself to potato.

'Actually, I'd no choice in the matter. The Bombay mills are going to be sold because wages have got so high, they're pricing us out of the market. Would you have preferred Singapore?'

'I'd have preferred not to go abroad at all,' I lied. 'Not without being asked.'

'But you're my wife.' Genuine hurt had crept into Ewan's voice. 'Surely you want to go wherever I go.'

'Without even discussing it?'

'There wasn't anything to discuss. It was my uncle's decision.'

Duty to the family. Would it have occurred to me, in Ewan's place, to question Garnock Fraser's decision?

'I thought you'd like to go back to China,' Ewan's eyes were bright with injustice.

'How the devil do you know what I'd like?'

Shoving his plate away, Ewan suddenly lost his temper. 'It

doesn't matter whether you like it or not, because we're going and that's all there is to it.' He took a deep breath and ran a hand through his hair as if an electric current of anger might have stood it on end. Ewan hated losing control of himself: it was a vulgarity he despised. He took a deep breath.

'You'll love it, darling, once we're there.' Reaching across the table, he covered my hand with his own. 'We'll have a much bigger house and as many servants as you want. It'll be a far more comfortable life than if we stayed here. In the office, they reckon Britain's in for a rough time over the next few years.'

There was some truth in that, I knew. Perhaps Ewan was right to have agreed to go abroad. A few months earlier, the keel of the first of Oliver's Heavenly Twins had been laid with great ceremony in a Clydeside yard, but there had been long faces among the directors attending the official luncheon that followed. The building of the two monster ships meant an enormous capital investment, even for a company as large as ours, and we'd always assumed the government would foot part of the bill in return for the ships being built to serve as armed cruisers in the event of a war – as they'd always done with our larger vessels in the past. Yet even now, though the hull of the first Twin was actually rising in her building berth, there was still no sign of the expected subsidy and without it the all-important project was beginning to look distinctly risky.

My father's head seemed to have become silver overnight. 'I know for a fact the French have put up money for this ship the Compagnie Générale's building for the Atlantic run – and yet all I hear from MacDonald and his henchmen is the need for a programme of public works and unemployment insurance. Dammit, our ships *are* unemployment insurance! If the government would only help with the cost, we could employ half Clydeside and put bread in the mouths of these wretched families they're so concerned about. Isn't it better to let a man work at his trade than give him dole money?'

In the spring of 1931, with the government still refusing any subsidy, my Uncle Kit proposed a tigerish solution. 'Warn MacDonald we'll stop work if he isn't prepared to help. We'll bring the yard to a halt. Not a plate will be moved, not a rivet, nothing. Tell the government we can't afford to complete the ship without a subsidy.'

'I doubt if we can complete it.'

'Then go and say that to the Prime Minister.'

My father went. But Ramsay MacDonald was no Baldwin, and his government had just been forced to set up a Committee of Enquiry into its own handling of the nation's finances. Rumours were spreading that the country was well-nigh bankrupt, and Edward Oliver came back empty-handed.

Kit's fury laid bare the resentment that still smouldered between the two brothers. 'My God!' he exploded. 'Father wouldn't have put up with this nonsense for a second. Can't you even sort out a gang of damned socialists?'

My father rounded on him coldly. 'Do you expect me to listen to a man who can't even manage his own daughter?'

My father had struck a raw nerve, for Rose had reacted to the growing national crisis in her own way, regardless of any embarrassment to Kit. Months with the Cadzows seemed to have turned what had started as little more than an affectation on Rose's part into an iron conviction that revolution was inevitable – and that she, Rose, could be its inspiration, if not its Boadicea.

With Leonard Cadzow's son Elliott in tow, she'd become a familiar speaker at rallies of the National Unemployed Workers' Movement among the South Wales miners, standing up before them a bright, slender torch of revolution, her inky hair flying. She could have spoken in Russian and still seduced them – except that to Rose, no sexual coupling ever approached the thrill of seeing grim columns of marchers in the streets and knowing she'd helped to send them there.

Guy, who'd often said that Rose's looks were wasted on a damned radical, found her latest manifestation a thoroughgoing embarrassment. As far as Guy was concerned, the streets were for motoring through and demonstrators had better stay out of his way. At the beginning of that summer he bought a monster eight-litre Bentley sports tourer as long as a house and with two hundred and twenty brake horsepower packed under its bonnet, had it painted livid scarlet and black and topped its radiator – as befitted the heir to the Oliver empire – with a massive silver mascot of the company flag.

In a spirit of lofty amusement, he drove down to Merthyr to watch Rose speak at a rally. While he lunched in a nearby hotel, somebody smashed his windscreen with a brick.

Then, at quite the wrong moment, Margot made newspaper headlines by spending a great deal of money on a Rubens portrait of a woman with a looking-glass: Kit flew into a rage and made her sell it again at the next auction – and that was splashed across the newspapers, too. Margot, icy with humiliation, left for the Côte d'Azur and Kit disappeared for a week into the arms of his lady in St John's Wood.

'Awful for you,' I said to Alice, over lunch at Sovrani's. Our table was placed between two mirror-glass pillars and I could see endless reproductions of Alice's back shrinking smaller and smaller and my face a vague, concerned oval confronting her.

Alice's thousand backs shrugged in unison. 'It's much the same as usual, actually, except this time there are no telephone calls from France.'

'I hate it when people don't speak. And now they're all at it – your father and mine, and then your parents – and, of course, Rose going off and being a revolutionary. Doesn't it worry you sick?'

'What can I do?' Alice glanced up defensively. 'I get on with my life, as well as I can. Did I tell you I'd started to help in a soup kitchen in the East End? Well, I have. And I see people there who have a hundred times more to worry about than I do. They know what suffering really is.'

Alice flung herself back in her brocaded chair and stared fiercely at the ceiling. 'It makes me feel so guilty for being unhappy, and yet—' She thumped her fists on the chair arms. 'I get so *angry*, sometimes, I want to scream.'

She was thinking, I knew, of Stephen Morgan. I wriggled my knees uncomfortably, beginning to wish I hadn't suggested lunch. And yet for me, who had everything, Alice's impotent hunger for another human being held the fascination of an open wound.

'Stephen,' I suggested.

'Not any more.' Alice swallowed hard, leaned over the table and began to crumble a roll.

'I wish I believed you.'

'You can believe me. I know it's all over.'

'How do you know?'

'I know.' She raised her head and gave me one of her careful stares. 'After all – I wasn't the one who brought up his name.'

Two days after my lunch with Alice, my father called at Cheyne Walk in the middle of the afternoon, an unheard-of event. He seemed weary, almost bewildered, and astonishingly old. I wanted to turn my eyes away, embarrassed, as if I'd found him half-dressed on my doorstep, the victim of some sudden delusion.

'Tea?'

'If you aren't going out. I hardly seem to see you these days.'

Absently, he accepted the cup I gave him and circled a spoon in it for some time.

'We've stopped work on No. 683.' No. 683 was the construction number, I knew, of the first of the Heavenly Twins.

'For how long?'

'Who knows?' He passed a hand over his eyes in a gesture I'd never seen before. 'Until we find the money from somewhere to build her, I suppose.'

'From the government?' I held out a plate of biscuits, but he waved them away.

'Not from this government. MacDonald's made that perfectly clear.' He shook his head slowly, like a dreamer. 'Three thousand men walked out of the yard last week and not one of them knows when he'll work again. Three thousand men, Clio – and heaven knows how many more, all over the country, who depended on us.'

'What does Kit say about it?'

My father frowned at his shoes. 'Kit says we'll have to

reduce our overall tonnage. Sell ships. Save money. Put more men out of work.'

'And what happens if we don't build the Twins?'

'We'll lose business to Cunard and the others on the Atlantic run. And we need those Atlantic profits, badly.' Suddenly realizing he'd allowed his tea to grow cold, he set the cup down on the table.

'Let me pour you another.'

He shook his head. 'Don't bother. I'm not really in the mood for tea.'

'There's whisky, if you'd rather.'

He raised a hand in gentle dismissal and let his eyes linger for a moment on my face. 'I just wanted to talk. As I said, I see so little of you nowadays.'

A soft melancholy had stolen into his expression and I felt a pang of guilt for having neglected him. Yet it had never occurred to me that I might be needed.

'Guy's still at home,' I reminded him.

'Guy—' Once more, his hand softly pushed the idea away. 'Guy has his own friends.' He gave a long sigh. 'Besides, it's different now, being here with you. You're grown up, a married woman. You were always such a mystery as a child.'

His sad, apologetic smile explained it all. Now that I was no longer dependent on him, Edward Oliver could lay aside the mask of fatherhood he'd found such a burden. He was weary of trying to be superhuman, of keeping up the trick of costume and light: now he'd brought me the real man, the flawed, indecisive aesthete whom his brother despised.

'Will you go and see our old home, when you reach Shanghai?' He leaned his cheek on one hand. 'Do you remember the firecrackers on your birthday and the stiltwalkers who danced in the garden?'

'And the camellia tree beside the verandah. And my lacquer sedan.'

'And Liu Ling.'

'And Sumei.'

'And Sumei,' he agreed softly.

I saw his eyes become bright with moisture beneath their parchment lids and his frailty completely unnerved me. Like a coward, I exclaimed, 'Good heavens, is that really the time? Ewan will be back at any moment.'

'Of course.' My father pulled himself to his feet.

'You don't have to go.' I felt like a murderer.

'It wouldn't be the same.' He straightened his back and then added in a long sigh, 'Though nothing's the same, somehow, nowadays.'

On the doorstep he asked in distress, 'What's happening to our family, Clio? What's gone wrong with the Olivers?'

'I don't know, darling. I wish there was something I could do.'

His slender fingers clutched at my wrist with the vehemence of the drowning. 'Don't let it spoil your life, that's all – your life and Ewan's. Be happy in your own way, whatever that may be.'

I watched him step into the Rolls, then turn and wave as the door was closed. Suddenly I couldn't wait to set off for Shanghai.

Part Two

Chapter Twelve

EVEN TODAY, crossing the concrete apron between my aircraft and the stark halls of the Shanghai terminal building, I seem to sniff again that strange and unsettling aroma, at once sweet and acrid, that is the breath of the world's most populous city. The airport lies on its outskirts. In 1931, as Ewan and I stepped gingerly from our ship's launch into the heart of Shanghai, the smell was unmissable. In those days, the city was still the 'Whore of the Orient' – a whore who cooked garlic and ginger in her teeming lanes, offered her smoky streets to trolleybuses and rickshaws and shoving, swarming humanity, tipped her refuse heedlessly into creeks and rivers and strutted forth after dark in search of excitement, drenched in the headiest of French perfumes.

And yet, walking through it now, I can see that somehow Shanghai has kept its old swagger, its street-savvy, its winking fairy lights – and that urgent pulse throbbing visibly below the thinnest of skins. There's no gentleness about this city, such as you might find in Beijing. Shanghai is an unsparing place, full of dark, quick people running hard in order to keep up with the rest. *Change your money? You English? I want to speak English!*

A traffic policeman leaves his point duty in the middle of Fuzhou Road to chat to me and immediately a hopeful crowd collects. *London Bridge is fall-ing down!* Maybe it is – I've lost track of when I saw it last.

A T-shirt seller tells me he's made the equivalent of £20,000 in twelve months. Who needs a university degree and six hundred a year? No one here sits casually on the pavement's edge, a telephone to one ear, tied by its cable to the nearest shop, as they do in Beijing. I look in vain for the old men with patient eyes, nursing their screwtop jars of green tea, or children like those in the park at Coal Hill, cradling ducklings between their palms and sliding, laughing, down the marble slabs at the side of the pavilion steps.

And there don't seem to be so many bicycle parks. Here, they tell me, bicycle theft is viewed with extra contempt: in this new, progressive China, the Shanghainese have rediscovered how to steal cars.

Onward, upward, bigger, richer – where did they hide, I wonder, when Mao's word was law and the common good was king?

When Ewan and I arrived here in 1931, it was August – hot and humid enough to send a trickle of sweat down the cheek of the red-turbaned Sikh policeman at the customs jetty gate. Long before we disembarked, I stood at the ship's rail, gazing across an untidy tangle of junks and sampans to the Bund, that crescent of ponderous stone buildings which seem to rise so oddly from the tumultuous life at their feet – a row of granite Canutes, lapped by a restless tide. This was journey's end, the final line of the old spell that ran *Colombo, Penang, Singapore, Hong Kong* – a spell that had turned our ship's sun-scorched deck to shimmering quicksilver and the blue China Sea to mustard where it swallowed the flood of the Yangtze. What would it make of us, of Ewan and me, this alchemist city?

'My God, is it always as hot as this?' At my side, Ewan looked unusually crumpled in his light flannel suit.

'It gets bitterly cold in winter – you'll see. In the meantime, why don't you have some suits made up here in silk or cotton, something light? That's what everyone else does.'

'Is it?' Ewan tapped his fingers irritably on the rail while I cursed myself silently for my impulsiveness. I'd noticed that frown once or twice before on our passage east, when I'd become more than usually carried away in describing our house in Shanghai and Liu Ling and the tulip trees and windmill palms, and birthdays and firecrackers, and old men who made spun-sugar monkeys on street corners for the enchantment of passing children. Perhaps the alchemist's spell was already at work. In England Ewan had considered it amusingly exotic to have a wife born in Shanghai. Now it seemed to annoy him that I didn't feel as alien here as he did, but almost like a returned exile. I'd caught him watching me, sometimes, with a doubtful expression, as if he suspected some shameful un-Britishness might have crept into my blood like a tropical disease.

For my father's sake – and for my own, too – I blessed the instinct which had kept me from telling Ewan about Sumei or Gardener's Little Sister.

A year earlier, my father's old friend Sir Victor Sassoon had opened his Cathay Hotel on the corner of the Bund and Nanking Road, by common consent the most sumptuous hostelry in the Far East, as lavish and elegant as anything in Vienna or Paris. After our little doll's house in Cheyne Walk, Ewan and I revelled for a month in the cool spaciousness of its marble halls while we searched for somewhere suitable to live. Every day, Ewan would leave for his office, and I'd go off to view possible houses, returning in the heat of the afternoon, sticky and footsore, to plunge into a silver-appointed bath filled with purified well-water from the outskirts of the city.

Ewan loved the Cathay: I think he saw it, in all its bronze and cream marble solemnity and clubbish atmosphere, as a monument to the fact that some £300 million in British funds was currently tied up in China, two-thirds of it in Shanghai itself. Sir Victor Sassoon, for one, had flung himself into local property and finance as if Shanghai offered a chance of profit unequalled anywhere else in the world. Like him, Oliver's, Jardine Matheson & Co. and Ewan's own company, Fraser, Dunsinane, had trusted firmly in the city's endless riches and so far they'd all been proved right. Even when the Japanese marched into Manchuria in the north of China a month after our arrival in Shanghai, it did no more than bring nervous investors scuttling for the shelter of the foreign concessions, driving up the value of buildings and land even further.

The invasion was still the main topic of conversation when

we had dinner with Victor Sassoon a fortnight later in his penthouse on top of the hotel.

'In my opinion,' he declared, 'the Japanese army simply sees this Manchurian business as a way of flexing its muscles. The generals want to show their people at home they can make Japan a force to be reckoned with.'

'Though some people think Manchuria's only the first step.' Ewan had been canvassing opinion in the business community. 'Tony Keswick told me he wouldn't be surprised if the Japs tried to bite off another piece of China in a year or so.'

Victor Sassoon's long, Semitic features assembled themselves into an elegant smile. 'Maybe so – though I don't see him scrambling to move Jardine Matheson's assets out of Shanghai.'

Noiselessly, members of Victor's staff began to move behind our chairs, removing the delicate porcelain bowls which had held our caviar and bringing an exquisite terrine of duckling.

'And now, of course,' Victor went on, 'the Chinese are doing their best to make life difficult for the Japanese community here in Shanghai. This boycott they've organized is closing down Japanese shops and factories in Hongkew at the rate of a dozen a day.'

'Hongkew's just across the Garden Bridge from here,' I told Ewan. 'It's so full of Japanese, it's known as "Little Tokyo".'

'I know that,' he hissed. 'For goodness' sake, Clio, I do have a map.'

'You must have seen all the cargo piled up on the wharves.' Tactfully, Victor Sassoon ignored the interruption. 'There are hundreds of thousands of tons of it now, left to rot because the Chinese banks won't honour any Japanese bills of lading. Only last week, there was a report in the *News* about pickets attacking people boarding a ship for Nagasaki and pitching them into the river.'

'I've seen the posters,' I said. '"Kill All The Japanese".'

'Doesn't involve the foreign settlements, though.' Ewan sliced precisely into his terrine.

Across the table, Victor Sassoon nodded thoughtfully. 'And so far, it hardly amounts to an invitation to invade.'

We'd long since decided the safest – and by far the pleasantest – place for us to live was among the tree-lined streets of the French Concession. This was the French-controlled area of Shanghai stretching back from the waterfront alongside the International Settlement – which, by the same unique diplomatic balancing act, was officially under British and American jurisdiction. After inspecting a great many houses, we settled at last on a large, recently built villa near the French Park with a vaguely Tudor air to it and a thicket of rhododendrons and camphor bushes packed into its garden. I'd have liked a more open outlook, but space was at a premium now in central Shanghai and Ewan had dismissed the idea of living far out on Bubbling Well Road or the Avenue Foch.

'After all,' he pointed out reasonably, 'one day you'll have Achrossan, with whole hillsides to look out on. Then you can have as much lawn as you want – and flowerbeds and pergolas as far as the eye can see. That's a promise,' he added with a grin.

I suppose I'd been trying to resurrect the past. Ever since I'd accepted that we were bound for Shanghai, I'd nursed a secret hope of finding my old home, with its verandah and its tulip trees, empty and available for us. But our Eurasian house-agent soon made it clear there was no chance of this. The place had passed into other, less innocent hands.

'Green Society boss lives there now,' he warned. 'Not top boss, but one of the others.'

'What on earth's the Green Society?' Ewan was frowning again – here was yet another fact to learn about this extraordinary city.

'You never hear of Du Yuesheng?' The agent looked up in disbelief. 'He's the boss of all the Greens. Very powerful man.'

'You mean he's a gangster?' Ewan looked startled.

The agent shook his head. 'I never said gangster.' He glanced towards the half-open door of his office. 'Maybe sometime, nobody could buy or sell opium without a say-so from Du Yuesheng, but now he's a member of the French Municipal Council and other men do the work for him. The chief policemen are his friends. Bankers, too. *Taipans*, heads of companies. Everyone gives favour for favour here, right down to the sampan-men and the officers on the customs jetty. Like Freemasons in England, I think.'

'Hardly.' Ewan drew in his chin. 'I don't believe even Masons buy and sell opium.'

'Things are different in Shanghai.' Proudly, the agent squared his shoulders. 'Here you can buy and sell policemen.'

Yet even if we couldn't live in it, my old home called me to visit it again and its garden where I'd once held a funeral for a shrew, trying to learn more about love and death. One day, while Ewan was in his office, several floors up in one of the stalwart stone buildings of the Bund, I went by rickshaw to spy on the house which still sometimes figured in my dreams.

I'd forgotten how isolated a life I'd lived there, as solitary as a princess behind our whitewashed walls. The iron gates were as tightly shut as ever. Only the upper windows of the house were visible, small-paned under the overhanging eaves, their woodwork picked out in the ubiquitous Chinese shade of warm clove-brown. Standing up perilously in my rickshaw, I could see the first few inches of the verandah roof and even the topmost leaves of our old camellia – but the tulip trees had certainly gone. No doubt they'd grown too big for the garden, or perhaps they'd offered too much cover for assassins and would-be kidnappers.

Two burly Chinese, lounging by the gate, began to push themselves forward from the walls and take a rather menacing interest in me. Chastened, I told the rickshaw puller to take me back to the safety of the Avenue Joffre.

When I mentioned at cocktail time what I'd seen, Ewan immediately became concerned.

'For goodness' sake, Clio, you mustn't go wandering off on your own like that! These men are criminals – they're dangerous, even if they do drive around in Cadillacs and sit on the local council. Anywhere but Shanghai, the blighters would be behind bars.'

Dutifully, I let the subject drop. On the whole, I found it harder than Ewan to condemn the subtle shades of patronage and obligation by which the Orient arranged its affairs. He'd been brought up to recognize only good and bad, black and white, virtue and villainy – and with dogged rectitude, he somehow managed to fit everything he came across into one of these categories.

For instance, he simply refused to believe that a system of 'squeeze' governed the daily shopping of our own household, just as it did every other transaction in Shanghai. Yet I knew perfectly well that by ancient custom, the tailor who came to measure Ewan for a new suit paid 'squeeze', or commission, to our Number One boy and simply added the sum to Ewan's bill. The flower-seller paid our porter for letting him in to deliver his blooms; the provision-merchant paid our cook for giving him our trade and our cook paid our Number One for being allowed to keep his job. This pyramid of 'squeeze' was ultimately added to all our bills, though so invisibly that Ewan was able to insist that *our* staff, unlike every other mortal in the city, were too high-principled to indulge in such things. Yet it seemed quite fair to me that in return for his substantial income, our Number One boy kept the whole time-hallowed system of cheating and bribery within bounds.

'That seems reasonable,' Ewan would say, carefully checking a bill presented by a Chinese. 'Thank you, Mr Chen, that'a a very fair price.'

And the tradesman would bow and smile over his padded accounts and praise Ewan's shrewdness. No doubt he was thinking of the sum he himself would later have to pay to the agents of Du Yuesheng, to be allowed to continue in business.

None of this struck me as remotely strange, so perhaps Ewan was right to suspect me of harbouring un-British standards. I suppose I must have been slipping quite rapidly back into the ways of Shanghai, since Alice's first letter from London, which reached me two months after our arrival in China, felt like the touch of a forgotten hand on my shoulder, quite startling and unexpected.

'Things are becoming pretty grim here,' she reported. 'Everyone's very tight-lipped and trying not to show it – and the newspapers are utterly dismal.'

We'd already heard, shortly after leaving London, that Ramsay MacDonald had resigned as prime minister and, amid scenes of high drama, had combined with the Conservatives to form a National government. It was the only way, he'd declared, of fighting the deepening slump which had gripped the country. Two months later, the British people apparently decided he was right and voted by a huge majority to continue the arrangement – yet it seemed there was still no money to spare for the building of ships.

'All the government can suggest is that Oliver's should join up with Cunard or White Star into one single company, so there wouldn't be such competition for profits. I needn't tell you,' added Alice, 'what Papa said to *that*.'

I hadn't expected her to write so soon, in view of the reserve which had grown up between us during the past year. But as I read her letter I realized she'd written it to herself as much as to me. I was simply an excuse for an outpouring of frustration which it hurt her to contain. I was eight thousand miles away, a memory of a cousin, a postbox for Alice's fretfulness.

'Mama came back from the south of France, having "gone sunburn" in the most fashionable way – you'd never guess she was forty-five in July. She's brought absolute *trunkloads* of clothes from Patou – coats dripping with astrakhan and little turban hats with cock's feathers – which is usually a sign she's about to declare war on the human race, or at least on Papa. She still hasn't forgiven him for the Rubens, I'm afraid.'

I raised my eyes from Alice's letter in time to see a scarlet-painted rickshaw fly past, its double headlamps slicing the dusk ahead and another lantern swinging between its wheels – a popular singsong girl dashing between engagements, her body-guard pounding in her wake. With an effort, I dragged myself back to Alice's news.

'Grandmother Kate has been ill, I'm afraid.'

Certainly, it had struck me that I hadn't had a letter from

Kate for some time, but I'd simply put that down to her being busier than usual. It wasn't like Kate to be unwell.

'The doctor says her heart is weak,' Alice continued. 'He told her she ought to rest, but as soon as he'd gone she insisted on coming down to the East End to see my soup kitchen in action.'

I couldn't help smiling: to Kate Oliver, defiance had been the elixir of life. Against the dark panes of my Shanghai windows I summoned up an image of my grandmother as I'd last seen her, when Ewan and I went to say our goodbyes. As soon as he'd left the room, sent off to see what had happened to the sherry she'd ordered, Kate had leaned conspiratorially towards me.

'So different,' she declared. 'He's so different from the Oliver men – by which, of course, I mean the *Gaunt* men, since Matthew was only ever an Oliver in his head.' She tapped her temple with a finger. 'Hard men to live with, both of them.. Eyes set on the stars and a mortal horror of being tied down.'

I waited, holding my breath. I knew Margot had always suspected that Grandmother Kate had been Adam Gaunt's mistress before marrying his son and I wondered if now, at last, Kate might be about to hint at the truth.

But the moment passed and she glanced in the direction of the drawing-room door. 'Ewan isn't like that. He wants everything exactly the same from one day to the next, just as it always has been.' She put her head on one side, like a cockatoo under a crest of white hair. 'You'll do well enough together, provided *you* never start this itching for the stars. You're a Gaunt too, remember.'

I'd never thought of the Gaunts in connection with myself. After all, I was a woman: in my motherless, Chinese-influenced childhood I'd been brought up to believe it was a husband's role to stand firm on his principles and a wife's to wind herself round him like ivy on an oak, shaping her ambitions to his. Ewan certainly thought so – and even Margot, the most independent woman I knew, returned periodically, like a circling comet, to her husband's side.

I looked round guiltily when Ewan returned. The light from Kate's table-lamp seemed to glow about him like a halo.

'They were about to decant a new bottle from the cellar. I told them just to bring it as it was.' Kate's ancient butler padded in Ewan's wake, a naked bottle on his tray and an expression of deep mortification on his face.

Kate hardly touched the sherry which Ewan poured. 'How long will you stay in China?'

Obediently, Ewan craned forward to shout into her ear. 'My uncle expects us to stay for five years before coming home. And then – well, we'll have to see what happens next.'

Once or twice after that, I noticed Kate watching us – wondering, perhaps, if she, already eighty-five years old, would be alive to welcome us home again. And now, according to Alice, Kate had been told to rest, to save that fierce heart which had been bruised by so many family wars.

'As for Stephen—' Here Alice's writing changed, as if she'd laid down her pen for a moment and then taken it up again with determination. 'As for Stephen – I think I've only seen him once in the past two months, when Harry Dunstanheugh (Lord Rockall's eldest, do you remember?) took me down to Calshot for a flying display and Stephen was there with a friend and a couple of girls. And just to prove I'm absolutely over him, I swear *I didn't mind in the least* and introduced him to Harry without a twinge.' Alice's underlining had been so vehement that her pen-nib had split apart, leaving a broad, passionate double track across the page.

At that moment, Ewan arrived home from his office.

'Oh, do get a move on, darling! We're supposed to be at the Cathay at eight for drinks and dinner, remember?' He began to loosen his tie as he crossed the room and his valet, running behind, neatly relieved him of his jacket and then swept up the discarded tie without breaking step. 'If we'd been going straight to the Lyceum at nine-thirty it wouldn't matter, but as things are—'

Thoughts of Britain and grimness fled from my mind. Already, I'd discovered that if one chose, life in Shanghai could be a continuous party, an endless parade of bunting and tinsel, a constant banquet at someone else's expense. If it wasn't a diplomatic event (the Fourth of July – ice cream and cakes in the shape of the Stars and Stripes) or a charity ball (dance partners auctioned off to the highest bidder), then it was bound to be a circus party, or a shipwreck party, or a children's flower party arranged by the great ringmaster of Shanghai, Sir Victor Sassoon.

To a certain 'set' in the city – the Country Club crowd, the diplomats, the bankers and the *taipans* of the various companies – Victor Sassoon was a bountiful host, though privately, I knew, Ewan wasn't entirely an admirer. 'Too much Baghdad, if you see what I mean, and not enough Harrow.' Yet he never suggested we refuse an invitation – few people did if they wanted to be in the social swim – and after the first few tentative weeks Ewan had thrown himself enthusiastically into the frantic whirlpool of European life in Shanghai. As Garnock Fraser's nephew he occupied an honoured lunchtime place at the hundred-foot bar of the Shanghai Club; in off-duty hours he hacked round the golf course, trailed at a safe distance by a Chinese caddy, and when golf palled, there was always the race course.

Fraser, Dunsinane & Co., like many other firms, kept a handful of sturdy, hard-mouthed little Mongolian ponies at the Shanghai Race Club to run under company colours; and during the spring and autumn ten-day race meetings, business in the city more or less closed down at eleven a.m., as *le tout Shanghai* converged on the race course to cheer on their favourites.

The races were followed by dinners and parties and visits to nightclubs like Ciro's, where we could dance, if we liked, until dawn. For single, unattached men – or men who could shake off their wives – there were jazz cabarets and countless brothels, where 'Olga' or 'Li' paraded naked on the tables, swinging their hennaed hair, before offering their customers cocaine and twenty dollars' worth of whatever diversion their fantasies suggested.

Shanghai was every bit as much a city of 'whatever you want' as it had been a decade earlier, when my father had indulged his taste for young girls – at least, as far as the foreign community was concerned. I remember hearing at one party of a drunken young Englishman thrown out of a cabaret for tossing a dollar (heated with a cigarette) under the buttocks of a dancer who specialized in picking up coins with the lips of her vagina. Later, disgusted, I watched the story make its way round the room, accompanied by shrieks of brassy laughter from both sexes.

The atmosphere of sensual adventure was as pervasive as the petrol fumes in the streets: what else, ran the logic, was Shanghai for? As we stumbled to bed at four in the morning, Ewan and I would laugh hysterically at the latest thinly veiled offer which had come with a fatherly pat on my knee from an eminent banker or diplomat.

'You never know,' Ewan would remind me, struggling to control his mirth. 'You might be glad of a fur coat in a month or two.'

At that time, for us, it was all the most innocent fun. We were young, we were sophisticated and Shanghai, the most fascinating city in the world, was at our feet. More than that, we had each other. In the mornings I could still watch Ewan shave, taking a proprietorial pride in the strong column of his neck and the capable squareness of the fingers which held down his cheek for the razor.

'Imagine, if I hadn't been outside your window, that night on the *Concordia*,' he used to say. 'Suppose it had been someone else and we'd never met.'

'Imagine how unhappy we'd both be now.'

'Gosh, yes.'

'Love you, darling.'

'Mmm – me too.'

'We don't want babies yet, do we?' It was early one evening and Ewan and I were changing to go out. In the afternoon I'd noticed a flock of amahs airing their charges in Jessfield Park and the scene had instantly carried me back to the simple sanctuary of my own nursery and to memories of Liu Ling.

'Babies? Good Lord, no!' Ewan's hands dropped from his

collar-stud and he peered at me in the mirror. 'Why? You aren't pregnant are you?' Reassured, he tugged down the front of his shirt. 'There'll be plenty of time for that sort of thing when we go home.' He laughed and reached over to ruffle my hair. 'We can't have the heir to Achrossan born out here among the heathen, after all.'

It was just as if he'd slapped me. Suddenly hurt beyond words, I watched him fasten his cufflinks. *I'd* been born in Shanghai, after all, among the 'heathen' he despised. What secret depravity did he think it had seeded in me, this city which was good enough to make money in and enjoy oneself in, but not to be born in?

I stood there, rigid, a necklace dangling from my fingers, suddenly aware of the utter impossibility of explaining in any language Ewan would understand that it was *my* city he was talking of. It wasn't his city, or Victor Sassoon's and certainly not the ex-pats' who paraded the ballroom of the Cathay Hotel, dressed up as birds of paradise, or listened to the self-important oompah of the band on the consulate lawn.

We can't have the heir to Achrossan born out here among the heathen.

Poor Ewan, he hadn't realized what he was saying – and, because I was sure I loved him and wanted to be loyal to him, I tried to forget the remark. Yet the words refused to fade or to mellow, until in the days that followed I found myself thinking of little else. I remembered my governess's horrified reaction to my childish question 'Am I a barbarian? If I'm not Chinese, then I must be a foreign devil of some kind.' *Good gracious, you're English, child, and very fortunate to be so!* No doubt she could have said American, or French, or German – anything but Chinese.

Our friends clearly shared her opinion. Now, at parties, I'd find myself drawing apart from the crowd, listening to the general chatter, but not contributing to it. I became conscious of a gradual awakening from a self-indulgent dream which had filled my head as thickly as opium fumes ever since we'd arrived. As I raised my eyes, I saw for the first time that there was another Shanghai beyond the lights and the music, a city where children of eight were sold to chromium-plate workshops, to be locked all day in a dark hell of metal-dust and din – and where the Corpse Collecting Society filled its carts each morning with the frozen bodies of the homeless. I saw whole families crammed into damp, urine-smelling huts, their meagre bodies barely covered by our own cast-off garments, long fallen into rags, and their short lives sustained by rice gruel and a handful of vegetables.

What was needed, the bankers' wives would say briskly, was a charity event here, a new infant school there – *noblesse oblige*, after all, and let's face it, some of the Chinese are quite *awful* to their own. They thought I was a trifle odd, these women: sometimes, in my enthusiasm, I said 'us' instead of 'them'. But I was certain now that this was my city, too. I had people of my own here: and, no matter how disloyal I felt to Ewan, the question of what had happened to Liu Ling and her family had begun to obsess me.

Finding myself at dinner next to the director of our consular police, I plagued him with questions until Ewan came to his rescue. But I'd already rushed down to Siccawei Creek, only to find it almost entirely filled in and its community of sampans long since scattered to the waters. Enquiries at the American consulate had also drawn a blank: whichever official Liu Ling had worked for near the Avenue Joffre had long since left for home or another posting.

In desperation, I enlisted the help of our Number One boy – who, I should explain, was a dignified gentleman in his forties who padded about our home in a long, immaculately pressed gown and silk slippers. When I'd finished my story he scrutinized me for a moment in grave silence. I knew it disturbed him to work for a Mississi who could speak a certain amount – and understand even more – of the Shanghai dialect. (Though I'd only spoken Chinese once in Ewan's hearing, when he stared at me in such alarm that I never did it again. 'Boy,' Ewan would say in pidgin at the door of a friend, 'Master just now have got, no have got?' and the servant would shake his head, and agree, 'Yes, no have got,' which to Ewan seemed a perfectly sensible conversation.)

My Number One boy, having considered this new eccentricity of his Mississi, at last gave a resigned little bow. 'I will see what can be done,' he told me in Chinese. 'I will ask my friends in the city.'

Two weeks passed and I began to suspect I'd been put off in the usual polite oriental manner. Then one afternoon our Number One stepped out of the shadows in the hallway as I returned from buying warm gloves in the Avenue Joffre. He held out a small rectangle of paper with something written on it in Chinese characters.

'Mississi, this woman worked for your father, a long time ago. She lives in Chapei, across the bridge.' He handed me the square of paper, bowed and retreated with the air of a conjuror who'd just pulled out of his hat a particularly handsome rabbit.

I thrust the scrap of paper into my pocket. Later on, alone, I could decide how best to make use of it; in the meantime there was a temporary distraction, a letter from Guy, on the drawing-room table.

As usual, my brother had compressed all his news into two sides of a single page – the fact that the first Twin was still at a standstill in her Clydeside yard, that Guy himself had been quite outrageously arrested and fined for 'furious driving' and that Margot had moved out of Kit's house in Belgrave Square and into a suite at the Savoy. Guy's longest comment was a complaint about Stephen Morgan.

'The fellow's a bloody nuisance, as usual. He's got some bee in his bonnet about Oliver's starting an air passenger company instead of building bigger ships and he won't let it alone. All he has to do, I told him, is stick to the job he's paid for and leave policy to the Oliver directors. Aeroplanes – imagine it! Where does he get these ideas?'

I'd wondered much the same when Stephen gave me the antique screen, with its fish and its sinuous cormorant. It was stored in London with the rest of our furniture and I hoped it hadn't come to any harm. I'd have liked to bring it with me, but as Ewan pointed out, it would have been madness to drag it all the way back to China. 'There must be any number of the things out there,' he'd assured me. But, in fact, I'd never seen one the same – not precisely the same as Stephen's.

Squeezed along the bottom of the paper under Guy's flamboyant signature was a minuscule PS. 'Keep it under your hat, but I've just heard Father's to become a viscount and Kit's getting his K at last. Bloody government,' he'd scribbled underneath. 'What we need is cash to finish the ship.'

Absorbed in my coming mission to Chapei, I only remembered to give Ewan Guy's news at breakfast the following morning.

'A viscount?' Ewan glanced up from his toast and marmalade. 'About time, I must say. What will that make you?'

'An honourable, I suppose.'

'Ah.' With a nod, Ewan returned to his breakfast. 'Not that you aren't perfect the way you are, of course, darling.' He licked marmalade from his thumb with schoolboy relish. 'What are you planning to do today?'

'I thought I'd go round to Marion Trenchard's and see if she needs any help with her charity dinner.' This was perfectly true. What I didn't add was that after Marion's, I intended to make my way into the dense mass of streets across the Garden Bridge in pursuit of the address I'd been given.

'Fine,' said Ewan. 'I'll see you at six.'

I didn't take our car and its driver – not that I was trying to hide my mission from Ewan in any way. Naturally, I meant to explain it all – when the time was right – and to try to make him understand why I simply had to find Liu Ling and some trace of my childhood. Yet I still felt uneasy as I told the driver to leave me near our consulate on the Bund, where I could look round for a likely rickshaw.

In the end I opted for a pedicab, a sort of tricycle affair with a hooded seat for its passenger, which took me quite swiftly over the bridge towards the rows of red-brick houses round the famous Hongkew market. In normal times, the smells and sounds of the huge, five-storey building enveloped it in its own pungent, clamorous atmosphere and announced it downwind with a sharp scent of oranges mixed with the honeyed sweetness of melons, with the comforting, nutty perfume of warm loaves and the cooing of pigeons, all overlaid with the salt tang of fish and squid hauled fresh from their tank in a writhing knot. Now, thanks to the boycott, the market had a sad and derelict air. An elderly Japanese dragging a handcart of vegetables towards the entrance leaned on his shafts for a moment to watch me pass, his face a mask of suspicion.

Somewhere to the north – only the inhabitants could have said exactly where – the streets ceased to be the province of the Japanese and became the tangle of lanes and grim factories which made up the Chinese district of Chapei. Near the smoky marshalling yards of the North Railway Station, my pedicab man halted for a consultation. I held out my paper again and after tracing the Chinese characters carefully with a finger, he moved perhaps a hundred yards further down the street, spat, and indicated the narrow mouth of a lane leading off to the right. Beyond that, he told me, he'd never ventured. I'd have to ask.

I paid the man and watched him pedal away into the stream of handcarts and trudging pedestrians which flowed endlessly towards the surging thoroughfares of the city. Already, passers-by were watching me curiously – a European lady alone and on foot, so far from her own kind. An old man carrying two white ducks crushed like cushions in a bamboo cage peered into my face with almost invisible eyes; a mop-headed infant, hidden among the blue-trousered knees, reached out to feel the fabric of my skirt, frightening us both. I showed my scrap of paper to a woman who might have been the child's grandmother. She frowned over the Chinese characters, her lips moving silently, and then pointed down the lane, to where an upper storey jutted further forward than the others.

'There,' she said.

The alley was dark, and cluttered with shop signs, galvanized buckets and rows of preserved fish, twisted like old sandals, set out on tables for sale. Overhead, poles of washing slumped in the narrow space between opposing balconies, while below, in the shadows, a man threw rice-cakes on a griddle to fry, a pile of brazier coal dribbling out among the feet of his customers.

A hardware shop occupied the lower floor of the building

I'd been shown, hung about with bamboo sieves and filled with towers of enamel bowls which rose unsteadily like ribbed worms among the fat clay steamers. The balcony above had been part-glazed with tall latticed windows: in the open section a parrot hunched on its perch, tied by one foot, and what looked like a bedcover swung in the oily smoke of the rice-cake man's brazier.

The hardware-seller scuttled out at once and began to praise his stock in a shrill stream of Shanghainese, laying hold of my arm to pull me inside. I shook him off and without allowing myself time to consider what I was doing, plunged into the narrow passage beside the shop, where a flight of steep and rickety stairs seemed to lead to the upper floor.

She must have heard me coming. Even if the sensation I'd caused in the alleyway hadn't already given notice of my arrival, her staircase groaned like nothing on earth. She was waiting at the entrance to her single room – grey, round-shouldered and stooping, wearing loose trousers and a padded blue cotton jacket fastened by toggles at one side. But what drew my eye, just as surely as they'd done in the days of my childhood, were the tiny, crippled stumps on which she stood, their mutilation hidden by a pair of obscenely small black slippers.

It wasn't Liu Ling after all, but Sumei.

Chapter Thirteen

FOR ALMOST half an hour Sumei hid behind a blank stare and evasive politeness. We sat in her room above the hardware shop, she on her simple bed against one wall, I on a wooden chair against another. Flaked green paint covered the walls as far as the windowsills and above that the surface was bare and stained. A wooden cupboard stood in a corner, a grim witness to our battle of wills, and a small, smoky metal stove squatted on the floor between us, the elbow of its chimney supported on bricks. The only feminine articles in the room were a thin, folded red and white quilt on the bed and a small white lace cloth on the table by the cupboard.

For thirty minutes I talked to Sumei of the two years we'd spent under the same roof, while she observed me round her dusty tin chimney as if we were complete strangers. Then all at once, she lifted her head triumphantly.

'You speak Chinese like a cargo lumper.'.

'That's how I learned it from Liu Ling.'

Sumei's minnow-shaped eyes glittered and the tip of her nose turned under as she sneered. 'That doesn't surprise me at all. Can a monkey teach an oriole to sing?'

The cruelty of the sneer startled me as much as her sharpness. As a child, I'd never suspected her of disliking Liu Ling. Now she wrinkled her nose fastidiously, as if a sour smell had drifted through her casement.

'Sampan people,' she said. 'Hardly suitable companions for a *taipan*'s child.'

'Sumei, I have to find Liu Ling. Do you know where she might be living now?'

Sumei glared at me and tugged back her thick hair, stranded with white. I noticed she was still vain enough to fasten it with a silver metal clasp.

'Why should you care about Liu Ling? She has a husband and a son to support her. What do I have?'

I was unable to stifle a gasp of pleasure. Liu Ling must have married after we left Shanghai.

'So you know where she lives? You've seen her recently?'

Sumei straightened her back, offended. 'I haven't set eyes on her since I left your house. I don't keep company with sampan people.'

'Then how do you know about her son?'

'Because she used to run off to see him, sometimes, when she was supposed to be looking after you. At night, when you were asleep. He was a year or two older than you, her son, but no one was supposed to know.' Sumei tilted her chin in satisfaction. 'But *I* knew.'

I stared at her, stunned. 'You mean, all the time Liu Ling was with us, she had a son of her own – and a husband – and she couldn't live with them?'

'Naturally. How could she have done her work, otherwise?'

'But where did they live, then?'

'With the rest.' Sumei wriggled her shoulders in distaste. 'In the sampan, on the creek.'

My mind flew back to the huddle of yellow-brown bodies under the curved roof of the sampan – grizzled heads and infant mops together, living like one many-limbed, many-mouthed organism among the cooking pots and the fluttering washing. Like a princess, I'd condescended to visit, smug in my absolute ownership of Liu Ling. And all the time, one of those round-faced toddlers was the dearest thing in the world to her and she couldn't show it.

Sumei had been watching my reaction and growing resentful.

'Why should Liu Ling have a son?' she demanded. 'What use was a child to her? Now, if I'd had a son—'

I already knew the rest. The daughter of a well-to-do family, Sumei had been given in marriage to the eldest son of a wealthy house. But though several years passed, no children were born and when Sumei's husband died of drinking bad water, she was left a childless widow, despised by her mother-in-law and with no status in her husband's home.

They sent her back to the house of her birth; but her parents had died and the family had fallen on hard times. Sumei, the extra mouth, was the first to be disposed of, traded off to my father as a concubine for as long as he cared to keep her.

He'd given her money when we left Shanghai, but the cash had obviously long since disappeared, no doubt wasted on finery and wild business speculation. The shop below, said Sumei, was her brother's: she was dependent on the charity of his family. 'If only I'd had a son!'

Now she looked far older than her years, though her dainty hauteur remained. She shuffled out to the head of the stairs with me as I left.

'Your father could have taken me to England. He had no wife in those days. He could have married me.'

'He still talks about you.' Yet it was the childlike face of the young Sumei that my father recalled, not the bowed shoulders and pinched features which had lain in wait. Somehow, she'd managed to counterfeit that combination of beauty and unawareness which always aroused him – as it still did, if Guy's accounts were true of the various typing girls who'd left Oliver's employment with glowing references and musquash coats. Yet I'd always thought of my father as an aesthete, not a lecher. He must have hated the sordid manoeuvrings necessary to indulge his taste in England, so different from the delicate sensuality which had entranced him in China.

Sumei pointed proudly to her tiny four-inch slippers – no sampan woman, she.

'Your father liked me for being a lady,' she said, 'and also for this.' She touched her crotch. 'The foot-binding made us strong here, you see, to please our husbands.'

Her face lost its light and became hard and old. 'In England

I'd have had a son. Then I'd have had a daughter-in-law of my own to bow to me and bring me sweet pastries.'

I'd almost reached the bottom of the stairs when she called after me, 'She had a brother, your sampan woman, didn't she? A brother who worked for the English newspaper?'

'Of course! So she did! Oh, thank you so much, Sumei.' But she'd already gone; I could hear the scrape of her slippers as she hobbled back to her stove.

'You look tired,' Ewan told me that evening. 'You shouldn't go wearing yourself out on these committees of Marion Trenchard's.'

It took me a couple of moments to remember where I was supposed to have been. 'I went to explore a few shops afterwards.'

'Look—' Ewan paused in the act of checking his bow tie in the mirror. 'Why don't I go off on my own to this party at the club and leave you to have a quiet evening at home? You could have a nice, relaxing bath and then an omelette in bed. Ten to one this "do" will be such a bore I'll be back in half an hour, anyway.'

I glanced up sharply – and then immediately felt ashamed of myself. This was what came of secret visits and the lies they bred. Guilt at having deceived Ewan had translated itself into suspicion – suspicion of Ewan, the most straightforward, the most transparent of creatures! Good heavens, I could even tell from Ewan's face when he'd bought my birthday present – he wore an expression of such comical stealth, such happy, wholesome expectancy, that it took all my acting skills to pretend surprise when the string of pearls or the bracelet was finally handed over. Soon, I promised myself, I'd tell him about Sumei and my quest for Liu Ling and everything between us would be back again as it had been.

I'd fallen asleep by the time Ewan returned, but I was roused by the creak of his bed as he lay down. Half-awake, I drifted into vivid dreams of stolen sons in a maze of courtyards, dreams through which Liu Ling wandered like a wraith, always just out of sight. Yet Sumei had given me hope, a new direction in which to try.

The following Friday I went to the offices of the *North China Daily News* on the Bund, and asked the doorman if he remembered a boy called Liu Tung, or Sammy Liu, who'd once worked there as a messenger. The doorman whistled and scratched his chin, and for a moment my heart sank.

'There's a Sammy Liu in the case-room,' he suggested at last. 'One of the comps. A compositor, that is. But he isn't in today – you'll have to come back some other time.'

'What does he look like?' I asked, tearing a page from my diary in order to scribble a message.

The doorman stared at me as if the question had been ridiculous. 'Like a Chinese,' he said and shrugged.

Next day after an outbreak of trouble in Hongkew, five hundred Japanese marines marched ashore from the battleship *Idzumo*, anchored in the river. The first I knew of it was on the following Monday, when Ewan returned from his office.

'What do you think they're going to do?' I asked him.

'Nothing much, I expect. But the fact that they're here will reassure the Japanese in Hongkew and remind the locals to mind their manners. In any case, they won't dare lay a finger on the foreign concessions, so there's absolutely nothing for you to worry about.'

'Then why did the defence committee hold an emergency meeting this morning? Marion Trenchard told me,' I added before Ewan could ask. 'Esmond went off to it looking dreadfully serious, but wouldn't say why.'

Ewan picked up his pipe from its place on a jade ashtray and began to fill it with elaborate care. He'd only recently taken up pipe-smoking, but already I'd noticed that the ceremonies of filling and lighting and scouring out often seemed to coincide with finding answers to awkward questions.

'It's a minor thing, really.' He tamped the tobacco with one finger and then sucked experimentally through the stem. 'A few soldiers have turned up outside the city – Chinese chaps from the Canton area, who seem to be hanging about a bit. They claim to be nationalists – Chiang Kai-shek's lot – but the defence committee thinks they're probably out for whatever they can steal for themselves.'

'How many of them are there?'

This time Ewan made a great play of lighting his pipe. 'Oh,' he said at last, 'there are about thirty thousand of them.'

'But—'

'There's absolutely nothing to worry about, darling.' His smile was disarmingly candid and wreathed in confidence-inspiring pipe smoke. 'Trust me. If I thought you were in danger, don't you think I'd be the first man out there with a rifle?'

The following day, martial law was declared throughout the Chinese districts of the city and barricades went up on the street corners; foreigners were warned to stay in the International Settlement and the French Concession. I imagined Sumei gazing disdainfully down from her balcony – then I tried to imagine Liu Ling and her family, and for the first time I hoped they were somewhere far away.

Late on Saturday night a large detachment of Japanese marines, reinforced from newly arrived warships, left their quarters in Hongkew and drove into Chapei. Ewan and I had gone to a party at the Race Club in honour of a judge from the British Consular Court, and knew nothing at all of the Japanese move until Esmond Trenchard arrived in a state of high excitement to round up extra men for the Volunteer Corps.

'The Japs tried to take over the North Station, but the men from Canton were waiting for them – the Nineteenth Route Army, or whatever they call themselves. Didn't you hear the shooting?'

'Thought it was firecrackers,' somebody called out.

'Are you sure it isn't some local festival or other?' demanded a loud male voice. 'They're always letting off fireworks round here.'

Esmond Trenchard's ginger head projected indignantly from the collar of his Great War overcoat. 'Come and see, if you don't believe me. It's safe enough as far as the post office.'

There was a chorus of delight. 'Oh, yes – let's! What a
wheeze! We can take my car. Muriel, are you coming? Esmond
says we'll be perfectly safe, as long as we stay clear of the
shooting.'

'But of course it's safe, you old silly! They're shooting the
Chinese, not us.'

'Bring a bottle, then, there's a good chap. No need to hold
up the party.'

Almost at once I found myself being bundled out into the
street, towards a waiting motor car. Ewan had managed to find
my wrap and slipped it over my gauzy shoulders.

'This is a bit of excitement, darling, isn't it?' He squeezed
my hand in his. 'Hold on tight now, in case we get separated in
the crush.'

Dumbly, I did as I was told and a moment or two later,
enclosed in the cool, dark, leather-smelling interior of someone's
motor, we were swept away towards the battle. The evening
had become even madder than my dreams. In North Szechwan
Road we tumbled out of our cars to join the crowd already
there, laughing and chatting like theatre-goers waiting for the
interval bell and stamping our thin slippers against the chill.
Somewhere ahead, in the darkness which had followed the
shooting out of the house lights, motorcycles roared to and fro
and bursts of rifle fire flew in startling echoes through the
streets. Not a hundred yards away, Japanese troops struggled to
build a wall out of sandbags.

Marion Trenchard appeared at my side and pushed a mug of
coffee into my hands. 'I brought it for Esmond, but he told me
not to be silly. Cigarette? No, of course, you don't.'

The coffee had been laced with whisky and burned its way
down my throat.

'Say what you like about the Chinese,' said Marion, 'those
fellows from Canton have more spine than most. Esmond
reckoned they'd push off at the first smell of the Jap marines,
but look at them now – all set to make a fight of it.' She shivered
in her fur coat. 'Glad I'm not one of those poor devils in the
lanes round the station. They'll get the worst of it, I should
think.'

A sudden thought struck me. 'Marion, you have children, don't you?'

'Two little girls.' She laughed. 'Esmond calls them the "bunnies". "Bring out the bunnies!" he says to the amah when he comes home.'

An unexpected burst of sniper fire spattered the roadway a few yards ahead. Brocade and gold lamé flashed in the car headlights as people scrambled clear, squealing in excitement and shedding chiffon roses as they went.

Firmly, Ewan took my arm. 'It's getting too hot for comfort here, darling. Tony Tattersall's taking Evie back and he's offered to see you and Marion safely home on the way.'

'What about you? Aren't you coming?'

'I've told Esmond I'll hang on here for a bit in case I'm needed to help put out fires in the Settlement.' In the yellow glare of the headlights Ewan looked as handsome as any film star. 'Don't worry, darling – this'll be over before you know it. And I promise I won't get into any trouble.'

It was still far from over by the time Ewan came home in the small hours of the morning; if anything, things were getting worse. Driven back by the defenders, the Japanese spent Sunday shelling Chapei from their warships and bombing it with planes; incredibly, the fighting had escalated in a matter of days into a full-scale war. Shut up in our house in the French Concession, I could hear the distant thump of explosions, but I was starved of news until Ewan came back on one of his periodic visits to change his clothes or snatch some food.

'Don't worry,' he repeated whenever I asked. 'You're safe as houses here.'

'But the Chinese aren't. Not in Chapei.'

'Well, no – of course not.' He glanced at me in surprise. 'But that's hardly our affair, is it?'

'But the Japanese aren't just killing soldiers,' I persisted. 'They're killing ordinary people – people who wouldn't know how to fight, even if they had weapons.' In those days, even after the Great War, the slaughter of civilians still seemed an unthinkable outrage.

'That's China for you.' Ewan munched a sandwich out of

the packet our cook had prepared for him. 'Look, if I'm not back by six, send my driver down to the office, will you, with some more of these?'

I could taste the devilled ham on his lips when he kissed me and I hung on tight, afraid, in spite of his confidence, that it might be for the last time. Then he was gone and I returned to waiting.

The battle went on for six weeks and, unlike the earlier Japanese 'adventure' in Manchuria, this time it attracted the world's attention. The Nineteenth Route Army was beaten back in the end, but not before the story of young men in their late teens and early twenties trying to shoot down bombers with rifles – their only weapons – had appeared in newspapers all over Europe and America.

'Imagine – firing rifles at aeroplanes.' Ewan shook his head. 'Those boys were never a match for the Japs. The Chinese were bound to get a bloody nose in the end. Now they'll have to make the best terms they can.'

I begged him to get permission for us to go to Chapei – or what was left of it after the bombs and the shelling had done their work. A month and a half earlier, six hundred thousand souls had lived and worked there: now its houses and factories were blackened ruins or rubble-fields strewn with pitiful scraps of cotton and discarded shoes. Here and there, a few uncollected corpses still slumped in their trenches among a litter of gifts from the local people – cigarettes and empty brandy bottles and the odd keepsake paper flower. Even the living we saw seemed dazed, stumbling like sleepwalkers among the mountains of broken brick. Most of those who could escape had fled with their children and a few belongings into the streets of the International Settlement, or had set off along the brigand-infested road to Suchow.

The North Station had been devastated. The marshalling yards were a mass of torn and twisted track, ruined sheds and ripped-up trucks, while the streets round about had been reduced to a moonscape where those few buildings that still sagged above the skeletons of the rest fluttered with the white ribbons of mourning. It had been hard enough to find Sumei's lane at the best of times: now it was impossible and pointless, in any case, since it had almost certainly been destroyed. How far had Sumei managed to run on her cherished lily feet?

At least Liu Ling was safe. Her brother brought her to see me a week after the battle had finished – smaller than I remembered and with her lively, intelligent face polished like a nut by a decade's labour and creased into a web of fine contour lines whenever she smiled. Brother and sister were astonishingly alike, constantly sharing bright glances as we talked, as if each point had to be checked against some huge store of private happiness.

Liu Ling's son was studying to be an engineer, she told me, and her husband was a pharmacist, with a shop in the old Chinese city of Nantao which lay between the French Concession and the river.

'Not one of those places selling deer antlers and porcupine quills and all sorts of roots and frog skins? Can I come and see it tomorrow?'

Liu Ling's face assumed a severity I remembered of old. 'Not tomorrow,' she said. 'And not alone. My brother will bring you one day.' Another shining glance passed between them.

I ordered tea and while I poured and passed the cups Liu Ling watched me in speechless wonder, her hands pressed together between her knees. Then she burst out laughing.

'My little girl,' she crowed, pointing. 'My English daughter.' She covered her face with her strong, flattened fingers and rocked to and fro. Her pride in me made me ashamed.

'Why did you never tell me about your son? I'd have helped you to see him more often. We could have played together.'

'I was always afraid someone would give me away, if I brought him to the house.'

I told her about Sumei and the ruins round the North Station. For the first time, the brightness left their faces.

'The Nationalists should have helped us against the Japanese,' Sammy Liu exclaimed bitterly. 'Where was Chiang Kaishek? Why didn't he come to protect the people?'

This time Liu Ling's glance was nervous. She turned to me.

'My brother thinks the Nationalists are wrong. I tell him he spends too much time drinking tea with those know-all poets in Szechwan Road. If the people at the *News* heard him say these things—'

An eloquent gesture of her hands completed her meaning. Her brother was a Communist – no doubt a supporter of the political rallies that revolved round the Shanghai College and a distributor of the underground magazines produced by writers like Lu Xun, whose trenchant views on the rot of the middle classes had made the authorities put a price on his head. With the Nationalists in control of so much of China, only Shanghai's foreign settlements had offered the Communists a tenuous safety, and even there the gangster Du Yuesheng was always ready to help his friend Chiang Kai-shek, his blood brother in the Green Society.

'I tell Sammy to say nothing,' Liu Ling confirmed. 'People disappear.'

This was undoubtedly true. I'd heard of hundreds of young people being kidnapped and dragged away to their deaths; only the year before we'd arrived in Shanghai, five Communist writers – the youngest of them twenty-one – had been handed over to be shot by the Nationalists on the outskirts of the city. Clearly, those five had been Communists of a completely different kind from my cousin Rose. If they'd lived, could they have helped the children who slaved in the chromium workshops or picked feathers in the stifling dust of the godowns?

'Nothing will happen to me.' Sammy Liu's smile was confident. 'I work for the *News*, for foreigners. The secret police can't touch me.'

He was still cheerful as they left, though I fancied Liu Ling's smiles in return had taken on a troubled air.

Liu Ling's visit brought back a flood of memories.

'Do you remember the story,' she'd asked, 'of the cormorant fisherman and the enchanted peach-blossom forest he found? That was your favourite – you used to beg your governess to tell it over and over again.'

'Did I always get my own way? I must have been a horrible child.'

'No, you were just a little girl.' Liu Ling shook her neat head. 'Fortunate in some ways, not so fortunate in others.'

I could have kissed her hands. I felt as if at last I'd found solid ground beyond the peach-blossom forest of European Shanghai, that false paradise of fun, as airy and insubstantial as laughter.

The trouble was that having touched reality, I couldn't bring myself to let it go. In spite of all my good intentions – in spite of having resolved only to *find out* and then be satisfied – from that day, without ever intending to, I began to lead a double life, half inside the magic valley, and half out. It wasn't by any conscious choice: I simply couldn't help it. It seemed to be my fate, no matter what I did, to find my loyalties divided.

To salve my conscience I confessed to Ewan that Liu Ling and her brother had called, but said nothing about Sammy Liu's Communism. And Ewan, whose road through life ran broad and straight, reproached me mildly about the dangers of soft-heartedness where the Chinese were concerned.

'Didn't they ask you for money, or try to sell you something?'

'Of course not.'

'They will – just you wait. Now they've found you, they'll be back with the whole family – grandma, babies and all.'

I didn't attempt to correct him, but managed to feel guilty for letting down both Ewan and Liu Ling.

A few days later, a batch of letters arrived from London; I recognized Guy's bouncing scrawl on one envelope and Alice's painstaking hand on another. I was just about to leave the house when the letters arrived, but I couldn't resist having a quick glance at Guy's – always the shortest way of catching up on the news.

He certainly didn't disappoint me this time. 'Guess what?' whooped his letter, hardly wasting a line on the usual prelimi-naries. 'Margot's taken off for Rio with the trumpet player from the ballroom band at the Savoy (a dashing *café noir* Cuban called

Diaz who apparently blows a pretty electric rumba) and Kit has not only put in for a divorce, but he's taken up with an American cutie less than half his age (with a very rich daddy, of course).'

At this point I took my hat off again and sat down to catch my breath.

'Did I tell you Margot had been living at the Savoy since she fell out with Kit at Christmas?' Guy's scribble swooped happily across the page. 'She bought a perfect rat of a dog for company (a vile poodle *en papillon* that pissed and bit) but naturally, being Margot, she began to hanker after something larger and more useful – hence the Cuban, hot from the ballroom, instrument at the ready. Even then, I reckon Kit might have managed to turn a blind eye, but when Margot took the fellow to a cock-shoot in Norfolk and introduced him to all and sundry as her long-lost brother Llewelyn, even Kit decided enough was enough.

'The newspapers made a meal of it, of course. *Lady Oliver Leaves Home With Darky Busker* – and you know what Kit's like when his temper's up. Within a week he'd started divorce proceedings and was walking out with the lovely Mamie Brand of Brand's Grizzly Bear Beer – a Yankee girl of twenty-two with a face like a buttercup and nice legs, but more bosom than I'd care for myself. Pa Brand is rumoured to be less than delighted, but his little gal's dined with the Prince of Wales and there's no stopping her now.

'The best thing about it all,' Guy added blandly, 'is that with Mamie to keep him busy, Kit's been letting me run everything in the office and I've already made a few people jump pretty smartly, if I say so myself. After all, as I pointed out to Kit, Father's fifty next birthday, which is bound to slow him down a bit, so the time's approaching when I'll have to take over the whole shooting-match, anyhow.

'PS. I've had a slight smash with the motor, but don't worry, I've only got a few bruises. (More than I can say for the milk-cart we demolished!!)'

Alice's letter confirmed all Guy had said, though being Alice, she tried to take everyone's side at once. Even Margot's trumpet player had 'a very sweet smile' and had been quite

227

famous for his ability to play *Whispering* while standing on his head. The only one who came in for criticism was Mamie Brand and on that subject Alice was uncharacteristically savage.

'Mamie has a big, bold stare and a juicy pout, and a habit of pawing over any man she's introduced to – "Well now, Mr Jones, I declare there's a blonde hair on your collar – however do you suppose *that* could have got there?" And out goes her little hand to flick away the hair, smooth a lapel, fasten a button – all very fast and common in an English girl, but in an American it's called "snap" and is supposed to be awfully amusing. I do hope Papa gets tired of her soon.'

Poor Alice. And poor Margot: I was surprised to find myself quite concerned for my wayward aunt. I wondered what had gone on inside that imperious, scornful head to have made her cast off the Olivers with such blazing thoroughness – for Margot never 'went too far' unless she intended every inch of it. *Love* had certainly had nothing to do with her disappearance: no one else's wishes had ever mattered to Margot, least of all any man's – it had been part of her allure. According to Alice, her mother had money of her own, but what else did she have? I wished I could have spoken to her before she left. There were so many questions I wanted to ask.

'I suppose she'll write,' concluded Alice, 'when she has a moment.'

'But family is very important,' insisted Liu Ling the next time she called. 'How else do you know where you fit into the world? Your father and mother are your past and your children are your future. You should give your husband a child, then you would be content.'

Why should she imagine I wasn't content? I was perfectly happy – at least, most of the time I was – almost always, in fact, except for the occasional hot, humid night of the Shanghai summer, lying sleepless under the whirring fans, when the old restlessness I'd never quite cured would return and tempt me with treacherous imaginings. Then – and only then – I'd allow myself to wonder whether the answer to my fretfulness was to be found in the arms of other men; and my dreams would circle the bed like the scarlet rickshaws of the singsong girls, sweetly enticing. I'd remember Tony Tattersall's hand sliding warmly down my spine on the dance floor, and Esmond Trenchard in his Volunteer Corps greatcoat, calling one evening, unannounced and amorous, when Ewan was fire-watching in Szechwan Road.

Nothing could have been easier than to slide into an affair – after all, this was Shanghai. But Margot had taught me a horror of furtive intrigues and besides, I now knew that at the end of that road there was nothing but a Cuban trumpeter, playing *Whispering* while standing on his head.

In any case, my dreams always fled when the morning light revealed Ewan once more, patently honourable, trusting me to be worthy of him. I was sure I still loved Ewan – not exactly as I'd expected to love him on the day I walked down the aisle of St Margaret's in my white and virginal Molyneux gown, but in a comfortable, reassuring, habitual sort of way, because I accepted that, unlike so many of the people we knew, Ewan would always do what was right and decent and good.

In the beginning I'd thought of him as the stout oak round which I'd wind my slender stem, but now – I suppose because we were in Shanghai and I was surer of myself – I rather thought of us as two silvery willows growing together, each one supporting the other, unwilling to stand alone.

Perhaps Liu Ling was right and there were other paths to contentment.

'The Trenchards have children,' I reminded Ewan. 'Two adorable little girls.'

'Who always seem to have sunstroke, or measles, or something filthy they've picked up from eating uncooked peaches. Esmond's an ass. China's no place for children.' He glanced at me. 'Marion isn't making you broody, I hope.'

'Oh, no fear.' I made an effort to sound unconcerned. 'As you say, we have all the time in the world.'

We went on into 1933. Liu Ling's son qualified as an engineer and the three of us celebrated with a secret feast of dates and sesame candy from the street stalls set out for the New Year Festival. The air was twitching with new beginnings. In far-away Scotland, building had even started again on the first of the Heavenly Twins and in London Mamie Brand (Mamie Oliver since May) had given birth to Kit's son.

It was Alice who broke the sensational news.

'Do be kind,' she warned, 'when you write to Guy. He came to see me yesterday, almost in tears of vexation – he's waited so long and now the company will never be solely his after all. Papa's been desperately tactless, I'm afraid, absolutely gloating over little Georgie and dishing out champagne to everyone who'll stand still long enough to drink it. He's already making wonderful plans for his son – so there'll always be another Oliver looking over Guy's shoulder and expecting his share.'

Margot had sent the baby a silver chamber-pot engraved with his initials – from New York, where she was now living. History didn't relate what had happened to *Whispering*.

It all seemed half a world away from our little universe of Shanghai. In Britain, Alice reported gloomily, although the building of the new Oliver ship was going ahead at last, three million people were now out of work. There'd already been disturbances in London and Belfast, and when the Birkenhead protest marches turned into several days of rioting on Mersey-side, my cousin Rose was convinced that the glorious revolution was about to happen at any moment.

When Guy announced that pay for all Oliver employees would have to be cut by ten per cent, Rose stationed herself outside the company offices in Leadenhall Street carrying a placard bearing the legend 'CAPITALIST OPPRESSORS'; when this failed to have any effect, she rushed off to chain herself to the railings of Fulham Labour Exchange, followed by a scrum of newspaper photographers, eager for a picture of her exquisite face peering from the maw of a Black Maria.

The results were disappointing. To Rose's fury, her father's solicitor soon had her released from police custody without charge. And since her intrigues in Gloucestershire had turned the Cadzows' happy commune into such a battleground they'd asked her to leave, she was temporarily reduced to creeping back under Kit's roof for bed and board. There was no comfort even to be had in the dingy bed-sitters of her Communist acquaintances: the British Party, claimed Rose, had been over-run by fashionable intellectuals and petit-bourgeois deviationists.

Where, oh where, was the glorious revolution? Not in Britain, it seemed; and, later that year, when the Comintern in Moscow ordered British Communists to co-operate with the despised trade unions against the growing power of fascism, Rose's disillusion was complete. What had happened to the hard, pure flame of class warfare? Where was Rose's glory, and her revenge?

The result of all this was Rose's arrival in China as an unpaid and self-appointed correspondent for the *Daily Worker*, desperate for excitement and drawn by the thrilling scent of danger which surrounded the Communist movement in Shanghai.

Chapter Fourteen

'*GOD HOW* I loathe Guy!' Rose sat cross-legged on the floor of our drawing room near the French Park, her beautiful face a caricature of disgust and her cheeks vivid pink. 'To *think* he almost married Alice!' She flapped her hands, dispelling the notion like a fog, while I tried hard to keep my temper.

'Guy is my brother, remember. He does have some good points.'

'He keeps motor mechanics in work, I suppose, but I can't think of much else.' Rose sniffed and dragged the back of her hand across her perfect nose. I wondered where she'd learned the gesture: thank heavens Ewan was safely in his office.

From the start, Ewan had been deeply unhappy about Rose staying with us in the French Concession, even for a while. Ewan was one of the few men I knew completely immune to Rose's tempestuous, flashing-eyed beauty; in fact, when I first confessed I'd replied to her letter, offering her a home until she found a place of her own, he was extremely angry and almost made me write again, withdrawing the invitation.

'What will people think, when she trots out all her Communist rubbish? What about our neighbours?'

'If you mean the Wangs, I shouldn't think they'll notice.' Our nearest neighbours were a Chinese film-producer's family whose daughters trooped out in the latest French couture from the Avenue Joffre and with whom we shared lively dinners of Yanchen Lake crabs and soft-scaled river herrings. The Wangs, I was sure, would be above such suburban fixations as wondering what their neighbours thought of them.

'They must be used to odd westerners by this time.'

'I wasn't thinking of the Wangs. I meant Victor Sassoon and Esmond Trenchard – people like that.' Irritably, Ewan began a ritual pipe-filling. 'Rose is quite capable of deliberately setting out to offend them.'

'If I know those two, they'll be too busy staring at her face and her ankles to notice her politics. You know what the club's like – there's an absolute race to bed anyone new.'

'Hardly.' Ewan drew up his legs with a curiously spinsterish movement. 'That's a bit of an exaggeration.'

'Oh, Ewan, it's true! You told me yourself that Esmond Trenchard had slept with the entire female chorus of *The Gondoliers* last season, not to mention the wardrobe mistress and the girl who sold programmes at the door.'

'I said that was what he *claimed*, not that he'd necessarily done it.'

'Of course he did it. The opera group bed one another like rabbits – it's something to do with the smell of greasepaint. And as for Evie Tattersall—'

'This is just gossip, you know.' The words were distorted by the stem of Ewan's pipe. 'These rumours get wilder and wilder, the more they go round.' He got to his feet, his head enveloped in a cloud of smoke. 'Did someone say the newspapers had come from home? I'll be in the morning room, then, if you need me.' In the doorway he stopped again. 'I suppose we're stuck with Rose for a while, if you've already invited her. But not for long, Clio, please – and do try to make her behave herself while she's here.'

It was a hot day, sultry and airless enough to make my blouse cling uncomfortably to my spine. There had been times – more of them, recently – when Ewan's righteousness was more than I could bear. Now the words popped out before I could recall them. 'What a dreadfully pompous thing to say!'

Framed by the doorway, Ewan removed his pipe from his mouth and stared at me, flabbergasted. 'I beg your pardon?'

'Pompous, I said. Priggish, if you prefer it.' Flushed and reckless, I stood my ground. 'This is my home too and I'll invite Rose if I want to.'

'This is the first time I've heard you have anything good to say about the woman.' Ewan's face had begun to colour. 'And as for being pompous – I was simply telling you what I thought.'

'And what about me? Doesn't it matter what I think?'

Ewan stared at me, angry and perplexed. 'Well, of course it matters. I just assumed—'

'You've no right to assume anything! I won't have it, Ewan. I won't!'

He drew himself up. 'Obviously not. I'm sorry if I've offended you in some way – though I can't honestly see what I've done that's so bad. Now, if you don't mind, I'm going off to read the papers.'

After he'd gone I calmed down quite quickly. It had been unfair to attack Ewan for being precisely what he was – exactly the same man I'd married. I went along to the morning room to beg his pardon.

'I can't imagine what possessed me, darling. You're right – I don't even like Rose very much.'

'Well, never mind. It's this damnable heat that makes us short-tempered. I feel it too.'

'Do you?'

'Of course.' Ewan put an arm round my shoulders, curiously awkward, like someone embracing an almost grown-up child. 'I hate it when we have rows.'

'Me too. No more falling out.'

'Nothing but sweetness and light.'

'Love you, darling.'

'Mmm. Me too.'

Fortunately for the peace of our household, Rose was no more anxious to linger than Ewan was to put up with her.

'His sort will all be swept away when the workers seize power,' she informed me cheerfully one morning, after a long argument over breakfast had ended in Ewan's outraged departure. 'And a damn good thing too. The McLennans have bled the peasants dry for generations and lived off the profits of the poor devils' labour. And Guy too.' Rose eyed me severely over her teacup. 'Honestly, Clio, I know he's your brother, but he's just like some rotten old Victorian mineowner, cutting the wages of the poor wretches who work for him and blowing the savings on enormous, obscene motor cars.'

I was stung by Rose's contempt for my brother. 'But Guy's supposed to be thoroughly progressive! What about his plans for building refrigerated ships and bigger tankers and concentrating on specialist cargoes?'

'Those weren't *Guy's* ideas.' Rose eyed me scornfully. 'Stephen Morgan's the one with the brains in that office. All Guy did was write down what Stephen's been saying for ages – but, of course, when he presented his grand plan to the directors, he pretended he'd thought it all out himself.'

'I don't see how you can possibly know that.' This was too much. Ewan had been absolutely right: even as a guest in our house, Rose was determined to offend us.

'That's just another lie, made up by your Communist friends,' I told her. 'And if you're going to spend your time here being rude about my family and Ewan's, then the sooner you find somewhere else to stay, the better!'

'I'm sorry! I apologize.' Rose lifted up her hands, her expression penitent at once. 'I really am sorry, Clio. I am, honestly. You know how I get carried away. You've been very kind and I've been thoughtless and ungrateful.' She touched my arm in graceful entreaty. 'You don't really want me to leave, do you?'

'Well—'

'It isn't as if I'll be here for long. If you could just put up with me until I find a place of my own, I'll be gone before you know it.'

She watched me for a moment, waiting for my reaction.

'You'll have to promise to stay off the subject of politics. One more argument with Ewan and you're on your own.'

'Not another word, I promise. But as a matter of fact—' She settled herself back in her chair. 'It was Alice who told me about Guy pinching Stephen's ideas.' She smiled sweetly. 'And Alice knows it's true, because Guy told her. He reckoned he'd pulled a fast one on Stephen and he was pretty braced about the whole business.' She leaned towards me significantly. 'I bet Guy wishes he'd got Alice to marry him years ago, instead of messing around with fast cars and cheap women. But he won't get Alice now, because Papa's got Georgie for an heir – and anyway, Harry Dunstanheugh is first in the queue for Alice.'

'Do you think so?' I temporarily forgot my annoyance, full of new hope for Alice's happiness.

Rose reached out for another piece of toast and buttered it vigorously. 'It's a pity Harry's one of the Rockalls – hopelessly doomed, just like the rest. Anyway—' She dug in the marmalade pot. 'The silliest part of it is, Guy's such a stick-in-the-mud he's missed the point of Stephen's most sensible suggestion yet.'

'Really?' My voice came out in a stiff little squeak – Rose just couldn't help being offensive. 'And what, exactly, is this particular stroke of brilliance?'

'Aeroplanes. Stephen reckons Oliver's should start an airline of their own, or at least buy a large stake in someone else's before they become too successful. Did you know Imperial were starting a service to Singapore this year?'

Now I was on surer ground. 'Well, I happen to think Guy's absolutely right. I wouldn't go up in one of those things, not for the world.'

'That's what Guy says. "We're a shipping company, not a circus." I heard him chortling about it one day with Papa and Uncle Edward. It's the only idea he gave Stephen any credit for – because he thinks it's so mad.'

'Well, it is mad, in a way. It must be every bit as boring as standing in a lift. Ewan reckons flying's just a passing fashion for people who care more about making an entrance than travelling in comfort.'

Rose pursed her lips and carefully sucked her knife. 'I'm not so sure. You don't see much of life, you know, cooped up here in Shanghai.'

Cooped up I might have been, but I was right in one respect, at least. As soon as Rose's arrival in Shanghai became known, various male friends began to arrive on the slenderest of excuses to inspect her. Tony Tattersall carried her off on a tour of the city in his newly imported Railton, bought her coffee in the

Renaissance Café and assumed she was joking when she described a bemedalled White Russian at the next table as an 'old bloodsucker'. Esmond Trenchard offered to find her a flat and promised that if Ewan wouldn't bring her to the Christmas dance at the club, he would – with Marion, of course.

'I knew Rose would cause trouble.' Ewan watched sombrely from the window as my cousin was helped into a motor car by yet another married acquaintance, this time bound for a pony sale.

'Let me see.' I joined Ewan at his post. 'As I remember, you said they'd all loathe her, but that doesn't seem to be the problem. In fact, I'd say that so far she's been one of the most popular people in town.'

Rose had told me quite frankly she'd 'been getting to know the place' by allowing herself to be squired around the city by men of a class she normally despised. It was just as well, I thought, that they'd no idea of her real opinion of them; for an hour that morning, I'd been treated to Rose's gossip about some of our acquaintances, passed on quite freely by her new-found friends.

'I told you Evie Tattersall had a lover.' I poked Ewan happily in the ribs. 'Apparently he brings her cockerel-and-seahorse powders from a Chinese pharmacist, so they can go on longer in bed.'

'Does he, indeed.' Ewan turned away, picked up his empty pipe from its place on the jade ashtray and blew sharply through the stem. A few specks of ash flew into the air and settled on the lapels of his suit.

'Don't you think it's a hoot?'

'Not really,' Ewan scratched intently at the grey worsted and then glanced at his watch. 'Time to go to the office, anyway.' He bent to kiss me on the cheek. 'Bye, darling – see you at six.'

I stared after him, astonished. Really, Ewan seemed to have lost his sense of humour in the past couple of months. I put it down to the hard work of running Garnock Fraser's empire in Shanghai.

★

Fortunately, after setting our home on its ear for six weeks, Rose found a large, modern, air-conditioned flat near the Avenue Edward VII which she decided was perfect for her needs. Another month crawled past while its walls were covered with startling murals of jungle animals and exotic greenery. Then, on the morning Rose moved in, three different married men turned up at our gates to help.

They didn't know Rose as I did. If all she'd wanted was a love affair, she had no need to come to Shanghai to find one. Rose was in search of something quite different. She wanted drama: she wanted blood.

Predictably, she soon made it clear to her admirers that she had no real interest in them. She despised golf, dismissed bridge as middle-aged and grew bored at the races. Before long the gentlemen had given her up as a dangerous extremist and, since Ewan never mentioned her name if he could help it, even her connection with us was largely forgotten.

Yet I didn't want to lose touch with Rose altogether – though I wasn't so much afraid for her safety as of what she might get up to in that irrational, explosive city. From time to time I called at her jungle-painted flat or arranged to meet her in a café, and for that reason one of my abiding memories of Shanghai is of Rose's huge, calculating, long-lashed eyes staring through a blue stream of cigarette smoke as she considered how much to tell me of her adventures.

For if Rose had sunk out of sight of the European section of Shanghai society, it was only to move more freely on her own subterranean level. By groping her way from one contact to the next, she'd made herself known surprisingly quickly among the radical students and the bookshops which secretly sold Marxist literature from under beds and floorboards. She had no fear for her own safety: the passwords and whispers involved in her new life simply exhilarated her. As she told me how she'd dodged the Nanking government's secret policemen, her eyes would shine and her lips grow soft and curved like those of a girl recalling a lover. Her passion frightened me. I began to long for the day she'd grow bored with it all and decide to go home.

But too many exciting things were happening in China for Rose to give it up. Late in that year of 1934, the Communist army broke through the Nationalist cordon which had contained it in the south-east and set out across the country in a straggling column of men, women and children. It was to take them a year to find a refuge in Yenan, 6,000 miles away to the north-west in the wind-scoured Shensi Hills, and three-quarters of their number were lost in the process; but in the meantime, the news of the battles and hardships which haunted their bloody trek was followed avidly by their comrades in Shanghai.

'Do you see?' Rose would lean over the café table, her eyes alight. 'Do you see what these people will do for the sake of the Party? Oh, I know at home there's plenty of talk, but when it comes to the point, no one will *do* anything.' She drew deeply on her cigarette and half-closed her heavy eyelids. 'But here . . .'

We'd just left Kiessling & Baader's coffee house one day when I spotted a familiar figure weaving through the crowd on Bubbling Well Road and stopped out of habit to chat. After an hour of Rose's baleful pronouncements I was so desperate for light-heartedness and laughter that I didn't even notice Rose, at my side, falling unusually silent, left out of the conversation.

'There's a race meeting at the Canidrome tonight. I can feel in my blood that I'm going to be lucky.' Sammy Liu rubbed his hands and his smile, like his sister's, brought his face alive, sunlight dancing on water. 'Oh, yes, the dogs are going to run well for me today.'

'I was born under the sign of the dog,' I told him. 'I suppose that gives me my faithful nature.'

'Well then, I'll shake your hand, Madam Dog, and be twice as lucky.' His face sparkled with merriment. 'You see how we were fated to meet?'

I didn't usually find Chinese men attractive in a physical sense – I prefer tall men, for one thing – but Sammy Liu was different. In serious mood he was capable of flights of almost poetic reflection on a world he loved profoundly; when he was happy, his warmth drew men and women alike. 'He's a terrible rogue,' Liu Ling used to say lovingly of her brother. 'He'll come to a bad end.'

When Rose enquired later about the stranger, I answered unthinkingly, 'Sammy Liu? I thought you'd have heard of him. Isn't he one of the Creation Society people who send out all the pamphlets?'

'He's a Party member?'

'I should think so – though since he works in the case-room at the *News*, perhaps he has to keep his political ideas quieter than most. To the *News*, a Communist Chinese is next thing to the devil himself.'

That was all I said – and I even laughed as I said it. Sammy Liu was my dear Liu Ling's brother and firmly on the side of the angels.

'He speaks English very well.' Rose was still staring in the direction Sammy had taken. 'How strange I should never have noticed him before.'

It was Esmond Trenchard who gave me news of what followed, at a fancy-dress party at the club. He loomed over me, a gangling Robin Hood, and I realized he'd been drinking; his speech was slurred, his face was blotched with crimson and he was scowling petulantly under his feathered hat.

'That cousin of yours—' He supported himself on his longbow. 'That cousin of yours prefers to hob-nob with the natives, does she, when she comes out east? 'Sthere something wrong with the rest of us?'

'You're drunk, Esmond.' I looked round for Marion.

'Jus' a tiny bit whistled.' He held up a finger and thumb and then, leaning down, puffed alcohol into my face. 'You didn't know, did you? Hah.' He swayed upright again and his scowl gave way to an expression of puzzlement. 'A Chinese feller. God knows why,' he added profoundly. 'God knows why.'

For all I cared, Rose could sleep with anyone she pleased – but this wasn't anyone, this was Sammy Liu and I was afraid of whatever was stirring in that lovely, dangerous head of hers.

240

Already, everyone seemed to know of the relationship. Rose and her lover were seen in all the radical cafés; they turned up at every political meeting and were spotted one midnight, splashing defiantly in the fountain in the riverside park, officially out of bounds to Chinese. It was just as if Rose had dropped out of sight into the oily depths of the city and then surfaced again, clutching Sammy Liu as her trophy.

Now I kept overhearing Rose's name in conversations that were choked off abruptly as I approached.

'The Oliver woman. One of the shipping people.'

'He's a Communist, you know—'

'My dear, they both are. My brother in Hampstead says—'

'—painted her nude, several times, and you could see *absolutely everything.*'

'They write these terrible things, apparently, about the government in Nanking – of course, it's all in Chinese, so one can't be certain—'

'Just stirring up trouble.'

'Exactly what I said to the Consul-General.'

Before long, the management of the *News* could no longer ignore what was going on. Sammy Liu was a good and popular worker, but there had been too many complaints: if he couldn't behave more discreetly, he'd lose his job. Rose immediately instructed him to resign. Who needed the paltry wage the *News* provided? Rose's allowance was easily enough to support them both.

When Sammy refused to give up his post, she hinted at the presence of other men, eager to relieve her boredom while he was at work. This time Sammy gave in and resigned, surrendering his last piece of independence. I couldn't blame him, mesmerized as he was by Rose, her voracious passion and her political energy. I could understand what Sammy found so irresistible in the relationship, but Rose . . .

Liu Ling was as worried as I was. 'Can't you speak to your cousin? Remind her of her duty to her family. Ask her what her parents will think of her, living openly with a lover.'

'It isn't like that in Britain, I'm afraid. If you have enough money you can get away with these things.'

Liu Ling's brows drew together in concern. 'Her parents don't want her to marry well?'

'They've rather given her up, after all this time. Rose has always been difficult.' I glanced at Liu Ling. Her face was printed with fear of the danger Sammy was courting – a danger Rose couldn't, or wouldn't, understand and to which she'd blinded her lover. 'Can't you speak to your brother?'

Liu Ling raised her hands pathetically. 'I've tried. My husband and my son have also tried, but he doesn't hear anything we say. It's just as if something has blocked his eyes and his ears, and his mind, too.' She gazed at me in such silent distress that my heart ached for her terror.

'I knew you wouldn't understand.' Rose surveyed me with contempt when I tried to warn her of the danger. 'Nothing's ever gained without taking risks. We all know that.'

'But it's Sammy who's taking all the risks, not you. Liu Ling says—'

Rose shook her head violently and waved the name aside. 'His sister doesn't like us being seen together, that's all. It doesn't look nice for the family.'

'She's worried sick that something will happen to Sammy – can't you see that?'

'Liu Ling is an interfering busybody – I can see that all right!' Rose moved to the door to indicate that the interview was over. 'And now she's got you running errands for her.'

Ewan's solution was simple. 'You'll just have to leave Rose to make the best of it. You've tried. There's nothing else you can do.'

'But she's my cousin. I feel responsible.' In the silence of my head, I added the words 'for any harm she brings to Sammy Liu'.

'I shouldn't think you need worry – Rose'll be all right.' Ewan stared out of the drawing-room window into the tree-lined avenue beyond our gates. Bizarrely, it occurred to me that I seemed to spend a great deal of time these days addressing remarks to his back.

His voice echoed against the windowpanes. 'I expect we're

the ones who'll be left to smooth things over when Rose has gone home. Just you wait and see.'

'Is there something going on out there, darling?'

'Nothing at all.' Ewan turned and strolled over to a table where Shen Fu, our Number One boy, had laid out a tray of bottles and glasses. 'By the way, talking about your relatives, I hear that fellow Morgan's coming out to take over the Oliver's office.'

'Stephen Morgan?' My mind was so full of Rose that for a moment I could hardly take in what he'd said. 'Stephen's coming to Shanghai?'

'So I'm told.' Holding the measure up to the light, Ewan poured French vermouth into a cocktail shaker. 'I take it, then, that you haven't invited *him* to stay.'

'I should think Stephen's quite capable of looking after himself.' I was irritated by the news and doubly annoyed with Stephen – first for being cleverer than my brother Guy and second for bringing his distracting presence to Shanghai when I already had my hands full with Rose.

'We can always give him dinner or something, once he's settled in.' Ewan tipped the shaker from end to end, then unscrewed the cap with a practised flick of his wrist. He raised his voice: 'Shen Fu – where the devil's the strainer? No, wait, it's all right, I've found it.' He lined up two glasses and began to pour. 'I can't say I've ever actually taken to your cousin Stephen, but he is new here and we'd better do something for him.'

Stephen duly came to dinner and said very little, though I saw him study each of our guests in turn, making judgements, I suppose, as he usually did. I hated to think what those judgements might be. Esmond Trenchard, for one, had clearly been drinking before he arrived; he was already silly and grew sillier as the evening progressed. I squirmed with annoyance as I saw Stephen's hard grey eyes appraise him and then coldly pass on.

What right had Stephen Morgan to despise us and the way

we lived? For once, I felt a rush of indignant kinship with the Trenchards and the rest. What harm had they ever done anyone? Yet in my heart I knew Stephen was only seeing what I saw, day in, day out – and forced myself to ignore, to be the wife Ewan expected.

For the rest of the evening I avoided speaking to Stephen unless we happened to find ourselves in the same chattering group. Let him watch me from a distance, if he must, and guess whatever he could. In an hour or two he'd have gone back to his hotel, swept away on a noisy tide of departing Trenchards and Tattersalls and friends from the club, and I'd be safe from his careful scrutiny. I felt sorrier than ever for Guy – the contest between them had been so uneven.

'According to Stephen Morgan,' Ewan reported later, 'Kit and your father have sent him out here to see if there's likely to be more trouble from the Japanese. He claims they're worried about the safety of company assets – the wharves and the dry-docks and the office buildings and so on.' For a moment Ewan gazed thoughtfully round our graceful drawing room, where our servants were diligently collecting the lipstick-stained glasses and scattered coffee cups.

'But that's obviously just an excuse.' He swung back to me, his hands in his trouser pockets. 'Everyone knows the settlements here are as safe as houses. No – I think it's far more likely there's been some falling out in the London office and Stephen's been sent out east to cool his heels for a while. He has the air of a remittance man, don't you think? That manner that warns you a bash on the nose is never very far away.'

'He didn't have much to say for himself, certainly.'

Ewan snorted. 'He doesn't need to say anything – he just *looks*. You'd think poor old Esmond was something we'd fished out of the drains.'

'Esmond was dreadfully drunk, Ewan. There was no need for that joke about the prostitute with three legs. And as for Evie Tattersall – I thought she was going to slide out of her dress, she was laughing so much. In fact, I can't think why you insisted on having the Tattersalls in the first place.'

But Ewan had already moved out of earshot, limping

across the room to retrieve an earring he'd spotted under a table.

By sheer ill-luck, I ran into Stephen again a few days later in a painting and calligraphy shop in Fuchow Road. It was one of my favourite places in the city, full of soft, mouse-grey, museum-like calm and unnecessarily beautiful objects – exquisitely decorated carbon ink-blocks lying next to brushes with fat tips shaped like chestnut buds, and velvety rice paper beside ink-stones as smooth as skin to the finger. I went to look and to smell and to feel, as often as I went to buy, but the smiling owner seemed to understand my weakness and followed me from counter to counter in wordless complicity.

At first, because of the shadows, Stephen was only a silhouette against the light of the street; he'd come near enough to touch me by the time I looked up from a delicate fan of bookmarks and recognized him. At once, my pleasure turned into dismay. What business could Stephen Morgan have in that shop, which had been my own, personal discovery? I replied coolly to his greeting.

He'd come for brushes, he said, promised to a girl at home who painted. Hoping to speed his departure, I translated for him and then, irritated, remembered my rule never to speak Chinese in front of acquaintances. That was the trouble with Stephen – that unsettling feeling he carried with him, which always managed to make you forget your firmest resolve.

His presence had destroyed the serenity of the calligraphy shop. Writing materials are smooth, passive, pliant things: Stephen's stillness was uncanny, but it was the stillness of a wound spring, the containment of hoarded energy, a kind of simmering anger without focus or reason. While the proprietor took the brushes away to wrap them with his usual elaborate care, Stephen prowled a few steps along the counter and then, almost at once, returned restlessly to me.

'I hardly had a chance of a word with you after dinner last week.'

245

'Hostess – you know.' I forced myself to sound airily apologetic. 'Circulating and all that.'

For a few seconds his eyes probed mine, before swinging away to comb the gloom of the shop. 'You seem to have made a lot of friends since you came out here.'

'We know plenty of people, that's true. Though I wouldn't say they were all friends, exactly.'

His gaze swept back towards me. 'Good enough friends to gossip behind your back. The people in this city seem to take pleasure in everyone else's scandals. Don't you mind that?'

I assumed he was referring to the stories about Rose. 'I shouldn't believe more than half of it, if I were you. Shanghai's a dreadful place for rumours.'

I wished he wouldn't stare so: it was one of his worst habits.

He leaned on the nearest counter. 'How much longer will you be staying in China?'

'We're supposed to go back to England in '36. That means another year and a half.'

'No sooner?'

'Oh, no – Ewan loves it here, now he's used to the summers. He has his golf and his racing and his club . . . Though, of course, we'll have to go back in the end. There's always Achrossan.'

'So Ewan's in his element.' Stephen reached out to turn over a painted bookmark. 'What about you?'

'Me? Oh, I love it too. I've never minded the heat – and I like all the colour, you know, and the bustle . . .' I tried to remember the things I ought to have liked. 'And the gardens – and the parties—' I was saved from struggling further by the return of the shopkeeper, who presented his parcel with a bow.

Stephen slid the box into his coat pocket. 'Have you time for a coffee somewhere? Tea?'

'No, I'm sorry.' Quickly, I drew on the glove I'd removed and glanced out into Fuchow Road, where the light was perceptibly failing. 'I must get back. Ewan will be home before long.'

Conscious of having sounded abrupt, I added on impulse, 'Another time, perhaps.'

'Another time, then. As you say.'

On the way home I wondered what Stephen had heard about Rose. Someone was bound to have supplied him with details – by now Rose was as notorious for her raffish household as for her political views. Artists, writers, radical film-makers and actors – Rose's home was always full of a shifting population who argued, drank, spilled their food among her jungle murals and fell asleep in corners, to the constant despair of her staff. In fact, for someone who claimed to be one of 'the people', Rose treated her servants very badly. But then, logic had never been Rose's forte. She was all volatility and reckless action: I expect her pamphlets sounded better once Sammy Liu had translated them into Chinese.

The long northward march of the Red Army had exercised a profound influence on Rose. From her safe distance, she'd followed the horrors of the trek with growing excitement. With such an example before them, only cowards pledged their support in whispers! It was time to denounce the Nationalist government in Nanking to anyone who would listen, the more openly the better – to shout aloud how corrupt the Nationalists were, how they traded in opium and grew fat on the profits of usury!

'They're racketeers,' her leaflets proclaimed. 'Givers of bribes to judges and policemen. Brothers of gangsters.'

'Rose,' I warned her, 'the Nationalists have powerful friends in Shanghai.'

She gazed at me with abstracted eyes. 'The truth is more powerful than the gun or the knife.'

At the start of 1936 Rose paid for the printing of a journal in which only the most extreme political writers found a voice. She helped Sammy Liu to write a play about striking factory workers which was put on at the Golden Theatre and immediately made its author a celebrity. When he appeared at a rally at the Shanghai College, two men suspected of being Nationalist spies were almost beaten to death.

Liu Ling was in despair. 'What can I do? He thinks because

your cousin is a foreigner, that will protect him. I say, it may protect *her* but not you too.'

I had no comfort to offer and it became painful for us to meet. In spite of our closeness – no, because of our closeness – Liu Ling and I began to see less of one another than before, and the loss of her wistful tenderness left a void in my life.

Without Liu Ling for company, I began to realize how little of each day Ewan and I now spent together. When we'd been married first, we'd talked about everything under the sun; now, with a shock, I realized we hadn't even made love for weeks. I blamed the pressure of business which kept him at his office – all the men at the club complained of it, now that world trade was at last beginning to emerge from the slump which had gripped it for more than five years. I knew from my father's letters that the Oliver Steam Navigation Company, which had paid no dividend on its Deferred Shares since 1932, had not only declared a respectable four per cent but had restored wages and salaries to their previous level and launched the first of the Heavenly Twins with the name *Gloriana*. Ewan's firm, Fraser, Dunsinane, was equally determined to take advantage of the recovery and as often as not, Ewan would call from the office, suggesting I went on alone to whichever dinner or party we were due to attend that evening, where he'd catch me up later.

It was all so different from our early days together; and yet, weren't marriages supposed to mature and develop as time went on? Guiltily, I wondered if I was the one who'd changed – if I was now so far from the tremulous virgin Ewan had married, the young girl who'd looked to him for strength and guidance, that he found the difference disquieting. Poor Ewan, he hated anything to change. Even our love-making had settled into such a familiar routine that I apparently hadn't noticed its absence.

I must be to blame. Ewan loved me and was still exactly the same man I'd married – still steady and honourable and honest to a fault. I had everything any woman could ask for: and if I sometimes found myself wondering whether this truly was *all* – then it was my own unsettled, divided nature which was to blame, not Ewan. I resolved to make an enormous effort to put matters right – to show Ewan our marriage was still my rock and my refuge.

'You're working too hard, darling.' We'd just returned from the opera group's *Merry Widow* and Ewan, too weary to undress for bed, had stretched out in a chair in the drawing room. I poured him a brandy and perched on the arm of the chair at his shoulder. 'I'm beginning to worry about you, you know.'

'Surely not.' Ewan reached up for the glass. 'It's very sweet of you, but quite unnecessary. I promise you, there's no need to worry about me.'

'But you seem to work such long hours nowadays. Look at tonight. Esmond Trenchard managed to arrive in time for the first act – and most of the others, too.'

Ewan hoisted himself up in the chair. 'I have to justify my salary, that's all.'

'But you earn every penny of it! I don't see why you have to work harder than anyone else, just because you're Garnock Fraser's nephew.' I slid an affectionate arm round his neck and felt him stiffen. 'You're a hero, darling. You always have been.'

'Nonsense.' He leaned away from me a little and cleared his throat. 'What's the time?'

'About two, I should think. Are you coming to bed?'

'In a moment. I must look over some papers I brought home.' He unwound my arm from his neck and brushed my fingertips with his lips. 'You go on upstairs. Don't wait up for me.'

'I don't mind waiting. I'll sit here and read a magazine.' Playfully, I ruffled his hair and he reached up at once to smooth it down.

'I'd rather you didn't stay, actually.'

'But I thought – if you weren't going to be long . . .' I felt like a child begging for a sweet and embarrassment sharpened my tone. 'I remember when you didn't have to be reminded to make love to me.'

He raised his head at once, flushed and startled. 'What an extraordinary thing to say!'

'It's perfectly true. You come home so late now, there never seems to be any time.' Was it disloyal of me? Ewan was working so hard for our future and all I could do was complain. Yet I so much wanted to be held in his arms again, to recapture the tenderness and the intimacy of the early days and to have everything back the way it used to be.

He followed me upstairs and undressed in a methodical silence which made me so abject that I slipped into bed while his back was turned.

'If you don't want to—'

'Of course I want to. I'm just a bit tired, that's all.'

Grimly, we made love, exchanging meaningless endearments and fraudulent kisses, united only by a desire to be finished with the business as soon as possible.

At last it was over and Ewan slid away from me at once, across to his own bed, knotting his pyjama trousers. 'Do you mind if I go to sleep now? I really am damnably tired.' Incredibly, within a few seconds his breathing had taken on the deep and regular rhythm of unconsciousness.

I lay awake for hours afterwards, listening to the faint Westminster chimes of the clock in the hall. I couldn't remember ever having been so miserable – so crushed and valueless. Had it been so much to ask, to be allowed to offer proof of my love? It seemed so. My punishment had been a hideous parody of the heart of a marriage, a cold, relentless coupling which made us ashamed, even while we pursued it.

Why?

I couldn't understand how we'd drifted so far apart, Ewan and I. I'd been completely faithful: I'd entertained Ewan's friends, run his household efficiently, tried to take an interest in his work – and never, ever, as far as I knew, let him doubt that he was everything in the world to me. How had I failed in my duty as a wife?

I heard five o'clock chime from the hall, and I still had no answer. After that, I must have fallen asleep from sheer exhaustion.

★

Some time later, while I slept fitfully in the bed alongside Ewan's, a terrified rickshaw puller pounded on the door of Rose's flat near the Avenue Edward VII. In the pale glow of the street light, he tipped his burden on to the pavement, springing back with a moan as it rolled towards his naked feet.

It was the severed head of Sammy Liu, cut off cleanly at the third vertebra.

Chapter Fifteen

THE RULERS of Shanghai – not the *taipans* or the consular officials, but the real rulers who kept their manicured fingers on the throat of the city – had their own way of dealing with irritations. A snatch in an ill-lit lane – a grip on the hair, dragging the head forward and down, extending the neck for the hiss of the sword . . . and everything's finished, without troubling the court that deals with 'reactionary activities', the verdict written as a stain in an alleyway: another Communist gone, another thorn in the Nationalist government's flesh disposed of.

Two hours after the delivery of her lover's head, Rose arrived on our doorstep, her face still hollow with fear. The *commissaire* of the French Concession police had questioned her for almost all of that time – questioned her as if she were a criminal and the dead man's Communist friends the most likely suspects for his murder.

'Go and speak to your crony Du Yuesheng!' Rose had shouted at him. 'Arrest the gangsters and the extortionists! Question the judges who do the Nanking government's dirty work for them – then you might find out the truth.'

'If Madame has proof of all this, most certainly I shall make enquiries.' The commissaire lit a cigarette, without offering one to Rose. '*Do* you have proof, Madame?'

She had nothing to offer except belief. The rickshaw puller had long since fled to the shelter of his thirty thousand comrades. All that was certain was that Rose's lover had left a friend's wedding in order to return home and no one had seen him alive since then.

The commissaire accompanied Rose to the door of his office. 'Perhaps, if we find the *rest* of the unfortunate victim . . . Forgive me, Madame, but we policemen cannot afford to be squeamish.'

Rose arrived at our door grey and trembling. I had no comfort to give her: I could only think of Liu Ling – and of Sammy, whose merry, quicksilver smile I'd never see again. He'd received no mercy at all from his murderers – or from Rose.

'Have you sent anyone to tell his sister?'

Rose gazed at me, her eyes blank and inward-looking. I sent one of our own boys off at once to the pharmacy in Nantao, and then sat down to watch Rose light one cigarette after another, only to grind them out violently, half-smoked, until the ashtray became a bone-yard.

From time to time a tear fell sizzling into the ash and her nostrils flared as she tried to stifle the others.

'I suppose you'll all blame me for this!' Rose swept back a lock of hair and stared up at me with eyes drowning in self-pity. 'You do blame me – don't you! How was I to know something like this could happen?' She rubbed her hands, dragging her palms over one another as if some clinging horror had soiled them. 'My fault! It's always my fault!'

For the second time in my life, I wanted to attack Rose – to tear and scratch and destroy the exquisite features she'd used so ruthlessly to get what she wanted. And what she'd wanted, I now realized, had been revenge – on Margot, on her father, on all of us, on the world that had produced her: she'd wanted the power to grind hearts, to raise despoiling armies with herself at the head of them, and make us as miserable as she was herself. Beside that, the enslavement and death of one poor, besotted man had been a small price to pay.

Another tear hissed into the ashtray. At that moment what Rose wanted most was absolution – and I sat in steadfast silence, repelled, ashamed and determined not to give it to her.

After a while Ewan reappeared, dressed for the office. I couldn't believe he was capable of going off to do a day's work as if nothing had happened.

'You aren't going to leave us here alone, surely?'

He glanced at Rose with dislike. 'You don't really need me, do you? I mean, I wish to God it hadn't happened and I can't forgive Rose for dragging you into the mess with her – but the poor fellow's dead and there's nothing we can do about it now. It's in the hands of the police and we'll just have to leave it to them.'

Rose raised her head and silently hated him through a cloud of smoke.

Gathering up my dressing-gown, I ran downstairs after Ewan to the front door. 'But what about me? What am I supposed to do?'

His hand on the latch, he turned in surprise. 'You aren't in any danger, darling, I promise you. Shen Fu and the others will take care of everything.' He glanced over my head towards the upper floor. 'And with luck, Rose will go home in an hour or two and leave us in peace.'

'For God's sake, Ewan. A man has died. Doesn't that mean anything to you?'

'It wasn't our fault. We had nothing to do with it.'

'Well, yes – in a way I did. I keep thinking that Rose might never have met Sammy, if it hadn't been for me. How can I ever face Liu Ling, after this?' I wound my hands round his arm, imprisoning him and laid my head on his shoulder. 'Oh, Ewan, why did it have to happen?'

Ewan sighed and ran his fingers through my hair, combing it gently back from my brow. 'I've always been afraid of something like this. Because we don't belong here, darling – not really. We could stay in China for ever and still be outsiders – even you. You'll just have to accept it – there's a gulf we'll never be able to cross.'

'But I was born here!' The thick wool of his overcoat was rough against my nose and lips. 'That must count for something.'

'Twenty-six years – against an inheritance of five thousand.'

My tears were making a damp patch on the shoulder of Ewan's coat. Gently, he detached me. 'I must go in to the office this morning – there are some people I have to see. But I'll come back in time for lunch. Will that do?'

I nodded, and sniffed and wiped my eyes on the sash of my dressing-gown.

'You can always phone me, if something comes up. I'm only fifteen minutes away.'

I nodded again, already missing his comforting solidity. Somehow, tragedy had released the tenderness I'd looked for in vain the night before.

He bent to kiss me on the cheek. 'Remember, you're quite safe here. There's absolutely no need to worry. No one can touch you.'

Later in the morning, feeling more confident, I took Rose back to her flat, but a crowd had camped at her gate and press photographers were perched like crows on a nearby wall. I was forced to tell the driver to take us straight home and to send off Shen Fu instead with a suitcase and a list of clothes. By the time Ewan returned at lunchtime, Rose was installed in our home once more.

She didn't take lunch. She didn't appear downstairs for dinner that night either, but her brooding presence in our house overshadowed the meal. I was in no mood to eat in any case, but by the time coffee was served, my nerves were as taut as fiddle-strings.

'I'll go upstairs and see if Rose wants anything.'

'No you won't.' Ewan reached out to push me firmly back into my seat. 'You've done enough for her today. If Rose wants to be pampered, she can go home to her own flat. In the meantime, Shen Fu can take a tray up to her room, in case she feels like eating.'

'Miss Oliver, catchee some bad inside,' he told our steward, unintentionally putting his finger on the truth. And Shen Fu, who doubtless knew the whole story better than any of us, silently did as he'd been asked.

For three days, Rose stayed in her room. I wondered what she was thinking – of supple, scented summer nights, naked with her lover below wide-flung windows? Somehow, I doubted it.

Forty-eight hours after Sammy Liu's head had been delivered to Rose's front door, the rest of his body was found, its wrists still tied, behind a pile of crates on the Jardine Matheson wharf across the river. The police commissaire brought us the news, but already he seemed to have lost interest in the case. Madame Oliver needn't trouble herself: the dead man's sister had identified his remains. As for who'd carried out the murder – the commissaire pursed his lips and spread his hands wide. Who could tell? Even the resourceful police of the French Concession were mystified . . .

Rose drew strength from the headlines in the press. She took to wearing black, and had herself driven back to her flat, a Communist martyr by association; but the reporters and photographers had gone and on the wall someone had scrawled the outline of a fox, the Chinese symbol of an immoral woman. Sullenly, she returned to us and sent a note to Nantao, asking when the funeral was to be held. Her enquiry was ignored, though I heard later that Sammy had been given a third-class burial, with eight men to carry the coffin and a band playing *Dixie* in Chinese time. Liu Ling had worn white, the colour of the mourning streamers at Chapei.

By now Rose was more of an incubus in our home than a guest. Not long after the funeral – no doubt starved of the attention she felt was her due – she smashed a mirror in her bedroom, hacked at her wrists with the shards of glass and was found by one of our house servants, smeared with blood and still sawing away pathetically at a few incompetent little slits on either arm.

'Wouldn't it be better if she went back to her own flat?' suggested Ewan once the doctor had left.

'Her servants have all gone. The place is empty. Shen Fu says they ran off because they were afraid.'

'Surely Shen Fu can find her some more.'

'I don't see how. No one wants anything to do with her.'

'Oh, for goodness' sake!' Ewan gazed round helplessly. 'What are they afraid of? Ghosts?'

'Of whoever murdered Sammy Liu, I should think.'

'But Rose is perfectly safe! Even Du Yuesheng's people would never dare to attack a British woman. The consulate would get involved at once and even Du's friends in the police wouldn't be able to help him then.'

But, as Sammy Liu had discovered, the rulers of Shanghai had their own way of dealing with these things. One day while Rose still lay upstairs in our house, her wrists elaborately bandaged, Shen Fu drew me aside with a warning gesture.

'Missisi, there is a beggar outside this house.' The expression on his face indicated what I should understand by 'beggar': the eyes and ears of the brotherhood of dark lanes. Shen Fu, as our steward and Number One boy, had taken it upon himself to negotiate with the spy.

'The beggar knows your cousin is here. He says the men who ordered the killing of Liu Tung also know.'

'But why should they bother about my cousin? No one pays attention to anything a white woman says. How can she harm them?'

'She has made them lose face, Missisi, through Liu Tung's writing. She made fun of them, instead of being respectful.' Shen Fu's gaze was steady. 'I think it would be best if your cousin left Shanghai.'

'But surely she's safe enough here, with us.' Ewan had assured me there was no danger – categorically, none.

'Accidents can happen, Missisi. Even in your own home, if the fates decide.' Shen Fu's eyes travelled round our peaceful drawing room and I realized he was talking of a world whose existence Ewan would have denied. *Say 'boo!' to the dragons and they disappear.* Not in Shanghai, they don't.

'It would be better for you, too, if your cousin went away.' Shen Fu fixed me with a sad, benevolent stare. 'Very soon, Missisi.'

I went up to Rose's room to tell her. It crossed my mind to wait until Ewan came home and discuss it with him, but I wasn't afraid any more, I was furious – too furious to hold back.

Rose had brought this upon us – Rose, who cast her malevolent shadow over everyone who became involved with her. In my bitterness, it began to seem that my life in Shanghai had been an idyll before Rose arrived.

At first she didn't believe me.

'You're making this up.' She stared at me accusingly from her pillows. 'You want me to go back to England because I've embarrassed the family.'

'I'm not making anything up. Ask Shen Fu. He actually spoke to the fellow who's watching the house.'

Rose's gaze flew to the window. '*Now?* Someone's watching us, right at this moment?'

'Someone's watching you, at any rate.' It was needlessly cruel of me, but surely she owed something to Sammy – a little terror, perhaps, if not remorse for the appalling calamity she'd brought about.

'What more can they do?' she demanded. 'He's dead, isn't he?'

'Sammy is. But you aren't.'

When the tears came, they took me completely by surprise. Yet even then, they weren't tears for Sammy Liu. Rose was weeping from sheer, unadulterated dread, her fingers white where they pressed over her eyes.

'Don't let them find me! Offer them money – anything they want. Tell them I don't deserve to die!' Her fingers slid wetly from her cheeks as she raised her face to mine. 'What have I done to them? I didn't write the articles – I can't even speak their stupid language.'

I despised Rose then, more than I'd ever done. In that moment she was ugly, inside and out – yet it hurt me to see such beautiful features grown suddenly shrunken and old, like Sumei's once age and bitterness had shaped them. I had to steel myself not to feel sorry for her.

'Ewan will know what to do.'

'No!' She lunged across the bed to clutch my arm. 'Ewan will go to the police – I know him. And everybody knows the police here take their orders from Du. You saw the commissaire for yourself.'

'Ewan will simply ask for police protection until you leave Shanghai.'

'No, that's too dangerous! All it needs is for one man to turn his back – just for a second.' Rose clung to my arm, as pitiful as a broken flower.

'You can't stay here.'

'Oh God, no. Find me a ship, any ship, and I'll go tomorrow. Tonight, if it's possible. But Clio, I beg of you – don't breathe a word to the police.'

'We must telephone Ewan, then. He'll make arrangements.'

'No – no. Not Ewan – Stephen Morgan.' Rose's fingers tightened painfully on my wrist. 'Stephen Morgan will understand. He doesn't believe in rules and regulations. And he has to help me – I'm an Oliver, after all.'

'I don't see what Stephen can do that Ewan couldn't manage.'

'It's just . . . I trust Stephen. I've never liked him much, but I'd trust him in something like this.'

I tried to prise her fingers loose, offended on Ewan's behalf. How could anyone doubt Ewan's loyalty?

'I suppose I could ring Stephen Morgan and see what he says.'

Rose shook her head at once. 'Not the telephone. You must go and see him yourself, in the Oliver offices.'

'Surely they can't listen to our telephone calls?'

'Please, Clio – go and see Stephen right away. Tell him I'll take any ship he can get me aboard.'

'But—'

'Now!' She'd resisted my efforts to dislodge her and her fingertips were digging into my flesh. 'Right away, this minute. And not a word to Ewan.'

'I'll have to tell him something.'

'Not until I've gone. Promise!'

What could I do? Rose's fingers were bruising my arm; the terror in her eyes approached madness. I'd have done as much for a stray dog.

★

The Oliver offices on the Bund hadn't changed at all since my father's time. Tall galleries of impassive marble soared away from a central hall, dwindling – out of sight of the visitor – into glass-partitioned pens where the shipping clerks toiled over insurance contracts and bills of lading. Stephen Morgan had inherited my father's airy office overlooking the river – and had moved his desk, I noticed, to give himself a view over the scramble and clamour of the waterway, as if to confirm that water, and not ornamental marble, was the company's proper concern. My father, the aesthete, had always sat with his back to the window.

I'd seen surprisingly little of Stephen, though more than a year had passed since his arrival in Shanghai. Company business, he said, had taken him to Singapore and Hong Kong, as well as inland to Nanking, Peking and the other major cities of China, but I suspected this was at least partly an excuse for indulging his taste for travel. It wasn't like Stephen to be at peace for long in any one place, or among any particular group of people. He certainly seemed to have nothing to do with the set from which Ewan and I drew our friends.

'Leave it to me.' Stephen simply nodded when I'd finished my account of Rose's adventures. 'I'll take care of everything.'

'Everything? Are you sure?'

It had been such a squalid, shameful story, and I'd have given anything to be able to take back my part in it. Stephen hadn't made the telling any easier by listening in noncommittal silence, even though he must have known some of the details already – but then, without any hesitation, he'd given me this calm, astounding assurance that everything would be taken care of.

He didn't leap into action; he didn't fling himself on the telephone, shouting instructions, or ring bells for assistants; he simply met my eye with cool, slightly pitying detachment and promised me all would be well. I felt oddly let down. Ewan would immediately have become protective, enveloping me in plans and revisions and adjustments and all the paraphernalia of command. Stephen had simply told me the problem would be solved, and nothing more.

'What about customs formalities and paperwork?'

He smiled fleetingly. 'There's always a way round those.'

I had to wait while he fished in a drawer for a map, apparently no more at home in this office than anywhere else. He spread the map where I could see it and used a pen to point out landmarks.

'There'll be a Gothic Line passenger ship lying here, off Woosung, tomorrow night, waiting to clear for Calcutta. If you can bring Rose to the watchman's hut in the Upper Harbour at six – do you know it? – I'll have a sampan waiting to take her down-river. I'll wire our Calcutta office to do the needful at the other end.'

'So you do think there's a danger.' That in itself was the greatest relief. In the marble fortress of the Oliver offices, I'd begun to wonder if I were shrinking from shadows.

'Certainly, there's a danger.' Stephen folded the map and leaned back in his chair. 'I believe Rose is a danger to you, while she stays in Shanghai.'

'And to herself, surely, even more.'

Stephen laid down his pen precisely between us. 'Frankly, I'm not greatly concerned about Rose.'

'Ewan says—' I suddenly felt a need to haul Ewan into the conversation; I heard my own voice, as brisk and cheerful as any colonial matron's, rallying the ex-pats. 'Ewan says we're all perfectly safe here – but then, he believes being British still counts for something.'

There was a pause. 'Ewan is—' Stephen hesitated, and then finished carefully, 'an optimist.'

Stephen met us by the watchman's hut at six the following evening, wearing a nondescript mackintosh over his business suit. Behind him, squeezed between the rust-streaked hulls of a pair of cargo vessels, a sampan nudged the wharf like a down-at-heel slipper, vapour rising from a stack of bamboo steamers on its stern. The evening was hardly cold, but even on the short journey from home Rose's fingers had trembled so much she could hardly guide the latest of her incessant cigarettes to her lips.

'I'll go down to Woosung with her, to make sure there are no problems.'

'Stephen, I'm terribly grateful. You've no idea.'

'For heaven's sake don't keep thanking me. Rose is my cousin, too, remember?'

'Of course she is. I'm sorry.'

Rose had brought a single suitcase. Everything else would be boxed and sent on. I watched her make her way to the wharfside, a small, diminished figure overwhelmed by a square-shouldered travelling-coat. On the point of stepping aboard the sampan, she turned and came back to where I stood and kissed me unexpectedly on the cheek. Her hair smelled of cigarettes; I wished her lips hadn't felt so cold against my skin.

'Thank God for Stephen Morgan,' she said.

'That's true. Good luck, Rose. Safe journey.' I forced myself to embrace her, but when she didn't respond I let go at once.

She examined me for a moment, her eyes darkly turbulent. 'You think I'm to blame for Sammy Liu's death, don't you, Clio? You despise me, you and Ewan.'

'That isn't true.'

'Oh yes, it is. You think everyone ought to be married and cosy and wrapped up in one another, just as you are.'

'I've never said—'

'But you've thought it. "Why can't she be happy like me? What she needs is a good husband to settle her down."'

Her eyes flicked over my face as if she were memorizing it, storing it away in some archive of dislike. In that instant I knew I'd joined Margot and Kit and most of the world in Rose's pantheon of resentment: she'd never forgive me for the mess she'd made of things. Her lips pressed together for a moment, then she seemed to make up her mind.

'It isn't true, you know, all this happy marriage business. You've nothing to be smug about.' She swept back a dark curl which had blown over her brow. 'You see, I happen to know your precious Ewan's been having an affair – with that woman Evie Tattersall. It's been going on for ages. Everyone knows about it.'

For a moment she regarded me almost with compassion.

'None of them are saints, you see. Not one. That's my parting gift to you, if you like.'

Her coat flicked out as she turned away, the old, unsparing Rose once more, stalking off to freedom. My face felt numb, as if I'd been slapped. Dumbly, I watched the sampan slide into the lanes of shipping, the long oar at its stern scrawling a lazy farewell across the black water.

As soon it was out of sight, I recovered my senses.

How like Rose, to strike out wildly, consumed by jealousy and resentment! I'd never heard such lies. It made my blood boil to think of her lying there under our roof, searching for a way of spoiling our lives. Well then, she should have invented a better story. Ewan might have his faults, heaven knows, but if anything he was *too* honourable, too decent – too conventional. To imagine that Ewan would . . . with a woman who dyed her hair white-blonde and had a butterfly tattooed on her ankle! Good heavens – he even squirmed with embarrassment whenever Evie Tattersall's name came up in club gossip.

As I walked back to the car, an image of Ewan looking uncomfortable superimposed itself on the huts and godowns of the wharf. I'd only to say 'Evie Tattersall—'

And yet, that's curious, when you come to think of it. Why Evie? Who else's name produces that effect?

Don't think of such things. That's exactly what Rose wanted – to make you miserable, to sow doubt in your mind.

I quickened my pace towards the car. I wouldn't even bother to tell Ewan what Rose had said to me on the wharf: it wasn't worth repeating. For goodness' sake – Evie Tattersall had fleshless, muscular calves which dwindled into gnarled little hollows at the ankle-bone, and that indigo butterfly, tinted green by the yellow cast of her skin. And white-blonde hair – baby hair, in helpless little curls on her forehead. And high, hard, vigorous buttocks she showed off on the golf course in flannel slacks.

Forget Evie Tattersall. Dammit, put the woman out of your mind.

But some men find her attractive. Esmond told me he did – and that Evie was aware of it. 'She wears those wide-legged French knickers,' he said, 'and sits with her legs apart.'

'How do you know that?'

'I dropped my cigarette lighter, didn't I?'

Ewan loathed vulgarity of that kind, thank goodness. He disliked excess in anything: I doubted if he'd ever dropped a cigarette lighter in his life.

'Home, please,' I told our driver as I stepped into the car. I looked at my watch, wondering if I'd be home before Ewan arrived.

I don't need a watch to tell me the answer. When was the last time Ewan came home at six o'clock? He even follows me to parties late – and won't hear of my waiting at home for him.

Ewan works extremely hard in the offices of Fraser, Dunsinane.

And almost always works late. And when he does come home we don't make love any more – except for that last grisly episode, when we came to one another like strangers.

Now you're playing into Rose's hands, Clio. You're walking into her trap.

But everyone knows Evie Tattersall has a lover who brings her powders from a Chinese pharmacist, so they can go on longer in bed.

Ewan wouldn't take an aspirin without a doctor's prescription. And besides, he loves me – my husband, my admirable, decent –

Shen Fu was waiting for me when I reached home. I peered at him carefully, a newly minted suspicious wife. *If anyone knows the truth, he does – one way or the other.*

'The beggar has gone, Mississi. Just after you left with your cousin.'

'The beggar? Oh, yes, of course.'

'And Mr McLennan telephoned. Very sorry, but he has to work late again tonight. He won't be home until eight o'clock, maybe nine.'

'When did he phone exactly?'

'Half an hour ago, Mississi.'

'Thank you, Shen Fu. Oh, by the way, if you see the beggar again, tell him Miss Oliver has left Shanghai and she won't be back.'

'I think he knows, Mississi. The beggars know everything.'

And I know nothing at all. I'm even having to learn how to be a proper, mistrustful wife.

There was a telephone extension in the drawing room. Wherever I sat, it seemed to draw my eyes to its smooth curves, blackly seductive. One call: one single call would put an end to my agony. Oughtn't I to tell Ewan Rose had left?

I don't want to be suspicious! I'm entitled to trust him. The wedding veil and the falling blossom: that's why I married him.

Let's make it a game, then, with forfeits. If Ewan answers, I'll black his shoes with my own hands every day for a fortnight. That'll serve me right for doubting him.

I telephoned Fraser, Dunsinane, and asked for Mr McLennan's office. His clerk answered. 'I'm sorry, Mrs McLennan, he left here half an hour ago. I dare say you'll catch him at the club, if he isn't home yet.'

'I thought he might be working late tonight.'

The clerk sounded surprised. 'Late? No, things are quite slack just now. I'll be off home myself any minute.'

I phoned the club.

'Can't find him at the moment,' admitted the secretary, then added at once, 'Which isn't to say he isn't here, of course. Might be on the stairs, or powdering his nose, or whatever.' He laughed, a bark of male solidarity. 'Is there a message, if I see him?'

'There's no message.'

Ewan came home at nine o'clock and dropped into a chair with a sigh of righteous weariness.

'Gosh – I'm whacked. Any chance of a whisky and soda, darling?'

As I held out the glass, I examined him closely, amazed at how boyish he seemed, only weeks after his thirtieth birthday. His smile as he took the whisky was the faint grimace of a weary child, grateful and dependent. He had an air of virtue – of trials endured and hard work accomplished.

He can't be having an affair. There must be some other explanation.

'Rose has gone.' I told him about Stephen Morgan and

the Gothic Line vessel waiting at Woosung. 'Shen Fu saw a beggar watching the house yesterday and Rose became frightened.' It was easy now to make it all seem insignificant. Compared to what had happened since, nothing mattered at all. 'Rose decided to leave as soon as possible, in secret, and Stephen arranged it.'

'You should have told me. You didn't have to go to Stephen Morgan.'

'I suppose Rose felt she'd caused you enough trouble already.'

'Well, good for Morgan.' Ewan tilted his glass, thoughtfully swirling the ice. 'Strange chap, but he's certainly done us a favour this time. I couldn't have stood much more of Rose.' He stretched out his legs, closed his eyes and folded his fingers round his glass, the picture of honest contentment.

'Shen Fu told you I'd phoned, did he?' With his eyes shut, Ewan missed the expression on my face. 'You've no idea – the blasted office is like a battlefield just now. One thing after another – as soon as my desk is clear, some fool brings along another pile of paper.' He half-opened his eyes to be sure of draining the last of his whisky, sighed, then let his head drop back again. 'That business would fall to pieces if I wasn't prepared to work half the night on it.' He extended an arm. 'Be a brick and fill this up again, darling, will you?'

'Fill it up yourself, you bastard.'

We had a nasty, sharp, well-bred row, conducted in the lowered voices of those accustomed to having servants within earshot.

'Of course it was unforgivable! But I beg you – at least try to understand. Clio, please!'

'But I *can't* understand! You, of all people – '

Servants are the salvation of men like Ewan: their wives are forced to hiss and mutter when instinct tells them to tear and scratch and scream out unmentionable truths.

Above all, I was appalled at how glibly he'd lied, this honest man. I was bewildered by how casually he'd broken my trust and how minor he felt his sin to be.

'Darling, you know how these things start in a place like Shanghai.' Ewan stood up and spread his hands, grotesquely helpless. 'Everybody else is doing it and somehow it doesn't seem so bad – and then it happens once, when you've had a bit to drink, and after that . . . I've behaved contemptibly, I know I have – but it isn't as if I'd been going to leave you, or anything. Not with Evie Tattersall, for heaven's sake. Damn and blast Rose! How could she hurt you like this?'

I raged at him, *sotto voce*: it wasn't Rose's fault, but his – his – his.

'But it was never *important*, darling. Not really.' He groped for a way of making me understand. 'It's different for a man, you see. Women like to think they're in love with a chap when they do it, but chaps can have a bit of fun with other women and it doesn't mean a thing.'

'Are you telling me Evie Tattersall has fallen in love with you?'

'Oh, no – not Evie.' He gave a nervous little laugh. 'Evie's more like a chap in that respect.'

I ran to our bedroom and locked myself in. It was all too much – first the tragedy of Sammy Liu, which had robbed me of dear Liu Ling, and now this sordid affair, which seemed to have robbed me of my marriage. I buried my head in my pillow and wept.

After a while, I heard Ewan's voice at the door – circumspectly, since Shen Fu might cross the hall below at any moment. 'Clio – darling – please let me in. I have to talk to you. I want to explain.'

'Go away! Go and explain to Evie.'

'Clio . . .' He tried the door handle. 'At least let's talk about it. We can't leave things like this.' The spring in the handle twanged again. 'Please, darling – if you've ever loved me . . . give me a chance.'

I unlocked the door and returned to sit on my bed – the same bed on which, I'd realized, we'd held our last, dreadful sexual encounter.

Ewan pressed the door shut behind him. 'Thank you.' He glanced at me across the room, taking in my white, swollen face and red eyes. Almost at once, he looked away. 'I can imagine what you think of me. It's no worse than the way I think of myself.'

'But how *could* you? That's what I don't understand. You, of all people.'

Perplexed, Ewan passed a hand over his hair. 'I suppose it was curiosity, more than anything else. And it was flattering, knowing that another woman wanted to go to bed with me.'

'But Evie Tattersall will go to bed with anyone!'

'No!'

'Of course she will. You should hear Marion on the subject. The professional at the golf club – that fair-haired under-secretary from the American consulate—'

'No, no.' He gazed at me, pained. 'That isn't true.'

Incredibly, for a moment I actually felt sorry for him.

'I never thought of leaving you,' he said pathetically. 'Not for a moment.'

I didn't want him to be pathetic. I was so furious I shouted at him, 'And what if I left *you*? What if I told you our marriage was over and I was going back to England to arrange a divorce?'

He actually staggered, as if I'd hit him. His face went pale and collapsed like melted wax. 'But you wouldn't do that! You're the most precious thing in my life, darling. You always will be.'

'Why should I believe that?'

'Because it's true—' He seemed genuinely stricken. His lower lip trembled like a woebegone child's and a hollow appeared in either cheek. 'Of course it's true! How would I manage without you? I couldn't.' He gazed, horrified, round the room. 'I just couldn't.'

The stupid, damnable, ridiculous thing was – he meant it.

'Darling, don't look at me like that.' He sat down quickly on his own bed, his knees almost touching mine. 'I can't bear it.'

'How am I looking at you?'

'As if you hate me. As if I'm a stranger.' He reached for my hands and gazed at me in distress. 'You must know how much I need you. I can't think what I'd do if you weren't here every morning when I wake up and when I come back in the evening.'

To my horror, his eyes actually began to grow moist. 'I don't deserve you – and that's the truth. I was tempted and, like a fool, I gave in.' A fat, oily tear swelled over his lower lid and slid down the crease of his cheek. My hero. My warrior.

He took a deep breath. 'If you don't forgive me, I don't know what I'll do. Kill myself, probably.' He squeezed my fingers with reckless strength.

'Don't be so silly.' Inwardly, I cursed myself for speaking. Simply by uttering the words I'd accepted my role in his pantomime of contrition.

'Kiss me, then, and tell me you've forgiven me for being so stupid.'

'I can't, Ewan. I'm still too angry. I don't know if I'll ever be able to forgive you.'

'At least promise you'll never think of leaving me again.'

And, forsaking all other, keep thee only unto her . . . How much are promises worth?

'Promise, Clio,' he repeated. 'I won't let you go until you promise.'

'Now you're being stupid again.'

'I'm perfectly serious.' His face was set, full of crazy purpose. 'It's true – I couldn't face my life without you. Not a week of it – not even a day. And the worst thing is, I'll know I'm the one to have thrown it all away. If you don't promise to stay with me, I can't answer for what I'll do.'

There was a desperation in his voice that was quite unlike Ewan. My resolution wavered. I couldn't believe he'd do anything reckless . . . and yet there was a nobility, a strength, even in that. Hopelessly adrift, I snatched at straws.

'All right – I promise. I promise to stay for a while, at least – until I can think about things sensibly.'

'Darling, you'll never regret it.' Ewan raised my hands to his lips and kissed them. 'You're an angel and I don't deserve you.' He kissed my hands again and again, until I pulled them away, revolted.

'Tell you what.' Having won his reprieve, Ewan leaned forward, the words tumbling out in his relief. 'You and I will go off to the mountains for a few days. To Mokanshan, perhaps. Just us two and no one else – except the cook, let's say, and one or two of the other servants. How would that do?'

'I'd rather not go away, if you don't mind. Not the way I feel at the moment.'

He hooked a finger under my chin and tilted it. 'When you're more settled, then. Just say the word, and we'll go.' He kissed me gently on my closed lips. 'Whatever you want, darling – because I couldn't bear to lose you. You must believe that.' He gazed down at me, his expression misty with affection and the shiny tracks of tears on his cheeks.

'Let's never do anything to upset one another again.'

Extraordinarily enough, Ewan imagined making love to me that night would somehow put things straight between us – all right as rain, as if nothing had ever happened.

'Don't touch me!' I lashed out at him and turned my back, and he returned, puzzled, to his own bed.

I spent most of the next day thinking, like a drifting raft in search of solid ground. All the assumptions I'd made about strength and decency and honour had been swept away in a matter of hours: now, when I thought of Ewan, I found myself seeing what was left through another woman's eyes – a merciless, clear-sighted woman whose coldness sometimes shocked me. I wondered if Evie Tattersall had noticed how pipe tobacco had begun to yellow Ewan's teeth, or if she'd minded him dropping into a deep and sonorous sleep as soon as his sexual needs were satisfied.

To my surprise, I found I could adjust to the fact that my husband had made love to another woman. If that had been all – a mere physical fact – I might have been able to go on believing in my marriage and believing in Ewan.

What filled me with dread was the discovery that I was tied to a man quite different from the honest, honourable, high-principled one I thought I'd married. This new husband of mine could lie fluently to me and to himself; he could shed tears of self-pity, but none for me, except for the possibility that he might have to learn to manage without me. Now it appeared I'd promised to remain married to this new Ewan, this weak self-deceiver, without trust, without respect and without the strength which had supported our life together.

They should turn mirrors to the wall, in the house of a woman whose husband has been unfaithful. A passing image – a profile, an unguarded glimpse – was enough to pull me back at once, close to the looking-glass. Had my skin grown dull in the smoky air of Shanghai? Had the sun drawn fine lines under my eyes, or coarsened the flesh at the base of my throat? Was I matronly, was I blowsy, had I let myself go so far that my husband had preferred a dyed blonde head and a tattooed ankle?

The mirror assured me I was none of these things. My face, perhaps, was a little thinner and marked by a gentle melancholy; but my lips, if anything, seemed fuller by contrast and my forehead was still smooth above dark, delicate brows and eyes whose blue-grey sadness had absorbed depths of sapphire. Why shouldn't I do as others did – Marion, Evie, Margot and (I supposed) my mother – and take a lover of my own? Yet I didn't want a lover. What use was another man, to smile and cheat and murmur the same hollow lies about faithfulness?

Babies, on the other hand, do not lie. Babies tell you what they love and hate, and when they fall asleep at the sanctuary of the breast, their faithfulness is perfect. I decided I wanted to be a mother. That way, I could remain married to Ewan, but I wouldn't need to be alone.

Ewan came home early, his arms full of conciliatory flowers, and I told him of my decision. 'We must have a baby now. Right away, without waiting.'

I'd taken him by surprise: I watched his expression freeze as he considered how badly he'd sinned and how much he might have to surrender in consequence. Then he crossed the room towards me and I allowed him to take me in his arms. *She'll come round*, said his face. *She's still angry, but she'll come round in the end.*

'Next spring, darling, I promise – when our five years are

up, and we go home. Then we'll have an heir for Achrossan and lots of girl babies for you to dress up and show off to your friends. You'll have a lifetime to fill the nursery.' He put on his most winning smile. 'And in the meantime, you can look after your penitent husband.'

Wisely, that night he left me alone.

To the south of the city, the peach trees were coming into blossom, heralding the Feast of the Dead, the time for Sweeping the Tombs. With the utmost care, I chose wreaths of paper flowers and sent them to the pharmacy in Nantao, to be burned at Sammy Liu's grave. The crimped, blush-coloured petals rustled an irresistible prayer for a happy life in the Western Sky, but Liu Ling sent them back, with a note in characters which I had to ask Shen Fu to translate.

'She thanks you, Mississi, but this is a Chinese time. A time for the family only.'

By the following afternoon, I couldn't bear to be alone in the house any longer. I ordered the car to take me into town, to the waterfront, to be near the core of Shanghai – that swelling, surging, siren-wailing, shabby, shoddy, rusty, never-still river that was the heart of the city. I walked from the Rue du Consulat to the Public Garden and leaned on the park railings, watching the junks wallow past the moored freighters, sails wide like tea-coloured wings, boxy moths riding the current.

Out in mid-stream, beggar-boats swarmed along the side of a liner, clinging under the galley gutter in the hope of a shower of delectable waste. Downstream, the gaunt shoulders of an American warship rose from flounces of awnings like a frivolous aunt, while 'honey-boats' passed under its nose in a cloud of stench, hauling their treasure of ordure to the bean fields up-river.

At the mouth of Suchow Creek, sampans were jostling – sampans like the one where I used to visit the Lius, ramshackle tunnels of matting and salt-stained boards, playing-card houses flying a bunting of indigo washing among their herb-pots. Brown-limbed children clambered in and out at the many openings or dangled fish-hooks into the litter under the hull, just as Sammy Liu must have done, while a very old man, curled like a cat on the point of a stern, stared out from the shadow of his straw hat. *Not long to wait now. Next tide, perhaps, and the voyage is over.*

A plump baby, as round and shiny as a brass button, crawled over his feet: his great-grandson or great-great-grandson – tomorrow's horizon, chasing a beetle.

Sammy Liu had left no children. I'd been denied any – now, when I needed them most.

I crossed the Bund to the marble and bronze mausoleum of the Cathay Hotel, dropped into a leather tub armchair in the lobby bar and ordered an Old Fashioned. An under-manager came to inspect me gravely from behind a pillar, recognized me, bowed and retired to his counter and his bronze clocks showing the time in Paris and New York.

In Paris at that moment, mistresses would be bathing and anointing themselves and setting out to spend; there was still half a day to go before the merry-go-round started up for *les cinq-à-sept* and all debts had to be paid. In New York the honeys and cutie-pies would still be fast asleep, while their sugar-daddies snored by the side of vinegar-mommas and dreamed of the firmness of ambitious young flesh. As for me, in Shanghai – it was high time I grew out of my romantic dreams. What hurt was the realization of how little else remained.

After my fourth Old Fashioned I took off my flower-pot hat with its fetching quill, laid it on the next chair, dropped my gloves, picked them up again and ordered another cocktail. A movement at my elbow made me glance round, assuming the waiter had returned.

'Are you waiting for someone? Or may I join you?'

It was Stephen Morgan, all amber under the art deco lamps. I toyed with the idea of telling him to go away, but decided that would be churlish. It had been kind of him to take Rose off my hands.

'I doubt if I shall be very good company.'

'I'll risk that.' He moved my hat and gloves to the table and sat down beside me. The waiter appeared with my drink on a tray and over the rattle of the ice I heard Stephen order a whisky and soda. I felt dimly resentful that he should have interrupted my self-pity.

'How odd to see you in the Cathay.'

'I live here.' He crossed his legs casually. 'I have a suite on the eighth floor.'

'What – all the time?'

'There didn't seem any point in taking a house on my own. This way I've no domestic worries and I can come and go as I please. The perfect solution.' He regarded me speculatively. 'I might ask what you're doing here today.'

'Looking for a solution of my own, I suppose. This is obviously the place.'

He glanced round the lobby, empty except for a group arguing volubly in French. 'Where's Ewan?'

'Who cares?' I shrugged extravagantly and a few drops of liquor slopped out of my glass to run down my wrist. With great care, I dried it on my skirt.

'You've had a row.' Stephen reached out for his whisky.

'Not at all. We couldn't be closer, Ewan and I. Haven't you noticed?'

'This isn't like you.' He indicated the glass in my hand. 'Do you want to know what I think?'

'Not particularly.'

'I think you've discovered something that's upset you. Something to do with Ewan and another woman.'

'What have you heard?'

'More than I cared to.'

'Oh, God—' I stared at him, suddenly desolate. 'If you know, I suppose everyone else does, too.' The cocktail glass in my hand fixed me with its unblinking oval brown eye. 'You must think I'm a real fool – the poor, bloody, slighted wife. Who told you? Was it Rose? Did she laugh about it on the way down to Woosung? You probably know more than I do, then. I seem to have been the only one kept in the dark.'

'It wasn't Rose. I was told soon after I arrived in Shanghai – so that I wouldn't put my foot in it, I gather. Wouldn't upset the status quo.' His voice was sharp with contempt.

'Oh, it's most important, the status quo. Stiff upper lip, mustn't rock the boat. After all, adultery built the empire.' I raised my glass to it.

There was an awkward silence, then Stephen asked, 'Are you going to leave him?'

'You aren't supposed to ask that question. Bad form.'

'But are you?'

'Mind your own business.'

I'd meant to put him off, but he simply let the silence grow longer and longer until I was forced to speak. 'For your information, I'm not going to leave Ewan. Not over a whore like Evie Tattersall. Besides – he's made me promise not to.'

'He can't force you to stay.'

'I don't seem to have any choice.' I took a long swallow of liquor. 'Ewan needs me. Can you believe that? It's actually true – my husband was quite devastated when he thought I might go. He was like a little boy, lost in the dark. What can I do?' I noticed that my glass had mysteriously emptied itself. 'Could I have another of these, do you think?'

Stephen signalled to the waiter and murmured instructions.

'Look—' I waved a hand to attract his attention. 'Forget all this. I shouldn't be saying these things.'

'Why not, if they're true?'

'Because I'm just feeling sorry for myself, that's all. I keep thinking how people must be laughing at me, all over Shanghai. "Poor Clio, what a fool." Yet, you know—' I leaned towards him. 'I could bear that, if Ewan would only let me have a baby. Just one – little – tiny – baby. I could love a baby, you see.'

I couldn't decipher Stephen's expression. 'And Ewan doesn't want that?'

'He won't allow babies while we're still in Shanghai. He takes great care not to get me pregnant, you know. Oh, golly, I shouldn't have said that either.'

Another glass had materialized in my hand, reassuringly fragrant with Angostura. All at once I began to understand my plight with cosmic clarity. I leaned forward again and lowered my voice. 'I think Ewan's afraid it might not be his, you see –

not in Shanghai. And there's Achrossan to think of. The ancient blood line and so forth.'

'You don't seriously believe that?'

I shrugged, the glass at my lips. My new wisdom had made me despondent. 'I've never wanted anyone else's baby, you know. I'd be quite happy with Ewan's, even after all this. You believe that, Stephen, don't you?'

'I do.' He tilted his glass to allow the last of his whisky to collect in the base and tipped it down his throat.

I was descending rapidly into misery. 'Everything goes wrong for me, you know. They cut Sammy Liu's head off – and so Liu Ling won't speak to me any more. And now I can't have a baby, because Ewan wants to be a baby himself and depend on me.' Tears had begun to blur the bronze lamps and craze the pillars. 'But you mustn't pity me, Stephen. I couldn't bear you to feel sorry for me.'

'I don't.' His denial was immediate. 'You had everything, you and your brother – everything I never had. I don't feel sorry for you in the least.' He watched me for a moment and then added, 'But I will take you home.'

He removed the glass from my hand and picked up my hat and gloves from the table. 'Come on, my car's outside.' He waited while I negotiated a complex route round the chairs and tables.

'I'm not drunk, you know.'

'I never suggested you were.'

'I walked all the way along the waterfront this afternoon. I'm just very tired.' With dignity I ignored the arm he offered. 'Just tired. Tired of everything.'

He rang two days later, by which time my hangover had subsided.

'Oh . . . Hello, Stephen.'

'How are you feeling this morning?'

'Ashamed of myself. More or less as you'd expect, after five Old Fashioneds. Or was it six?'

'Five. The last one had no bourbon in it.'

I wondered why he'd rung. Perhaps he wanted to lecture me on the sin of drunkenness. At any rate, I hoped he'd say his piece and leave me alone. It appalled me to think how much I'd told him.

Fortunately Ewan hadn't arrived home by the time Stephen deposited me at our door, and when he did appear I was already undressing for bed. I told Ewan I was ill, which was more or less true. At least it spared me the ordeal of another silent, reproachful dinner.

'I expect I bored you with a lot of nonsense,' I said to Stephen. 'Don't believe any of it, please.'

'You told me to mind my own business, I remember.'

'I'm sorry. I shouldn't have been so rude.'

'I shouldn't have asked questions.'

I struggled to remember how I'd answered them. My insides were shrivelling in embarrassment and I scrambled towards a natural end to the conversation.

'At any rate, it was decent of you to see me home – and to help out with Rose. She'd no right to put you to so much trouble. I was going to write you a note.'

'You're doing it again.' His voice sounded suddenly sharp. 'Shutting me out with politeness. Making a stranger of me.'

'But you are a stranger – more or less.'

'After all this time?' The question buzzed indignantly from the receiver. 'It's more than ten years, you know, since we first met in Norfolk – nearer twelve, in fact.'

'What difference does time make?' Flustered, I blurted out the truth. 'Stephen, if I'd seen you every day of those twelve years, you'd still be a mystery to me.'

'Oh.' I heard what might have been a sigh and then a short, apologetic laugh. 'I suppose I'm a mystery to myself as well, sometimes. But I'd rather hoped we were friends.'

'Well, yes, of course we're friends.'

'Then you'll meet me somewhere this afternoon?'

'I don't think so, Stephen, thank you all the same.'

'Just for a stroll in the park. And some tea, if you don't think that's too boring.'

'That's unfair of you. Tea would be perfectly all right. *If*

I were to meet you somewhere – which, as I said, I'd rather not.'

'Look, I'll see you in Kiessling & Baader's at three and if you're still upset with me you can tell me to mind my own business all over again.'

'Stephen, I know why you're doing this.'

'Do you?'

'Yes – and I don't need a shoulder to cry on, and I certainly don't need you to feel sorry for me.'

'I've told you – I don't. You and Guy and your cousins were given everything in the world on a golden plate. If it hasn't made you happy, that's your affair. You might say we're even at last. But that doesn't alter the fact that I still want to see you this afternoon.'

'What on earth do you expect me to say?'

'Say "I'll meet you at three o'clock, in Kiessling & Baader's."'

For a moment, I hesitated. Then I heard myself say, 'Oh, what does it matter?' At least I wouldn't have to sit at home, brooding, for another afternoon. 'Yes, all right, if you're so determined.'

'At three, then.'

Chapter Sixteen

HALF-WAY TO the coffee house, I almost changed my mind. Somewhere – Rue Admiral Bayle, I think – I caught a glimpse of a woman whose short step and earnest, slightly bowed head might easily have been Alice. The resemblance was so uncanny that I craned round in astonishment. The woman was half as old again as Alice, in daisy-printed silk and a frying-pan hat, yet the impression lingered of Alice at my elbow, invisibly proprietorial, lending me Stephen for an hour or two to restore my tattered self-respect.

Certainly, Stephen Morgan was a handsome man – if you discounted the unease he brought with him and his disconcerting habit of staring. To be honest, that was the only reason I kept our appointment – a determined hope that the Trenchards and the Tattersalls and the secretary of the club would see us together and take note that Clio McLennan had no lack of attractive company when she wished for it.

Doggedly, now that I'd remembered her, Alice followed me all the way to the tea table and hovered, a silent spectator, at my side. Yet, in reality, Stephen had never been hers to lend. No matter how deeply Alice herself had loved him, I couldn't believe she'd even come close to the core of the man – or that anyone ever had, or could.

There had been a time when I could see Catherine Oliver in him. Even on the night Kate conjured him out of thin air at Hawk's Dyke, silent and wary in his apprentice officer's uniform, a trace of his mother's softness still lingered about the stubborn mouth and distrustful eyes. Now he was twenty-seven and the flesh clung starkly to the bones of a face which, for all its classical regularity, could become as dumbly impenetrable as a fist.

Alice continued to ask about him in her letters – always at the end, where afterthoughts were supposed to belong. Had I seen Stephen, by any chance? Did he race, did he golf, had he made friends at the country club? Not that she had any more than a passing interest in him these days, she assured me – it was merely something to fill up the page after telling me she'd had her ears pierced like the Duchess of Kent's, and the second of the Heavenly Twins had been launched as the *Patria*. Harry Dunstanheugh was no longer mentioned. Guy was certain Harry had asked Alice to marry him and had been put off. At any rate, he seemed to have passed out of her life and her letters, leaving nothing but her 'passing interest' in Stephen Morgan.

What could I tell her about that afternoon? For the life of me, I couldn't have written an account of our meeting at the tearoom. What did we talk about? Not about Ewan, I'm sure, and not about white-blonde women with tattooed ankles, or Alice, or Rose, or poor Sammy Liu, or any of the people we'd left behind in London. Stephen had no use for the halfpence and farthings of gossip. He preferred to live for the instant. I don't think I'd ever met a man so deliberately rootless, so contemptuous of the musty baggage of the past. Liu Ling would have been appalled – Liu Ling who'd taught me the sole object of life was to mould oneself into a worthy link between what had been and what was still to come.

To revere one's ancestors, honour one's parents and please one's husband – those were her articles of faith. Why did Confucius never bother to explain that a woman must die a little, in order to be a wife?

Ewan would not have approved of my walking the length of Nanking Road, pushing through the crowds like the Shanghainese themselves: and so after tea I suggested we did just that – walked back to the Bund under the shop awnings and the banners and the swinging signs, past the big Chinese-owned department stores like Wing On and Sincere, dodging the trolley-buses and the lines of overloaded carts.

Oddly enough – perhaps because for once I was part of it all – I couldn't remember having seen that street of wonders so full of life before. Stephen and I seemed to stroll in a tunnel of light and din, walled in on one side by a babble of neon lettering – for Italian restaurants or British furniture stores, Chinese silk shops or Russian haberdasheries – and on the other by the hooting, clanging, sweating stream of humanity which toiled past us on the roadway.

We paused at a junction to let a young woman cross ahead of us with a wheelbarrow hidden under a mountain of quivering pork carcasses crowned with a fan of fly-crusted ribs. A flock of bicycles pressed behind her, followed by a large American car with an armed bodyguard crouching on the running-board.

Stephen pointed. 'That's what I call style.'

'Which? The motor, or the Russian with the gun?'

But Stephen was already hustling me, zig-zag, to the next section of road, where a fresh row of little shops offered themselves to his eternal curiosity. Without warning, he'd disappear inside, pursuing something that had caught his eye, but more often, he dragged me with him. In the space of a few minutes he swept me through a wig shop and an incense-maker's, and then into an oiled-paper lantern store where we laughed so much over a sunshade painted with hideous faces that we had to buy an enormous pleated umbrella before we could decently leave.

'Why doesn't it rain?' Stephen demanded of the sky.

'We'd be bound to get wet. There simply isn't room to put that umbrella up here.'

'Not at all! We could rent out the space. Most of Shanghai could stand under it – wasn't that what the chap in the shop was saying?'

'No, he said your grandchildren would treasure it as an heirloom.'

'Hah.' Stephen frowned, stuffed the umbrella under his arm and thrust his hands into his pockets.

Long before I was ready, the shop signs began to thin out before the sober stone towers of the Bund. Stephen's motor was waiting at the steps of the Cathay Hotel, its driver reading a newspaper. Stephen tapped on the window and opened the rear door for me.

'You'd better have this.' He thrust the umbrella into my hands. 'Leave my grandchildren to get wet. I'll ring you in a couple of days.'

'You will?' It hadn't occurred to me that the invitation would be repeated.

'You want to try this again, don't you?'

'Well, yes.' I suddenly did, very much.

'Then I'll ring you.' He closed the door, raised his hand in a perfunctory wave and the car pulled away into the traffic.

I sat down to write to Alice as soon as I reached home. 'You'll never guess whom I happened to meet today—'

I tore up the page. Fibs were best kept for the ends of letters, where afterthoughts belong. Besides, Rose would be in London soon, giving her own version of events in Shanghai.

'If you see Rose,' I wrote instead, 'she may tell you some nonsense about a misunderstanding between Ewan and me—'

Ewan came home at his usual time, tripped over the oiled-paper umbrella in the hall and peered at me carefully.

'You look more cheerful, I must say. Been buying up the town, have you?' He swung down to kiss my forehead. 'Show me the spoils, then.'

'Actually, I've had my ankle tattooed.'

'*What?*' Ewan's stare flew from my face to my feet.

'That was a joke, Ewan.' I stretched out my legs, but he ignored them, glowering.

'That was cruel.' He limped to the window and then turned suddenly to face me. 'Look, Clio, just how long are you going to keep this up? I mean, I know I've behaved badly and hurt you very much, but I've promised to make it up to you in any way I can. I mean it. I'll do anything you ask. And yet you still won't . . . well, you still won't let me touch you in bed. Is there something more you want, for heaven's sake? And don't say "baby", because we've discussed all that and agreed to wait. Darling—' He spread his hands helplessly. 'I love you. What more can I do?'

I gazed at him, noting with surprise the newly acquired

droop of his broad shoulders and the single horizontal line bisecting his forehead.

'I don't think there's anything you can do, Ewan. You see, I think what I really want is something we had before – or I imagined we had – something that went missing without my ever noticing.' I reflected for a moment. 'Maybe it's just that I've never known you well enough. For instance . . . I keep wondering what it was that attracted you to Evie Tattersall in the first place, and whether it was different, making love to her, and how her skin felt to you, and how she smelled, and—'

'Oh, for goodness' sake!'

'I'm trying to understand, Ewan.'

'But not like that!'

'Then how? I ought to know you, surely, if I'm going to be married to you.' It was the exact truth. There was no animosity in it, no intention to wound. If I couldn't have back the Ewan I'd married, then I wanted to find out as much as possible about the Ewan I'd promised to stay with.

'No – no – this isn't the way.' Mortified, Ewan limped out of the room and tripped over the umbrella once more. I could hear him swearing, quite clearly, in the hall.

Exactly six days passed before Stephen Morgan telephoned again.

'Where shall we go this time?' His voice buzzed confidently from the receiver as if he'd never doubted I'd fall in with his plans. 'A cabaret? Blood Alley?'

'Good heavens, no.'

'Why not? I'm hoping you'll show me Shanghai, since you know it so well. For instance – have you ever been inside the Great World?'

'Of course not. Only the Chinese ever go there – and certainly not ladies.'

He must have known that already. The Great World was famous throughout the Far East, an extraordinary, six-storey amusement centre on the corner of Tibet Road and Avenue Edward VII, opened, it was said, by a Chinese pharmacist who'd made his fortune from a miracle brain-powder called 'Yellow'.

'You'll be safe enough with me.'

'You aren't serious?'

'Why not? Wear a scarf round your head and sunglasses, and no one will be any the wiser. They'll just think I've picked up a boy in Fuchow Road – one of those fellows with lipstick and enormous high-heeled shoes.'

'Stephen Morgan, you're quite mad.'

'Maybe so. But have you never passed the place and wondered what goes on inside?'

'I can imagine.'

'No, you can't. That's the point. You have to see for yourself.'

All of a sudden I did want to see for myself. I, Clio, wanted it, badly. For a second Ewan's wife hesitated and Stephen took this as a refusal.

'Never mind. I'll go on my own.'

'Tomorrow afternoon, you said?'

'That's what I had in mind. But not if you don't want to.'

'I do want to. I've decided. I want to go with you.'

As we pushed through the crowd towards the pillared doorway, the tower of the Great World scraped the sky above our heads. From where we stood it resembled a cascade of white pillars, topped by a leprechaun's hat. I didn't doubt for a moment there'd be Chinese leprechauns inside: it was that kind of place – deafening, vulgar, concocted from ancient sleight-of-hand and the magic of patent brain-powder.

A knot of men stood by the entrance, smoking cigarettes and spitting. They glanced at us curiously as we passed, but beyond the doorway the galleries were so dim and so densely packed that for the most part, people ignored us as we shouldered our way through the crush.

'Keep hold of my arm, whatever happens.'

'Don't worry, I intend to.' I buried my fingers in the fabric of his sleeve until I felt reassuring flesh and bone. A miasma of incense laced with acrid human sweat and the stink of hot fat seemed to have replaced the oxygen and I was already beginning to doubt the wisdom of our adventure.

'Scared?' He pressed my arm to his side.

'No,' I lied.

'I am.'

He was actually grinning. He hadn't the faintest idea of what lay ahead of us inside that place – visions of Armageddon or a murderer's knife – but the uncertainty only drew him on. Fear was like strong wine to him, intense and intoxicating.

On the ground floor, the crowd was thickest round some slot machines guarded by lounging desperadoes, and we hurried along its margin. Over the heads of the gamblers, under the glow of red lanterns, I could see the lithe limbs of acrobats flying into pyramids on satin wings, to the triumphant roll of a drum; further into the gallery, real wings fluttered among the shadows where orioles trilled from clusters of lacy cages dangling from the roof.

'Can't we stop to look at the birds?'

'I don't like cages.' Stephen's stride lengthened. 'Upstairs – come on.'

On the next floor, restaurateurs bawled their wares against the swooping howls of a dozen groups of actors. Earwax extractors fished delicately in their clients' ears, the better to let them enjoy the din. We climbed on, upwards, past lines of third-class singsong girls, their skin-tight tunics slit to their ribs and their lips promising what their eyes withheld.

Hands plucked at our clothing, offering herbal medicines, fighting crickets in tiny carved prisons, photographic portraits in borrowed top hats, hot towels, dried fish, erotic massage and the world's finest acupuncture. From raised platforms, barkers offered opportunities to dance the tango or publicly empty our bladders into new-fangled western lavatories.

'What's this old fellow writing, in the corner here?'

'Love-letters.' I'd leaned close enough to pick up a snatch of conversation between the hunchbacked scribe and his customer. The boy seemed bemused, a country lad hoping for a sprinkle of city magic. 'The old man has just promised him a lifetime's faithfulness.' A bleak thought struck me. 'I must ask him to write me one for Ewan.'

'You can't send a love-letter to your husband.'

'Why not?'

'You don't know?'

Stephen glanced down at me in amused disbelief, then his eyes slid away. 'That's what's so wonderful about you, Clio. In spite of everything, you're such a firmly married woman.' He indicated the madhouse all round us. 'I couldn't have come here with anyone else. You're as innocent as a nun, for all your silk stockings and chorus-girl shoes. That's something these creatures—' he pointed to the waiting singsong girls, 'will never understand. I'll bet you wear silk all the way down to your blameless skin.'

In the press of the crowd, he spun me round, bringing us face to face.

'Do you know – you're the most frightening thing in this building?'

I read the words on his lips; the clashing cymbals, the yowling of the actors and the drenching colours of the jugglers' costumes were making my head swim.

'But mercifully, you're married to Ewan McLennan, a man who needs you as much as life itself.'

'It's true. He told me.'

'And since he's a gentleman, we have to believe him. Have you had enough of this place yet?'

'No, please—' I glanced round. All of a sudden, I didn't want to go home yet, to a man who needed me as much as life itself. 'Let's go out on the roof.'

In the brightness of the flat leads, a tightrope walker squatted on his rope, dangling one leg like a flamingo. Strings of red firecrackers zipped and spattered – and there beyond the roof's edge, veiled by the smoke of the fireworks, sprawled Shanghai herself, denuded, undisguised and enticing, from the elephant-backs of her *hutong* roofs to the secret gardens of her mansions.

'Come right to the edge.'

'There's no rail.'

'That's to let the suicides jump over. Don't worry, I'll hold you.'

He held me and I looked down, delicious fear scraping every sense like a razor's edge, a nun in silk stockings compelled to put her trust in a brigand.

Released from that clamorous hell, we began to laugh like idiots, curled over our linked arms like the pliant bodies of the acrobats.

Later, restored to the modesty of my wifely self, I gazed round the ordered, tranquil home I'd created for my husband, uneasily aware that in some way it had changed. It was undeniably different. I could have sworn it wasn't the same house I'd left a few hours earlier, though Ewan's Panama hat lay on the hall chair, exactly as I remembered, and our respective families watched me as usual from their photo-frames by the drawing-room sofa.

I stood in the middle of the room, gazing round, the hair at the nape of my neck prickling like a cat's. Then I realized: my house knew. Somehow, my house had divined that I'd betrayed it, that I'd slipped out of its cloister to go sight-seeing in a hall of demons. Worse – I'd been enchanted by every fearful, wicked minute of my escape. My house was shocked by what I'd done.

That night Ewan and I went to a cocktail party at the American consulate. Afterwards, out of guilt, I let him come to my bed and believe our differences had finally been resolved.

'Home next spring,' the new Ewan breathed in my ear. 'Not long now, darling – back to London and Achrossan and as many babies as you want.' He sounded relieved and grateful – as if gratitude was what I wanted. 'That's a promise, darling. It's this wretched place that's changed us. No more Shanghai – we'll go home next year.'

I'd never minded Shanghai summers, even when the soaking heat was at its worst and each change of clothes had to be peeled off, drenched, within two or three hours. I'd never wished to go off to a seaside resort like the more delicate European wives – but in any case, nothing could have dragged me away in that summer of 1936, which Ewan had promised was to be my last in the city.

That year, the summer heat seemed to burrow inside me, reaching for something elementary it knew was there to be found. I began to notice with an almost animal enjoyment how the warm downpours dripped thickly from the trees long after the rain had passed. Now that the city and I were to be separated, I wanted to fill my eyes, my nose and my ears with such things – and, time after time, respectably in the afternoon, to continue to outrage the primness of my house.

'Have you ever been to those shops in Canton Road where they sell theatre costumes?' I'd known, even before lifting the telephone receiver, that it would be Stephen.

'No, never.'

'We'll go tomorrow. I'll pick you up at half-past two.'

I'd never thought of refusing and to ease my conscience I picked a quarrel with Stephen as soon as I'd settled myself in the upholstered luxury of his car. 'So you're playing truant from the office again? Suppose I tell my father, or Guy?'

'Tell them what you like.' He shrugged dismissively. 'I'll be gone for good soon enough, anyway.'

'But why?' I twisted round to gape at him.

'Because I never wanted to work for the company in the first place. It was Kate who insisted on it. She feels the family owes me a career – something to make up for all Matthew Oliver did to my mother and father.' He leaned back in his seat and studied the pleated cream plush of the car roof. 'I've promised myself I'll stick it out as long as Kate's alive and then I'll wash my hands of the whole lot of them.'

'But you know the business. You're good at your job. Even Guy says so.'

'I won't stay on to slave for Guy. Let him run the company into the ground if he wants.'

'But what will you do?'

'I'll be free of the Olivers, that's enough. Free – to come and go and do exactly as I please. Free to shake off the old black crow that sits on my shoulder. Don't you envy me?'

'I wish I knew what you were talking about.'

He laughed, that strange, harsh laugh which always took me by surprise. 'I tell you what we'll do today – we'll buy you one of those stage crowns with tassels and beads and a mass of silver pins, then you can amaze them when you get to London. Something with enormous tail-feathers whizzing out of it like fire-hoses. You can wear it to a gallery opening, or a charity tea.'

'They'd think I'd gone mad.'

'But you'd know the truth. Isn't that enough?'

There was no sign of amusement in his face, only anger stirring in his voice, and I didn't know how to respond to that.

Outside the costume shop he took my hand and pulled me out of the car. 'Here we are. Come on.'

Two hours later, dazed with colour and the impossibility of choosing one gorgeous silk before another, I fetched home my rolls of stiff brocade from the costumier's lacquered chests and wondered how on earth I was going to pack them for the journey to England.

I never asked where Stephen spent his evenings, or with whom. It was an unspoken pact between us, each to pretend the other had no existence beyond our shared afternoons. Stephen never offered information or asked any questions – yet I sensed that Ewan's ring on my finger, and Ewan himself, like an invisible chaperon defining our friendship, created an ease between us that might not otherwise have existed.

'Are you going to make a go of things with Ewan?' Stephen asked the question right out of the blue as he delivered me home from one of our jaunts, startling me with his directness.

'Yes – I suppose I am.'

It was a subject we normally avoided; yet it did seem as if I'd finally reached an accord with the new Ewan. Whole days went by now when Ewan's betrayal was only a word, no longer an open wound, and his relief was positively endearing – I could believe he'd been genuinely terrified that I'd leave him. I would stay: but I couldn't answer for the new, second Clio who'd been stirring inside me all through our time in Shanghai and who had now finally separated, like a dividing cell, from Ewan's wife, though she continued to share her skin. I'd thought at first that with the fading of my anger over Ewan's affair, the rift would heal. But time had passed and I'd had to accept that the two Clios would never again be one and the same and that this new half of me would continue to think thoughts and feel emotions that Ewan would never suspect and which I would never divulge.

We went greyhound racing at the Canidrome, Stephen and I, and blew our winnings on champagne. A week later we went to the cinema, to see *The Sultan* with Claude Rains, Karen Morley and Rudi Romanov.

'*Rudi Romanov?*' I clutched Stephen's arm. 'What nonsense!' I gazed at the melancholy eyes and deeply fissured cheeks which shone, silvery and giant-size from the screen. 'That isn't Rudi anyone – that's Igor Starozhilov, Aunt Margot's friend. I'd recognize him anywhere. How extraordinary!'

The sultan scowled and postured over his pretty white slave while I tried hard to believe those braceleted arms had once held me. Igor had so obviously been destined to be the whole world's lover, not to waste himself on wayward schoolgirls behind the backs of their aunts. Now, effortlessly, he could be every woman's fantasy and satisfy millions. He was bound to be a stupendous success.

'If you've had enough of this, let's go for a walk.'

We strolled along the waterfront, a view of which I never tired. As we leaned on the railings, watching a string of barges drift by, they reminded me of a conversation we'd had some time before.

'You told me Guy was bound to run the Oliver company down. Do you really believe that?'

''Fraid so. Old Matthew Oliver must be spinning in his grave.'

'Then what would you do, in Guy's place?'

Stephen stabbed a finger towards the sky. 'I'd buy aeroplanes and start up an air transport company. Breakfast in Glasgow, lunch in London, dinner in Paris – that sort of thing.'

'And one's stomach left somewhere in between? Ordinary people will never want that.'

'Yes they will.' His fingers were curled round the top spar of the railings; his eyes were fixed on the far side of the river and I was suddenly reminded of a boy who'd once sat on a dyke-bank in Norfolk, dreaming of spinning off on the wind, far above the sordid muddle of human affairs. Stephen had no doubts at all. 'Everyone will travel by air in future. Even freight will go by air – the most urgent stuff, at least.'

'Then the shipping business will be in a terrible state. Oliver's ought to fight that, surely.'

'Clio, tell me this—' He twisted round to lean one elbow on the rail. 'Exactly what is it that subsidizes our transatlantic and Far Eastern passenger services?'

'I don't know.'

'The government does, by handing out mail contracts. But if mail can be flown across the Atlantic in a day, or flown out here, say, in three or four days instead of six weeks, who's going to bother sending it by sea?'

'You mean Oliver's might not get any more mail contracts.'

'Exactly. That's why the company ought to start an airline of its own. But Kit and your father have been too long in shipping and Guy can't see an obvious move, even when it's under his nose.' He shrugged. 'My brief is to look after Shanghai and not to worry about company policy.'

Something Stephen had said weeks earlier now began to make sense. 'And so you're going to leave and set up an airline of your own.'

He smiled grimly. 'If only I could. But it takes capital to buy aircraft and I don't have any. Oliver's do – that's what's so stupid.'

'Then why not stay in the company and persuade them to do what you want?'

'Oliver's isn't my company.' He kicked the base of an iron post. 'Let the Olivers save it.'

★

As the summer passed, the scenes on the world's stage became more surreal. In July we heard that a dirty, cruel, civil war had erupted in Spain, where neighbour was being urged to murder neighbour and the fascist side had called upon their comrades in Germany and Italy to join in the mayhem. A month later, Adolf Hitler's rise to power in Germany was crowned by the drama of the Berlin Olympics – only for Aryan superiority to be exploded by the triumph of a black athlete. In Shanghai we noticed nervously that the Korean marathon winner had been forced to run in the colours of the Japanese Empire. Clearly, Japan had ambitions of her own – one of them tightening her hold on a large area of China.

Quietly, Stephen Morgan began to dispose of Oliver property in those parts of Shanghai beyond the protection of the foreign settlements.

'How much will you sell?' I asked him.

'As much as I can get away with. As long as the price holds up.'

'What do they say in London?'

He smiled faintly. 'I haven't told them yet. It's just a hunch I have that things could get awkward here before too long – and they put me in charge of Oliver Oriental, after all. Perhaps I'll be proved wrong and then Guy can hang out flags and celebrate in style.'

Alice wrote to say that my father's friend, Stanley Baldwin, who was once more Prime Minister, had been distracted by problems nearer home.

'The newspapers here won't print anything, of course, but we hear all the scandal because of Mamie, who's "in" with the American set. Papa says the King ought to be free to marry any woman he chooses, regardless of how many divorces she's had – but that's because he's been divorced himself and, naturally, he takes Mamie's part in everything. Mamie used to be very thick with Wallis Simpson in Baltimore, you see, long before the P of Wales thing began – and now she talks about her *dearest friend*, who's just the *sweetest person in the world*.

'Your father and Mr Baldwin think it's all frightful. Uncle

Edward calls Wallis "What's-her-name", and "that woman who wears girls' frocks". No one would care if the King was content to keep her as a mistress, but unfortunately he's obsessed with making her Queen and, really, her past is just too lurid for words.'

Near the end of her letter Alice enquired, 'Are you well, darling? Are you really happy?' from which I guessed Rose had arrived back in London and had started to spread her poison. The letter closed with Alice's usual plaintive aside, 'I don't suppose you've seen Stephen Morgan recently, have you?'

I answered as honestly as I could: I see him occasionally. The 'occasionally' was strictly a lie. In fact, I saw Stephen Morgan quite often, but always in the chaste afternoon, cousin-to-cousin, without any hint of impropriety, and so I described our friendship as 'occasional'. Yet in truth, I could no more have given up those afternoons than I could have explained the reason to Alice – unless it was that we two oddities, Stephen and I, seemed the only sane pair in a city rapidly descending into madness.

Cautiously, I'd asked Ewan, 'Do you believe the Japanese will invade? What will happen to your uncle's property here, if they do?'

'Well . . .' Ewan sucked in a whistling breath. 'It's possible the Japs might start something in the Chinese districts of the city, I suppose, but they won't dare to touch the foreign settlements. They'd have half the British Navy in here if there was any chance of a raid, never mind the Americans and the French. Still, I've reported the rumours to London. The old man can decide what he wants me to do about them.'

He leaned over my chair and kissed the top of my head. 'In any case, darling, nothing's going to happen before the end of the year and after that we'll be on our way home.'

My time in Shanghai was drawing to an end; with concern, I realized I'd heard nothing from Liu Ling for almost six months. At last, breaking all our rules of non-involvement, I asked

Stephen Morgan to go with me to Nantao, into the serpentine lanes of the old Chinese city, where Liu Ling's husband kept his pharmacy.

I'd been there several times before, but always with a guide. The shop was harder to find than I'd expected, hidden away among clove-brown alleys where the doorways of the horned houses gaped like dragons' mouths, extending tongues of stone flags. As we pushed on into the labyrinth, limbless beggars scrabbled into our path, beating our knees with twisted hands. Without warning, a dentist and his customer rolled out, kicking, at our feet, locked in a python embrace; impassively, their audience allowed them an inch or two, then crouched down for a closer view.

As the lanes grew narrower and more tortuous, we had to thrust aside shop-flags and duck our heads under the tufted bamboo poles identifying fireworks shops, or jade-cutters, or silversmiths, or dealers in opium lamps. From the fragrant doorway of an eating-house, men who might have been wrestlers watched us grimly, chewing with slow malevolence.

'I don't believe this.' Stephen murmured the words under his breath, but I was pressed against his side, near enough to hear.

'Scared?'

'You bet.' Yet his eyes were alive and avid for more.

'Look for an altar-maker. The pharmacy is next door.'

We found it at last, sunless under a brow of sagging tiles, its once crimson pillars faded to dirty magenta, the leaping-tiger sign under its eaves blackened with age. Just inside the entrance there was a shrine to Kong Mu, the apothecaries' patron, with his iron cane and bulging eyes, and his gourd full of medicines rubbed to a fine sheen by the kneading of anxious fingers.

Liu Ling's husband, Tao Ho, received us at the back of the shop behind jars of preserved snakes and an old glass aquarium full of ginseng roots. Even in the poor light, Tao Ho's skin had the greenish tint of an opium-smoker.

'My wife is ill.' His eyes roamed round his store of remedies and I guessed he was lying. 'She says you should go back to your own family, where you belong – back to England, to the home of your ancestors.'

'Can't I speak to her?'

Tao Ho gazed at me with empty eyes. 'My wife is ill, as I said.'

I left greetings for her, nevertheless, wondering if they'd be passed on, and her husband signalled to someone in the shadows. 'My sister's son will take you safely back to the iron gate.'

We left Nantao in silence and under escort.

It wasn't until the beginning of December that the mass of the British people at last learned of the constitutional crisis surrounding their king – something we in Shanghai had followed for some time in our French and American newspapers.

'Why can't he find himself a respectable wife and stick to her?' Ewan's indignation was quite genuine. 'That's his duty, for heaven's sake. It seems little enough to ask.'

In the end it proved too much to ask and by Christmas we had a new king, a shy, honourable former naval officer. Poor man, he inherited a throne already beset; one of his first tasks was to sign an act banning uniformed fascists from marching through British cities and another voting more money for the armed forces. In Britain, as in France, spending on national defence was being stepped up to match the millions invested by Germany.

One day in March, Ewan returned, somewhat put out, from the office. I'd spent the afternoon packing our porcelain into tea-boxes, ready for dispatch to London.

'Bad news, I'm afraid, darling. Garnock Fraser wants me to stay in Shanghai for a bit longer – just till the autumn, he says. He's sending someone out to take over the office, but the new chap hasn't been out east before and the Old Man wants me to stay on until he's found his feet. He's sorry, but there it is.' He looked at me anxiously. 'You won't mind another six months, will you, Clio? I mean, you've always liked Shanghai, after all.'

I didn't like Shanghai – that was the trouble. I *adored* Shanghai and at the same time I hated its cruelty with an equal passion. Had I been blind and deaf before? Sometimes now, when I explored secret corners of the city with Stephen Morgan, it was as if I'd never suspected its true nature before. To my heightened senses, its colours seemed to give voice like a choir – the deep hum of the reds, the soft fluting blue-greens of carved jade, the hot clashing of yellow walls and the cello-note of the shadows. In the lanes, the song of hidden orioles brushed my skin like rain. The incessant clicking of copper cash counted five at a time, Chinese fashion, from one hand to the other, began to march as an army of insects through my dreams. Even the bitter, syrupy, crude stench of the place was a psalm to the living. In those last months Shanghai was like a new city: it made my soul sing as nothing else had ever done.

But I'd counted on being clear of it in the spring. That was why I'd let my senses loose, clinging to our departure date like a charm against enchantment. Nothing too awful could happen because we were leaving, Ewan and I. It was the end of things; there was no time for a beginning.

And now we were no longer going.

I became unsettled. The whole world seemed to be on the move and yet we were trapped in Shanghai. Our newspapers reported that foolhardy young men from all over the world were flocking to Spain to fight for the International Brigade against Franco. Alice wrote to say that Elliott Cadzow, the artist's son, had made a vain attempt to persuade Rose to marry him, before rushing off to enlist with the rest.

'He's trying to prove something to her, I think. Rose was dreadfully cruel.'

Within a month, Elliott was dead, having proved, perhaps, something quite different from what he'd intended.

An unplanned summer crept upon us. Stephen Morgan continued to telephone and I continued to spend afternoons with him. I'd never intended it to go on, but by now we felt secure in our ability to remain mere acquaintances, in our determination not to understand one another any better. I was reassured by the air of finality which hung over the city like the poignant closing parade of a circus. The end was approaching: no promises were possible. There was no danger of *for ever*.

At the end of April our newspapers reported that Hitler's bombers had obliterated the Spanish town of Guernica in support of his ally, Franco. I hadn't forgotten the ruins of Chapei, littered with broken, dead young men – and now the fluttering white ribbons were coming closer again. In China, the Communists had urged General Chiang Kai-shek to make a joint stand with them against the Japanese occupiers, but he'd refused, fearing the Communists' ambitions more than the invader who held parts of his country. Everywhere, ambitions were stirring. Even in his coronation photographs, I thought, the new King George looked sombre.

In Shanghai, we knew that the Japanese, hungry for more of China, were only looking for an excuse to bite. In July shots were exchanged between the two sides on a river bank near Peking; yet somehow, the incident was contained. Then on 9th August the bodies of a Japanese sub-lieutenant and his driver were found, riddled with bullets, near Hungjao military airfield on the outskirts of Shanghai. The Chinese authorities protested that the shooting had been deliberately provoked – but the Whangpoo River began to fill up with Japanese warships nevertheless.

On the 10th, Shen Fu brought a note at breakfast and, when Ewan automatically reached out for it, elegantly sidestepped him.

'For Mississi,' he said.

The note was in Chinese characters and he read it for me. 'Men from the Japanese consulate are gathering all their people. The women and children are to be sent away to Nagasaki. You must go to your own home now and be safe. May you find there the five blessings.' He laid the paper precisely before me. 'It's signed "your friend, Liu Ling".'

★

297

Country people from the outskirts were streaming into the settlements for safety, bringing their cows with them, and Chiang Kai-shek's troops had begun to pile sandbags round the North Station, rebuilt after the previous Japanese raid. A horde of refugees had crammed themselves – men, women and children – into the galleries of the Great World among the birdcages, the dried fish and the slot machines. The Volunteer Corps stationed Ewan at the Union Church.

'I'll be back in a day or two, when this blows over.' At the front door he held me tightly. 'You mustn't worry. It's another false alarm, that's all.'

But the alarm continued. On the evening of Friday 13th, a race meeting at the Canidrome was called off; instead, people went out on the rooftops to watch the shelling begin over Chapei, just as they had five years before.

The following morning was wet and muggy, but by midday the cloud cover had lifted enough to allow a special show – Chinese bombers busy over the river, making low-level raids on the Japanese warships which had shelled the shore.

Finding me at home in the middle of the afternoon, my silent house taunted me with suffocating isolation.

At four o'clock I telephoned the Oliver offices and found Stephen still at his desk. 'There must be something I can do. Ewan's going to be away for days and I'm going out of my mind here, all alone.'

'You could come down to the Cathay, I suppose. At least you'd be with other people there. I'm trying to find a ship to bring some soldiers up from Hong Kong at the moment, but I'll meet you there in half an hour.'

The marble foyer of the hotel was crowded when I arrived, but Stephen wasn't among the throng. The receptionist phoned his suite but got no answer.

'I expect he'll be on his way.'

The sound of cheering drifted in from Nanking Road and the Bund, where the people of the International Settlement, going about their daily business, were enjoying the show put on by the bombers over the river. Spectators on the rooftops cheered each hit as if the whole spectacle had been laid on for their benefit.

I went out into the street and peered up into the sky with everyone else. A crack bomber squadron had appeared among the bi-planes, concentrating on the Japanese flagship *Idzumo*, anchored off the Bund. Time after time they made shallow dives, only for their bombs to fall harmlessly into the water.

'Come inside, Clio, it's safer.' Stephen Morgan materialized from among the crowd. For a second he hesitated, shading his eyes and glancing upwards with all the rest.

'That's odd,' I said. 'Look, some of them are coming this way.'

'They've given up, I should think. They're heading for home.'

Assuming the show was over, the people nearest to us began to turn away from the river. Suddenly Stephen shouted in my ear, '*Get inside!*' and hurled me towards the hotel entrance. But the pavement was jammed with terrified souls who'd seen exactly what he had: four black specks detaching themselves from the aircraft overhead and plunging towards us.

A fraction of a second later, I was sprawling flat on the pavement with my cheek in the dirt, crushed breathless by Stephen's weight above me, while the noise of the Apocalypse exploded in my ears.

Instantly, I could hear nothing. All I knew was that bright day had become an airless hell of hot dust, a copper light through which, instants later, a sleet of mortar and pieces of brick and sharp splinters of glass plummeted down on us where we lay, gasping for breath, on the ringing pavement. Overhead, slices of building seemed to pitch themselves into the street; and though my ears were now filled with a roaring which drowned out thought, I felt the concrete below my cheek throb with each new cataract of masonry as if the earth had opened to swallow us up.

The crashing stopped. There was sudden, absolute silence. Then, from a score of mouths, a wailing rose up – a disembowelled, unearthly shriek of pain. I heard Stephen's voice close to my ear, increasingly wild, and I struggled to answer.

'I'm all right. I'm all right. I'm not hurt – just—' He'd been lying over me; now he rolled aside and I sucked dust-laden air painfully into my lungs. 'Just bruised.' A hand appeared before my face – mine, trembling. I touched my hair and found it dry and tangled with debris. Overhead, the ochre sky still drizzled an ash-like litter. We hauled ourselves awkwardly to the wall of the hotel.

'Good God.' On the other side of the road, a bomb had cut a wedge from the two top floors of the Palace Hotel. Rooms lay open to the sky, curtains fluttering at gutted windows, their splintered woodwork gaunt against the light. On the lower floors, there wasn't a sheet of glass left intact; shocked faces peered out from the jagged holes, their expressions of horror vividly reflecting what we on the ground still couldn't take in.

I rose up to my knees, crunching glass. Yards from where we lay, a crater had swallowed part of the roadway. Round its lip lay the unmistakably dead – European and Asian together, limbless, headless, tossed aside. Here and there, a hand lifted in feeble entreaty, withered by pain. Moans formed a descant to the thin calling of voices.

Astonishingly, dust-covered figures were rousing around us, probing bruised heads and testing limbs for injury. The bombs had amalgamated us – rickshaw puller and society matron – into a putty-coloured race, floured into anonymity. From the debris people staggered to their feet, crawled to help others, or peered into strange faces, searching for friends.

'The crush saved us. If there hadn't been so many people . . .' I reached out to touch Stephen's arm and felt the sleeve of his jacket wet. The deep stain of blood bloomed against the pale dust on my fingers.

'You're bleeding—' I moved round: the cloth of his jacket lay dark and shredded over his shoulder blade and upper arm, glittering with particles of glass. 'We must find you a doctor.'

'I'm all right.' He shook his head and leaned against the wall. 'Let them see to these poor devils first.'

Hotel staff were moving among the injured now. A Sikh policeman had run up from his traffic duties on the Bund and was vainly trying to take charge. The uninjured were waved back. 'Away! Go home!' Stephen's bloodstained jacket caught his eye. 'Inside, inside.' He pointed towards a group shuffling into the doorway of the hotel.

The foyer of the Cathay looked amazingly normal. An injured doorman lay on his back in front of the reception desk, but even that had been managed with exemplary neatness. Quickly, however, the atmosphere of calm was swept away by the groaning, limping, bleeding survivors of the blast, trailing stained clothing as they came and leaning on one another for support. An elderly man called for brandy for his wife, while a child whimpered inconsolably in a corner; several voices demanded the attention of a doctor, while others begged for patience.

Stephen shepherded me through the throng. 'Let's get out of this.' Mercifully, the lifts were working, though my hand was still shaking so much that I could hardly push the button for the eighth floor.

I'd never been in Stephen's suite before. It reminded me of the one Ewan and I had shared when we first came to Shanghai – panelled in some cool, light wood, luxurious in its clean lines and ebony detail, a world away from the mayhem downstairs. Like Stephen's office, it looked out over the river, where the Chinese bombers continued to harass the *Idzumo*, oblivious to the catastrophe below.

I caught sight of myself in the engraved mirror above the desk – chalk-white, red-eyed, wild-haired and filthy, but alive and uninjured. Automatically, I ran my fingers through my dust-stiffened hair and somehow this small vanity helped me to pull myself together.

'We must get you a doctor.' I went to the telephone.

'Yes, sir?' The voice from the reception desk was calm and professional, only a distant babble of voices betraying the chaos beyond. Yet for once, the Cathay Hotel could not provide what was required.

'I regret, madam, the external telephone lines are temporarily out of order and we've had to send out for medical assistance. Our own doctor is engaged with the badly injured people in the road outside. Is Mr Morgan in severe pain? Perhaps, a bromide while he's waiting—'

There were scissors on the desk and I took them into the bedroom.

'Let's get your jacket off, at least.' I began to cut it round the shoulder seam and up to the collar, moving the scissors as gently as I could. 'You can see I was never much of a tailor.' Underneath, Stephen's shirt was stuck to his shoulder in bloody ribbons. 'Or a nurse,' I added lamely.

His face was ominously pale under its tan, but he managed a smile.

'It isn't nearly as bad as it looks. Don't worry.' He sat down heavily on the bed. 'You might bring me a whisky. That would help.'

'But we have to do something. You could have blood poisoning by the time a doctor gets here.'

'Have a go at it yourself, then. You must have had lessons in first aid.'

'Not for anything like this.' I gazed at the oozing mess in horror. 'There's glass in there. I wouldn't know where to begin.'

'You can't make it any worse. Just clean it up a bit and pick out any glass you see.' Stiffly, Stephen rolled on to his stomach, as if sitting up had become an ordeal. 'I'll leave it to you. Do whatever you like.' He moved his uninjured arm up under his head and his voice became muffled. 'If you go into the bathroom, you'll find razor blades and so on in my shaving kit. And I would rather like that whisky, if you don't mind.'

The bathroom, like the rest of the suite, was clinically tidy and almost bare of personal possessions. I peered into cupboards, scooping up anything that looked remotely useful – towels, a bottle of iodine, a torch and, in desperation, some of the odd-looking instruments from a leather manicure case. There was an almost full bottle of Glenlivet in the sitting-room cocktail cabinet. I tucked it under my arm, picked up a glass and, after a moment's hesitation, added another.

It was only when I returned to the bedroom that I noticed

the gilt-framed picture hanging opposite the bed, curiously out of place among the chrome and sleek veneers. It was a study of a young girl in a ribboned hat staring thoughtfully from a window into a garden of hazy trees and speckled grass – and yet it was hardly a portrait, unless of a mood or a fleeting expression. The girl had been caught in a moment of soft, gentle melancholy, but the colours about her were flushed with all the luminous exuberance of a flower market. The play of the light reminded me of the Côte d'Azur and lazy evenings lit with gold.

'That's your Renoir! The one you sold your plane for.'

Stephen twisted his head to catch a glimpse of his treasure. 'It wasn't very clever of me to bring it here, under the circumstances.'

I was gazing at the picture, momentarily distracted. 'I'm glad you didn't leave her behind.'

The weight of the whisky bottle against my side dragged me back to reality. Yet even as I began to cut away the strips of bloodstained shirt, I couldn't resist another glance: the little picture seemed to flood that quiet room with the sustaining spirit of a rainbow. Beyond the window, though Shanghai as I'd known it was dying, it lived in me still, just as that triumphant garden sustained the cool, meditative face at its centre.

I worked in silence, with an emptied fruit bowl as a basin, gently washing away the blood to expose the places where the skin was torn. I'd never touched any part of Stephen's body before, except his hands or the crook of his arm when we walked. The distance between us had been understood – part of our need to remain strangers – so that now the novelty held all the thrill of broken rules. The whisky had steadied my hands a little, but shock and the sweet fumes of Glenlivet had combined to release the new Clio from her sister. I found myself relishing the smoothness of Stephen's skin under my fingers and the rounded undulation of bone and muscle.

The wounds made by the glass shards weren't deep, but there were many of them, as if a meteor shower had raked him while he sheltered me. I felt with my fingertips for the fragments which remained, then tackled them with tweezers or scissor-points, sometimes starting the bleeding afresh, dismayed by the vivid welling of blood over the pale parchment of his skin. Stephen never spoke, but lay there under my hands, with only the occasional indrawn breath and sudden tensing of his shoulders to show when I'd hurt him.

'I shouldn't be doing this.' His pain distressed me beyond words. 'You should have a doctor.'

He made a dismissive sound, deep in his throat, and I felt the throb of it below my palms, the vibration of living flesh. I wanted to press my cheek to the faint sheen of his skin, to count the beating of his heart against my lips. Instead, I closed my eyes and forced myself to concentrate on the harsh white disc of torchlight and the hunt for my glittering enemy.

From somewhere outside there came another distant explosion. Stephen rose up on one elbow, wincing. My hands froze.

'Another bomb?'

'It sounded like that. A mile away – maybe not so far.'

'Japanese, do you think? Are they going to shell the settlements?'

'I doubt it. They're too clever for that. They'll find another way. Hey—' With sudden vigour Stephen twisted round, clasped my hand in his and held it to his lips. 'Pour us both another drink.'

I watched him reach for his glass, fascinated by the smooth play of muscle and bone. Ewan had a virtuous, ramrod back, an inflexible vee. Stephen's back was pliant, as supple as the embroidered cormorant on my screen; I had a sudden urge to take it between my two hands and feel the voluptuous power of its coiling. Resolutely, I applied my lips to my whisky glass.

'That's the best I can do, but there are probably tiny pieces deeper down, where I can't reach them. You must let a doctor examine you.'

'All right, I promise.' He swung his legs slowly over the edge of the bed and sat up.

I made an effort to sound briskly medical. 'I don't think I

should put on bandages in case there's infection, but iodine is supposed to help.' Marion Trenchard had assured me she applied it to everything.

I soaked some cotton wool yellow-brown with iodine and dabbed firmly.

'For God's sake!' Stephen's shoulders flexed in sudden agony, his head flew back until I could see his tightly shut eyes and a cry of anguish escaped from his throat.

'Oh, I'm sorry! Stephen, I'm so dreadfully sorry, I didn't think—' My own eyes were pricking with tears. 'It said on the bottle "For cuts and scrapes".'

'You'd better put it on, then. Go ahead! Go ahead.'

'But—'

'Finish the job, why don't you? It hurts like hellfire, so it must do some good.'

'I don't want to.' But he sat in silence until I continued – more sparingly this time – and waited, rigidly suffering, until I'd finished. Then he turned back to me, smiled and stroked my cheek gently with a crooked finger.

'I'd no right to be rude. You've been wonderful.'

That simple contact destroyed the last of my control and great drops of misery began to run down my dusty cheeks.

'What's this? Tears? But why? Because of the bombs?'

Dumbly, I shook my head, dislodging more tears. 'I never meant to hurt you.'

'You aren't weeping for me? Oh, my dear, dear Clio – ' His uninjured arm slid round me, pulling me against him, cradling me in warmth and strength, and the smell of iodine. 'It's a very long time since anyone cried for me.'

The words sucked the soul right out of my breast. In truth, I was weeping for other things besides – for the glory of broken rules, for feelings I'd never known I had and for the certainty that something near to my heart was about to end, one way or another, in torment. The doleful eyes of the girl in the ribboned hat watched me from her frame over Stephen's naked shoulder. His hand had already found the tender hollow at the nape of my neck; now it moved irresistibly down my spine, sending its searching heat deep into my very essence. I buried my tears in the soft shadow of his throat, where a lover belonged: it never occurred to me to do otherwise.

Beside the bed, a telephone rang. Stephen glanced down at me, then reached out for it.

He listened for a moment and held the receiver against his chest. 'The telephone lines are open again. Someone's trying to get through.'

He listened again and I saw his face become expressionless. 'Yes,' he said. 'She's here. She was just outside the hotel when the bomb went off, but she's quite safe. Just a few bruises.' He held out the receiver. 'It's Ewan. He's in a pretty bad state.'

Ewan was almost incoherent. He sounded as if he were sobbing with anxiety. 'Thank God,' he kept saying. 'Thank God you're all right. I've been phoning everybody. When I rang home and Shen Fu said you'd gone into town and hadn't come back . . . Oh, my darling – don't ever frighten me like that again.'

I perched, embarrassed, on the edge of Stephen's bed, powerless to stop the flood of Ewan's distress and a little frightened by its intensity. Stephen made no attempt to move out of earshot. I watched him pour himself another large whisky.

'Did you hear the other bomb? The one that fell later?' Ewan was gabbling in his relief. 'Esmond reckoned the Chinese pilot was trying to drop his load on the race track, but it went straight into the Great World instead. There's a crater fifty feet wide at the road junction, and burnt-out cars in all directions. Esmond says there must be at least a thousand dead – it was full of refugees, you see. Pieces of them were flying everywhere.

'Thank God,' he murmured again. 'Oh, thank God you're safe.'

Carefully, I replaced the receiver. 'Ewan's coming here to collect me and take me home.'

Stephen nodded into his whisky. 'He sounded upset.'

'I've never known him like that before.' I clasped my hands in my lap, wet with tears. 'Oh, what a mess.'

'Time to go.' Stephen got to his feet and walked to the window. 'It's time to close down the circus.'

Chapter Seventeen

THE VOLUNTEER CORPS allowed Ewan to sleep at home that night, and for a few desperate hours shock revived the tenderness of the first weeks of our marriage. I clung to it blindly. All I wanted was to be comforted and held safe in somebody's arms and assured that everything was simple and straightforward – knowing perfectly well that it wasn't and never could be again.

A mile beyond our gates, as the blood-soaked sawdust dried to a stinking mat on the pavements round the Great World, the residents of the foreign settlements stumbled about their business, appalled by the sudden, brutal demonstration of their vulnerability. A rumour went round that the bombing hadn't been a mistake after all, but a deliberate attempt to drag the Great Powers into China's war with Japan. We all waited – but the Great Powers showed no sign of coming to Shanghai's rescue.

Marion Trenchard telephoned to say she and her children were taking up the Consul-General's offer of evacuation to Hong Kong, while Esmond stayed to look after the interests of his bank. Later that day, a cable came through from Garnock Fraser in London, instructing Ewan to come home without delay.

'I suppose Mother's been on the phone, giving the old boy an earful.' Ewan handed me the cable form. 'You should leave, certainly. There's no question about that.' He chewed his lip. 'The trouble is, Esmond's staying, Tony Tattersall's staying and quite a few of the others. It's a bit embarrassing, being ordered home like this.'

We left, all the same. Fierce fighting was going on to the

north of the city and the Japanese bombing and shelling of the suburbs beyond the foreign settlements was already worse than their previous raid. The British Navy sent bluejackets ashore to march through the International Settlement, raising morale, yet in their hearts everyone knew it was the beginning of the end of our lease on Shanghai.

I saw Stephen Morgan once more, on the day before we left, when he came to supervise the transfer of our possessions to the basement of the Oliver offices, for dispatch as soon as conditions permitted. His wounds were healing – he flexed his arm to prove it – and he was staying behind, oh, certainly he was. He avoided looking at me, but I saw a stormy light in his eyes that made me afraid for him.

If we'd been alone I might have tried to persuade him, but Ewan was with us.

'The Old Man's determined to have me home.' Ewan stuffed his hands into his pockets and rocked on his heels. 'Otherwise I'd have stayed, naturally.'

This time Stephen glanced curiously at Ewan and then at me, but didn't reply. He held out a package he'd brought with him, sewn into a canvas cover.

'It's the Renoir. The girl in the hat. Do you think you could take it back to London for me? I wouldn't ask, but it's possible I might have to get out in a hurry.' He twitched his shoulders apologetically, then noticed the expression on my face. 'Not that I expect to, of course.'

'I'm sure it'll blow over before long.' Ewan beat me to the package. 'But we'll take good care of this, in any case.'

'Funny,' he remarked as Stephen's car pulled away from our gate. 'Never took him for the sort to buy pictures – did you?'

The Navy were to escort us as far as Hong Kong. I had thought that Stephen might come to see us off, but of course, he didn't. Why should he? I was the one who'd overstepped our carefully drawn boundaries and brought my feelings into the equation. No doubt he was relieved to see me go.

Yet thoughts of Stephen continued to catch me unawares,

all the way to Hong Kong. I'd glance at my watch and find myself wondering whether he'd gone out with the Volunteer Corps or had spent the night safely in the Cathay Hotel – or, when my imagination ran riot, whether the Cathay itself had been shelled to ruins, taking its marble and chrome and Stephen Morgan along with it. Always, when I thought of Shanghai, I saw Stephen there, alone – alone in our city of bombs and blue shadows, and dragons which waited with swords in dark lanes.

In more sensible moments I knew perfectly well that in a state of shock people do silly, emotional things, entirely out of character. It was the bomb, and nothing else, which had awakened in me this sense of overwhelming, irretrievable loss. I felt as if I had lost . . . my city, I suppose, and the sense of wonderment which had gone with it. In truth, my peach-blossom forest had never existed anywhere, except in my head – I recognized that now; but the loss of a dream can be even more poignant than reality.

We stayed in Hong Kong for several days, while the Oliver agents found space for us on the old *Alexandria*. Normally I'd have enjoyed being at sea, but this time I found the prospect of a six-week passage dismaying. On our way from Shanghai we'd been buoyed up by relief and the difficulties of 'making do' in a crowded vessel. There'd been an atmosphere of defiant cheerfulness, born of the need to support those whose husbands and fathers had been left behind. Now, aboard the *Alexandria*, Ewan and I suddenly found ourselves more alone than we'd ever been in our life together. Even our personal servants had been left behind in Shanghai.

'We'll manage,' Ewan assured me. 'And after all, it's only for a few weeks until we're back in London.'

We sailed from Hong Kong at the tail of a typhoon, which was unfortunate, since all the people we might have met at official cocktail parties stayed shut in their cabins for more than a week and by that time the atmosphere of the voyage was established. The ship was full of home-going Europeans, which meant that all the suites had already been taken and we were forced to make do with a double cabin, where there never seemed to be enough space for our possessions and ourselves.

Ewan didn't seem to mind as much as I did. Every morning he flung himself at the apparatus in the ship's gymnasium until he was exhausted and then returned like a faithful puppy to my side.

On our eighth day at sea, he reported a grand total of forty-three press-ups, four more than the day before. Glowing with virtue, he sank into the armchair next to mine in a corner of the lounge and poured coffee into the second cup on my tray. Yet I could tell, by the persistence with which he chased the brown nuggets of sugar round his cup, that there was something on his mind and, after what must have been a hundred circuits of the spoon, I was proved right.

'You don't think I should have stayed in Shanghai with the others, do you?'

For the umpteenth time, I reassured him. 'You were entitled to go. We were supposed to leave months ago.'

'It's just that, well, when men like Stephen Morgan are prepared to stay on, it makes you think.'

I laid down my magazine with resignation. 'I shouldn't worry about it, Ewan. I'm sure they'll be all right.'

In fact, I'd been driven to distraction by the lack of news: I was desperate to know what had happened to the city, and to Stephen, and the Lius, and our old servants, yet Shanghai was hardly mentioned in the ship's daily news bulletins. The start of the British football season seemed to arouse more interest. But our flight from Shanghai was such a sensitive subject for Ewan that I tried to keep my anxiety to myself.

Fortunately, as the beleaguered city receded into the distance, he seemed to have become more reconciled to our leaving it.

'Someone had to take care of you, after all. You've been jolly brave about being caught in the bombing, but you're still not yourself.' Leaning across the table, he patted my knee affectionately. 'If I'd been sitting in Shanghai last week, knowing you were off in that typhoon, I'd have been worried sick.' He picked up his coffee cup and drank, eyeing me over the rim. 'So you really don't think I ought to have stayed?'

'No, I don't.'

His face brightened and he gazed at me with genuine tenderness. At the end of the voyage I discovered the other passengers had assumed we were a honeymoon couple, and that was why they'd left us alone.

'Told you we'd manage on our own.' Ewan had mastered the knack of tying his own bow tie on our fourth evening afloat and was immensely proud of his new accomplishment. 'I sometimes think we get too used to having servants around. Makes you think you can't do anything for yourself.' He dug in a drawer. 'Put the studs in this collar for me, darling, will you?'

We arrived in London at the beginning of October 1937 and found ourselves in a city which had no interest in our war: it was too busy rehearsing for a war of its own.

My father came to meet us and, between family news and his own foreboding about the situation in Europe, I managed to establish that the bombing and shelling of Shanghai was still going on, with an even crueller effect on the Chinese districts than the battle of 1932. This time the fighting had spilled over into the countryside beyond, laying waste much of the land which fed the city. To the best of my father's knowledge, although shells frequently howled over the settlements between invader and defenders, Stephen Morgan had managed to keep himself alive and unharmed.

'But it doesn't look promising,' he concluded.

In the dimness of the Rolls, my father seemed tired. Age had accentuated the feminine delicacy of his features, giving him an air of distinguished fatigue.

'So many problems,' he said. He examined his manicured fingers. 'And Kate's ill, I'm afraid.'

Three weeks earlier, my ninety-one-year-old grandmother had suffered a stroke; but instead of dying immediately as her doctors had forecast, Kate had lived on, half-paralysed and unable to form the words which struggled in her mind.

'At first she kept trying to speak, but now she just lies there,

311

watching us.' My father sounded irritated, as though he'd have preferred his mother to make a more graceful end. 'You will go and see her, Clio, won't you? And take Ewan with you,' he murmured in my ear. 'Rose has been spreading all sorts of silly nonsense. It might cheer Kate up, to see the two of you so happy together.'

They'd moved Kate to a large bedroom which looked out to the back of her house, instead of her own room at the front which was noisier but got more sun. Beyond the window, a few black, scraggy trees were losing the last of their leaves. I wondered if she minded.

The nurse rose from her chair as Ewan and I went in.

'Not too long, now.' Her starched uniform creaked as she crossed to the door. 'We're a wee bit tired today.'

My first thought was that Kate herself had disappeared while we'd all been too busy making a fuss to notice. Then I saw a tiny, blanched figure in the bed – white hair and stark white skin against bleached pillows – already half-way to being an ancient angel, all spirit and no flesh, like the flame of a wax taper. The invalid made an effort to turn her head as we approached, her eyes flicking from face to face, loaded with enquiry.

At my shoulder, Ewan cleared his throat. Illness made him uncomfortable. 'Sorry to hear you haven't been too well, Mrs Oliver.' Because of her deafness, he had to raise his voice, making the remark sound banal.

I drew the nurse's chair as close as I could and took Kate's hand in mine. It was as frail and dry as one of the fallen leaves beyond the window. It was her paralysed side; I hoped she could still feel the warmth of my fingers. I bent close to her ear.

'I'm glad you waited for me.'

Kate allowed a long, whistling breath to escape and let her gaze rest on mine, silently questioning. As I began to tell her about Shanghai, and our house, and the parties, and the bombs, I realized my father had been wrong. Kate could still make herself understood, if only through the sudden, amused elongation of an eyelid, or the interrogative swelling of a pupil, or a blink of astonishment. My heart went out to her, trapped in that helpless, nursling body. *We're a wee bit tired today.*

Behind me, Ewan cleared his throat again and Kate's glance flew over my head.

'Do you think she'd mind,' he murmured in my ear, 'if I went downstairs and made a couple of phone calls?'

A faint hissing sound issued from the pile of pillows. On the far side of the bed, Kate's good hand twitched a dismissal.

'I don't think she'd mind at all. You'll find a telephone in her old room across the passage. The nurse will show you.'

'Back soon.' Ewan nodded towards the bed and escaped. Kate watched him go, and then her eyes probed my face, her irises ringed by the pale corona of nine decades.

'I suppose Rose told you Ewan had an affair while we were in Shanghai?'

Kate's tightened lips informed me she had.

I stroked her hand, smoothing the tendons like milky ropes and sliding on down to the pearl-blue nails.

'I was bitterly upset at first, of course – and angry. But Shanghai's that kind of place – lots of people seem to have affairs all the time and it hardly seems to matter. And the woman, the one Ewan was involved with . . . it wasn't as if he ever thought of leaving me and going off with her. It was just an impulse, I suppose.'

And I understood impulses. I hadn't forgotten a hotel room in Shanghai, with the rubble of a bomb-blast in the street outside and a girl in a ribboned hat looking on.

I shouldn't have said any more, but I'd begun to think aloud, beguiled by the silence of my listener.

'It wasn't as difficult as I'd expected – forgiving Ewan for the lies and having slept with someone else.' I addressed the words to Kate's fingers. 'The hardest thing was that I'd always thought, "Not Ewan, never." I'd loved him for that – for not being like the others. And now . . . I'm still fond of him, I still care, but in a different way.'

I couldn't stifle a sigh. 'I even feel sorry for him, sometimes. He was like a frightened child, you know, when he thought I might leave him. I never realized he needed me so much.' I was frowning now, reaching for the nub of the problem. 'He seems to expect *me* to be *his* strength, and now I feel trapped, Kate – even though I never really thought of leaving him. It isn't as if there was anyone else.'

The unearthly white hand resting in mine shamed me into honesty.

'Except . . . there was a moment, it's true, when I thought I'd begun to love another man. Then, later, I realized it was only because he'd been there when I was miserable and I'd no one to turn to. I'm sure of that now. No—' I shook my head, clearing it of any lingering doubts. 'It's me, Kate – I'm the problem. Ewan's doing his best to make amends – I couldn't ask for more – but our marriage has still become something I never expected. Is that what marriages are always like, Kate? Is that how you felt, living with Matthew Oliver?'

From her pillows, Kate's eyes offered wordless understanding.

'Matthew needed you, didn't he? Even though he could be heartless and cruel, he needed you and you couldn't leave him.'

A stealthy dusk had crept into the room, softening its silence. On the other side of the bed, Kate's good hand crept like a blind white beetle towards the photographs on her bedside table. It stopped by a particular frame, stroking the image, summoning up the name I'd avoided.

'Stephen Morgan?' I made my voice light. 'Oh, Stephen's well. At least, he was the last time they heard from him in the office.' Kate's attention had returned to my face, as sharply focused as a needle-point. *Tell me more.*

'Stephen was absolutely determined to stay on in Shanghai. I think he was actually looking forward to the war. You know what he's like – he had that look on his face that says, "Now, *here's* something!" as if it was just what he'd been waiting for all his life.'

I stopped, unable to go on pretending I didn't care. I confessed softly, 'It makes me afraid for him, when I see it, that look. Do you know the expression I mean?'

Kate's head moved slightly in acquiescence. *Oh, I know. I know.*

'You've seen it before? Where? In Stephen's father? Was that why Catherine fell in love with him?'

Kate's eyes indicated *No*, and slid away, hoarding their secret.

'Not Robert Morgan? And not Matthew Oliver, I imagine. But someone you loved, all the same.' Resolutely, Kate's glance avoided mine and I made a wild guess. 'Adam Gaunt. The man in the picture downstairs – my great-grandfather and Stephen's. Was it Adam, Kate?'

She turned back to me, her eyes suddenly lustrous, her face quite beautiful in its pallor.

'Oh, Kate—' I gazed at her, suddenly despairing. 'So he was your lover, after all. The man who fixed his eyes on the stars and couldn't settle for anything less.'

Kate's hand lay almost weightless in mine, empty now of the passion which had once quickened it.

'You told me it was a curse, this habit of star-gazing. I remember your saying so, just before Ewan and I left for Shanghai. You told me all would be well, as long as it never took hold in me. Well, I think it has, Kate. All of a sudden I'm afraid of my own feelings and I don't know what to do. Is there a cure for it? Is there something I can do?'

Very slowly, Kate's head rolled on the pillow, a fraction to the right and then to the left. *No. There's no cure.* Her attention wandered away from me towards the weeping trees outside the window.

We'd shared that twilit silence for some time before the door opened and the nurse returned, followed rather self-consciously by Ewan.

'Time for our rest now, Mrs Oliver. We find visitors a wee bit much these days, don't we?'

I bent to kiss her cheek, and found it damp and crumpled like the thinnest silk.

'Goodbye, Kate. And thank you.'

★

Two weeks later, Kate Oliver died and the family returned to Norfolk, to the cemetery of Stainham St Agnes, to leave her between Matthew, her husband, and Adam Gaunt, his father, who'd once been her lover. More than half a century had separated Adam's death from hers – I scraped the lichen from his stone to make sure, and moved aside some faded flowers. I guessed on whose instructions they'd been placed there. Kate had touched stars of her own and never forgotten.

'Well, that seemed to go off all right.' Ewan came across the grass to join me, pausing to scrape some soil from his shoe on the corner of a nearby headstone. He glanced back at the rectangular pit which the gravediggers had already begun to fill. 'Your uncle's wondering how much she's left you all.'

Kate had left me precisely as much as she'd left to my father, my uncle Kit, Guy, Alice and Rose: a small amount of money and the right to choose one memento from her home, up to a certain value. Her lawyers had worked for years to make sure that everything else she'd possessed, including Hawk's Dyke and her house in Chester Square, would go to Stephen Morgan.

Kit was homicidal. If Stephen had been there in person, I think Kit would have done him a physical injury.

'Not a penny to George!' he fumed at my father. 'Everything to that creature Morgan.'

'Ah well.' My father nodded philosophically. 'It isn't as if the boy's going to starve.'

'It's the principle of the thing!' Kit waved a finger stiffly under my father's nose. 'That was family money.'

'True – but Stephen is family.'

'Hah!' Kit stalked off to share his outrage with someone less logical.

It wasn't, perhaps, the best moment to meet Kit's new wife for the first time, but since Mamie Oliver hadn't come to the graveyard, it was the first chance I'd had to see her. And certainly, apart from the sullenness in her face, Mamie looked exactly as Alice had described her, 'as slick as a whistle', as the

Americans put it, bandbox-smart from her snappily tilted hat to her high suede heels. I cringed for Alice. Mamie's severe black crêpe frock hugged breasts like apple-pips above a tiny waist; her face seemed almost too thin for its load of mouth and eyes. Someone, I guessed, had coached her in smiling – mouth only, honey, or the camera will lose your eyes.

Mamie had every reason to look disgruntled. I happened to know that she and Kit had already removed Kate's best pictures to the walls of their own house 'for safekeeping', and now they'd have to take them all back.

Mamie's hard little voice cut through the room like chalk on a slate. 'Stephen probably doesn't even want the pictures. I bet he'll sell them off without looking at them.'

'The fact remains,' said Alice stoutly, 'they're Stephen's pictures. You'll have to give them back.'

'That was brave of you,' I told Alice afterwards, when we went for tea together. 'Won't it make things pretty hot at home?'

'No worse than they are already.' Alice tugged at her cardigan suit, rumpled by sitting. It was an elegant suit, but spoiled as usual by a fussy blouse. Yet a perceptible change had come over Alice in the years I'd been away. Several people had told me how her East End soup kitchen had been a major success during the hungry years, funded by whatever she could beg and borrow from friends and acquaintances. Alice herself confessed that she'd enjoyed the work and had been surprised to discover her own capability.

She still resembled a mouse, in spite of having at last curled her fringe away from her huge, tremulous eyes, but she'd become a tenacious mouse, a mouse with a small, set, determined mouth and a bony little nose which hinted at strongly held opinions.

'I'll tell you something else,' she informed me now. 'Every time Mamie went over to visit Kate, she stuck her card on the back of another piece of furniture, with "Deliver To" at the top. Isn't that the vilest thing you've ever heard? I used to pick them off again when no one was looking.'

'You've been terrific. Stephen would be proud of you.'

Alice blinked gratefully and brushed something invisible from her sleeve. 'I know you'll think I'm silly, but I'm still quite fond of Stephen, in an abstract sort of way. He's become a bit of a habit, I suppose, after all this time.'

'I don't think that's silly at all.' I felt a sudden need to fuss with the teapot, to lift the lid and peer in.

'Don't you?' Alice sounded surprised. 'You always used to say I should stop mooning over Stephen and find somebody else. Clio,' she demanded, 'what on earth is so interesting in that teapot?'

'Nothing.' I let the lid fall with a clatter on my jealousy.

'Anyway, there is nobody else at the moment. There was Harry Dunstanheugh for a while, but – I don't know – somehow it all seemed so pat and so organized and so fearfully dull, and everyone started taking our marriage for granted. There was no . . .' Alice flapped a glove in frustration. 'No *thrill*. Do you know what I mean?'

'I know exactly what you mean.'

Alice drew the glove carefully through her fingers. 'I sometimes think even a man who was occasionally unfaithful would be better than a bore. I mean, you and Ewan are still together, aren't you? Not that I believed half of Rose's nonsense,' she added quickly.

'We're still together, it's true. Still marching on.'

'Oh, darling, I'm so glad.' Alice clasped my hands impetuously. 'I *do* like Ewan, and I'm so fond of you. You were always exactly right for each other. You are lucky, Clio, to have everything so perfect.'

I continued to trawl the press for news of Shanghai. The guns had fallen silent at the end of October, not long after we reached London, but only at the price of a Japanese stranglehold on the city. The occupiers had taken over the municipal services and moved into the industrial half of the International Settlement. They'd put censors into foreign cable companies, isolating the businesses of the Bund. My one consolation was that the Chinese in Nantao seemed to have been preserved from the worst brutality of their new masters by the courage of a French Jesuit priest. With luck, Liu Ling and her family would be safe.

Now that Kate was dead, I wondered if Stephen Morgan would come back to London. I'd taken his Renoir out of its canvas cover and propped it on a chair in my bedroom, from where the girl in the ribboned hat reproached me gently for my moment of madness. But the weeks passed and Stephen didn't come.

We all went in turn to choose our mementoes of Kate. My father picked a Georgian desk which had been Matthew Oliver's, Mamie chose a bronze cupid for Kit, Guy found a pair of shotguns, Alice a brooch and Rose a set of books in antique leather bindings which seemed amazingly cerebral for the cousin I remembered.

I'd hoped that by now Rose might have changed – that she might feel some shame for the part she'd played in the deaths of two young men – but I should have known better. Real life is seldom so equitable. If Rose seemed intent on changing herself back from a butterfly into a caterpillar, it was simply because she'd become obsessed with a lecturer at London University, an intense, bearded man whose skull looked enormous enough to have a climate of its own.

The attraction, I believe, wasn't so much that Kit and Alice couldn't stand the man – which they couldn't – but more importantly that Roger Woade was not obsessed with Rose. It was the first time Rose had employed the full power of her allure and gone unnoticed. Compared with his study of *Jane Austen – Parlour Marxist*, Rose's angelic face and haunted eyes had hardly caused a ripple on the surface of Roger's life, and she was deeply and humbly impressed. She understood as little of what went on in Roger's mighty mind as she'd understood of the politics of China, but one thing was clear to her: Roger was the only male creature she'd failed to enslave when it suited her – and she worshipped and wanted him more than anything else in the world.

Roger, unfortunately, had heard something of Rose's reputation. Consequently, we were seeing the birth of a new Rose, in horn-rimmed glasses and a severe skirt, with leather-bound volumes under her arm and a studious expression on her face.

My own appointment at Kate's house was for three in the afternoon. Her solicitor opened the door himself.

'Take your time, Mrs McLennan. You may not remember the house as well as the others, having been abroad for so long.'

I didn't hesitate. I'd known what I wanted from the moment Kate's will was read: I wanted the portrait of Adam Gaunt which had hung on her dining-room wall, the face of a man who'd set his eyes on the stars and refused to be deflected, and whose memory had lived for more than fifty years in her heart.

Ewan went north to visit his parents at Achrossan, but I stayed in London, where my father had become ill with bronchitis. Hitler had just driven into Vienna, to a storm of orchestrated cheering and my father was infinitely depressed by the prospect of war.

Guy, too young to remember much about the Great War, was almost elated.

'Wars are good for shipping, that's the important thing – because suddenly the world is full of people wanting to be somewhere else. *Patria* and *Gloriana* are sailing full on each crossing, as it is. So much for buying aeroplanes!' he crowed. 'I said we should stick to ships and I was bloody right.'

All the same, I was sickened to discover Oliver's were charging five times the normal fare for German Jews sailing to Shanghai. I'd seen a cable from Stephen on my father's desk, querying the passage rates, and Guy looked so shifty when I tackled him on the subject that I knew it must have been his idea, or Kit's.

'We're simply asking what the market will bear. Everybody's doing it – and we aren't charging the most, by any means.'

It wasn't even as if the foreign settlements of Shanghai offered a safe refuge any longer. After making a bloody conquest of Chiang Kai-shek's capital of Nanking, the Japanese army had opened fire on British and American warships on the Yangtze River. The veneer of foreign neutrality was wearing perilously thin.

But it was hard to get information on a Chinese war, when British newspapers were full of the fact that our own government had authorized the building of air-raid shelters in towns and cities and British schoolchildren were drilling with gas-masks in their playgrounds like so many little Chinese dragons.

Just at this depressing point Margot Oliver came to Europe from the United States to cheer us up, and arrived in London wearing Mainbocher and hats by Lily Daché – and with the twenty-five-year-old son of a Boston family whose ancestors had come over with St Brendan.

Margot summoned me to dinner at the Savoy, while Kit took her young companion to dine at his club.

'So civilized, don't you think?'

Margot, at fifty-one, was still an extraordinarily beautiful woman, still wrapped in the sensual hauteur which had made her the tantalizing erotic summit of so many male ambitions. Even so, I doubted the wisdom of sending her current lover to spend the evening alone with her ex-husband.

'Kit will probably tell him all sorts of tales. Shouldn't you have gone with them?'

'To Kit's club? My dear, I can't imagine any place designed for men and used exclusively by men being at all attractive.' She wrinkled her nose. 'Think of gentlemen's lavatories.'

'Don't you worry, one day, about being left all alone?'

Margot surveyed me with her enormous eyes, so like Rose's. 'Darling, I've never minded being alone. That's what men regard as such a challenge – the possibility that one can do perfectly well without them. People see me as such a man-eater, but really, you know—' She stretched voluptuously on her sofa, somehow preserving her cocktail from spilling. 'I'm the helpless little victim every time.'

I burst out laughing. 'Margot, you're such a fraud! You're the most ruthless person I know. I've never forgotten how you reduced poor Igor Starozhilov to jelly aboard the *Concordia*.'

Margot raised herself on one elbow. 'Only because you were

distracting him from his duties, you torrid little monster. And besides, look at him now – *Rudi Romanov*, no less, up there in lights with Gable and Cooper. "Sleep with the *men*, darling," I told him. "They can do so much more for you than the women."' Margot sipped elegantly from her glass, leaving a red stain like a flower. 'It was probably the best advice he ever got.'

'I wondered how he'd done it.'

'And now we're plagued with his horrible sister, who seems to have been one of your father's little weaknesses. You do know she's turned up in London, demanding money from him?'

'Nina has? Nina Starozhilova?'

'I don't suppose he told you.' Margot reached out to refill her glass from the crystal jug. 'That's the trouble with indulging in little bits of naughtiness. They do crawl back later to haunt one.'

This seemed unfair, coming from her. 'And how old was Cad Langham when you were seeing him, Margot? Nineteen?'

'Yes, darling, but he wasn't under age – that's the point. I gather this Nina person was barely out of the baby-carriage. Even in Shanghai, you see, there's always someone watching. I hope you've been careful about your own little *amours*, my dear Clio.'

'I'm afraid I haven't had any little *amours*, careful or otherwise.'

'What? Nothing at all?' Margot looked dismayed. 'Not even when Ewan was running after that terrible Tattersall woman? Rose told me everything.' She wafted a hand. 'Absolutely everything. And I thought to myself, "What Clio needs is a beautiful, impulsive lover to sweep her off her feet and make her feel life is worth living again." Your glass is empty, darling.'

Preoccupied, I allowed her to refill it. 'Perhaps you're right. Perhaps I should have found someone else. And yet – you've always had lovers, Margot. More of them than I can count.'

'Darling—'

'It's true, though, isn't it?' I put down my glass and examined her across the room. Now that I was looking for it – beyond the glossy, hard carapace and brilliant colours which dazzled Margot's men – I could detect a curve of habitual disappointment in the line of her eyelids and two stars of tiny, bitter lines at the corners of her mouth which disturbed her perfect enamelling. Even the line of her chin was an instinctive challenge to those who might imagine she wasn't the most blessed of women.

I pressed on with my point. 'What I'm wondering is – all these lovers, Margot – have any of them actually made you happy? I mean, happy for good – not just for a week or two when it was all new and marvellous fun?'

Margot pouted, deepening the lines at her lips, and rearranged the folds of her moiré skirt. 'Gracious heaven, we are getting deep, aren't we? Who knows what's *happy*, for goodness' sake?' She swirled the last of her cocktail in the base of her glass and solemnly watched the liquid settle. 'I suppose – if you swear never to tell him – Kit Oliver made me the nearest thing to happy, when I knew him first. He's always been *such* a bastard, you see – never to be trusted for a second. One never knew what he was thinking, it made one feel so *alive*. Am I making sense, darling?'

'Yes, Margot, you are. More sense than anyone else, in fact.'

'And then I found out about the woman in St John's Wood. So meanly suburban – three children and a semi-detached villa! How is one supposed to survive something like that?'

'So you took a lover.'

'A very young and beautiful lover, darling – I thought I might as well enjoy it.'

'Just to pay Kit back.'

'To make a point.' Margot wriggled on her sofa. 'You could say I've been making the same point ever since.' She yawned elaborately. 'But oh dear, you've no idea, sometimes, how tedious it can be. To know you're *obliged* to do your hair and *obliged* to do your face and squeeze into something seductive, just so a randy little boy can disarrange it.'

'Margot – I love you, do you know that? I wish you'd been my mother, instead of Alice and Rose's.'

'Oh, come now. You'll be asking me for advice, next.'

'No need, darling – you've just given it.'

★

Sane now, and beyond the reach of the tumultuous mysteries of Shanghai, I could see how things must be. There was no real magic – none that would last, at any rate; I might search and search and still find nothing. Indeed, I was fortunate to have as much as I did – a husband who needed and valued me. It looked as if Liu Ling and Confucius had been right after all: loyalty and duty were the lot of womankind.

Some time in the future, Ewan would take me to his empty land where the stars were surely far out of reach and where his silent mountains would make me feel small and content. Achrossan – the Place of Briars – would be my salvation.

And so, in April 1938, when Ewan's mother telephoned us in London with the news that Sir Cato McLennan had died suddenly while landing a fish in his favourite pool, I went forward willingly to what seemed my destiny.

Part Three

Chapter Eighteen

I'D BECOME a city woman, and for months the hush unnerved me. Then, little by little, I learned to replace my sprawling rooftops with waterfalls of cloud which tumbled hypnotically over the lip of the glen, and the hard ring of pavements with mornings of milky-green mist on the loch, where silent islands drifted like visions between the smoking shores. Now, in the evenings, instead of being swallowed up behind uncaring brick, my sun drifted softly to the western sea, tinting the topmost crags with rose-pink and leaving a dusty twilight to gather round us in the valley.

Yet even there, peace was not to be had.

It cost almost a thousand pounds, I believe, to install Sir Cato in his newly cut rock tomb on the island in the loch where McLennans of Achrossan had been laid to rest for three centuries. As the burial-boat left the shore amid a wailing of pipes, the sky blackened and the rain came down in torrents. It was all highly satisfactory, Ewan reported, and worth every penny.

'Not that money's any problem, of course. In fact, I've been making a list of projects we ought to get cracking on – like a new turbine for electricity, up on the hill. I'm afraid Father let things go a bit in the last few years.'

I, too, had been making plans, secret schemes to modernize the house: the first dwelling on the site had been built in the seventeenth century and then extended during the 1860s in a style which owed more to Sir Walter Scott than to the pioneers of plumbing. The core of the Victorian section was a stone-colonnaded hall, aglow with stained glass, where the family traditionally gathered in the evenings, pressed as close as possible to the towering fireplace. The bathrooms were tiled like morgues from floor to ceiling, crowded with thundering brass and so cold that an early morning bath could bring death from exposure before one of the gigantic tubs was filled.

Ewan loved it exactly as it was. 'When I'm dead, you see, Achrossan will go to my eldest son, just as it was left to me. It's my duty to look after it in the meantime.'

I could almost hear Liu Ling and Confucius applauding.

For a week Ewan shut himself in his father's business room to overhaul the books of the estate, while barrow-loads of files and ledgers passed between the factor's office and our garden door. The ledgers, I noticed, became tattered and more fragile as Ewan burrowed into the history of his inheritance. On the eighth day he left for Edinburgh to consult Clantavish & Prosie WS, his father's solicitors. He returned the following afternoon, limping heavily, as he often did when he was tired.

I was sitting in the hall, examining a book of fabric swatches I'd had sent up from London. Without taking off his coat, Ewan dropped into a seat by the hearth and gazed round the great chamber for a few moments in silence. I remember thinking how much better his new gravity suited him than the ferment of Shanghai. He'd grown in dignity since Sir Cato's death, as if the wind-scoured granite of his native mountains had quietly reclaimed its son.

When his fist crashed down on the arm of his chair, it made me jump.

'All this—' In his frustration he banged the chair again, his voice ringing with betrayal among the pillars. 'All this – and yet nothing. Can you believe it? This whole charade kept afloat, year after year, on nothing but promises and bits of paper?'

He stared round the walls as if the truth should have been plain to see among the targes and Lochaber axes.

'What charade, Ewan, for heaven's sake?' I moved to the edge of my seat, to be nearer him. 'There are outstanding debts, do you mean?'

'Debts? There's nothing *but* debt. The estate hasn't turned a profit since the '45. The last time anyone made a penny out of it was in the 1820s, when they managed to sell some kelp from the shore for fertilizer.'

'Then what did your family live on?'

'Other people's money.' Ewan flung up a furious hand. 'My great-great-grandfather seems to have started it all by issuing bonds over some of the land – and his son and grandson followed him, piling up borrowings, mortgaging land, selling a few acres here and there if they absolutely had to – but putting off paying for ever, if they could.' He waved impatiently in the direction of Sir Cato's business room. 'There are bad debts in those books going back to the Clearances, never mind taxes and death duties – all unpaid, except for a thousand or so on account whenever the government twisted the screw.

'In other words—' His voice broke on the final syllable and dropped to a murmur of pain. 'Achrossan is a bubble company – a sham – floating along on a bogus impression of old money. "If the laird can afford to go round with the seat hanging out of his trousers, he's obviously got more cash than he knows what to do with."'

He gave a short, despairing sigh. 'And, of course, since the old man was Lord Lieutenant and chairman of every blessed council and committee, people didn't like to dun for their money. So when he had to sell – when the bank called in a loan in 1931 and he had to get rid of the whole north end of the Conachan peninsula – it was the worst possible time to get a decent price for it.'

Ewan chewed his lip for a moment and then burst out, 'He'd no right to sell that land, Clio! I used to fish for mackerel there, when I was a boy.'

He held out his empty hands and in that instant the child Ewan gazed through the grown man's eyes again – robbed of his fish, bewildered by the treachery of his forebears.

He let his hands fall and shook his head. 'And now that my father's dead, they'll come down on us like a flock of crows – the banks, the lawyers, every damned parasite in the place. God knows how we're going to pay them.'

'Oh, Ewan . . .' I went to kneel on the floor beside him, drawn by the distress of the fisher-boy. 'You could always sell more land, I suppose, if there's no other way.'

Ewan stared at me, speechless with anguish and outrage. Too late, I realized I might as well have asked him to hack off an arm or a leg. Then his eye fell on the fabric swatches, abandoned on my chair, and he jabbed a finger at the frivolous pool of colour.

'You'll have to send those back where they came from, for a start. It's going to be hard enough to hang on to what little is left, without wasting money on anything new.'

We'd never had to economize in our lives before, and it was difficult to know where to begin. We laid up the thirsty Daimler and bought a Ford tourer to replace it – then had to bring out the Daimler again because Ewan's mother refused to be driven to church from her dower house 'like a commercial traveller'. Virtuously, we cancelled *Blackwood's*, but it was apparently impossible to do without the piper who marched round our table at formal dinners and we continued to bawl conversation to our neighbours over the skirl of *Lady McLennan's Fancy*.

Tradition had to be maintained – as had a pair of Queen Anne armchairs whose needlework seats had sagged and split open and whose arms had been criss-crossed with string to show they could be admired, but not sat on. I'd hoped to exchange them for a modern bathroom, but Ewan's distress was too great.

'Those chairs came to the family with the Maid of Ness.' In pain, he gazed at the spilled stuffing. 'No, no – we can't sell those.'

None of the keepers could be let go – they'd worked for the family for generations, as had the stalkers, the foresters, the gardeners, the cook and the housemaids. Not surprisingly, our efforts to save looked ridiculous beside the sums that were needed. Even the dowager Lady McLennan's house at Finglas had a mortgage outstanding. In the end, Ewan was forced to concede that the only solution was to sell land to pay his creditors – moor by moor and farm by farm – though as he signed away each title I knew it was as agonizing as parting with his own flesh and blood.

Even so, for a long time he refused to ask my father for help – and when he did, to make matters worse, my father insisted on putting the thousands of acres he bought into my name alone. 'After Shanghai,' he told me with a significant nod.

I couldn't make him understand that to Ewan, even land which had passed to his wife was still land lost to his sacred Achrossan. Yet if anyone was to blame for Ewan's frustration, it was his own ancestors, not my father and I. They were the false gods, the broken links in the chain.

Paradoxically, as the Achrossan estate diminished, Ewan became more and more obsessed with the need for a son to inherit what was left.

'Not yet, Ewan, please. Can't we wait a little longer, until we're properly settled here?'

'But you'll have nine months. Won't that be enough?'

'I just want . . . to wait for a bit, that's all.'

More than anything, I wanted a child – and yet I was afraid of having one, because a baby would bind me even more tightly to Ewan, would give a final wrench to the jaws of the trap . . . Help me, Kate! What can I do? I haven't diminished enough yet, I'm not passive enough for that final surrender.

Ewan would dump himself down on his bed in his dressing-gown, his face heavy with dissatisfaction. 'I hate using these bloody rubber things. I did think, after we'd left China, I'd seen the last of them – and now you're the one who's insisting.'

'Only for a little while—'

'If you're trying to punish me for that business in Shanghai—'

'Of course I'm not.' This was true, as it happened – the problem was something else entirely: but for a few seconds the name of Evie Tattersall would hang in the air between us, driving us apart.

Then Ewan would go through the usual arguments: his

mother had hinted, the tenants on the estate were starting to wonder why there were no children up at the big house. I was twenty-eight and time was passing.

With the matter still unresolved, we'd lie in our separate beds and glare silently at the ceiling.

'It's all very well to say *wait*,' Ewan muttered one night, 'but there may not be as much time as you think. If all this talk of war turns into the real thing, I might have to go off and fight these blasted Germans. And then I could be away for heaven knows how long.'

Through a haze of resentment I heard the flutter and snap of white mourning ribbons. 'Could it really come to that?'

'Don't see why not. And this time, it won't be like Shanghai. No one's going to be able to say Ewan McLennan ducked a fight.'

Britain itself was still trying to duck the fight, while continuing to prepare for the worst. Neville Chamberlain returned from Munich clutching a precious, hopeful scrap of paper, but in London the Admiralty had already decided which Oliver vessels they'd need for naval service. In early summer of 1939 the first wave of young men were conscripted and then in August the military reservists were called up. Before long all the younger men had gone from Achrossan and those who were left began to talk of taking up arms in defence of their homes.

Alice telephoned from London, breathless with news. Stephen Morgan had returned from Shanghai, where he reckoned the Japanese were only waiting for an excuse to make a clean sweep of the foreign settlements. He'd done all he could to transfer Oliver assets out of China and he'd no intention of staying on to be bullied or imprisoned by the Japanese. Alice's voice quickened with excitement: Stephen had resigned his job at Oliver's, volunteered for the Navy and been sent to Skegness to train.

'I expect they'll give him a commission, since he was an officer before. By the way,' she added, puzzled. 'He said would you mind keeping something for him, just for a bit longer. A girl in a hat. Does that make sense to you?'

'The girl in the ribboned hat. It's a picture. He asked me to bring it back with me from Shanghai.'

'Oh,' said Alice. 'I see.'

Stephen had left the company, just as he'd warned me he would, breaking the last links with the past he'd disowned. I'd guessed he would join up, sooner or later. Even now, I only had to close my eyes to see him stride again over the roof-leads of the Great World, impatient to be tested by whatever risks lay ahead.

'He isn't coming back,' I told the girl in the hat, staring sadly out of her peaceful window. 'Not for a long time, perhaps.'

The news about Stephen seemed to spur Ewan into action. We travelled down to London by train and found the city infused with grim endeavour. Kit and my father had been co-opted to the new Ministry of Shipping and had turned over the day-to-day running of Oliver's to Guy. Yet in spite of at last having the freedom he'd always wanted, Guy seemed oddly subdued and for the first time I suspected my brother was nervous of taking charge alone.

'Trust Stephen to leave the company,' he complained, 'as soon as he got his hands on Kate's cash.'

'He's gone into the Navy,' I pointed out. 'I'd hardly call that taking things easy.'

'No, which just goes to show you how crazy he is. Why on earth does he want to go and get his head blown off when he could be sitting safely in a shipping office?'

'In a reserved occupation, like you.'

'It's an important job.' Guy tapped an after-lunch cigarette on the side of his gold case, lit it and then waved it in a smoking arc. 'Someone has to stay at home and run the show.'

Ewan returned miserably from an Army medical, turned down for active service because of his wasted leg.

333

'This cursed leg! This bloody, cursed leg!'

With wretched defiance, he'd walked all the way back to Rutland Gate; his face was brick-red from sunburn and effort and his sandy waves curled tightly with damp.

'I feel so damned useless! Did you see the way Bertie Headington looked at me at lunch today, showing off his bloody uniform in front of all the women?'

'Bertie's an ass, darling. Pay no attention. There must be heaps of useful things you can do without joining up.'

'Such as?' Ewan's eyes were painfully blue. 'Such as, exactly?'

'Well, I don't know. But there must be something.'

'Nothing I'm fit for.' He gazed at me morosely for a moment before turning away. 'You despise me, I know. You don't even want my child.'

'Oh Ewan, that isn't true.' In that instant I'd caught another glimpse of the boy Ewan, humiliated and downcast, and the urge to lift his spirits had overwhelmed my doubts. 'Of course I want your children. In fact, I don't think we should wait any longer.'

There was plenty for Ewan to do, even out of uniform. By the time war was finally declared on 3rd September, he'd been put in charge of pretty well everything on the Conachan peninsula, from the issuing of ration cards and identity papers to the slaughtering of cattle and the marshalling of our elderly keepers and farm workers into a band of Local Defence Volunteers. The Achrossan estate might be dwindling to a shadow of its former magnificence, but as long as local memory lasted, Sir Ewan McLennan was still a descendant of Roderick *Dubh* and the giant Alexander.

We were given orders to watch the loch at all times, in case the Germans chose it for a midnight landing; a gun emplacement was built at Boddanish, where our loch emptied out into the Sound, and plans were drawn up to close our single road with farm-carts and boulders and to disable all the local transport.

Before long, the Achrossan housemaids began to leave, heading south to the well-paid munitions factories which taught them to paint their nails and wear lipstick, to the infinite distress of their parents. Already, the war had done what Ewan had refused to do: emptied our house and brought silence to the land. Yet one thing transcended it all: Ewan watched me covertly, waiting for a sign that I was pregnant with his son.

'Not yet, Ewan. Not this time, I'm sorry.'

Hitler, too, kept us waiting, with our barricades ready and our field-glasses trained on the loch. The war had already begun at sea, where U-boats were sinking Allied shipping, yet for us ashore there was nothing to do but wait and keep ourselves busy.

'Would you believe it – Roger's married Rose,' reported Alice, when she wrote. 'So now she'll be Rose Woade – isn't that heaven? None of us were there, I may say, and there's no sign of a ring. Papa reckons Roger only agreed to get married because he thought it might keep him out of the Army, but it won't, of course. He says he won't fight under any circumstances or even carry out medical duties and Rose is hoping for an enormous fuss. I hope they just lock him up quietly – I think he's an absolute weasel, when all sorts of other people have gone.

'Oh, by the way—' As usual, Alice had saved the best until the end, where afterthoughts belonged. 'I've joined the WRNS. And before you say it – I know I'm thirty-one and most of the girls will be much younger, but Fay Standish was recruiting and she remembered my soup kitchen from six years ago and said at least that meant I could *cook* – none of the young ones want to do it. You probably think I'm mad, but I just couldn't sit around here doing nothing, when so many of the men have joined up.'

After that, her final piece of news didn't surprise me at all.

'Papa says S. M. has gone off on convoy escort duties in the North Atlantic.'

The war still seemed very distant from us at Achrossan. Even after our tall iron gates had been dragged away for salvage, there were times when I felt as safely shut up among my make-believe turrets as I ever had in my childhood home in Shanghai. Somewhere beyond our mountains – beyond the wall, among the barbarians – people were dying in fear and ugliness. All we had to endure was an echo of their cries, a shadow-play of their calamity.

I remember that first winter as particularly bad, even by the standards of the Scottish Highlands, though down by the loch we were spared the worst of the blizzards that blocked the passes and bleached the head of sheltering Creagruadh. In the little sitting room I'd taken for my own, the wireless hissed its measured bulletins and I looked out into a wilderness of weather, wondering how it must feel to toss on a ship in the freezing North Atlantic, knowing that somewhere unseen, the U-boats waited.

As the winter of 1939 began to bite, a huge red deer hind came down off the hill and ate every chrysanthemum plant in the formal garden. It didn't matter. By the following summer Belgium and Holland had fallen to Hitler and our flowerbeds were furred with carrot-tops to feed the Home Fleet in Loch Ewe.

By now the whole of Britain seemed to be filling with the temporarily homeless, as the country absorbed everyone from the Free French to the Dutch royal family, just as Shanghai had taken in the White Russians and most lately the German Jews. As Hitler's troops advanced on Paris, an international flotsam poured out of the city – writers, artists, musicians – anyone who feared their race or profession might make them a German target.

Even so, the last thing I expected was to find Nina Starozhilova turning up on our doorstep at Achrossan.

She and the glum little man she introduced as her husband, Oscar Besson, arrived one day at the end of May, the bus from the station having set them down at the end of our drive on its way to the village. They'd carried their bags and cases for the remaining half-mile – Oscar drooping like a melting candle, trailing after the relentless Nina.

'We had to escape. The Germans were almost in Paris.' Nina held out her hands in dramatic appeal. She was wearing black, and cracked, dusty shoes, and she'd had her hair fiercely cropped *en gamine*, like a prisoner. Knowing Nina, she'd planned her entrance down to the last detail – the flight of the hunted refugee, seeking shelter with all she possessed in the world.

'Oscar is a sculptor.' She reached out for him, earning a wan smile. 'But his work is banned in Germany. "Degenerate", they say.' Nina's eyes rolled up to the ceiling. 'If we'd stayed in Paris, they'd have locked him up – locked up Oscar Besson himself!' She leaned forward. '*Jüdisch*, you see.' At her side, the sculptor nodded sadly at the floor.

'Then I thought of the Olivers, in London – of your so-generous father and of my dear Clio, married to her Scottish lord.' Nina threw her arms wide.

'Hardly a lord,' Ewan put in hastily, scratching his nose. 'Just a baronet, I'm afraid.'

Nina's smile enfolded him – the café dancer searching for a patron at the bar. 'Such a beautiful house. You're so lucky.'

I tried to deflect her. 'But you must go to America – mustn't they, Ewan? The Americans would love a famous sculptor like Oscar. And isn't Igor in Hollywood, making movies? Well, there you are! You could stay with him.'

'America . . . Ah—' Nina fluttered her hands. 'Unfortunately there was a small incident at the American embassy in Paris. A gentleman friend, you understand – for some reason he thought I'd tried to rob him. And now they tell me I'm not wanted in the United States.'

She wasn't wanted at Achrossan, either – but alas, we had no Ellis Island to keep out unwelcome visitors.

A sudden burst of sun behind our stained glass splashed Nina with the harlequin gaiety of her old cabaret costume from Shanghai – and for the first time I caught sight of the fear in her eyes, the badge of the lifelong fugitive, an instinctive dread of the barbarians beyond every wall that had made her run all the way to the west of Scotland. Her eyes were outlined in black, which gave them the bright menace of a rat's. I doubted if there was anything Nina wouldn't do to secure her own safety and that of Oscar Besson.

'I saw your father in London.' She emphasized each word,

in case I missed her meaning. 'So busy, with his ships and his work for the Ministry. Such an important man! I didn't like to make trouble and ask him to find us a little house . . .' She wriggled her shoulders. 'But I thought maybe, for his sake, you'd help us.' Her bright, rodent eye conveyed a clear message.

The sins of the fathers . . . Silently, I reproached mine for his self-indulgence.

My father telephoned from his office an hour later, in the guarded tones of a man aware that if his secretary wasn't listening to our conversation, our local postmistress would be.

'That Russian woman, darling – Nina Starozhilova – do you remember? She's apparently in London, with some sculptor fellow she has in tow. She seems to think I ought to find her a safe billet for the rest of the war. I don't suppose she'll find her way to Scotland, but I thought you ought to know—'

'They're here, I'm afraid. They arrived this afternoon.'

'Oh, damn. I'm sorry, darling. This is all a bit awkward.' My father coughed delicately. 'Nina could actually be . . . a bit of a nuisance . . . if you see what I mean.' His voice trailed off for a few seconds. 'Would it be a great bother to find them a little place, somewhere out of the way? Just until things quieten down?'

Over dinner that night, Nina was at her most charming. She sparkled; she let off explosions of wit, like a firecracker. As usual with Nina, there was a little too much of everything – too much colour in her face-powder, too much cigarette smoke in her voice, too many violent, theatrical gestures – but always with that tragic, underlying poignancy which, even in Shanghai, had lifted her dancing from a twenty-dollar turn of poses and grinds to a passionate assault on the emotions. Throughout, Oscar Besson watched her with the eyes of a devoted hound and every so often, when she remembered, Nina would reach out one of her busy hands to pat his paw.

As we undressed for bed, Ewan was still smiling to himself over some of the stories she'd told and her enchanting habit of calling him 'Lord McLennan'.

'She's an engaging creature, isn't she? I can't think why

you've never told me about her before, if you've known her for so long.'

'I've never really *known* her. Her brother taught me to dance when I was a child, that's all.'

'Ah yes – Margot's boyfriend from the *Concordia*. Rudi Romanov, no less.' Peeling off his wristwatch, Ewan chuckled again. 'That was a wonderful story of Nina's, the one about Clark Gable's false teeth. Do you suppose it's true?'

'I shouldn't think so. Not if Nina Starozhilova told it.'

'It was wonderful stuff, even if she did make it up.' Ewan put out the light and lay down. 'Goodness knows what a woman like Nina sees in a dull dog like Oscar Besson.' I could tell he was still smiling by the sound of his voice. 'You know, it really cheered me up, this evening. I was beginning to feel a bit low, what with one thing and another, but now . . .'

Such a long silence followed that I thought he'd fallen asleep. Then he spoke again.

'Old General Munro at Ardlarach has taken in a Belgian concert pianist and her husband. Charming pair, he says. And they keep the Bechstein in tune.'

I should have remembered the old tradition of country house hospitality, where guests arrived for a fortnight and remained for a year, fading unnoticed into the leisurely life of the rural gentry. Moreover, there was a war on and we had to 'do our bit'; most of the time, all we could manage was to follow the progress of things on the wireless and pretend that by being stand-in postmen and growers of beetroot we were doing something to help. Months later, the whole district felt better when a German pilot, lost on his way back from bombing Belfast, dropped the rest of his load on the hillside behind the church and we had a genuine air raid at last.

In the meantime, Nina and Oscar *were* the war. At Ewan's insistence they stayed at Achrossan for a week while somewhere was found for them – and then, in the absence of a suitable 'small house', for another week, burrowing like mice into our daily life. Nina, that creature of mirrors, had instantly turned herself into a hausfrau. As often as not, I'd find her in the white-tiled kitchens, hunched over steaming pans of hay, bottling early plums or gooseberries, while Oscar Besson wandered around outside the house, making exquisite sketches which he'd present to us later with infinite dignity. In due course, Police Constable Archie Matheson cycled out from the village to interview our guests and after a couple of large whiskies from Ewan's private reserves, wobbled back again to report that the laird's refugees were no threat to the security of the realm.

'There you are,' said Ewan. 'And you can't say they aren't making themselves useful.'

I tried to object. I pointed out that we were supposed to be economizing: if we couldn't afford to repair the glasshouses and put a new roof on the north turret, we could hardly justify a pair of penniless house-guests at Achrossan. But Ewan brushed my objections aside and before I knew it, a month had passed and Nina and Oscar's ration books lay piled with our own.

About this time, to my great delight, Alice was transferred to Scotland to work on a cipher machine in Rosyth ('Can't explain, darling, it's all top secret'). Now, every so often, I set off by bus and crowded train to meet her in Edinburgh. Our usual rendezvous was Crawford's tearoom, where I could indulge myself in a slice of mock lemon meringue pie and covertly envy Alice's uniform, short enough to reveal her knees on the stool next to mine.

Denied any opportunity to wear ruffles and bows, Alice looked cool and smart, while I'd had nothing new for ages except a pair of very necessary dungarees and a frighteningly expensive coat Guy had shipped over for me from New York. It was far too luxurious to flaunt in the village – or anywhere else, for that matter, in austerity-minded Britain, but it made a wonderful dressing-gown.

'No babies yet?' Alice would glance critically at my waistline.

'Nothing yet. Maybe I've left it too late and it won't happen now.' I'd never suggested this possibility to Ewan, but I was sure he must have wondered about it.

'I shouldn't worry,' said Alice confidently. 'Grandmother Kate was years older than you when Uncle Edward was born and then she had two more. We're late breeders – it runs in the family.' She licked her fingers. 'Did Guy tell you a bomb came through the roof of the Oliver building last week? Fortunately, it didn't go off and they managed to defuse it.'

'The last time Papa telephoned, he said Connie Headington had dragged a woman out of a burning house. She's a big wheel in the Red Cross now, apparently, and organizing everybody.'

Alice wrinkled her nose. 'I wish I was in London just now. I can't help feeling I could be more *use* down there. All I do here is push out messages and receive what comes back.' She dissected her sultana tart with precision. 'We're all listening out for a Polish submarine at the moment. The crew are so charming – you've no idea.'

Her fork, half-way to her mouth, returned to her plate. 'Although sometimes it's bad news and people have been killed. Those days are awful. And I can't help thinking . . . suppose something happened to Stephen's ship and I was the one who took the message?' She peered warily round the crowded tearoom. 'I'm not supposed to say this, but they're having a dreadful time of it in the North Atlantic at the moment.'

For several seconds we reflected on this in silence.

'Don't worry.' I forced myself to be cheerful. 'I can't believe anyone who tries as hard as Stephen does to get himself killed will ever actually manage it.'

'Mmm,' said Alice, gazing doubtfully at the wreckage of her sultana tart.

In the autumn of 1941 Oscar Besson left us to live with a gentle, asthmatic poet in his cottage near Ballachulish. I wasn't surprised – I'd always had my doubts about the relationship between Nina and the 'husband' she treated with sisterly affection. Coming in from an evening walk, I'd sometimes see Oscar alone at their bedroom window, watching night fall on the pearly ribbon of the loch – and as often as not earning us a reprimand from Chief Warden Hector Mackinnon, patrolling the shore road in the hope of catching Achrossan breaking the blackout regulations in one of its innumerable windows.

Far from being dismayed by Oscar's disappearance, Nina seemed to grow more vigorous with each passing day. All she'd ever known was adversity; a life of luxury would probably have killed her with tedium and over-indulgence. Now, in warbound Britain she was in her element, salvaging treasures from the rubbish cart with gull-like cries, and begging, borrowing, adapting and bartering anything which fell into her tight little fists.

'You have given me a *home*,' she would say, clutching at my wrist. 'I don't forget that. We work *together* – all of us, to make what we do not have.'

With tireless ingenuity, she made wine from the potatoes we grew in abundance and traded it for tea. She gathered dangerous-looking mushrooms under the autumn beech trees and swapped them recklessly for honeycombs – and in return for enough rabbit skins to line a coat, I discovered she'd told Donald *Mór* Macrae, the biggest poacher in the region, when the Achrossan keepers would be busy with a Home Guard exercise and not looking out for him on the hill.

If mankind bombed itself to dust, Nina Starozhilova would survive. I sipped her bootleg tea and tried to fight down the suspicion that sooner or later she'd make an attempt on the greatest prize of all.

'That silly woman,' Ewan observed mildly one day. 'Wandering through the wet grass in high-heeled boots and a thin silk jacket, just to watch us overhaul the electrical turbine. As if the inside of a machine would mean anything to her! Of course, coming down the hill, I had to carry her across all the burns, or her feet would have been soaked.' Ewan smiled to himself at the recollection.

I'd just come in from delivering potatoes to the depot. I was wearing grubby, shapeless overalls and old rubber boots with their soles held on by tape and I didn't relish the comparison. I was about to point out hotly that Nina Starozhilova had no interest at all in electrical apparatus, but appeared to be developing one in my husband, when – right out of the blue – I fainted.

It was typical of the place that Dr Campbell informed Ewan of his wife's condition before confirming it to me. Ewan was ecstatic, absolutely convinced the baby would be a boy. There was to be no more hoeing for me in the vegetable beds, and no more salvage collection: it was only with the greatest reluctance that Ewan agreed to my keeping up my mail deliveries for another month or two.

'Dr Campbell says you need lots of rest, darling, and I'm going to see that you get it.'

Perhaps, after all, the peace of the mountains had done its work, or perhaps it was simply the tranquillizing effect of pregnancy, but instead of being stifled by Ewan's fussing, I was touched by his concern. I hadn't seen him so genuinely happy for ages – and his happiness and pride were like a blessing on our marriage. For the first time in years we spoke in a private language of our own – silly, affectionate word-games to do with the baby's name.

'You still awake, darling?' Ewan's voice would issue sleepily out of the midnight darkness.

'Mmm. It's your friend Hector, I'm afraid, tramping around in his size twelves.'

I'd hear a smile in Ewan's drowsy murmur. 'Sounds as if little Roderick's got his mother's feet, then.'

'Oh, darling, not Roderick! I thought we'd decided against that one.'

'All right—' Ewan would turn over on his back. 'Hamish Torquil Ranulf McLennan – "Hamish of the Big Feet", they'll call him.'

'Hamish the Handsome. Hamish the Wise.'

'Hamish the Sleepless, if we don't get some rest.'

And Ewan, fully awake now, would come to my bed and take me in his arms, selflessly cradling me until at last I slept. Sometimes, when Nina completed our evening semi-circle by the wireless, I'd see her eyes flicking from Ewan's face to mine, probing the strength of this new bond between us. And as my body swelled, the gentle anaesthesia of approaching motherhood made me confident at last. Our coming child would surely keep me earthbound and benign and content to be Ewan's wife.

Margaret Dulcie McLennan was born on 6th July 1942, a minor miracle among the mouse-coloured loaves and dried egg of a Fort William nursing-home. From the very start, her astonished flower face earned her the name of 'Daisy', though Mrs Stott, who helped out in the house, called her 'the wee thing' and was stiffly jealous when red-haired Mary Macrae was brought in from the village as nurse.

Ewan assured me he was delighted with his daughter, but – sensitive as only a new mother can be – I thought I detected a forced note in his cheerfulness.

'She's wonderful, honestly. You both are.' And yet he seemed puzzled. I'd see him reach out a tentative middle finger to her fuzzy head, as if this outrageously female creature already belonged to a strange and arcane sisterhood, something he hadn't bargained for when he'd taken his own youthful .410 shotgun so eagerly out of its case to be cleaned and oiled, just a few weeks earlier.

'A practice run,' declared his mother. 'Next time, it'll definitely be a boy.'

In September, Alice, now promoted to third officer, came to spend her leave with us at Achrossan.

'Gosh, you look tired, Alice. Was it a ghastly journey?'

I'd planned to drag Alice to the nursery at once to show off my glorious daughter, but her waxen skin and the dusty shadows round her eyes shocked me out of my excitement. There'd always been such firmness to Alice, even at the height of her passion for Stephen Morgan; she'd loved him with determination, never in a feeble, languishing sort of way. Yet now, for the first time, she seemed listless and without direction. Her uniform jacket hung on her hollow shoulders as if she'd draped it over a coat-hanger and it seemed an effort for her to raise her eyes to the level of our faces.

When I took her to meet Daisy, a vague frown cast such a

shadow between her brows that I wondered if it had been tactful of me to bring her. After all, she was older than I was: perhaps regret for her own childlessness was at the root of Alice's trouble.

'Did it hurt much? Having her, I mean.' Alice studied my daughter from a couple of paces away.

'Oh, gracious, it hurt like the dickens at the time, I can tell you. But it isn't like being ill. You know you'll have a baby after it's all over.' In her cot, Daisy struggled into wakefulness, pummelling the air with her fists and ripping her slumbers from end to end. Then, breathless with achievement, she demanded imperiously to be embraced.

'Would you like to hold her?'

'Oh goodness, no.' Alice stepped backwards, her hands behind her back. 'I'm hopeless with babies. I'd be bound to drop her, or something. Look – I'm simply dying to change out of this uniform. Why don't I go and do that and I'll see you at tea?'

Alice's detachment persisted. She was curious about Daisy, but her questions were almost scientific and she avoided any contact with my daughter's warm, milky reality. Sometimes she'd come with me when I went upstairs for a feed, but as soon as I was settled serenely in a nursing chair, with Daisy busy at my breast, the conversation would become fitful and awkward. In that respect she was like Ewan, who tried to mask his unease with strained humour.

'Two girls together – three, now you're here, Alice. High time I made myself scarce, I'd say.'

But Alice never lingered in the nursery. Instead, she'd go off for a walk alone by the loch or climb the flank of the Fiddler or the ridge of Creagruadh behind the house. When it rained, as it often did with us, she'd take refuge by the fire with a book, mechanically turning the pages as if her mind were on something else entirely.

Only Nina's presence seemed to stir her.

'I don't know why you let that woman stay here!' she burst out one morning, her cheeks quite pink with indignation. 'I've never liked her. Don't you remember her fighting with Rose, on the dining-room floor in the Villa Oléandre?'

'Nina isn't so bad, when you get to know her – and she absolutely adores Daisy. She's made a beautiful quilt for her out of scraps of fabric and she sings funny little Russian songs to make her sleep. Besides,' I added, as I'd repeated so often to myself, 'Nina will be off as soon as the war ends. This place isn't nearly glamorous enough for her.'

But Alice's attention had already wandered; as swiftly as it had come, the brief colour drained from her cheeks.

'Come on.' I tugged her out of her chair. 'We'll leave Daisy to Mary Macrae, and see if we can reach the top of Creagruadh before lunch.'

We set off in the clear brilliance of a morning unfolding to sunlit, honeyed sweetness. Far below us, the loch was frosted with dancing light; somewhere in the roof of the world, lapwings pierced the air with their cries, slivers of sound in a cobalt vastness. I turned to share it all with Alice – and found her climbing doggedly in her sensible shoes, as though the hill and the morning and the lapwings were obstacles to be overcome by sheer persistence.

There seemed no point in going on to the summit. Still some way below it, we threw ourselves down on a thin mat of grass among the wind-scoured ribs of the hill.

'Gosh, I'm so out of breath these days!' Pillowing my head on my arms, I stared up into the endless blue. It seemed incredible that under such a sky there was room anywhere for the squalor of war. I turned to look at Alice: her arms were wrapped round her knees and she was staring straight ahead, hugging her thoughts to herself. I don't imagine she'd even heard me.

It struck me again how much she'd changed from the cheerful, practical Alice of our conversations in the Edinburgh tearoom. And then, as I remembered some of the things we'd talked about there, an awful possibility dropped like a stone into my mind. Had Alice learned some tragic news from one of her coded messages that she wasn't allowed to share?

I made an effort to keep my voice steady.

'Alice, if you don't want to tell me what's the matter, I can understand that and I won't ask.' Like a dreamer, she half-

346

turned towards me. 'But it's obvious something's making you unhappy and I must know – is it anything to do with Stephen Morgan? Has something happened to him?'

Alice examined me, her eyes clouded with incomprehension.

'Stephen's perfectly well, as far as I know.' With her hand, she shaded her face from the inquisitive sun. 'And there's nothing the matter with me, really. I just need a little peace and quiet, that's all. Somewhere to sit and think for a bit.'

At the end of her leave Alice went silently back to Rosyth and her cipher machine, and the war, which I'd managed to push away beyond the top of Daisy's enchanting head, became depressingly real again, if only in the shape of those young men who'd left us and hadn't returned. Bertie Headington was reported killed at El Alamein. 'Cad' Langham had already been taken prisoner at Dieppe. In the village, our postmaster's son was missing, believed shot down over Danzig: the postmistress could be heard sobbing as she switched telephone lines in the exchange.

Ewan's frustration returned tenfold. No amount of Home Guard exercises, shore patrols, tons of turnips grown or licences for pig-slaughtering could make up for the fact that he, an active man of thirty-six, was safely at home, rubber-stamping government forms, when most of his generation were involved in the raw reality of war. Ewan wasn't a complex man and I knew his jealousy was genuine. All he'd wanted was a chance to do the right and honourable thing, to prove himself among his peers. Instead – it was written plainly enough on his face – he'd stayed at home and sired a daughter.

A daughter was doubly disastrous. As far as Ewan was concerned, Daisy was mine – a female child, a companion, drawing me away from him into womanly mysteries he neither understood nor thought it proper to understand.

In October, news came through of desperate fighting at Stalingrad; Nina, who insisted on calling it *Tsaritsyn*, became distraught and had to be comforted.

Tea and sympathy were not enough – or perhaps it was

simply that others were looking for comfort too. One day in November I came home early from a paper salvage collection to find Ewan and Nina coupling energetically on the hearthrug in Princess Mary's Chamber. If Nina hadn't made so much noise I might never have opened the door; I'd assumed Ewan's springer spaniel had been shut in by mistake.

'For heaven's sake, Clio!' Ewan pursued me to our bedroom. 'This has nothing to do with *us* – with you and me. You must know that. It was just a spur of the moment thing. You warned me yourself what Nina was like. When she lays it all on a plate, it would take a bloody monk to resist her.'

Bluster makes me savage. Ewan followed me, still blustering, from our bedroom to my dressing room next door.

'I swear to you, Nina means nothing to me – nothing at all. You're *my wife*, dammit, the mother of my child – and I love you. Nothing can change that. Something like this doesn't matter.'

Doesn't matter? I glanced at him, incredulous. How could he pretend it didn't matter? I was the last one to forget how things could happen on the spur of the moment – I'd only to close my eyes to remember a shaded hotel bedroom, with bombers swooping and diving outside the window – but if anything had taken place between Stephen and me on that Shanghai afternoon, then it certainly would have *mattered*. It would have meant the beginning and end of just about everything in my life. How could Ewan look at me with that expression of injured righteousness and try to pretend it didn't *matter*? That was what made me so angry.

I took a suit out of my wardrobe and threw it past him, over a chair-back. The sight of it injected a note of anxiety into Ewan's voice.

'Look, I know it was wrong of me – I know it – my God, of course I know it. But try to understand how hellish it's been here for me – first of all, finding the estate in such a bloody mess and then being stuck at home when all the other men are fighting. Sometimes I feel so useless. And you've been completely tied up with Daisy, you didn't want me. And Nina just happened to be there and she was unhappy too and – Clio, at

348

least look at me! Come out of that damned wardrobe!' He tried to swing me round to face him, but I pulled away and tossed a dress down on top of the suit.

Now his tone became aggrieved. 'You expect too much of me, Clio – that's always been your problem. You wanted to marry a hero and instead you found yourself with a fellow who turned out to be lumbered with debt and cursed with a bad leg. Let's face it, I've been a disappointment to you from the day we were married.'

'Shut up, Ewan!' I shook a pair of shoes in his face. 'And stop whining! Be a sinner if you must, but for heaven's sake be an honest sinner and don't blame your misdeeds on me.'

I swept up the clothes I'd selected and set off back to the bedroom with Ewan loping at my heels.

'What do you think you're doing?'

'I'm packing, Ewan. And tomorrow I'm taking Daisy and going down to London for a while. That'll give us both time to decide whether there's any point in going on with this marriage.'

Taken aback, Ewan stared at me. 'You aren't serious? You wouldn't really leave Achrossan?' With remarkable speed for a limping man, he crossed the room towards me.

'Clio, please – at least wait until you can see this clearly. Clio – ' He ran a hand through his hair. '*Please* . . . I know I've got no right to say this – but what is there left for me, if you go? I'm miserable enough already, for heaven's sake. I don't know what I'll do, if you leave me.'

'Shut up! Shut up! I won't listen to any more of this.' I covered my ears and took a deep breath. I could feel the two Clios inside me struggling for mastery and the second Clio – the one who had no time for excuses and self-pity – thrusting aside her docile sister.

'Turn that woman out of our house.' I was surprised at the cold clarity of my voice. 'Tell her to get out. Now. At once.'

'But how can I send her away at this time of night? Where could she go?' Ewan's expression dissolved into uncertainty, like the face of a small boy trapped between two demanding aunts. Mulishness and dismay battled in his countenance until I felt such contempt I wanted to kick him. 'At least let her stay until she finds somewhere else. I promise never to touch her again.'

I pulled a dressing-case out of the cupboard.

'Mrs Stott can drive me to the station in the morning. You know where to find me after that. Now excuse me, I have to see to Daisy.'

'Clio, please!' I heard his wail behind me as I slammed the door

Mary Macrae having balked at the idea of London, it was more difficult than I'd expected to convey Daisy and her baggage from train to crowded, blacked-out train as far as the capital and, in spite of the willing help of fellow travellers, we were both exhausted by the time we arrived. I was shocked to see the devastation in London; no wireless report or newspaper photograph had even half-way conveyed the reality of whole streets crushed to unrecognizable rubble or homes blasted open to the rain and the wind, robbed of their simple dignity, their flayed wallpaper fluttering like the mourning streamers I remembered from Chapei.

'So this is Daisy. Well, well – she *is* a beauty, isn't she?'

My father pretended to be fascinated by his first grandchild, while I told him I'd simply taken it into my head to show Daisy off to the family. If he suspected there might be another reason for my visit, wisely, he didn't ask for details. Ewan telephoned two days later and found himself discussing the war in North Africa for several minutes before my father consented to hand over the phone.

'It's taken me hours to get through.' Ewan sounded harassed. 'The postmistress couldn't get a line.'

And now that she had, I was pretty sure she'd be listening in to it. Ewan obviously thought so too.

'Your father sounds better,' he said pointedly. *'Bearing in mind how ill he was when you had to rush off to London.'*

So that was the excuse he'd given everyone. I picked up my cue. 'Papa is a little better, thank you.'

'I wondered, perhaps, if you were thinking of coming back sometime soon.' There was a pause. 'I miss you very much – you and Daisy.'

I took a deep breath. 'Has Nina gone?'

'Not exactly.' Ewan's voice became slightly muffled, as if he were glancing over his shoulder. 'It's a bit difficult.'

'Is it?' The second Clio, with her clear mind, saw no difficulty at all, beyond weakness and self-pity. She almost shouted that fact . . . and then heard a sniff on the line – or it might have been the scrape of a hairpin – which didn't sound as if it belonged to either end.

'I don't think I'll be able to leave my father for a while,' I said carefully. 'I'm sure you understand the situation.'

'But Clio, darling, I need you here!'

'It's more serious this time, Ewan. In fact, as things stand, I really can't say what might happen.'

A sigh of frustration whistled down the line. 'What am I supposed to do, then?' The telephone lent a rasping quality to the words.

'Do whatever you think best, but let me know when you've made up your mind. That's all I ask.' With sudden decision I laid down the receiver.

When the telephone rang again in the middle of the following morning, I let my father's elderly butler answer it, afraid it might be Ewan once more. In fact, it was Alice, asking to be picked up at King's Cross. She sounded desperately weary and relieved to discover I was in London.

'Can I stay for a day or two, do you think? Will Uncle Edward mind? It's just that I don't want to go straight to Belgrave Square.'

'But what on earth are you doing in London? And where's your uniform?'

Small and vulnerable in our monumental hallway, Alice tilted her pointed chin. 'I've been discharged from the Wrens.' She swallowed hard and clutched the folds of her voluminous coat. 'I'm six months' pregnant, you see.'

All at once her self-control dissolved and she threw her arms round my neck. 'Oh God, Clio – help me tell the family.'

My mind whirled with questions – questions I couldn't ask, since that was why Alice had come to us in Rutland Gate rather than to Kit's. At least now I could understand her torment, when she'd stayed with us at Achrossan in September. She wouldn't be the first – or the last – unmarried woman to become pregnant in the middle of a war, but that didn't mean it was any less of a disgrace. The back-street abortionists and the unofficial adoption arrangers had flourished on the reckless passions that had blossomed during three years of war – though Alice didn't seem to have considered either solution to her 'mistake'.

Whose is it? More than anything, that's what I wanted to know, although I was sure I hardly needed to ask. It could only be Stephen Morgan's baby – Stephen's child – conceived, no doubt, during some brief spell of leave: there had only ever been one man in Alice's life.

We were sitting in the drawing room. I'd made her put her feet up on a sofa to rest, but she insisted on talking.

'I want you to know everything, Clio, the whole story.'

I wasn't sure I wanted to hear it. *Stephen's baby – Stephen Morgan's child.*

By the time I forced myself to listen, Alice was already half-way through her tale. '. . . and I went with them once, to Gibson's in Princes Street – do you know the place? They have tea-dances on the first floor, not with a band, but with Victor Silvester records – just like *Dancing Club* on the radio. *South of the Border . . . down Mexico way . . .* ' Alice smiled shyly. She'd rolled her hair into the fashionable sausage, I noticed, although, freed from the brim of her uniform hat, her incorrigible fringe had tumbled down once more to hide her eyes.

'It's quite respectable, Gibson's.' Alice's expression became earnest. 'Well, more or less respectable. But of course, I never expected to see *him* there. I'd assumed he was thousands of miles away – and there he was, on leave, just popping up in Gibson's as if it was the most natural thing in the world. And then he took me to dinner and we arranged to meet again.' Here Alice halted, chewing her lip. 'And then, somehow, everything suddenly became terribly serious, because we had so little time and we both knew he might even be killed before too long.' Struggling for honesty, Alice wound her fingers into the rug covering her knees.

'I just couldn't bear the thought of him dying far away, without anyone. I wanted to *give* him something – so that he could believe someone cared.' She fastened her enormous eyes on me and her voice dwindled to a whisper. 'And we were all alone one day and I found myself wanting him . . . so much. Can you understand that?'

I nodded, overwhelmed by a wave of such shameful, agonizing jealousy that I couldn't trust myself to speak. Yet even then, I believe, it wasn't so much Alice's triumphant possession of Stephen Morgan's child which hurt me, as her freedom to love any man so unconditionally. My dismay must have been printed on my face – I rested my forehead on my hand so that Alice shouldn't see. Could I understand? Oh yes – alas, I could understand perfectly.

Entirely self-absorbed, Alice didn't notice my confusion.

'And then he was posted away. He told me where, but of course he'll have moved on from there by now.' Alice shrugged philosophically and ran her hands over the mound of her belly. 'That's all there is to tell, really.'

'So he doesn't know about the baby?' I couldn't imagine how Stephen would react to the arrival of a child. In my overwrought state I even became indignant on his behalf. 'But surely he has a right to know, if he's the father. He's bound to find out, sooner or later.'

Alice's head snapped up, her eyes dangerously bright.

'Why should he ever find out?' She twisted round towards me. 'Clio, he mustn't ever know. That's the whole point. This is *my* baby, not anyone else's. I'm not ashamed of it – and I don't want to be forced to get married, or anything like that. David will probably go straight back to America after the war and there's no need for him ever to know – '

'*David?*' I stared at her. Several seconds passed before I realized my mouth was still open.

'David Spencer,' she said. 'I told you. Don't you remember

going over on the *Concordia* to spend August with the Spencers at their summer house in Newport – you and I and Mama? Ewan was staying with friends, somewhere near by.' Alice scraped at her fringe. 'David's father shot himself after the Crash and now his mother has married a lawyer from Philadelphia and David's in the Army. He's something rather grand to do with building bridges.' She peered at me curiously. 'I said *David* at the start. Didn't you hear me?'

Kit flew into a rage, torn between a desire to murder the scoundrel responsible or to book St Margaret's for a shotgun wedding.

Doggedly, Alice refused to name the father. 'I don't want a husband,' she kept repeating. 'Just my baby.'

'This is all Margot's fault!' The ridge of Kit's handsome nose had gone white with fury. 'This is what comes of your mother's example.'

'What rubbish!' Alice's mouth had formed a determined line and for the first time I saw the resemblance between Kit and his elder daughter – that grim resolve to hold on to what was theirs, come what may. 'Mama had her children in wedlock,' she snapped at him. 'You had yours in St John's Wood.'

Rose came to see us at Rutland Gate to make sure of what she'd heard. I noticed with surprise that Rose's beauty hadn't lasted as her mother's had done. Nowadays she scraped her hair into a bluestocking bun which gave no hint of the wild, dark curls of her youth, and her imperious, winged cheekbones had disappeared into twin pouches of discontent. She was already the mother of one little Woade and her straddling walk and the tilt of her spine indicated that another was hatching under the folds of her smock.

Rose had served two weeks in prison at the start of the war for trying to obstruct the call-up, but Roger Woade had been locked up for longer and even now was picking brussels sprouts in a Leicestershire field while composing socialist tracts in his enormous cranium.

Rose's views on Alice's pregnancy were, as usual, the opposite of anyone else's. 'Don't let them make you get married,' she instructed. 'If the father's one of these war-mongering murderers, then you're better off without him, in my opinion. You could always put the child up for adoption.'

'I will not give my baby away!' Alice's eyes sparkled as she confronted her sister. 'Can't you understand? I love this baby already, simply because it's mine. It's the only thing I've ever loved that no one can take away from me. I'd die, sooner than give it up.' She spread her fingers tenderly over her abdomen. 'And you don't have to worry. I'll find somewhere to live and bring up my child, far away from any of you. Then you and Papa and your precious Roger can pretend I don't exist.'

Dismayed, I realized I couldn't even offer her the sanctuary of Achrossan. Instead, one day, while Alice was taking her afternoon nap at Rutland Gate, I went round to see Kit.

'No one in this family seems to have learned a thing from the past,' I told him. 'You're all turning your backs on Alice, exactly as you did to poor Catherine, your sister.'

'Nonsense.' Kit pronounced the word with conviction, but closed his mouth without explaining what the difference might be.

'Catherine Oliver hated her father until the day he died. You and Papa both loathed him – and yet now you're going to do exactly the same thing, all over again. Do you really want to lose Alice for ever?'

Afterwards, Alice gave me the credit for the compromise which was reached, though I'm sure Kit would have come round in the end, once the first shock had worn off. In the end, Alice reluctantly agreed to wear a wedding-ring and call herself 'Mrs Buckley', and to pretend her baby was the result of a whirlwind marriage to a pilot almost instantly shot down. For their part, Kit and Mamie redecorated their nursery in Belgrave Square for the late Flight Lieutenant Buckley's child (Kit had held out for Squadron Leader, but Alice felt the deception had gone far enough), and Alice and I, besotted mother and mother-to-be, spent Christmas playing with my six-month-old princess and sharing the baby-talk Alice had denied herself until then.

Shortly after New Year, my father finally broke his silence on the subject of my marriage. 'You'll have to sort things out with Ewan, you know, sooner or later. What was it all about? Another woman?' He tugged uncomfortably at his earlobe. 'After that business in Shanghai, I thought it might be.'

'If you must know, this time it was Nina Starozhilova.'

'Ah.' My father looked chastened. 'Of course.'

'Though if it hadn't been her, there would have been someone else.'

'And you mind that very much, do you?' He gazed at me sadly over his fine Roman nose and I had a sudden vision of Steward's Niece and Gardener's Little Sister playing with a ball under our tulip trees in Shanghai.

'Shouldn't I mind? Shouldn't I care if my husband has other women?'

My father examined the carpet. 'You have very high principles, darling. I don't suppose you learned them from me.'

'Or from Kit, either – or from Margot.' I noticed he didn't attempt to contradict me. 'In any case, it has nothing to do with principles – it's the hypocrisy I can't bear and the self-righteousness. Ewan doesn't only lie to me – he lies to himself.'

'We all have our weaknesses, darling.' My father's face had settled into its gentle, old-womanish folds, as if he'd long since lost the struggle with life's expectations. 'You mustn't be too hard on Ewan. On the whole, you know, he's a decent man and I'm sure he cares for you in his own way.'

'You're saying I expect too much of people.'

'Try to remember we're only ordinary mortals – that's all.' Comfortably, my father folded the hands which had caressed Sumei and Gardener's Little Sister. 'We're tempted and we fall. That's what being human is all about.'

'You're telling me I should forgive Ewan and go back to Achrossan.'

'I think you should try to understand him and mend your marriage. Stop looking for perfection, darling, because you won't find it.'

Alice's baby son was born on 14th February 1943, St Valentine's Day. When he was four weeks old, a letter arrived from Ewan, begging me to go home. Nina, it seemed, had been gone from Achrossan for ages: Ewan admitted he'd been stupid and he humbly hoped I'd forgive him. He'd missed me a great deal and missed Daisy too, and Mrs McAngus the minister's wife was beginning to enquire with some asperity when my father's health might be expected to improve.

He gave me news of the estate and of the village as if he assumed I'd be anxious to know what had happened in my absence.

The postmaster's son, he reported, had turned up, alive, in a POW camp, but almost at once the blacksmith's boy had been lost in the North Atlantic, just when the fortunes of war seemed to be turning at last. Chief Warden Mackinnon's daughter had come home on leave from the ATS with platinum curls, causing much wringing of hands in his grocer's shop, and Lady McLennan's hens had produced such a glut of eggs that an inspector had come all the way from Oban to find out how she'd fed them.

It was like a dream of another world and, little by little, I found myself seduced by it. My dutiful self pointed out that Ewan was Daisy's father, that he loved us to the best of his abilities and that Achrossan was the home I'd no right to deny her; and if the other, indefatigable Clio tried to insist this wasn't enough, then I clung to my father's advice. We were all ordinary, fallible mortals; we were tempted and we fell. I should settle for what I had, instead of looking for more.

In the end, I went back to Achrossan, accompanied by Daisy's new nurse, Nanny Tarrant, who had relatives in Glasgow and was happy to go north with us. Ewan and his mother were waiting at Achrossan to welcome me home: any signs of Nina Starozhilova's occupancy had been swept from my hearth and there was remarkably little to show I'd ever been away.

'This is how it should be.' In the evening, after the rain had cleared, Ewan and I strolled a little way along the shore of the loch, to where we could look back at Achrossan, rising like a fairytale castle at the foot of rose-tinted Creagruadh. Ewan had taken to walking with a long horn-topped crook and he stopped to lean on it now, putting an arm round my shoulders.

'Yes – this is how it should be.'

No, I wanted to say. *This is how it is, not how I longed for it to be. But I've discovered that I can't change you and I can't change myself, and perhaps I was wrong to imagine I could do either. Help me to accept you as you are, Ewan, and to learn to love the good in you. But you must keep my eyes forever looking down this glen: don't let me lift them to the stars.*

Ewan hugged me against his side. 'This is where we belong, you and I. Nothing can change that.'

Alice telephoned one morning a month later. I could feel her tension fizzing down the line. 'Got to be quick. I'm phoning from Papa's office – priority line.'

'What's wrong? Has something happened to the baby?'

'No.' Alice cut me short, anxious to dispose of the preliminaries. 'The baby's fine. Eating me up at every feed. We're definitely calling him Hugh. Hugh Christopher Oliver.'

'Not Buckley?'

'Buckley-Oliver, then. I think that's how Papa's put him down for Eton. Look, Clio—' Alice cut me off again. 'I've had some bad news about Stephen Morgan and I wanted to tell you right away. I had a call from a friend who's still working you-know-where, to say Stephen's ship was torpedoed, somewhere south of Iceland. A U-boat sank one of the merchant vessels in the convoy and Stephen's destroyer was hunting for it when another of the pack got off a torpedo.'

Alice's voice was deceptively brisk, but my heart turned over like a stone in a swollen river. How long could a man survive in the sea south of Iceland? Four minutes? Five?

When I was a girl, Sumei once told me how she used to visit a Buddhist temple in Shanghai, not to pray to the great Buddha in his red silk grotto, but to take a pair of baby-shoes as an offering to gentle Guan Yin to relieve her childlessness. Guan Yin, said Sumei, is also Captain of the Boat of Salvation which carries men's souls over the seas of life and death to the Pure Land. In the instant's pause Alice had left, I thought of Guan Yin. As a sea captain and a goddess, she must understand both the secrets of sailors and of those who waited for them.

From a long way off I heard Alice's voice continue, 'Stephen's in hospital in Glasgow. He's quite badly hurt, I think, but I don't know any more.' Such profound silence followed this news that I thought for a moment we'd been cut off.

'Alice? Are you still there?'

'I don't want to see him, Clio. I'm not even going to write to him. I have Hugh now and that part of my life is over. But I must know Stephen's going to get well.' There was another pause. 'Clio?'

'Yes.'

'You're the only person I can ask. Will you visit Stephen for me? Please, just once, to see how he is – and then let me know?'

Chapter Nineteen

THE HOSPITAL was on the outskirts of Glasgow and looked as if it had been built at the time of Charlemagne, with even more pepperpots than Achrossan. The receptionist slid a finger down her list. Lieutenant-Commander Morgan, she informed me briskly, was in Ward 16, though the visiting hour was still twenty minutes away and Sister Gilfillan had never been known to let anyone in till the stroke of three.

It took me all of twenty minutes to find the ward. The tall cream corridors ran like pale veins through the flesh of the hospital, filled with an echoing din of voices and the clash of enamelled basins. Bandaged men – some with battledress tunics thrown over striped pyjamas – lingered in groups in niches and corners, or fumbled their way along the walls, fuelling the fear which had grown inside me with every mile from Achrossan.

'I'm sorry, Lady McLennan, but we're not allowed to give details over the telephone. Lieutenant-Commander Morgan's condition is stable – that's all I can say.'

A figure groped towards me, head wadded in white and dressing-gown trailing, moaning for a nurse. It was as much as I could do to go on. I stared at the nearby sign for several minutes before the words meant anything at all. Ward 16 had cream and verdigris paintwork and beds like slices of white bread, cut thin, each one spread with a broken body; half-way along, a cube of drawn green curtain gave out the sound of gargling regurgitation, until the impulse to turn and run brought guilt rising to my own throat.

The only ruddy faces here belonged to the visitors clumped

by each bed, murmuring reassurance while their eyes stared round. Nurses rustled past in a gale of Lysol, their shoes sucking the linoleum. Why does no one bring flowers to a men's ward?

In a bed near the heavily taped window I found a white-faced man I knew but hardly recognized, like a photograph on a stranger's wall.

'Stephen?'

He'd been staring out through the dirty lozenges of the window and it took a few seconds for his eyes to readjust to the rationed electric light.

'Clio.' He rolled his head on the piled pillows to inspect me. His lips were cracked with half-healed frost-sores; it must have hurt him to smile.

'"Of all the wards in all the hospitals in town – you have to walk into mine." Is that how it goes? I haven't seen the film yet.'

Casablanca had just been released and the dry Bogart one-liners were everywhere. I matched his light-hearted tone. 'Here's looking at you, kid.'

'Have a seat.' Stephen indicated a white-painted chair with a cork seat by the side of his bed and I sat down, trying to ignore the hump of a surgical cage under the bleached cotton bedspread and the bandages that rolled out over his wrist and hand from the left sleeve of his pyjamas.

'How did you know I was here?'

'Alice phoned. A friend in the Wrens heard you'd been wounded and passed on the news.'

'And you were sent to make a damage report.' He examined me from under blue-white eyelids, raw with sleeplessness, and then pointed to the tented bedspread. 'Compound fracture of the tibia, they call it here, two broken ribs, lacerations to the left arm and a few other bits and pieces. Laid up for repair until further notice.'

I gaped at him, relief making me stupid. 'What – nothing else?'

'What else would you like?' He twisted his head to survey the ward. 'Help yourself – they've got everything in here, poor

361

devils. Legs and arms missing, blinded, hacked up by shrapnel. All of that, some of them.' He turned back and the bitterness left his voice. 'You're right, I've been lucky. I should get back on my feet again eventually, provided they've cleaned out all the infection.'

'And if they haven't?'

'Bad news.' He made a snipping motion with his fingers. 'But it won't come to that.' His gaze travelled over my country tweeds. 'How's Ewan these days?'

'He's fine. Busy trying to beg some ammunition for the Home Guard. And Daisy's fine, too.' I hesitated. 'Did you know I'd had a baby?'

'Someone mentioned it.' Stephen searched my face as if he expected to find some visible sign of motherhood. 'Congratulations.'

'Thank you. Ewan was awfully bucked.' There was an awkward silence and I rushed to fill it. 'Daisy's more than a year old now. Hard to believe – they change so quickly. One moment they're just like little grubs and then suddenly they're pulling themselves up to snatch everything off the table. Daisy's got four front teeth, believe it or not. Ewan swears she says "Achrossan" quite clearly, but of course she doesn't. It's just her own private language.'

I realized that I, too, had begun to babble. And I was running out of trivia. I held out the rectangular parcel I'd brought.

'No grapes for the invalid?'

'You'll be lucky! Just a couple of books to read.' I glanced at his immobilized left arm and started to unwrap the parcel myself. 'These are both to do with the sea. There's a book by "Taffrail" about pirates, and this one's *The Loss of the Titanic*, by someone called Beesley—'

Our eyes met above the crumpled, several-times-used brown paper.

'A shipwreck,' he said gravely. 'I'll enjoy that.'

The utter stupidity of my choice had struck me at the same moment. There was complete silence between us as we stared at each other: then Stephen's shoulders began to twitch and he started to laugh helplessly – and I burst out laughing too, laughing so much that my eyes filled with tears and I simply couldn't stop. The sheer irreverence of laughing in such a place only made us worse: it was like making love on a park bench, all the more shockingly intimate for being in full view. I hugged the silly, inappropriate books that were the excuse for it – knowing full well our laughter had nothing at all to do with them, but with a shared city of lanterns and tense years apart and the wonderful accident of being together again in a cream and verdigris hospital ward.

Tears ran down the blue hollows of Stephen's cheeks as he wrapped his arms round his painful ribs. I'd forgotten how harsh his laugh was; a woman and a boy beside the next bed craned round in surprise.

'Dear God, you know how to make a man suffer.' Stephen wiped his eyes with his bandages. 'Remember the iodine in Shanghai?' He began to gasp all over again, but returning pain forced him to sober up with a groan.

'This bloody leg.'

'How long should it take to mend?'

'The plaster should come off in two months, but they say I'll need crutches for another two after that. It could be Christmas before I get back to sea.'

'You'll have to go back?' I hadn't looked so far ahead – but this was 1943 and we'd already endured more than three years of fighting. Surely there had to be an end to it some time. 'Maybe the war will be over by then and they won't need you. They say the Germans are getting the worst of it in North Africa.'

Sister Gilfillan, her pleated hat squared like a topsail, bore down the aisle, ostentatiously consulting her watch.

'Ten more minutes.' Wearily, Stephen allowed his eyelids to close and his face, unguarded, relaxed into an expression of such touching helplessness that I was glad he couldn't see it himself. I wondered what he did see, in the dimness behind those almost transparent eyelids. The last anguish of Shanghai? The hunting of the Atlantic? I couldn't even guess – he'd left me so far behind.

ALISON McLEAY

I couldn't ask, either: he'd made that clear when I arrived. Everything was to be light and superficial: *Of all the wards . . .*

Yet somewhere behind those closed, enigmatic eyelids was a memory of the sickening impact of a torpedo – of pain and the black chill of the water – of realizing, perhaps, that this was how death had come to his father and that the world would soon go on its uncaring way without him. And I could share none of it.

I fastened my coat. 'I'll visit you again, as soon as I can.'

His eyes blinked open. 'I probably won't be here much longer. They're running short of beds.'

'Then where will you go?'

'To a convalescent hospital in Ayrshire, they say.' Stephen shrugged, exposing heartbreaking hollows by his collarbones. 'I don't have much choice in the matter.'

Sister Gilfillan's rubber soles squeaked meaningfully up the ward.

'I'd better go.'

'It's time. Go and make your damage report.'

'I wanted to come, you know. It wasn't all Alice's idea.'

He raised a hand in acknowledgement, but didn't answer. I felt I'd been dismissed, fended off at arm's length: I wondered if he was afraid of a messy goodbye.

'Give my regards to Ewan – and whatever you give babies to Daisy.' He was already reaching for one of the books I'd brought and starting to leaf awkwardly through the pages. 'And thank you again for these.'

Sister Gilfillan was standing by the door, watching jealously as the last of the healthy trickled out.

'Excuse me, Sister – have you a moment? What exactly is a compound fracture?'

She thrust out her downy chin and eyed me severely. Satisfied, she drew herself up. 'You mean Commander Morgan. Yes, well, when he was picked up, I understand, the broken ends of his shin-bone were sticking out of his leg – and, of course, the longer a wound like that goes untreated, the more likely it is to become infected. I'm talking about hours, you understand, not days – and the commander spent some time in an open boat.' Sister Gilfillan clasped her hands over her silver belt-buckle. 'However, the ship's surgeon made a fair job of cutting out the infection and packing the wound while they were still at sea. Dr Fraser reckons the freezing air probably delayed the onset of gangrene.'

'Gangrene?' Alarmed, I repeated the word more loudly than I'd intended.

'*Please.*' Sister Gilfillan scowled. 'Think of my patients.'

'I'm sorry. But – Commander Morgan is going to be all right, is he?'

'If the bone in his leg heals properly, he'll be as good as new, given time.'

'And if it doesn't heal?'

Sister Gilfillan held open the door. 'We only look on the bright side in this ward, Mrs Morgan.'

'A frightful convalescent hospital, for months and months?' Alice's indignation wailed down the telephone line. 'But that's awful! Poor Stephen, the nurses will try to jolly him along and fat women will bring him socks. He'll hate it.'

'There's always Hawk's Dyke. They'll probably let him go down there when he's better.'

'Hawk's Dyke has been let to the Air Ministry – I thought you knew that. And Kate's London house was sold months ago.' I could almost hear Alice thinking, rummaging around in that tidy brain of hers for a way of solving what seemed such a simple problem. Inevitably, she came up with the one solution I'd feared. 'You could take him, Clio! Achrossan would be a marvellous place for an invalid. You eat far better than any of us down here and Ewan would probably be glad of the company.'

'But Stephen will need drugs and physiotherapy and our nearest hospital's at Fort William, almost forty miles away – and we've hardly any staff these days to look after him—'

'There's a nurse in the village, isn't there? And a doctor somewhere?'

'Well yes, but—'

'In any case, once the broken bone's healed, these things are just a matter of exercise.' Alice's voice quacked from the receiver, exactly, no doubt, as she'd chivvied her Wrens. 'Oh yes, Clio – Achrossan would be perfect. You can telephone the superintendent in Glasgow tomorrow. He's bound to agree – Lady McLennan of Achrossan and all that. Pull rank, darling, that's what it's for.'

'You sound just like Margot.' I resented Alice snapping like a sheepdog at my heels, driving me in the last direction I wanted to take. 'What if Ewan doesn't agree? He doesn't actually like Stephen very much, you know.'

'Oh, for heaven's sake – put them at opposite ends of the house, then. Don't be so wet, Clio. There is a war on, you know.'

'You were quite prepared to take in Nina and Oscar,' I reminded Ewan as we got ready for bed that night. 'And Stephen Morgan is family, after all.'

'I suppose so.' Ewan dropped his dressing-gown on the end of his bed and slid between the sheets. 'What's wrong with him, anyway?'

I explained the nature of Stephen's injuries and Ewan whistled. 'Poor devil, it sounds as if he'll be crippled for life now.'

'No. The doctors say that given time, he should recover completely.'

'Naturally, that's what they'd tell him.' Ewan's tone was dismissive. 'They wouldn't come right out and say he'll have a busted leg for the rest of his life. But he will, all the same. Dash it, I should know.'

Ewan lay on his back, gazing, unseeing, at the elaborate cornice overhead, one hand on the switch of his bedside lamp, about to close our marriage down for the night. He'd been relieved to have me back – grateful, even, that I'd returned – yet at the same time he seemed to resent his need of me, as if I were the one holding him back, preventing him from being all he should. We'd hardly ever made love since my return and when we had there'd been such tension about it, such forced politeness that we'd been reluctant to try again.

Now, I could imagine what was going through his head. He'd never liked Stephen Morgan; something about Stephen's determined iconoclasm had always made Ewan suspect an attack on himself, as if Stephen were laughing at him behind his back. Stephen had stayed on in beleaguered Shanghai while the shells whined over the settlements and the Japanese prepared to march in; Stephen had joined the Navy; Stephen had been wounded in action and would arrive at Achrossan a hero, in the uniform Ewan coveted.

Sitting up in my own bed, I waited for a decision, trying to guess what his frown implied.

'Yes, why not?' Ewan clicked the switch, plunging half the room into darkness. 'By all means tell them to send him here.'

Three weeks later I drove over to collect Stephen from the railway station. The Ford was cramped, but the Daimler had been deemed too wasteful of precious petrol.

It was the first time I'd seen Stephen in naval uniform, with the rippling lines of gold across his sleeve. His colour had returned, though his face was thinner than I remembered it from Shanghai and a fan of upward-curving lines at the corner of each eye testified to anxious hours of watchkeeping.

The station master hurried over at once to the carriage door. 'Ye'll need a wee hand, sir.'

But Stephen had already mastered the use of his crutches and refused any help.

'I hope you don't feel I'm interfering.' I was still annoyed I'd allowed Alice to manoeuvre me into this position. Until the moment I caught sight of him at the grimy carriage window, I hadn't really believed Stephen would let us take care of him.

'Not at all. I'm very grateful.' He swung himself so rapidly along the platform that I had to run to keep up.

'The convalescent home was a bit grim, I expect.'

'Full of invalids.'

'Not like you.'

'Not a bit like me.'

I'd arranged with Mrs Stott that Stephen should have the ground-floor morning room as a bedroom until he was more able to deal with stairs; I'd even hung up his painting of the girl in the ribboned hat to welcome him. But when we got back to Achrossan I discovered that Ewan had changed everything.

'I told Mrs Stott to make up one of the tower rooms overlooking the stable yard. Much quieter.' He indicated the silent mountains beyond the windows.

'But that's up two flights of stairs, Ewan!'

'Will that be a problem?'

'None at all.' Stephen swung himself forward. 'I'll manage.'

'Ewan—'

'I'll manage. Don't worry about me.' Swinging his plastered leg like a pendulum, Stephen stumped steadily towards the oak staircase as if he couldn't wait to prove his self-sufficiency. 'This way?'

'Turn right at the top,' Ewan called after him. 'Mrs Stott will show you where to go after that.'

'How can you possibly expect him to climb all those stairs? Stephen—' I turned to follow, but Ewan caught my arm, holding me back.

'If Stephen thinks he can manage, I've no doubt he will.'

At the foot of the stairs, Stephen tucked both crutches under one arm and, by gripping the broad wooden rail with his free hand and alternately hauling on it and sprawling over it, succeeded in clearing the first two steps.

'There you are, you see.' Ewan threw an arm firmly round my shoulders. 'Stephen doesn't want to be mollycoddled. I knew there wouldn't be a problem.'

I could hardly bear to watch Stephen's tortuous progress. I could only imagine the pain wrought on two newly healed ribs by that awful ascent. 'I thought this might happen. I should never have brought him.'

'Nonsense.' Ewan smiled blandly. 'I shall enjoy having him here.'

★

In some secret manner of his own, Stephen had already made his way down again to the hall when I came downstairs for dinner. He'd propped his crutches against one of the Queen Anne chairs and was supporting himself on the stone chimney-piece, gripping it with one knotted hand, apparently absorbed by the pattern of flames in the hearth.

'Stephen, I'm so sorry. I had a room all ready for you down here. I can't imagine what possessed Ewan to change everything.'

'Don't worry about it.' Stephen smiled briefly and then returned to his contemplation of the hearth, his hair and the narrow bones of his face drawing fire of their own from the flames. 'I told you, I'll manage.'

'How long did it take you to come downstairs, for goodness' sake?'

'About thirty seconds.'

'*What?*'

'I slid down the banisters.'

There was no hint of humour in it. I felt deeply embarrassed for Ewan.

'Stephen, all this has nothing to do with you as a person, honestly. It's just that Ewan hates having to stay at home when everyone else is in uniform. You know what silly things people can say.'

'I didn't mean to impose on you. If Ewan doesn't want me here—'

'He does, really. We both do.' I'd seen that expression on Stephen's face before. For two pins, he'd have been off and away, the twenty-five-mile drive to the railway station notwithstanding. Now that he was here in flesh and blood, it was the last thing I wanted.

'Ewan will enjoy having another man around the house – really, he will.'

If I'd been about to say any more, I was silenced by Ewan's arrival.

'Splendid.' His voice echoed among the pillars. 'I see you've made it to dinner without any mishaps, Stephen. I told Clio you'd manage perfectly well. Now, how about a whisky before we eat?' Ewan headed for the decanters and glasses laid out on a silver tray under one of the galleries. Sir Cato McLennan might have been forced to let the Achrossan glasshouses collapse and rain come through the roof of the north turret, but to Ewan's great satisfaction, the one thing his father hadn't stinted was his cellar. Even in wartime, we could drink pretty well.

'Sherry for you, darling?'

'Please.'

'Room all right, Stephen?'

'Very comfortable, thanks.' Stephen pivoted expertly on his plastered heel. 'I must thank you both for looking after my Renoir for so long. I've missed the poor girl, believe it or not. It's like meeting an old friend again.' He spread his hands behind his back towards the fire. 'By the way, what's that hill behind your house – the one I can see from my window, where the rocks look red as the sun goes down?'

'That's Creagruadh. The mountain behind it is *Beinn an fhidhleir*, the Fiddler.' Ewan splashed whisky into glasses. 'Good stalking country, once you're over the ridge.'

'Creagruadh.' Stephen repeated the name thoughtfully. 'It doesn't look particularly high. I might try and climb it one day, when I'm on the mend.'

'Oh, I'd forget that, if I were you. Creagruadh's steeper than it looks.' Ewan held out the crystal tumbler like a consolation prize. 'Try something smaller.'

Stephen eyed him over the golden ellipse of his whisky. 'You can climb Creagruadh, can you?'

'Oh, certainly. I go up there all the time during the shooting season. It's quite a nice little walk all year round, just for a bit of exercise.'

'Then I'll look forward to climbing it too, one day.' Stephen treated Ewan to an easy smile. 'Just for a bit of exercise.'

After that, I guessed it had become a point of honour with Stephen never to be late for a meal. Before long he'd developed such a mastery of the Achrossan staircases that I wondered if Ewan hadn't been right after all: perhaps adversity had been exactly what Stephen needed.

★

'So you had to bale out of Shanghai, too, in the end,' Ewan remarked during dinner one evening. His voice betrayed a certain satisfaction.

'I'd no reason to stay.' Stephen regarded him levelly across the table. 'Most of the Oliver assets had been sold and the money shipped out through Hong Kong. Even the offices were only on lease. There was no point in staying to watch a few ships come and go.'

'No point at all. And, of course—' Delicately, Ewan picked up his fork. 'The Japanese were about to overrun the place.'

'As you say.' With an expression like flint, Stephen watched Ewan slice triumphantly into his fish. 'As you say, the Japs were getting closer to us every day. By the time I left, they were demanding protection money from most of the foreign companies in the settlement – and then, after the attack on Pearl Harbor, they simply moved in on the banks and all the other businesses.'

He glanced up, catching my eye. 'They've even run off with the radiators from the Cathay Hotel. I believe there's a Japanese general living in your house now.'

'Still,' Ewan persisted, 'you got out in time.'

'I did.' Stephen's voice had become deceptively soft. 'But lots of people didn't. For instance, I hear the Tattersalls are still interned in Shanshuipo.' He left a tiny, significant pause. 'You must remember Evie, Ewan – that woman with the butterfly on her ankle.'

'Oh, yes. Evie Tattersall. Yes.' Ewan swallowed, glanced at me and then dropped his eyes to his plate. 'D'you know – this must be the biggest sea-trout we've had all season.'

One day Stephen found his way to my little sitting room overlooking the drive. He moved awkwardly round its cluttered cosiness – not only because of his crutches – and refused to sit down. He examined my pictures, turned over my Sèvres bowl with the intensity of an auctioneer and moved on. Most of the time I found myself talking to the back of his head.

'Do you mind my having Kate's portrait of Adam Gaunt? When we were asked to choose, it was the only thing I really wanted. Poor man, he looked so lonely in that empty house, as if he needed taken care of.'

'He wouldn't have thanked you for it. I suppose you realize that.' For a moment Stephen stood nose to nose with our great-grandfather, exactly matching his expression of quixotic defiance. 'Kate used to say Adam Gaunt hated obligations. He loathed being in anyone's debt.'

'I think that's why Kate loved him so much. Do you know, there were still flowers on his grave on the day we buried her?'

'Hmph.' Stephen swung himself over to the window and levelled a crutch at the cormorant screen. 'Is that the one I gave you?'

'Don't you remember?'

'I wasn't sure it was the same screen. I remember buying the thing and then wondering if you'd like it after all. Odd sort of object to give anyone for a wedding present, I suppose.'

'I love it – though I must admit, I thought it was a strange thing for you to choose. But that was before I saw your beautiful lady-friend.'

A guarded expression had come into Stephen's eyes, as it did whenever I crossed into forbidden territory. He didn't ask whom I meant. He waited for me to explain.

'The girl in the hat. Your Renoir. The one on the wall in your room.'

'Oh, that.' He smiled then, and nodded, but for a long time afterwards I wondered what very private tenderness he'd imagined I'd been about to crush under my blundering feet.

'Ewan, for heaven's sake try to be nicer to Stephen!'

'I'm being perfectly charming.' Ewan's spaniel was dancing on the threshold, waiting for the order to get into the car. Ewan leaned forward to print my forehead with his lips. 'Sensitive creature. You're imagining things.'

'No, I'm not. You keep needling him, sniping at him –

about his leg, for instance, as if he'll never be able to walk properly again.'

'I don't treat him as something miraculous, simply because he was injured on active service, if that's what you mean. He may have you and Peggy Stott eating out of his hand, but he needn't expect that from me. I can't see why you should feel sorry for him.'

Ignored, the spaniel began to snuffle and whine.

'Ewan, if I feel sorry for Stephen, it's because you've made me feel that way – not because of Stephen, or anything that's happened to him. Can't you see what you're doing?'

Ewan peered at me, taken aback by my sudden intensity. Ewan, Daisy and I – we were such a fragile unity, held together by familiarity, and need, and affection, and forgiveness, and the putting aside of dreams. It was the road I'd chosen, persuaded that everything else was delusion: and now Ewan himself was putting that hard-won acceptance in jeopardy. It didn't matter what I felt for Stephen – sorry, or indignant, or resentful on his behalf. What mattered was that I *felt*. And that was Ewan's fault – Ewan's and Alice's.

Ewan reached out to touch my cheek in a sudden, uncomprehending rush of fondness. 'You've too soft a heart, you know. I can't think what I've done to deserve you.'

Embarrassed, he snapped his fingers at the dog. 'Quiet, Rhona.' He gave me a sheepish smile that touched me with its utter lack of insight. 'Must go. Old Jock Cameron needs a permit for a couple of cows, but he's made a complete hash of the form. Pity the Ministry doesn't read Gaelic. Go on, then, you stupid animal, get into the motor.'

I'd written to Alice, one day when Ewan's jealousy had been particularly obvious. By now I was dreading the moment when Stephen would decide he'd had enough and leave us.

'I don't know how much more of this Stephen can stand.'

'You might be surprised,' came Alice's reply, 'if what Guy tells me is true. Do you remember Basil Leslie, that rather divine third officer on the *Concordia* when we sailed to New

York? He's got a command of his own now – the *Jonas Oliver*, I think – but the important thing is, he was there, in the convoy, when Stephen's destroyer was torpedoed.'

Stephen had never said much about that night. All I knew was that shortly after the order to abandon ship was given, the vessel's boilers had exploded, breaking her back and hurling him into the sea. Several hours had followed in a freezing open boat before the survivors were picked up by one of the other escorts.

Now Alice had extracted the whole story from Guy. 'The captain went down with the ship, they reckon, because it sank so quickly that only the people who were in the water survived. Basil Leslie heard that the boats were either smashed up or still in the falls and, of course, it was the middle of the night and freezing cold – and there was a heavy sea running.

'A Coxswain Someone reported it all to the Board of Enquiry. Apparently there was one boat floating clear, but upside-down, with a little sub-lieutenant clinging to the keel – absolutely off his head with fright, poor chap, he was hardly out of grammar school – and Stephen managed to swim to it and organize enough men to right it, though they'd no way of baling and the sea could have swamped it at any moment. Apparently it was so cold the men were actually weeping with agony and they kept going numb and trying to sleep, and Stephen made them stay awake by shouting at them and giving them things to do, and they had to sit up to their chests in the icy water, with these frightful waves breaking over them—' Here Alice turned a page.

'And then a U-boat came straight for them in the darkness – shooting – and they thought it was going to run them down, except that it turned away at the last minute. And *still* they managed to pick up more men out of the water and call out to the others on rafts and keep everyone together. They had to bale the boat with their bare hands, even though they couldn't feel anything at all – can you imagine? But the important thing was, Stephen kept them alive until they were picked up, all except two poor fellows who were burned to bits and died in the boat. He kept them *alive*, Clio, Stephen did – they all said so

– even though his leg was just about hanging off and he was in ghastly pain. Can you believe it?'

I could believe it. Hadn't I seen Stephen plunging into the back streets of Shanghai, drawn by the danger, relishing the intensity of each moment made vivid by fear?

'I think it's absolutely wonderful,' Alice concluded crisply. 'I hope they give him a medal for being so brave.'

I didn't tell Ewan about Alice's letter, though whether that was for Stephen's sake, or for Ewan's, I never decided.

Now that he'd recovered some of his strength, Stephen was never still. If the weather was good, he'd set off down the drive or patrol the limits of the grounds, dipping forward with each swing of his plaster like a boat in a head sea. If it was raining heavily he'd stump the corridors of the house, up and down, until by the time he was due to report to the hospital in Fort William to have the plaster removed from his leg, he'd long since worn through the rubber knobs on the ends of his crutches.

Ewan had authorized extra petrol for the trip. 'You'd better drive him to Fort William yourself, if you're so concerned about him.'

'We're an ambulance this morning,' I told Stephen, fixing a Red Cross sign above the Home Guard sticker on the Ford. 'Wait till you see how we have to crawl up the hill to the pass. We'll fly down, coming back, but I always take a bucket in case we have to fetch water from a burn on the way out.'

From a distance, I heard myself, like an infant teacher rallying her tots. All I could think of was how much depended on this trip to Fort William. With the plaster off, the doctors would know if the bone in Stephen's leg was knitting as it should and if the ragged gash had healed satisfactorily, throwing out its packing of gauze.

'Do I get toy soldiers, Miss, if I'm brave?' Stephen regarded me balefully from the passenger seat.

'Not if you're going to make fun of me. What am I supposed to say?'

'Let's just get started. I can't bear any more hanging about.'

He stretched backwards as far as he could, flexing his spine with a groan. 'Anything to be rid of this infernal plaster!'

To Stephen's fury, though the news at Fort William was good, he was given a new plaster and new rubber knobs for his crutches.

'They warned you in Glasgow it would take twelve weeks for the bone to heal,' I reminded him as we drove home. 'They said it would be another month after that before you could put weight on it.' When Stephen didn't answer, I added, 'Look, I do realize how fed up you must feel.'

'No, you don't. You bloody well don't.'

His fierceness stunned me to silence. I drove the next quarter-mile without registering a single fact about it.

And Stephen's anger was still savage, still unappeased. After a moment, he burst out again. 'You haven't the slightest idea how I feel! You can go where you please, do what you like. How the hell can you understand?'

I could have wept with rage.

'All right, then, I don't understand. Have it your own way. Wallow in the unfairness of it all. Why should Stephen Morgan's leg take the same time to heal as other people's? Why should *anything* about bloody, pig-headed Stephen Morgan be the same as the rest of us?'

There was an awful silence, broken only by the grumbling of the Ford. Then I realized Stephen was grinning, in the seat next to mine.

'I don't suppose I'll get my toy soldiers now.'

'Not a chance of it.'

'That's fair, I dare say.'

Lazily, he stretched an arm along the back of my seat, slid his hand under my hair and gently began to stroke the nape of my neck. The sensation was so startling that the Ford made a wild swing across the road before I could stop it.

'Forgive me?'

'Of course I do.'

'I hate being helpless. It's torture having to wait, day after day, to be whole again. I even dream about finding some way of making it all happen sooner.' He gave a quick, resentful sigh.

'At first I couldn't even dress myself. I had to be helped like a baby. And you're the only person I can bear to tell about it.' He tilted his head back to watch me melt under his touch. 'That means a great deal, Clio.'

I knew everything about helplessness – clinging to the steering wheel while those strong, soft, insistent fingers swept like a bird's wing at the tip of my spine, rousing so many other drowsy, astonished parts of me.

'Do you understand what I'm trying to say?'

I knew I should stamp on the brake, right there in the middle of the steep and winding road, virtuously shouting *Don't touch me! My husband wouldn't like it.* Yet those warm little circlings on my skin were words, pledges, headlong declarations so precious and profound I knew I'd never hear them aloud.

'I understand – I do, now.'

'Everything?'

'Everything.'

Several seconds passed before he spoke again and then his voice was so low I could hardly hear him above the grinding of the engine. 'Why on earth did you ever come back from London?'

'How did you know I'd been in London?'

'I met Guy one day in January and he was pretty sure you'd left Ewan for good. "Another spot of bother with the fair sex" – that's how he put it.'

In the downy hollow at the nape of my neck, the circlings began to slow until they stopped altogether, leaving Stephen's fingers entwined with my hair.

'For heaven's sake, Clio, the man's a fool!'

'That isn't true—'

'You should have left him years ago, in Shanghai.'

'And done what? Where else should I have gone?'

There was total silence.

'I don't know. Somewhere.' Stephen leaned away, withdrew his hand and began to scratch absently at the long scars on the back of his left wrist. 'I only realized you'd gone back to Achrossan when you came to visit me in the hospital in Glasgow.'

'Then why didn't you say something, if you knew all the time?'

'It was between the two of you. It wasn't any of my business.'

Mercifully, the silence was filled by the deafening howl of the Ford cresting the pass. As we rounded the final bend, the flank of Creagruadh slid away before us, dissolving into a stubble of birch and a denser clustering of alder and willow where the long sleeve of the loch unrolled itself towards the distant sea. The air had the painful clarity of pure, cold spring water; I could see the toy towers of Achrossan, dazzlingly white, at the foot of the hill. I guided the Ford into the gravelly pocket of a passing-place and we stared at it all through the fly-studded windscreen.

Stephen's hand moved to the door handle. 'Let's get out for a moment or two.'

We crossed a patch of rumpled grass, passed a rock cairn reeking of the strong, sour smell of fox and sat down with our backs against a great boss of stone, printed with continents of lichen. Suddenly weary of the weeks of tension in the house, I found myself sliding against Stephen's shoulder and felt his arm instinctively curve to accommodate me. But it was a restless arm: before long it would be gone again, leaving me to make my way along the road I had chosen.

'There's Daisy now, you see. She needs a father, as well as a mother. And Ewan isn't a wicked man, or a fool – he's just . . . human, I suppose. I expect too much of everyone. I don't know why.'

Stephen's scarred fingers had found a resting place in the valley of my shoulder. His breath warmed my temple. 'You don't have to explain. I told you, it's none of my business.'

But I wanted to explain. I wanted his blessing, if that was all he could give me – that inexplicable, half-healed man, that creature of stone who'd once sold a beloved plane for the painting which had captured his heart.

High among the crags, a young buzzard mewed like a cat. Stephen's gaze was fixed on the horizon, following the blue and undulating line until it came to rest on the domed summit of

Creagruadh, almost level with where we sat, across a scree-filled corrie.

'When I've climbed that hill, I'll know I'm whole again. And then I'll go.'

Chapter Twenty

EWAN WAS in the carriage-yard when we got back, talking to Gillespie the factor. He turned to wave and his eye fell upon the new plaster.

'Told you,' he muttered later in my ear. 'It's no good pretending he'll ever walk normally again, because he won't.'

For another month, Stephen endured the torment of the second plaster – not patiently, but because he had no choice. Meanwhile, for both our sakes, I made a conscious effort to ration my time with him. In the mornings I had my postal round or my paper salvage duties to keep me busy, and on fine afternoons, with Ewan away on official business, Nanny Tarrant and I took Daisy out for a walk – waving like a queen from the enormous McLennan baby carriage – or down to the lochside to roll on a rug in the splashy shade of the alders.

As often as not, Stephen came with us to the loch, though I didn't really count it as time together because of the presence of Nanny and Daisy. Perhaps I ought to have done. Daisy, whose first birthday we celebrated on 6th July, adored Stephen and spent a great deal of time persuading him with coos and gurgles to throw fleets of round, knobby alder catkins into the loch for her amusement.

Nanny Tarrant admired the play of sunlight on the water. I admired the supple arch of Stephen's body as he threw and tried not to remember a fading afternoon in a Shanghai hotel room and what had almost happened there.

The second plaster was cut off in Fort William in the middle of July and Stephen travelled there and back with Mr McAngus, the minister. He returned with an ordinary bandage on his leg, two stout walking-sticks and instructions that no unsupported weight was to be put on the barely healed bone for another month.

At first I wondered if Ewan had been right: Stephen's unplastered leg was dismayingly weak. When he walked, his gait was almost a caricature of Ewan's, but the difference, as Ewan was grimly aware, was that Stephen could at least cling to the prospect of fitness. Sometimes I'd come upon him unawares, gritting his teeth over the exercises he'd been shown and trying to compel his ankle to flex by sheer strength of will.

Day by day, Ewan watched his progress. 'I see they've brought aircraft carriers up from North Africa now. That should sort out Dönitz and his U-boats. Perhaps there'll be no war for you to go back to.'

Stephen drove himself relentlessly. If he wasn't labouring over his exercises, he was out of doors in all weathers, lurching up and down the Achrossan drive and then, as his leg became stronger, forcing himself along the road to the village, where I found him one day, leaning on a dry-stone wall two miles from home, his face rigid with the pain of tortured muscles.

He limped across as I threw open the passenger door of the Ford.

'How on earth did you think you'd get home?'

'I'd have made it. I just needed a rest.'

One evening, with some embarrassment, he thrust a letter into my hands. It was from the Admiralty, to say that in view of Lieutenant-Commander Morgan's injuries, arrangements had been made for him to travel to Glasgow to receive his Distinguished Service Cross from the hands of Commodore, Clyde.

'Well, I'm blowed.' Ewan's eyes bulged a little with a major effort to be fair. 'I suppose he must have done something to deserve it.'

'I think it's wonderful,' I told Stephen when he brought the medal back in its leather case. 'I'm very, very proud of you.'

He inspected me curiously. 'I actually believe you are.'

Without warning, he reached out to pull me against him – to hold me, pressed close enough against his body to feel the heat of it.

'Please, Stephen, this isn't fair.'

'There's no one to see us. Ewan's off on one of his highly important missions and everyone else is in the garden. A moment or two won't hurt.'

'It'll hurt when it's over.' I buried my face in the fabric of his uniform jacket, which smelled of railway smoke and the alien scents of the city. 'And it'll hurt like the devil when you go.'

His lips moved in my hair in something that might have been a sigh.

After a moment he slid his hands up to my shoulders, gently eased us apart and folded my fingers round the flat leather box. 'You'd better keep this for me. I'll only lose it.'

'No one loses a medal!'

'Just keep it safe. I'll know where it is if I ever need it.'

Stephen's mind was fixed on the day he'd leave us. He'd thrown himself, heart and mind, into training for the climbing of Creagruadh, discarding one of his sticks and hitching his lame leg up and down Achrossan's steep bachelors' stairs to the point of exhaustion.

From time to time, Ewan would raise his eyes from his Notices to Agricultural Committees to watch Stephen trudge past the window. 'Still at it,' he'd say, and shake his head.

But I willed Stephen to succeed. He was like one of the eagles which nested in the most unforgiving crags of the Fiddler. All I wanted was to see him whole and wild again – and yet I couldn't prevent a small, selfish part of me from hoping Ewan was right and Stephen Morgan's wings had been clipped for ever.

'That McAngus woman trapped me for ages in the post office this morning.' Ewan scowled and mimicked the genteel burr of the minister's wife. '"Do you think the Commander would consider giving a talk to the WVS on how he won his medal? He's quite a hero in the village these days." *Hah!*' Ewan snatched off his hat. 'What does she think it has to do with me, for heaven's sake? I'm not the so-and-so's keeper. Why the devil can't she phone and ask him herself?'

'He'd hate it, anyway. You know what Stephen's like.'

Ewan refused to be mollified and glared towards the door as if he could scent Stephen lurking behind it. 'He's a rootless wanderer, if that's what you mean, and silent as the tomb when he wants to be. Even talking to him – there's nothing you can get *hold* of. Why the hell are women so impressed by fellows like that?'

At the beginning of September that year, 1943, Italy surrendered and Ewan decided the news was a welcome excuse for a celebration. 'Let's put on a ceilidh for the village and cheer everyone up. We could rent the hall, hire a band – lay on some beer and sandwiches, or whatever.'

A wistful expression stole over his face. 'My grandfather put on an enormous bun-fight to welcome the men home from the Great War. I remember driving out with him to the steading where the estate workers were dancing and being allowed to light the rockets for the firework display. Grandfather stood up in the motor and they all shouted "Achrossan!"' Ewan smiled fondly at the memory. 'The laird was always known as "Achrossan" in those days. Only the factor called him "Sir Alastair".'

'But this war isn't over yet,' I pointed out.

'Then we'll have another ceilidh when it is.' Ewan rapped the base of his crook on the flagstones of the courtyard. 'We ought to keep up the old traditions. When my grandfather was laird, you know, his chamberlain used to go up to the battlements every night after dinner to shout "McLennan has dined! The world may now sit down to its meat." Every night.' Ewan tapped his crook again. 'Without fail.'

Ewan pursued his plan with determination. Soon there

wasn't only to be a ceilidh in the village hall for the local people, but also a grand dinner at Achrossan for as many of the gentry as could be mustered in the middle of a war. As it turned out, dismayingly few of those Ewan was prepared to invite could actually come, and the doctor and the minister, who'd been down for the village hall, were reluctantly promoted to make up the numbers.

Dr Campbell arrived in a midnight-blue dinner jacket which made Ewan regret having invited him. The minister came in a kilt, and his wife, like all the ladies, in whichever pre-war dinner gown seemed least like the all-pervading, button-rationed Utility dresses. Eighty-two-year-old General Munro hurtled down from Ardlarach in his pony carriage, hauling the reins in his great knotted fists while his wife and groom and his Belgian musical refugees clung to their seats behind him. Sir Donald Fraser of Kilphail brought his wife and daughter and a dashing son on leave from the Army; Ewan's mother, the dowager Lady McLennan, was ferried down from Finglas, and Charles MacIlwham, a pump-manufacturer from Glasgow to whom Ewan had sold a shooting lodge in the next glen, brought Mrs MacIlwham and two house-guests who made rivets and gaskets respectively.

Altogether, twenty-four of us sat down to dinner under the pie-crust ceiling and the jealous eyes of McLennan ancestors. Even in wartime, with grouse and venison from the hill and salmon and lobster from the loch, Achrossan managed to provide a satisfactorily laden board and Ewan was able to look down the length of his table and see only two things which brought a frown to his brow – the doctor's blue dinner jacket and Stephen Morgan, his DSC ribbon splendid on his uniform, being lionized simultaneously by Miss Catriona Fraser and the pump-maker's blonde and comely wife.

We hadn't yet reached the baked apple pudding and Ewan was just suggesting that in an hour or so it might be amusing to look in on the village hall to see how the ceilidh was progressing, when I heard a commotion beyond the door – an agitated and increasingly shrill argument among the stone pillars. At last the dining-room door opened a crack, the apprehensive head of

Macrae the poacher peered round it and Ewan was beckoned frantically from his place.

In a moment he was back again, grim and a little pale, to murmur in the ears of the estate factor and General Munro and after them the other gentlemen at the table. The conversation had already died: now chairs scraped back as the men rose to their feet in a body and trooped out into the hall.

A chorus of female voices demanded to know what was going on.

'I'm sure there's no need for alarm.' Ewan stood very straight at the head of the table. 'But it seems that a submarine's been spotted, making its way up the loch.' There was a general gasp and Ewan held up his hand for calm. He seemed to have grown an inch or two taller in some mysterious way and his brow and chin formed two stern parallel lines. I could imagine his ancestor, Roderick *Dubh*, announcing the arrival of raiding galleys in the same quietly authoritative manner.

'As I say, there's no reason to worry unduly – the vessel seems to be alone, so it may well be damaged and looking for a sheltered bay to make a landing. At any rate, the most important thing is to call out the Home Guard to keep the sub under observation, until we see what it has in mind.'

By now the gentlemen were returning from the gunroom, armed with the best anti-submarine weapons Messrs Purdey and Holland & Holland could provide, and we went out to join them in the hall. Ewan had automatically assumed command.

'Donald, the General can go with you. Charles, you should have room for the doctor in your motor. McAngus, I dare say this isn't your sort of show—'

'I'm coming, don't you worry.' The minister scuttled to Charles MacIlwham's side, rubbing his hands.

'Very well, then. Gillespie—' Ewan turned to the Achrossan factor. 'Phone the people in Inverness and tell them what's happened. Say we'll have more for them when we've some idea of what the U-boat's up to.'

The gentlemen moved in a body towards the door. Stephen came forward with the rest, gripping his single stick, his limp a bizarre echo of Ewan's own.

'Ah, Stephen—' Ewan placed himself squarely in the door-way. 'You're hardly up to this sort of thing. Better stay behind, I think, with that leg of yours.'

'There's nothing wrong with my leg.' Stephen's face set hard with annoyance. He moved towards the cars revving their engines outside, but Ewan stood his ground.

'There's no transport for you, in any case. The motors are full.' He turned away from Stephen, raising his voice. 'If you ladies would like to gather your coats and so forth, I'll send Macrae up with his bus to take you all down to the village hall. It's just a precaution, so we know where you are and the Home Guard can keep an eye on you.'

He cast a glance over the fluttering Miss Fraser and turned back to Stephen. 'Now, why don't you look after the ladies? That's a good job for you. Can't leave them on their own, after all.'

'To blazes with the ladies. I'm coming with you.'

Stubbornly, Ewan held his ground, his eyes bright and glazed with perversity. These, at last, were *his* Germans, *his* submarine. This was the chance he'd craved to prove he was the equal of a dozen Stephen Morgans, and he'd no intention of sharing it.

'Sorry, Stephen. Can't be done, I'm afraid.'

From somewhere outside Charles MacIlwham shouted, 'Ewan, what the devil's keeping you?'

'Sorry,' said Ewan again and disappeared into the twilight.

'Bastard.' Stephen muttered the word under his breath, but I was standing at his shoulder now, close enough to hear. 'What the hell does he know about submarines?' Stephen swung round, daring me to speak, hurt and furious.

Behind us, the voice of the general's wife rang clearly through the hall. 'Come now, Tilly, we're not going to let a handful of German sailors upset us, are we? We shall take a few packs of cards and then we can play whist.'

The ladies ran about, fetching wraps and coats. Nanny Tarrant came down with Daisy on her hip, blinking like a fat owl, and Mrs Stott marching grimly in her wake, carrying a Moses basket. Pity help the German, I thought, who dares so much as look at my daughter while she's in the care of those two.

The general's wife marshalled everyone at the door. 'Mahjong is too complicated, Dulcie. We need something everyone can join in.'

With sudden decision, Stephen snatched his uniform cap from the table. 'I'll *walk* down to the loch, then, since Ewan's left me no choice.' He glanced at me over his shoulder, challenging me to take Ewan's part. 'You don't really expect me to go with you to the village?'

'Not for a moment.' I shook my head. 'But don't walk – take the Ford. It's round in the carriage house in the yard. George Stott finished work on the carburettor this afternoon.'

'Why didn't you say so?' Stephen wheeled round and set off for the door leading to the kitchen quarters.

'Clio, dear—' Ewan's mother held out an imperious hand and for a moment I hesitated. Stephen had almost disappeared: in the middle of the group of women, Daisy had fallen asleep again, her head pillowed securely on Nanny Tarrant's blue serge shoulder.

'Must go,' I said to Lady McLennan. 'First Aid post, you know.' Then I turned and ran after Stephen.

'I'm coming too.'

'You are not.'

'Oh yes, I am.' Dragging a waterproof shooting-coat from its peg by the game-larder, I kicked off my evening slippers and stuffed my feet into half-wellingtons. It was a warm September evening, but I didn't fancy meeting a boatload of Germans in a delicate broché dinner gown and one of the precious pairs of nylon stockings Guy had shipped specially from New York.

Stephen blocked the doorway and I cannoned into him. 'You needn't bother dressing up. You aren't coming.'

'And you' – I placed my hands on his chest – 'haven't got the car keys.'

'They're in the dashboard. They always are.'

'Not this time.' I pushed past him into the yard. 'George brought me the keys, just before dinner. I didn't have time to put them back.'

My wellingtons flapped as I ran across the yard and began to drag open the wooden doors of the carriage house. Stephen caught up with me just inside and seized my shoulders.

'I can't let you come. This is dangerous.'

'More dangerous than the lanes of Nantao? More dangerous than the roof of the Great World?' I reached with both hands to touch his face and the soft responsiveness of his skin took me by surprise, kindling all the old excitement. This was the man who'd held me over the edge of the roof of the Great World – terrified, helpless, but consumed by such a wild, exultant intensity of living that I'd never forgotten it.

'You aren't leaving me behind now.'

I ran over the cobbled floor, slid into the driving seat of the Ford and gathered the hem of my gown up to my thigh to reach the keys I'd tucked behind the ribbon of my suspenders for safekeeping. Stephen watched curiously as the deep red figured silk streamed over my skin.

'Next time, I'll know where to look.'

As we roared down to the bottom of the drive, Police Constable Matheson shot past on his bicycle, pedalling for all he was worth, his uniform tunic half-buttoned and his cycle clips askew.

'He's going the wrong way for the village.' I swung the Ford to the right, racing after the constable. 'The submarine must be heading for this end of the loch.'

The sun had just slipped over the horizon, leaving a stain in the western sky which brought a blush to the darkening breasts of the hills. Just over the hump-backed bridge, I saw Matheson skid to a halt, feet splayed. Charles MacIlwham's Rolls and Sir Donald Fraser's shooting-brake were drawn up on the grass verge and beyond them stood Mackinnon's van, its rear doors hanging open as if passengers had just clambered out of it in a hurry. The Home Guard had arrived from the village hall with commendable speed: Chief Warden Mackinnon, an elder of the Free Kirk, had sworn he would only come to the ceilidh to prevent it from spilling over into the Sabbath.

I was about to get out of the car when Stephen touched my arm.

'You wait here.' In the shadows, he reached for my right hand and closed my fingers round something cold and solid – a small automatic pistol. 'This is the safety catch – look. Now, it's only a .25, so you'll have to let them get pretty close. Between the eyes, if you can manage it.'

I gazed at the gun, appalled. I'd never forgotten the marks of gunfire on the broken bodies of Chapei, like some obscene infection. I couldn't imagine holding a gun to a man's face and pulling the trigger.

'How long have you been carrying this around?'

'Since Shanghai.' Stephen was already half-way out of the car. 'It was the only thing I saved when the ship went down. Quiet, now.' He held a finger to his lips and pressed the door shut with barely a click. In another moment he'd gone, hitching himself through the rough grass in the direction of the loch.

Pistol or no pistol, I'd no intention of staying behind. I could see figures stirring among the alders at the edge of the rocky shore; the occasional flash of starched shirt-front showed where one of our dinner-guests was levelling his shotgun at the alien presence on the water. As Stephen made his way cautiously between the trees, I slipped out of the car and followed. I felt ridiculous with the pistol in my hand; checking the safety catch, I dropped it into the pocket of my waterproof coat.

I guessed Ewan would be watching the loch from a point nearby where the trees divided round a pebbled inlet, giving an unrestricted view. The gales of the past few days had died away, leaving hardly a breath to stir the leaves as I crept through them, and before long, I spotted Ewan staring through field-glasses into the gathering twilight, with General Munro on one side, tall and string-like in his venerable kilt, and on the other the squat shape of the pump-manufacturer, MacIlwham.

'Too small for a Type IX,' Ewan murmured as I edged within earshot. 'More like a Type VII. Just nosing down the loch, weighing up our defences. Cameron—' he called out to the nearest trees. 'You've posted men right down the shore, as far as the village?'

'Indeed I have, Sir Ewan.'

'It's important to keep the sub under continuous observation. They'll probably try to launch a rubber boat under cover of darkness and sneak ashore. Our job is to hold them until help arrives.'

It sounded impressive, but I recognized a tremor of self-doubt which belied Ewan's apparent confidence. This was no Home Guard exercise, carried out according to Instructions. This was the real thing – the test of whether Ewan McLennan could take it and prove worthy of his ancestors. To Ewan, it was certainly the most important night of his life: every moment of the past thirty-seven years had led up to this, and now he was tense beyond belief. I saw him jump as Stephen materialized out of the dusk at his shoulder.

'Dammit, what on earth do you think you're doing, creeping up on us like that?'

Stephen braced himself on his stick. 'Have you any idea how far voices carry across water?'

'Well now, this is the fellow we need.' General Munro laid a bony claw on Stephen's shoulder. 'Give him the glasses, Ewan. Commander Morgan will soon tell us what kind of fish we've caught. Why the devil weren't you here earlier, man?'

In silence, Stephen levelled the field-glasses. 'How deep is the loch at this end?'

'It's about three hundred feet where the sub is now. There's a narrow shore here and then the loch starts to shelve pretty steeply.' Ewan pointed, saw his hand tremble and clasped it behind his back. 'This chap's got the cheek of the devil, coming so close inshore – you have to hand it to him.'

'A Dhia,' muttered a voice among the trees, 'they're devils, these Germans, right enough.'

Even I, straining my eyes, could now make out a sinister dark line on the water, with a raised section amidships and what looked horribly like a gun. At last, Stephen lowered the glasses and passed them back to Ewan.

'It's a tree.'

Ewan stared at him, speechless. Then he found his voice. 'Rubbish.'

'It's a tree. The tide's bringing it up the loch. It was probably knocked down in the last couple of days by the gale.'

Ewan flung up the glasses again and stared. 'You're off your head,' he concluded. 'Anyone can see it's a submarine. You have a look, General.'

'My eyes aren't what they were, you know.' General Munro shook his head. 'Perhaps it is a tree, after all. This fellow should know. Been shot at by the blighters.'

'It damned well isn't a tree!' Ewan almost shrieked the words. 'Charles – what do you say?'

Charles MacIlwham peered through binoculars the size of a brace of claret bottles. 'Well, you know, for a tree, it looks remarkably like a submarine to me. What do you think, Walter?'

The gasket-maker peered. 'There's a sort of periscope affair sticking out of the top. That's never a tree.'

'Well?' Ewan spun round to confront Stephen, his eyes bright and his chest rising and falling. 'Do you still claim it's a tree?'

'I do.'

'Then you're a bloody fool, Morgan – either that or you've lost your nerve. You'd have us all home in our beds and the hillsides crawling with Germans. If you're the best the Navy can muster, then pity help the country.'

Stephen had his back to me: I was glad I couldn't see the expression on his face at that moment. He couldn't know what I knew – that it was the fear in Ewan speaking, the dread of being tested at last and exposed as a craven.

I saw Stephen's right hand ball into a fist in a spasm of anger. For a moment I thought he was going to lash out with it – but rage had never been Stephen's way. Instead, he turned and limped off without a word, leaving Ewan to the General's grumbled, 'No need for that, you know. Feller might have a point.'

I scuttled back through the trees, caught a boot in a muddy gully and fell to my knees in my haste to see where Stephen had gone. I'd expected him to go back to the Ford or start to walk towards the gates of Achrossan, but he didn't do either. Instead, he set off along the road in the opposite direction, limping rapidly and jabbing his stick with each step as if the sharp spurt of gravel relieved his fury.

I couldn't bear him to know I'd overheard his argument with Ewan, but there was a wildness in his step which made me afraid to leave him. Fortunately, he was walking on the road, his shoes grating on the loose stones. I set off after him on the soft grass of the verge, hoping he wouldn't look back.

Just before the junction with the Fort William road, he turned aside, clambered over the tumbledown stone dyke and began to push through the screen of birches beyond. I didn't follow at once, afraid of betraying my presence among the papery autumn leaves. Beyond the trees, the flank of Creagruadh lay bare of scrub and though the dusk was gathering more steadily now, I knew I'd still be able to make out Stephen's dark figure against the paler grass.

I should have realized what was in his mind, yet it was only when I emerged from the trees and saw him toiling determinedly round an outcrop of rock that I knew he'd set himself to climb Creagruadh – the price of his freedom – and then to leave us for good.

In normal circumstances I'd have reached the summit in about an hour – even in wellington boots and a cumbersome waterproof coat – but I'd never tried it leaning on a stick and with muscles still wasted from months of confinement. Time and again, I saw Stephen halt to catch his breath or bend to rub his aching leg – or sometimes just to stare up at a particularly steep section, deciding how best to drag himself over it. And all the time it was becoming darker, until it began to look as if it might be full night before he came within reach of the top.

I knew there was no risk of his giving up and turning back to find me scrambling in his wake. He'd made up his mind to defeat that hill – to defeat Ewan, to defeat the pain and frustration which had tried so hard to claim him. His head never turned; he was quite unaware of me there behind him with the solid weight of his pistol banging against my leg, willing him to succeed, silently begging the hill to offer him its gentlest aspect.

And when at last I saw him stumble out across the indigo skyline, his arms wide to the triumphant night, I wanted to weep with relief and pride and infinite sadness, all mixed up together.

He stood there for so long, looking out over the loch, that the hills became no more than a fold in a sky of velvet and I lost sight of him against the blackness. Then, after a while I heard him, scraping down a rocky face, hunting for the grass slope by which he'd climbed up and discovering that the hill was a mistress of disguise. Even I, who knew the sheep-tracks and the rabbit warrens, would have hesitated to descend again in that blackness between sun and moon.

'We'll have to wait until the moon rises,' I called out to him. 'Then we'll be able to see our way.'

'Clio?' There was silence, except for a little scattering of stones. 'Are you there or have I imagined you?'

'I'm over here – under the cliff. This way.'

A moment later a shadow moved against the ashy slabs of the bluff, searching for me, waiting for me to speak again.

'What about the Germans?' I said.

'There wasn't a submarine. It was a tree.'

'I heard you tell Ewan.'

His footsteps slowed. 'Look, I've spent three years keeping watch for U-boats. I should know one when I see it.'

'And this one was a tree. I believe you.'

Without warning, we collided in the darkness and instinctively threw our arms round one another. He'd unfastened his jacket on the long climb and I slid my hands inside to pull myself closer against him, revelling in the kindly night.

'I made it to the top.'

'I know, I saw you.'

He didn't seem to find it at all strange that I was there, too, sharing his victory. He never bothered to ask, as if he took it for granted I was now too much part of him to be anywhere else. And perhaps it was true: before long, in that blacked-out world, I sensed our lips were going to meet and that I would do nothing to stop them. The moment for holding back had been passed years before, in Shanghai – or perhaps even earlier than that, on a ditch bank in Norfolk, where I'd followed him for the first time, all unsuspecting, into the night.

Even now, I never doubted that when the time came, he'd leave Achrossan. Nothing I could do would prevent him from packing his bags, parcelling up another set of memories and going back to the war or to wherever life summoned him next. And that would be the end of the matter – because men of Stephen Morgan's stamp never say 'Come with me'. They have no answer to the question 'Where to?' Yet I knew I had to go with him in spirit, or have no peace. The understanding between us had to be made complete, the last barriers torn down.

Nothing else was remotely important – not Ewan, not Germans, or trees or submarines: just two people in the bosom of a black hillside, sharing the unsayable on an old waterproof coat. We blessed the darkness and lived in texture: in the whisper of hair between the fingers; in the smooth, tempting warmth of skin released from laundered shirting, with its faint scent of singeing from the iron; in the round obduracy of buttons; the palm-filling delight of rolling muscle under supple flesh; the greedy sigh of nylon stockings. My burgundy broché flowed away like a cool black river in the darkness, leaving my body hot with longing. There's no surrender like the slithering retreat of silk undergarments, withdrawn by an unfamiliar hand, no exultation like the slow ascent to the pitch of heartbreak, step by step with the pleasure of another.

We had no need to speak. Our shamelessness told a thousand truths as we relished each new discovery: the cool niche between neck and shoulder, the swelling of a masculine nipple, brushed with the lips, the sweet scent which rose from my breasts as they yielded to the firmness of his hands, mellowed perfume overlaying the scorched smell of September grasses and the spicy, resinous odour from the skin of a fair-haired man intent on possession. Immodestly, in the tactful night, we searched out the voluptuous geography of one another's lust, caressing, kissing, tormenting to a pitch of agony. The curve of Stephen's body sheltering mine was the song of songs; the fierce tightness of his loins a psalm to the incompleteness of the lonely. We were two split halves, desperate to be matched, two hollow hemispheres, aching to be reunited.

Years before, he'd given me a city. Now, in that singing darkness, he gave me back my living, feeling self – and when, at the moment of abandonment, he became a creature of pure instinct, unguarded and helpless, he taught me more than he'd willingly have conceded about himself, too.

I wondered if he realized it, as we sprawled languorously, limbs thrown wide in the last, slackening eddies of desire. Softly, I laid my head over his heart and listened to it betray him with its rapid song.

He stroked my hair. 'I always said you were dangerous.'

My gently exploring fingers found his knee and below it, the glassy, ruffled flesh of dreadful scars. He'd never let me see the wound: now it seemed to have no limit and I thought of the pain our ardour must have cost him. He heard my gasp of dismay: 'I'd forgotten—'

He drew my hand to his lips, and kissed it. 'Never mind. So had I.'

A trace of ultramarine had begun to thin the blackness of the eastern sky. Little by little, the blue-black became slate, inking the mountain-tops while we rested in their shadow. By slow degrees, our combined mass became discernibly two bodies, one angular, one softly rounded, until the moon spilled over entirely into the glen, painting us in pearly splendour as we lay in a litter of crumpled finery and cast-off wellington boots.

We were no longer alone in the world. Far below, the loch aimed its bright blade at me, challenging me to look down at the bleached turrets of Achrossan. Yet I had the rest of my life to look at those trim pepperpots and only the space of a thought with Stephen Morgan. Already, where once the all-concealing darkness had drawn us into intimacy, the thrill of shameless nakedness had begun to stir us all over again. Stephen stretched his long, pale, hungry body against mine and, clear-eyed, I turned back to my lover of the night.

It was five o'clock in the morning when Ewan came to bed. I pretended to be asleep, but I was still as wide awake as I'd been at the top of Creagruadh, when Stephen and I at last started our moonlit descent. Back in Achrossan I'd found Daisy fast asleep in her nursery with an expression of angelic tyranny on her face and the door left ajar: Nanny Tarrant had slipped down to the kitchen to have a cup of tea with Peggy Stott amid the ruins of our dinner party.

'All's well, then,' I said, as briskly as I could. 'No First Aid required after all.'

'All that trouble for a tree.' Nanny Tarrant sniffed.

'And now there's mud all over the hem of your bonny dress.' Mrs Stott pointed to the damage with the Worcester plate she was drying. 'Those Germans are wicked creatures, to be sure.'

It had taken Ewan most of the night to disband his forces, clear the barricades and call off the might of the Home Fleet, C-in-C Western Approaches, Scottish Command and goodness knows who else. With half a bottle of whisky inside him, in the relief which had replaced his fear, his basic decency reasserted itself and began to make him ashamed of the way he'd treated Stephen. No doubt the massive pine trunk lying stranded at the head of the loch was an awkward reminder of his unfairness. At any rate, as soon as Stephen appeared for breakfast, Ewan stood up with his hand outstretched.

'I was unforgivably rude, and I wouldn't blame you if you'd taken a swing at me.'

Stephen glanced at me out of the corner of his eye, yet he'd no option but to shake the hand of the man he'd cuckolded. I tried not to watch.

'Decent of you,' said Ewan. 'I'm afraid we all got a bit over-excited last night.'

'I've taken nothing Ewan McLennan ever possessed.' Stephen stared out over the mountain lochan, his hair curling, damp and dark, spun with gold where the sun had dried it. We were lying together deep in the grass; tiny green spearheads of crowberry still clung to the glistening shield of his back, imprinted by the urgency of our desire. I prised them off with a fingertip as I'd once searched for fragments of bomb-blasted glass and kissed the empty spaces.

He wanted to be reassured that he'd taken nothing at all – that there'd be no lingering obligation, no reason to return. His leg was almost strong enough now for him to manage without a stick, the deep scars gouged into his flesh were shiny with repair, and I knew we had very little time left.

Avoiding my eye, he confirmed it.

'I have to report to the MO at the beginning of October.'

'And after that?'

'Wherever I'm sent, I suppose.'

High in the hills, the waters of the lochan had been icy enough to make our bones ache, forcing us to dive and twist like fishing birds in twining streams of bubbles, whirling vortexes which tickled the skin like the fingers of imps and demons. Stephen was the stronger swimmer, coiling round me, splitting the tea-coloured water with the turbulence of his passing. When the excitement became unbearable, we'd leaped out, tingling with cold and desire, and rolled in a hectic coupling among the mosses and the cotton grass.

Later, I watched his lids grow heavy with contentment until at last his eyes closed and he slept in my keeping, as trustful as a spent young animal. For a short while then he was entirely mine and it was possible to pretend I'd feel that heavy, enigmatic head against my breast for ever. Awake, the spectre of his leaving hung over us and made him ration his affection: he'd kiss me in sexual hunger, but never otherwise. And yet, at the height of his passion there was a desperate tenderness I wouldn't have given up for a blizzard of kisses.

Our private time was in the early afternoons, when Ewan drove off on highly important government business and the house settled down to naps and knitting. We didn't always end up in bed, though that was our truest and most candid place. Sometimes we walked, or if the post had arrived late from the station, cycled off on my letter round: but then we chatted about the village, or life at sea – anything except what lay nearest to our hearts.

One wet afternoon a few days before he was due to leave, as the rain drove against the window of his tower room, Stephen steered me to bed with a serious air and we began to undress one another with calculated slowness.

'Lady McLennan wears silk under her dungarees.'

It was true – I wore it for him and also for myself. I loved the feeling of my China crêpe sliding over my skin, recalling the bird's-wing brush of Stephen's touch. I loved to know he was watching me and thinking of it.

Those days were like my last months in Shanghai – the same feeling of imminent loss, the same greed of the senses for the experience of touch, smell, colour – all the heightened perception of a fever. I needed new-minted memories to store away against that final goodbye, when there would be no one to wear silk for, and the crowberries by the lochan would grow uncrushed by our impropriety.

I wanted to make our physical loving roar like a hurricane in those last few days – to suck Stephen into my very soul and feel him spent and triumphant inside me. Eagerness was all I knew: years of marriage to Ewan had left me such a novice. But as our time together ebbed away, Stephen taught me – I didn't let myself wonder where he'd learned it himself – a more subtle sensuality, a seduction of the mind which produced sensations of the sweetest and most exquisite agony.

On this particular day, with the rain spewing from the gutters and lashing the window, he halted, even as we rose towards a climax and my heart fluttered like a wounded bird, and made me lie on my back while he turned on his side to enter me, my legs over his hips.

'Don't move any more. Relax.'

Bewildered, frustrated, I lay back and strove for stillness . . . and discovered unexpected comfort in the tiny undulations between us – until gradually, as I released its tension, my body began to flicker and throb of its own accord, somewhere infinitely deeper than consciousness.

I became almost afraid and groped for Stephen's hand to give me courage – just as the sensation became overwhelming, dissolving into a vast inevitability that rose and beat against our determined stillness. Without warning we slid together, headlong, into a shuddering aftermath.

For a few seconds we remained indivisible, drunk with wholeness.

'Oh heavens—' I heard my own voice. 'However shall I live without you?'

He stared at me, light-headed, as if the reality of the situation had struck him for the first time. 'Come away with me, then. Leave Ewan and come with me.'

I couldn't believe he'd spoken the words. I was completely resigned to spending the rest of my days with Ewan – in a way, I suppose, I felt we deserved each other now, sinners that we were. I'd never dreamed those last few blazing weeks with Stephen could be any more than an island in a lifetime's sea. Confused, idiotic, I blurted out, 'Where to?'

He smiled, wistfully, and in that instant, I knew I'd lost him and he'd never ask me again.

'No, of course, you're right. You have Daisy's future to think about and I have this blessed war to finish, with whatever that may bring. Afterwards – who knows where I'll end up?' He swung his legs over the edge of the bed, stretched with slow relish and began to fish for his clothes.

'I'm going for a shower. And then, rain or no rain, I think I'll go down for a walk by the loch.'

Loathing messy goodbyes, he wouldn't allow me to drive him to the station. Instead, George Stott took him there in the Daimler, for which Ewan had somehow managed to find enough petrol.

'Perhaps he improves when you get to know him.' Ewan was already coughing as we stood on the threshold of Achrossan, watching the Daimler disappear like a fat black frog into the trees of the drive. Next day he considerately developed bronchitis and nursing him helped to dull the pain of Stephen's departure for several weeks.

I'd expected to feel guilty, but I didn't. Poor Liu Ling, I was completely free of her teaching now. Or perhaps it was simply that Ewan had placed the question of loyalty between us on a different basis: I'd returned from London to a marriage with no great expectations in that area – I'd accepted that Ewan, like my father and my Uncle Kit, would go on having other women in his life and that our marriage, if it was to endure, must be built on something other than faithfulness.

Stephen had been right when he said he'd taken nothing that Ewan had ever possessed. My marriage to Ewan was based on familiarity and need, and affection, and forgiveness – and Stephen had wanted none of these. While they lasted, Ewan and I would no doubt go on together and our marriage would endure.

Gradually, life returned to normal after Stephen's departure – or to the normality which had grown on us after four years of grinding war. Every day my postal duties took me round the village, then eastward along the lochside road by bicycle towards Achrossan, where I picked up the Ford to take letters and parcels on to Finglas and to some of the more isolated cottages. When his leg began to recover, Stephen had enjoyed coming with me – churning up the rutted tracks to the keepers' houses, or hiking over ditch and bog if the roads were deep in mud.

'Who lives over there?' he asked me one day, pointing to a steep-roofed stone cottage on the hill behind Finglas, whose cockeyed wooden porch gave it the look of an untidy parcel.

'That's Tigh Beag. It's been empty since the start of the war. Why?'

He shrugged. 'Just wondered. I thought I saw Ewan coming out of it yesterday morning, when I was out for a walk.'

'He was probably checking the state of the roof, after all the gales we've been having. He usually comes over to Finglas every few days to see his mother.'

It wasn't until a week after Ewan's bronchitis had finally cleared up that I had cause to notice the little cottage again, when a letter from someone's sweetheart took me to the door of the Land Girls' bothy on the opposite side of the valley. From there, to my surprise, I had a clear view of a thread of grey smoke twisting up from the chimney of Tigh Beag.

Curious to know who'd come to live there, I drove back to the main road and turned off towards Finglas, skirting the main house and its outbuildings and taking the track which led through the pines to the hill beyond. The tart, resinous smell of burning logs clung to the trees as I knocked on the cottage door. Feet scuffled on the stone flags of the porch: someone paused to peer out of the window and saw the Ford, perhaps, but not its driver. I heard a cry of pleasure as the door grated open, which turned at once into a gasp of dismay.

There, on the doorstep of Tigh Beag stood Nina Starozhilova, crossing her hands theatrically across her stony little bosom and wearing an expression of truly ridiculous distress.

Chapter Twenty-One

'THAT,' AS my elder son would say, 'was *then*, before either of us were born.'

He says it with an expression of such exasperated fondness, too . . . But why did you bring me back to Shanghai, my dear, if not for *then* – if not to search, like the poor cormorant fisherman, for the peach-blossom forest and the magical valley I once knew on this spot?

All I can see from my fifteenth-floor hotel window is a traffic roundabout, my hotel being one of a cluster of international glass palaces far out on Yan'an Road, on the way to the airport. The real China halts at its automatic doors, where an air-conditioned, theme-park China begins. Here in Shanghai this means copper pagodas on the wall of the coffee shop, where the copper gondolas hang in Venice and the copper kangaroos in Sydney.

For some reason the Chinese staff have adopted new names of truly international blandness. According to his label, it was Shane at the desk who shuffled my Foreign Exchange Certificates with the deftness of a Las Vegas croupier, while delicate Carly poured my coffee and Ringo found me a taxi at the door. Startled to hear halting Shanghainese coming from a white face and even whiter hair, Ringo admitted that his real name was Hu. After that Rumpelstiltskin-like surrender, Hu and I are now conspirators.

Strangely enough, though nothing like China, my hotel is very Shanghai – very *haipai*, as the Chinese say, after the showy style of the Shanghai Opera. And the city itself, even now, more than half a century after I last set eyes on it, is still unexpectedly Shanghai – still hard and flashy and fashion-mad – and still, at night, a city of lanterns, with uncountable miles of coloured lights to sweeten its brashness. I should say it's *once more* Shanghai, for the intervening years have been very different. This is now the People's Republic and nobody seems to steal the light bulbs.

Some things will never be the same again. My friend Hu sent me by taxi to Nantao yesterday – Number 11 trolley-bus goes round there now, he said, but a western lady should arrive with dignity, by taxi. Taxis? Trolley-buses? The ancient labyrinth has gone quaint; factory workers from Changsha wander round it now in light cotton anoraks, snapping one another in front of the winged roof of the Wu Xing Ting teahouse and nosing down the fairy-lit lanes.

For a moment, after determined searching, I thought I'd stumbled at last on the shop where Liu Ling and her husband had sold ginseng and lizard skins from dusty glass cases. But there was no leaping tiger above the door any longer and no finger-worn shrine to Kong Mu. The shop, if it was their shop, was full of panda rugs and tourists.

Liu Ling herself must be long dead now. To my great surprise, some months after the Japanese were thrown out of Shanghai, her son wrote to me at Oliver's, asking me to find an engineering textbook he needed for his studies. I sent off the book and afterwards we continued to correspond, even after the Communists took control in 1949 and he became a professor in one of the universities, honoured by the new state in its drive towards industrial strength. We exchanged letters, fitfully, while five-year plans came and went, and the communes and the hardships of the Great Leap Forward. Then, suddenly, during the upheavals of the Cultural Revolution, when academics were sent to plough the fields and repent their political backsliding, the letters stopped. I didn't dare to write again, in case letters from Britain were simply further proof of the professor's capitalist sympathies.

Now I've no idea whether he's alive or dead, exiled or enjoying honourable retirement in some provincial city. I've tried to make enquiries, here in Shanghai, but it's clear I'm only embarrassing people. If they do know what's become of Liu Ling's son, they're far too polite to tell me anything that might cause distress.

Surprisingly, I find I'm beginning to appreciate the air conditioning in my hotel. I must have lived too long in Britain: this is only May and yet the shock on walking out of the temperate foyer into a wall of warmth takes me by surprise.

Rose would love to hate this hotel, with its soft-handed businessmen and its fibreglass sampan. I sometimes think Rose hates most things, except her husband, Emeritus Professor Woade. Rose and Roger have retired to Berkshire, where they drive what I tell Rose is a 'university car' – Scandinavian, and earnest as a hearse, obliging Rose to excuse its size by claiming she needs it for grandchildren and bags of wholesale lentils.

Seven years ago, Rose wrote an autobiography, *Rebel in a Gilded Cage*, in which she gives a shamefully distorted account of the death of Sammy Liu, as well as a great deal of other nonsense. Lies notwithstanding, it has turned her into something of a media celebrity. Television producers love mad old women who don't care whom they offend – and what is the past, after all, but a thousand separate fictions?

It was in the spring of 1944, when I was living in London after the second Nina business, that Rose and some of her friends decided to crash the Savoy Hotel. It wasn't that Rose had anything against the Savoy in particular, except that it was her father's favourite. Wartime diners there endured the same Spam and dried egg as everyone else, but they looked as if they were enjoying it, which smelled of privilege to Rose.

It was lunchtime when the daughters of righteousness plunged through the lobby, heading for the restaurant, stripping off their coats as they ran to reveal the words RATION THE RICH printed across their chests. Alas, in the restaurant doorway Rose ran into Winston Churchill, who knew Kit well and who gave her such a wigging that for the first time in her life Rose retreated, abashed, without pausing to tie herself to a single pillar.

Her youngest daughter is now an asset-stripper in the City,

which pains Rose dreadfully. It's nice to know there's at least a little justice in the world.

As for Guy – did I mention that Guy married Connie Headington in the middle of the war? Poor Connie had lost a brother and a husband quite early on and threw herself into Red Cross work and, being as brave as a brick, she organized everybody and scored an absolute triumph. She was nothing like Guy's usual ladies, who tended to be small and giggly and got drunk quickly. Connie was big-boned and moved like a big-boned woman, with a no-nonsense tread and the kind of skin that powder never seems to cling to.

It was Guy who'd changed. I noticed it first when he found himself managing director of the shipping line, without his father to blame for any mistakes or Stephen Morgan to keep him from making them. What had seemed easy from the heir apparent's chair suddenly began to look amazingly complicated, more a matter of politics and foresight than pulling off one deal after another.

And as Alice pointed out, Guy was given an excellent start. On the whole, in spite of the awful toll of vessels and men, the war was good for shipping, in a commercial sense. It was afterwards that the problems began – but perhaps Guy was for once employing foresight when he married Connie, who organized him, organized the directors and their wives, organized the masters of the Oliver vessels, the marketing men, the publicity people and anyone else who would allow her to interfere in their work. Somehow, in the middle of all this, she also managed to bear Guy two sons to add to her previous one of each, so when Guy died in 1984, if nothing else, at least he'd left an heir to our father's title.

Kit (to his great satisfaction) outlived my father by six years – long enough to see his passenger ships overtaken by airliners, as Stephen had predicted, in the business of moving humanity round the world. There was still freight, but that too soon passed its glory days and Matthew Oliver's empire began a slow slide into a morass of laid-up tankers and flags of convenience.

Georgie – Sir George Oliver, Kit's son by Mamie Brand – is now chairman of the line, or what's left of it. Certainly, a new

Gloriana still plies between Southampton and New York, but so briskly there's hardly time to discover the captain's name before everyone is shaken out again on the opposite quayside. As for romance – in summer, on the Atlantic crossing, there's simply no time, and in winter, when the vessel cruises in the Caribbean, those who can afford her are largely past anything more than holding hands under their travelling-rugs on the sun deck. *O tempora, O mores!* Oh tango, oh foxtrot – oh assignations fixed by moody, passionate glances across the Turkish Grill . . . Would Ewan and I ever have got together, do you suppose, over an aerobics session or a fax from the Seattle office?

I've always expected too much from Ewan – my father told me so and Ewan's mother said exactly the same when she tried to explain why she'd helped her darling boy to bring his mistress back to Tigh Beag. My amusement puzzled her, and yet the situation had its ludicrous side: Stephen and I had been such secretive, careful lovers and all the time Ewan was cherishing Nina in the hills, aided and abetted by his preposterous mother.

I believed I was Ewan's for life; I still believed it, even after Nina reappeared. There'd never been a divorce at Achrossan – *duty to the family*, naturally – and after his first couple of strayings were forgiven I doubt if it crossed Ewan's mind that I might want one. All the same, I couldn't bear another episode of penitence and emotional splashing as Ewan floundered his way to the convenient moral rock he perceived me to be. He had one mother already: I left Lady McLennan to see to her demanding child and took Daisy to London to stay with my father for a while.

'What do you want me to *do*?' Bewildered, Ewan watched me pack my bags for a second time. I guessed Nina was applying pressure in her own particular way, but I'd no intention of riding to his rescue. 'What do you expect me to do? Just tell me!'

'I can't tell you. It's high time you decided that for yourself. In the meantime, you know where to find us.'

London at the end of 1943 was so different from Achrossan: resolutely determined to stay in business despite the awful scars of the Blitz, sorrowing over its losses, madly celebrating its little victories and soon, by the following spring, buzzing with rumours of an enormous military Something being prepared 'somewhere in the south of England'.

In June, D-Day brought, of all people, Igor Starozhilov, or Rudi Romanov as he'd become, passing through London on his way to entertain Allied troops overseas. I can't imagine why the soldiers should have wanted to see Igor, except that he'd recently had an enormous success in a film called *Tripoli Express*, about a jaded, mysterious Russian agent persuaded against his better judgement to help a beautiful young French girl spy for the Resistance. Naturally, it was all filmed in California, but it had added a bogus whiff of heroism to Igor's stunning allure and caused middle-aged waitresses to drop plates in restaurants where he ate.

I encountered him at a charity tea and let him take me to dinner. I thought it would be awfully good for Ewan, who'd never quite forgotten the way we'd met aboard the *Concordia*. Everyone knew Igor had recently been divorced from the actress Carole Duquesne, whom he'd married twelve months earlier in a blaze of studio publicity.

He shrugged when I mentioned her. 'After a few weeks I find we are both having affairs with the same director.' He regarded me across the table with the expression of world-weary rakishness which had turned a legion of female knees to water. 'One day I will go back to Shanghai. Once these Japanese guys have gone, and things are OK again. You, too, you will go back.'

'I shouldn't think so, Igor. I've come to realize the good times were nearly always make-believe.'

'All the better: make-believe is what you remember best! And besides, Shanghai gets into the blood.' He surveyed me for a moment and then swung an arm extravagantly. 'Come back to China with me. We'll dance together in the ballrooms – just like the old days.' Out of life-long habit his eyelids drooped, making his eyes ridiculously long and lecherous. 'We could go and talk about it in my room, if you like.'

★

And now here I am, in Shanghai – and people are dancing again, in the park by the river, couples shuffling to and fro in their lunch hour while the loudspeakers crank out old ballroom numbers.

Today Hu introduced me to his uncle, a man with a melancholy, intelligent face who serves doughnuts in the hotel coffee shop. Twenty-three years ago, Guo told me, he'd just secured a place at university when the zealots of the Cultural Revolution sent him out into the country, where he knew nothing of farming and almost starved. After Mao's death he was allowed to return, but by now he'd passed the age for university education in China: his only hope was to teach himself English in the little spare time allowed from his job and apply for a place abroad. At last, after years of labour, two universities in the United States said they'd accept him, but just as he was about to leave for America, the democracy demonstrations of the 1980s began, culminating in the events of Tiananmen Square and the imposition of martial law. Guo was told that as a good Chinese he must stay at home.

'Sometimes,' he told me in faultless English, 'I feel as if I've buried the best years of my life under the soil of our fields.'

'It's sad, isn't it,' Hu said to me later, 'what people will do to one another?'

Hu is too young to remember the worst of the Mao years, when neighbour spied on neighbour and families were encouraged to give up their own fathers, sisters and sons to be beaten and humiliated, and locked away in labour camps to break stones, or themselves. It came as no surprise to me. Those of us who remember the final months of Hitler's war learned then, when the full horror of the Nazi death camps was exposed, that there's no limit to what one human being will inflict on another in the name of belief.

I went to see my old homes yesterday; first the house of my childhood, which has lost the gangsters at its gate and become the headquarters of an educational publisher. The house has been painted bright mint and the verandah, the low eaves and all the woodwork picked out in the usual dark red. Our magnolia has gone the way of the tulip trees: in fact, the whole garden has disappeared under grey concrete huts which seem to have eaten themselves through a gap in the wall like a cluster of tumours. It saddens me, but I dare say the house serves a more useful purpose than it did when one small girl learned to foxtrot on its parquet floors.

The house where Ewan and I used to live is in a poor state of repair, inhabited by at least a dozen families, probably people who moved into the cities when the Japanese moved out, or were encouraged by the Cultural Revolution to bring their ideological purity from the countryside to fill the jobs in town. Weeds grow round the bases of our chimneys now and the walls have the stained, furtive air of dirty fingernails. Yesterday the windows were open, with shirts flung out of them on wire coat-hangers. Cream-coloured long johns flapped themselves dry on bamboo poles and there were mattresses and cooking pots on the balconies, and the rusting skeleton of a bicycle.

'You'll be shocked,' someone in the hotel warned me the night before. Yet I wasn't. We lived such messy lives there, Ewan and I. In our day the house was cluttered with the rusting skeleton of a marriage.

Hu has just rung from the concierge's desk to tell me the taxi I ordered is waiting to take me to Nanking Road – Nan*jing* Road, as I must call it now. He wonders if I had forgotten.

Forgotten? No. I was remembering how ecstatic Rose and Roger were when the new People's Republic was born in 1949. 'The people's revolution,' they said. 'Tomorrow, the world.'

Margot had returned from the United States by then, unthinkably alone. To blazes with revolution, Margot said – when Paris was liberated, that was when she knew Civilization was safe. In London, she made straight for the Savoy and, if the management there could still remember a poodle *en papillon* and a Cuban trumpeter who played *Whispering* while standing on his head, they welcomed her back nevertheless. She'd refused to stay at Rose's child-filled rectory, so Guy drove her down there one day for a visit.

'Oh, God,' she said, finding Rose in a print smock, pounding some unspeakable grains in an African mortar for one of Roger's treats. 'Darling, you never told me you were so *poor*.'

None of us knew what Margot herself lived on, after the lovers had gone, that is, and she began to metamorphose into one of those *grande dames* of great age and ghostly beauty who hold a magnetic fascination for the young. If she'd ever had money of her own, goodness only knew what had become of it. And yet to her dying day she preserved the most incredible chic, in a tiny London flat filled with brilliant shawls and enormous lilies and a constant gallery of admiring youths.

Her last Christmas card to me read, 'Darling, the bastards are the best. Didn't I tell you? Raise a glass to me, when you have a moment.' With the card was a suitcase-sized box of expensive chocolates. When I broke the seal I realized the gift must have been recycled from another, distant Christmas. The chocolates, like Margot, had the sad, grape-like bloom of perfection wasted.

My taxi circles round to stop at the door of the Cathay Hotel, facing up Nanjing Road once more, away from the Bund and the Huangpu River. The Cathay, of course, is now the Peace Hotel, together with the old Palace Hotel on the opposite side of the street, with its bands of red brick and soiled white tiles. And yet in spite of its change of name and the fact that during the Mao years (according to Hu) bicycles were sold from its ground-floor rooms, this Peace Hotel is spectrally familiar.

Today I found the marble and bronze lobby festooned with flags for an Asian athletic event, but the art deco clocks behind the reception desk assure me it's still 1937 in Paris and New York. And as I sit over coffee at one of the tables, I can almost will myself back to the day when Stephen Morgan found me here, drowning in self-pity and Old Fashioneds, and saw something in the wreckage he recognized.

I couldn't have taken a room here. I couldn't have borne the slow fading of each afternoon beyond the windows, or the Dixieland tunes played nightly in the coffee bar by the same six Chinese – now white-haired and rediscovered by some miracle – who played for us in the 1930s.

Alice warned me not to come, peering at me through her thick old-lady spectacles. 'All the way back to China!' she said. 'At our age?'

'I'm sixteen and the world is at my feet. You're trying to turn me into a geriatric.'

'You are a geriatric. They don't make aeroplanes for eighty-year-olds.' Alice was dead-heading her roses, slashing at Ena Harkness and Pascali with murderous relish. She waved her secateurs in my face. 'Hugh got food poisoning in Delhi.'

I forbear to say this doesn't surprise me in the least. Hugh Buckley-Oliver, at fifty, is the only human being I know to have gone down with dysentery in Bognor Regis. His mother says this is what happens to men who refuse to wear vests, even in winter, and Hugh, who is dry and funny and looks very like David Spencer, somehow keeps his temper, even though Alice's interference had a great deal to do with the break-up of his marriage.

Recently, however, Hugh has become close to another barrister in the same chambers and his mother has *hopes*. No one could be a more degenerate creature than his ex-wife, says Alice. The woman didn't even prevent Hugh from getting food poisoning in Delhi.

It's hard to see how any wife could have competed with Alice for Hugh's affections: over the years, Alice created a debt which no son could ever repay. Before Hugh was born, she fought Kit and Rose for the very idea of him. From the moment of his birth, she was utterly besotted, dragging metaphorical feathers from her own breast to keep him warm: Hugh needs me, therefore I am.

It seems so obvious now, and yet, when I went down to London after discovering Nina Starozhilova at Tigh Beag, it was meeting Alice I dreaded most. I couldn't believe that anyone who'd loved Stephen Morgan could ever give that love to another.

'Oh dear,' said Alice, when she saw me. 'Ewan again, is it?'

'Yes. No, not entirely Ewan.'

'Ah.' Alice surveyed me closely. 'Someone else, then?'

'Not really. I mean, there was someone else, but there isn't any more.' One glance at her face told me she understood. 'Oh, Alice, I'm sorry. I never meant it to happen. You must hate me for being so weak.'

She took my hands in hers. 'Has it made you happy?'

'I don't regret it, if that's what you mean. Not for a moment.'

Alice nodded. 'Thank goodness for that. I was beginning to think I'd made a dreadful mistake and hurt two people I love very much.' She smiled at my bewilderment. 'Who else would care for Stephen the way you did? He needed you, Clio. And I thought perhaps you needed him.'

I stared. Alice was pure Machiavelli, under that fringe. 'Do you mean to say you *meant* all this to happen, when you made me bring Stephen to Achrossan?'

Alice reached down to where Hugh was investigating my shoes, his dark head bent intently over the well-polished calf, his thumb glistening wet from sucking. Alice's smile became beatific as she stroked his curls. Absently, Hugh held fast to his mother's fingers while continuing to gaze at my feet.

'With Hugh it's for ever,' she said. 'That's all I wanted, you see.'

But nothing is for ever, neither pain nor pleasure: that is the secret of Chinese endurance. Everything passes, given time. Everything changes: the Cathay was a hotel, then a billet for American soldiers, then a bicycle shop, and for the present it's a hotel again, called Peace. Who knows what tomorrow will bring?

Achrossan is a hotel now, of course. Poor Ewan, the Labour government of the 1960s was the last straw which broke the McLennan finances. Death duties which had been jogging along, quietly unpaid for decades, were suddenly called in and all over Britain, family land began to pass into the hands of foreigners and financiers.

Charles MacIlwham made Ewan a handsome offer for Achrossan, but Ewan turned him down and chose instead to be the first of his line to earn a respectable living. If you visit Achrossan today, you'll find the Regional Council has built a fine new road over the pass and there's even a nature trail to the top of Creagruadh, with litter bins and places to sit and admire the view.

As for the house itself, there's a mock-ancient four-poster in Princess Mary's Chamber and central heating and whirlpool baths. As Ewan keeps reminding me, Achrossan has more staff now than Balmoral in its heyday. American visitors go mad for the Gothic pillars and the Lochaber axes, and Ewan often drives down from Finglas to tell them stories of Achrossan as it was, when his grandfather's chamberlain shouted every evening 'McLennan has dined! The world may now sit down to its meat.'

Ewan and I get on very amicably these days, but then, we have Daisy in common and the two hillsides my father bought for me that will one day belong to her and to our grandchildren. Daisy, bless her, emerged remarkably well adjusted from her parents' separation; I like to think that was due to the affable nature of our divorce – Ewan had always thought of Daisy as mine and was happy for her to remain so – but it may simply have been the result of her own happy, optimistic personality. At any rate, she and her husband have built up an enormous herd of pedigree cattle on their various farms and Daisy herself is heavily into daughters' weddings and Jacob sheep.

Nina, I'm afraid, still regards me with suspicion, though heaven knows, I give her full credit for the turnaround in the McLennan fortunes. Ewan's financial disasters were meat and drink to Nina and the hotel was entirely her idea. She was the one who borrowed and manoeuvred to finance it, saw it kitted out in the Grand Imperial style she remembered from her childhood and frightened the staff into reaching her exacting standards. Nina and Ewan's son, Alastair, is nominally in charge, though you may still sometimes see the second Lady McLennan – small and fearsome, in black, with highly coloured face powder – scolding the receptionist in the passionate and eccentric English it suits her to keep up.

Belatedly, I remember I've promised to be on the corner of the Bund and Nanjing Road at half-past twelve. Luckily it's only a few steps from the door of the old Cathay. Strange to think I was standing here – just *here* – when the bomb fell that started it all, when Stephen Morgan threw me to the ground and shielded me from the blast with his body. There's no sign now of that cataclysmic afternoon. The earth that melted and shuddered under our bodies has long since been rolled firm beneath the wheels of buses and taxis. It's incredible, this fickleness of concrete and stone. How can there be nothing to show – not a mark, not even a pitted wall – of a day which changed everything in my life?

In 1946, Stephen came back from the war and took me to dinner at the Savoy. Rationing was still in force, of course, but evening dress had come back at last and the war correspondents had gone from the foyer.

I told him about the secret resident of Tigh Beag.

'Nina's pregnant now. She must want Ewan very badly indeed.'

Stephen watched me carefully across the table. 'And what about you? What do you want?'

'I want . . . all sorts of things I can't have.' Suddenly overcome with weariness, I rested my cheek on my hand. 'Ewan expects me to wave a magic wand and somehow make all this mess come out right for him. And I wish I could – I'm still fond of him, heaven knows – but I can see he's going to spend the rest of his life getting into one scrape after another and expecting me to help him out of it each time. It just isn't the way I'd hoped marriage would be.'

In truth, I'd come to believe my marriage to Ewan was essentially over, but I didn't want Stephen to think I was looking for sympathy.

'It's probably my own fault for having my head in the clouds, but I'm beginning to understand how my mother must have felt, trying to live with my father.'

'That's a bad sign.'

He was smiling, but I sensed an undertone of regret, a passing echo of some old sadness.

'Why is it so bad?'

I expected him to change the subject as usual, to steer the conversation away from something too private to explain, and I was astonished when he suddenly began to speak about his own mother, Catherine. He'd hardly ever mentioned her before, though when we'd talked of other things I'd sometimes heard the faint rustle of her almond-coloured coat and seen that drawn, set face behind his own.

I'd never forgotten those two, standing close together in the churchyard, watching us bury Grandfather Matthew – more like defiant lovers than mother and son.

'You meant everything to her, I do know that.'

He nodded. 'I owed her so much. And yet she wanted the one thing I couldn't give her: my father, back again.' He glanced up at me, assuring himself that I understood. 'In the end I had to go off to sea. To find out who I was – to be myself.'

He'd never told me any of this before. I stayed silent, almost holding my breath, afraid of breaking the spell.

'It's become a bit of a habit, I suppose, always moving on.'

'Was that . . . an apology for something?'

He considered the question for a moment and then smiled slowly. 'Perhaps it was. My way of saying I'm sorry for what I am.'

I slid my hand across the table towards his and our fingers meshed instinctively. For a few seconds he studied our linked palms and then raised his eyes.

'Nothing's ever straightforward, is it? I still have dreams, sometimes, about the ship going down and being sucked under the water and feeling nothing at all – and thinking how easy it would be to give up and let the sea take me. No choices to make. Everything simple, for once.'

Yet even then it hadn't been simple: absently, his fingers had begun to mould mine, pressing my wedding ring into my flesh.

'The cold only hit me when I came back to the surface. That was when I realized there was no escape.'

In that instant I had a profound sense of a door swinging open, the door to Stephen's past, vigilantly guarded for so long. Somewhere, in the fear and tumult of war, he must have made his own way through it and found himself in a place inhabited by nothing but shadows, without the power to shame or to hurt.

Now he seemed to be waiting for me to test his new liberty.

'I've always wondered . . .' I remembered the drawn white face in the Glasgow hospital, hoarding its secrets behind closed, bluish eyelids. 'What does a man think about, injured and adrift in an open boat?'

'Oh, a reason for staying alive.' He gave a little inward smile. 'Something wild and impossible – like another man's wife, wearing silk right down to her skin – and how her naked body might feel, clasped against his.' Stephen's eyes told me which man's wife he'd wanted.

The Orpheans were playing something fast and jazzy, but the need to cling to one another was so irresistible that we ran out anyway on to the dance floor. I remember a quickstep and then a foxtrot, close and intimate as I'd been taught long ago, our bodies alive with the memory of a darkened hillside and the unearthly, unlicensed hour before moonrise.

We spent the night in one of the hotel's river suites with the windows flung wide to the night, healing the empty ache of more than two years' separation – not with wasteful passion, but with a gentle and unhurried tenderness which whispered of other nights to come, and still others, with no sense of finality or confinement or the need to set limits to our loving. I could feel it in the fingers that softly rescued the strands of hair which had tangled themselves in my lashes; it was there in the boyish wonder in his face as he realized the pleasure he gave, and in the hollow of his arms, held out for me to fill whenever we rested.

And when in the afterglow of a long, rippling release, Stephen murmured, 'Leave Ewan and come with me', and repeated it next morning – 'Come with me' – quite soberly, over the teacups, I didn't think for a second of asking 'Where to?' I said, 'Anywhere. Anywhere at all.'

Then we moved the breakfast tray from the bed and celebrated this astounding development.

We were married as soon as my divorce from Ewan became final; and Guy immediately tried to woo Stephen back to the shipping line with promises of directorships and divisions of his own.

'For heaven's sake, Clio, can't you talk him round? He knows the business inside out. He always used to come up with ideas to get us out of tight corners – and right now we need as many of those as we can get.'

I didn't even try to persuade Stephen. I already knew what was in his mind and that nothing would deflect him. Kate had anticipated it years ago, when she said the Olivers would come to regret it, if Grandfather Matthew had made an outcast of Stephen Morgan. Now, with Kate's money to start him on his way, Stephen was set on joining the rush to the air that would put long-distance passenger shipping out of business.

He began – no, *we* began, since I'd meant it when I said 'anywhere' – with an Avro XIX, operating charter flights and transportation for the Army, chipping away at the newly imposed state monopoly wherever we saw a chance. By the late 1950s, when the market opened up, Morgan Air was flying subsidiary services for British European Airways and we had established a second company in Canada, linking far-flung communities across hundreds of miles of wilderness.

Where Stephen went, I went, and, for most of her childhood, Daisy went too. Our first son, Adam, was born in Yellowknife, on Canada's Great Slave Lake, which was where we happened to be at the time. Adam's brother, Steve, was born two years later in Cairo. I can't remember why it should have been Cairo, except that Stephen was there, tirelessly setting up some route or other, while I hung on telephones in an airless city office, pretending to be my own secretary, until the contractions became so severe that I had to leave for the hospital.

We, together, Stephen and I, set up an airline; Liu Ling, are you listening? There's danger outside the garden walls, beyond the tulip trees, oh yes, but there's also *life* and self-discovery and fulfilment, even for girl children.

Stephen could never have borne confinement for a moment: he was never still, never in one place for very long. Even after the blossoming tourist market made the company too big for us to run every part of it ourselves, I soon lost count of the number of times I'd waited at airports for him to return from a last-minute dash to some trouble spot or urgent meeting. I became good at waiting.

And now I find that familiar places – smells, sounds – dissolve all sense of the passing years. There are new red and yellow tiles in the pavement of the Bund these days, but apart from that it has changed incredibly little from the years when I tripped along it in an afternoon dress and a halo hat. And at last, in the distance, I can see a beloved tall figure weaving through the crowd, a fair head among a sea of dark ones, a little late as usual, hurrying to be with me. I wave and receive a wave in return. My heart quickens when I see that step: automatically, I search for the narrow, intent features, that elusive wildness, never entirely quenched, although I know perfectly well it isn't – and never can be – Stephen.

I never doubted that one day Stephen would leave us, as suddenly and completely as he always did. Old age like mine would have been intolerable to him – the final prison from which he could never escape. One day in 1972, he simply fell out of the sky in a prototype aircraft he'd insisted on joining for a test flight, leaving, typically, hardly a sign of himself for us to mourn over.

It took a long time for Stephen to be able to tell me 'I love you,' without hearing the faint slamming of doors – yet he never let me doubt that he did love me, not once in twenty-five years.

'Sorry, Ma, didn't mean to leave you waiting on the corner.' My son Adam runs his father's company now. China, for him, is an exciting new market. He's spent weeks here, wooing the tourist authorities.

'Not tears, surely?' His expression softens, so like his father's. 'I thought this might happen if you came back. Look, let's go into the hotel here and sort you out with a drink.'

'I'd like an Old Fashioned, if they still know how. Ask them, Adam, will you?'

The old legend blamed the cormorant fisherman for making the peach-blossom valley disappear. If he'd only accepted the make-believe – taken his share of the blessed indolence he'd discovered, without letting in the harshness of the world outside – then the miracle might have lasted for ever.

I don't believe it. Peach-blossom valleys never last: it's part of their magic. Everything changes, sooner or later, just as every wall crumbles in the end. What endures – as Tao Chi'en's poem says – is the memory.

> *I walked in a dream, only to find the dream was reality,*
> *Where beautiful women shook down blossoms from their silken*
>   *garments.*
> *Where has it gone? The days are grey now,*
> *Yet on my tear-spotted sleeve there lingers one pink petal.*

But then: one petal is all I need, to remember.